Books by
Tim Dorsey

THE
BIG
BAMBOO

TIM
DORSEY

WITHDRAWN

HARPER

An Imprint of HarperCollinsPublishers

This is a work of fiction. The characters, incidents, and dialogue are drawn from the author's imagination and are not to be construed as real. Any resemblance to actual events or persons, living or dead, is entirely coincidental.

HARPER

An Imprint of HarperCollins*Publishers*
195 Broadway
New York, NY 10007

Copyright © 2006 by Tim Dorsey
Author photo by Janine Dorsey
Excerpt from *Hurricane Punch* copyright © 2007 by Tim Dorsey
ISBN: 978-0-06-058563-1
ISBN-10: 0-06-058563-3

First Harper paperback printing: April 2007
First William Morrow hardcover printing: April 2006

HarperCollins® and Harper® are registered trademarks of HarperCollins Publishers.

Printed in the United States of America

Visit Harper paperbacks on the World Wide Web at www.harpercollins.com

10 9 8

FOR LAWRENCE MCCONNELL

No one goes Hollywood—they were that way before they came here. Hollywood just exposed it.

—RONALD REAGAN

ACKNOWLEDGMENTS

Tremendous thanks again to Nat Sobel, Henry Ferris, and Lisa Gallagher.

THE
BIG
BAMBOO

LOS ANGELES POLICE DEPARTMENT

Y ou think this is a game? You didn't snuff some hooker. You killed Ally Street, the famous actress. You're facing the gas chamber!"

"I didn't do anything!"

The detective lunged. His partner restrained him. "We don't have the gas chamber anymore. Let me talk to the kid a minute."

The wormy young suspect sat at a plain metal desk. Dress shirt and slacks. Hands trembling. His untouched coffee was cold.

The second detective opened a notebook. "Maybe we can work something out."

"What do you mean?"

"A deal. Tell us what you know."

"But I'm innocent!"

"You're in deep shit!" yelled the first detective, the one named Reamsnyder.

"Take it easy," said his partner, by the name of Babcock.

The young man stared down at the scratched desktop. "I think I need an attorney."

A technician shot video from behind a two-way mirror. The interrogation room was an off-putting shade of mildew green that psychiatrists said would help to break suspects.

Babcock took a sip of his own coffee. "Sure, you can have an attorney. Whenever you want. But as soon as one arrives, we can't help you anymore. Maybe we can figure a way out of this."

The young man looked away.

"Still want that lawyer?"

No answer.

Babcock opened a folder. "Ford Oelman. That your real name?"

Ford nodded slightly, no eye contact.

"Says you work at Vistamax Studios. What do you do?"

". . . Props . . ."

"That's a good job—"

"Why are you being nice to this asshole?" said Reamsnyder. "He's a dead man! He's going down!"

"We don't need to talk like that," said Babcock. "He hasn't told his side of the story. Maybe it's not what it looks like."

"Bullshit! He was stalking her. We have witnesses. And just look at those eyes—some kind of pervert." Reamsnyder leaned into the young man's face. "Tell us where the body is, and maybe we'll ask the prosecutor for life."

Ford jerked back in his chair. "I didn't do anything! I don't know what's going on!" His head snapped toward Babcock. "You already questioned me last month, right after it happened. You believed me then."

"That was before we found you with those panties," said Reamsnyder. "The lab positively matched her DNA. And you'd just been fired. People heard all those threats you made when security threw you off the lot. Then there's your cell phone. How do you explain the ransom calls we traced?"

His whole body was shaking. "I— I can't . . ."

Babcock calmly folded his arms. "You have to understand how this looks from our side. It's not good."

"But I really am innocent!"

"You're a loser," said Reamsnyder. "Some lowlife who drove a golf cart around the set."

Ford wouldn't look at him.

"Hey, shithead! You still don't get it, do you? You don't realize who you killed." The detective seized the young man by the collar and yanked him out of his chair. "The weight of this town is about to fall on you like an anvil!"

Babcock jumped up and grabbed Reamsnyder again. "What the hell are you doing? Let go of him!"

The detective pushed Ford back down in his chair. "What did she do? Laugh at you? Make you feel small?"

Babcock squared around on his partner. "I think you need to go cool off."

"Fine!" Reamsnyder straightened his shirtsleeves. "I can't stand the stench in this room!" He slammed the door on the way out.

Babcock returned to his seat. "Sorry about that. He's actually a good cop. Cases like this get to him."

"I didn't have anything to do with it! You got to believe me!"

"I do," the detective lied. "But you have to give us something to go on. Any idea who's involved? I mean, you're connected to this thing at every stage. It can't all be a coincidence."

"But it is!" said Ford, eyes big and watery. "This whole thing is insane. A bunch of weird stuff just kept happening. If it made any sense at all, I'd swear I was being framed."

"Maybe you are." Babcock opened his folder again. "So, this started when? About four weeks ago?"

Ford rubbed his forehead.

"Why don't you tell me about it, from the beginning?"

Ford nodded and took a deep breath . . .

FOUR WEEKS AGO

Hollywood Tattletale

SHOOTING SCHEDULE DELAYED BY DEATHS

HOLLYWOOD—Three people were killed on the set of *All That Glitters* when a medieval catapult malfunctioned Monday, accidentally firing on several craft-service workers preparing lunch for the cast and crew.

The fatalities are but the latest in a litany of problems that have plagued the production of Werner B. Potemkin's ambitious epic. The film—intended to encompass the entire history of Tinseltown—is $120 million over budget and two years behind schedule. The death toll now stands at 18.

Filming was indefinitely suspended after Monday's accident when special effects coordinator Olaf Bløt stormed off in a rage. "I don't know why we even had a catapult. There's nothing in the script."

Potemkin is notorious for incessant rewrites on the set, not to mention a meticulous attention to realism bordering on the obsessive. Sources report that earlier in the day, Potemkin and Bløt argued loudly over the director's refusal to use a less powerful catapult. Hospital spokesmen revealed that the victims would have survived the lightweight foam boulder, but they were standing at the end of the full-scale weapon when the thirty-foot spring arm sheared loose and followed the fake rock down on top of the workers as they removed steam lids at the buffet table.

"You start cutting corners on catapult strength," remarked Potemkin, "next thing you're cheating on your wife with a blackmailing hooker named Candy. I mean someone else is."

The entertainment media quickly descended again outside the gates of Vistamax Studios, where police were called in to clear the driveway for departing vehicles.

"If only he had listened," Bløt said out the window of his baby blue Alpine-Renault. "Those caterers didn't deserve that."

On-set quarrels are not confined to the special effects chief. Movie insiders attribute a state of total chaos to Potemkin's brusque directorial style of perpetual shouting punctuated by sudden, unexplained bouts of weeping in the corner. Defenders, on the other hand, argue that this same tempestuous European approach was the genius behind such Potemkin classics as *The Deconstructionist's Dilemma, Anatomy of an Enigma* and *Die, Mr. Snodgrass, Die!*

As rewrites and broken deadlines mount, however, the friction has become the source of constant feuding with all the actors. The first four female leads have either been fired or quit, and the last— model-turned-actress Naomi Passious—had been seen fleeing the soundstage in tears on a daily basis before being replaced by newcomer-model- turned-actress Ally Street. Complicating matters was Naomi's on-again-off-again relationship with boy- band heartthrob Jason Geddy (see related story,

page 17), who was a regular distraction on the set
until being banned after mistaking one of his own
bodyguards for a member of an archrival boy
band and repeatedly striking him with the golf club
he always carries.

"That was a mistake," Geddy later said. "It's
time to move on."

Meanwhile, Potemkin's already strained relationship with the studio has become untenable in recent
months. Privately, studio brass are said to be furious
with the director's whimsical treatment of the shooting schedule as well as an utter intransigence in the
editing room. Vistamax is seeking a commercially
viable running time of 90 to 120 minutes, while
Potemkin refuses to budge on his ever-growing
eight-hour cut.

The director, in response, is said to be livid
about the studio's decision to target younger moviegoers by recruiting Snoop Dogg to perform the
theme song, "There's No Bizzle, Like Show Bizzle."

In other developments, tonight's cast party at
Skybar is apparently still on. Originally planned as
the "wrap party," it had already been postponed
six times before studio officials finally decided to go
forward with the event as a "midpoint" publicity
bash, issuing four times the usual number of press
credentials in an effort to offset chronic rumors that
the film is in danger of becoming the most expensive flop in Hollywood history.

A Vistamax spokesperson requested that in lieu
of flowers, donations be made to the Caterers,
Grips and Personal Assistants Home in Pasadena.

RELATED STORY, PAGE 17

PASSIOUS, GEDDY GET BACK TOGETHER, BREAK UP

HOLLYWOOD—No sooner had publicists confirmed the latest reconciliation between model-turned-actress Naomi Passious and boy-band heartthrob Jason Geddy, than the stormy relationship was reportedly off again.

The latest about-face came during a Sunset Strip altercation in the trendy Viper Room, where a melee broke out during a private party thrown to celebrate the star couple's reconciliation. The exact order of events is unclear, but witnesses generally concur Passious sparked the donnybrook by flirting with archrival boy-band singer Frankie Flatone. Before anyone realized what was happening, Passious and Geddy had both removed their matching Rodeo Drive belts with each other's name encrusted in diamonds, and began horse-whipping each other in front of the stage.

"It was like *The Passion of the Christ*, but worse," said one unidentified observer. "Everyone wishes them the best."

Bodyguards quickly separated the couple as members of the entertainment press rushed out to report that the volatile relationship was off again. Soon, however, the couple was observed sloppy-kissing on the dance floor, and journalists quickly refiled that the rocky courtship was back on. That's when Flatone asked to cut in and sustained blunt head trauma from a golf club. Accounts vary greatly, from a three iron to a sand wedge, but emergency room personnel place the official number of stitches at 36. Passious fled the lounge in tears with a support entourage of unemployed models and/or drug connections.

"I overreacted," said Geddy, wiping the end of the club with a bar napkin. "I guess I should send him something."

Just after midnight, Passious's publicist called a hastily arranged news conference and blamed the media. She attributed her client's behavior to "professional exhaustion" and pleaded for everyone to respect the star's privacy in high-profile nightclubs.

The couple's earlier troubles have been well chronicled in the celebrity press, particularly Geddy's volatile temper and intense hatred of paparazzi. Several lawsuits had been settled out of court before it came to a head last August, when Geddy was sentenced to a year's probation after a pistol registered to him discharged six times poolside at the Argyle. Fortunately, Geddy was holding the gun sideways to look cool, and didn't hit anything.

"It was a misunderstanding, as well as an accident," said Geddy's celebrity attorney, Calvin Sass. "He's become very respectful of firearms."

Then, of course, was February's infamous 72-hour weekend in Las Vegas that resulted in the panicked pair racing down to the courthouse Monday morning for an annulment, which was denied on the grounds that they had forgotten to get married in the first place.

"It was supposed to be an innocent joke," said Passious. "But it went too far."

Added Geddy: "That's what happens when you drink for three days without eating anything."

THAT EVENING

Just after dark, an endless convoy of stretch limos cruised down Sunset Strip with precision and social urgency. The vehicles were soon backed up for blocks, waiting to burp passengers onto the sidewalk at 8440, the address of Ian Schrager's landmark Mondrian Hotel.

The hotel was famous because it was the home of Skybar, the nightclub that was famous because you couldn't get into it. If you could get inside, you might see Cindy Crawford or Tom Hanks or Cher, but you couldn't.

The club's entrance was defended like the gates of a U.S. embassy in a refugee crisis, which described every night on the strip: dumpling-shaped tourists with Instamatics, autograph hounds with maps of the stars, barefoot street musicians, runaway wolf children, meth-monkeys, winos. A riot formation of block-shouldered bouncers in black dress shirts stood fast and held the Maginot Line, waving through the cultural elite with air kisses.

Tonight, Skybar's admittance policy was even more rigorous. The "midpoint" party for the runaway-train-wreck *All That Glitters*. A private function, which meant The List. Cast members, movie moguls, entertainment press and lower-rung studio employees who wangled extra invitations that floated around the soundstages like a separate form of currency.

Another limo pulled up. Paparazzi pounced. They'd been alerted by the studio, then reminded. The backdoor of the stretch opened. Cameras flashed. Which alerted more tourists.

"Look!" yelled a fan from Toledo. "It's Ally Street!"

Another limo. Sightseers stampeded across the boulevard. Traffic screeched.

"And there's boy-band heartthrob Jason Geddy!"

More photo flashes. More tourists flocked and fused tightly into a single screaming blob. More limos. The Bryl-creemed tumor of Middle America pulsed forward. Body-guards pushed back. VIPs shielded their eyes and ducked inside.

Next limo.

"It's the Glick brothers!"

Out came Ian and Mel, owners of Vistamax Studios and co-producers of *All That Glitters*. The Glicks had earned their way to the top of Vistamax by being born to the previous owners. Identical twins, the brothers exited the limo in identical, untucked white linen shirts, loafers and no socks. Their short, gelled black hair stood up in a crop of tiny sta-lagmites. Thick-rimmed reading glasses. In addition to being power players, the Glicks were style setters, and their sense of chic had become the gold standard. They under-stood that "hip" was a rapidly repeating cycle, and the brothers stayed so far out in front on the trend track that they often lapped those in the rear of the herd. Like tonight: All the fashion observers were uniformly wowed by every-thing the brothers had going on. They'd done it again, way, way ahead. Others at the party had the same look, but it was because they were so far behind, and they were aggres-sively shunned.

The brothers turned around one last time at the entrance, smiling and waving to the little people, then darted inside to more photo flashes.

Next: a crammed Malibu convertible. Five guys from the props department who roomed together and scored invita-tions from a third executive producer who hung out on the back lot with no obvious duties. The paparazzi didn't recog-nize them but took pictures in case. A bouncer found their names on The List and inside they went. Or *out*, to be more accurate. Because Skybar was located under the stars, spread across a poolside patio where unnatural concentrations of supermodels lounged with the sultry, bedroom eyes of people coming around after surgery. The decor was minimal, the big color white, lots of candles. The Hollywood Hills dropped off steeply behind the hotel, and the back of the club appeared to rest on the edge of a cliff, overlooking the vast, twinkling grid of greater Los Angeles, where the night air seemed to conduct voltage; the thick daytime haze, now invisible, trapping various wavelengths from fluorescent streetlights that gave the palm trees a slimy glow like low-budget porn.

The props guys couldn't hide their surprise. Despite countless attempts, they'd never made it inside Skybar before.

"Damn!" said Mark, the one with sideburns. "I can't believe we're in the movie business!"

"You mean *you* are," said Ford.

"Sorry, forgot about you getting fired," said Mark. "Let me get you something to drink."

"You know I don't drink."

"You should start. Take your mind off it."

Ford glanced around. "I just know I'm going to get thrown out. As soon as the Glicks notice I'm—"

"They're too busy figuring out who they're going to nail," said Mark, turning toward the loudest section of the party, where bookend vixens were fighting off all comers to stay attached to the Glicks' arms. The competition was fierce, despite—and because of—the brothers' reputation for spiking drinks and tag-teaming unconscious ingenues, who landed juicy movie roles in exchange for not going to the authorities. The brothers considered themselves fair men.

"Look at those jerks," said Ford. "I still can't believe what they did to me."

"You'll find another job. Besides, who'd have thought we'd make it this far?"

Indeed. A mighty long way for two guys who'd begun the year wearing paper hats at a Pretzel Depot in the food court of a deserted mall in unincorporated Zanesville, Ohio. Ford Oelman and Mark Costa. Both on the thin side with extra-young faces that suggested childhood histories of being picked on.

But they had dreams. Ford wanted to be a writer; Mark, an actor. The pair spent many an idle evening in the food court sharing a love of cinema, elaborately planning their shot at stardom. And that's as far as it went. Months passed. Inertia set in. Ford eventually worked his way up to interim weekend night manager before mall occupancy fell below ten percent and the shopping center was slated for demolition to make way for a new empty field.

Mark was crushed, but Ford saw the silver-screen lining. He knew opportunity when it knocked. That's right: Pretzel Depot had several franchises in southern California.

Westward ho! They landed evening gigs in a Burbank food court, where they served a steady stream of stagehands from Vistamax Studios across the street. Ford and Mark followed them back across the street one day and applied for jobs. Their big break came from the props department.

The enormity of the warehouse blew them away, like that scene with all the crates at the end of *Raiders of the Lost Ark*. It was a converted blimp hangar with endless, cavernous, interconnecting rooms. Hundreds of oil paintings, thousands of Tiffany lamps, two separate rooms for musical instruments, string and wind. They couldn't have been happier, zipping around the studio in golf carts full of wax fruit, fireplace pokers, caveman clubs, yacht pennants, cowboy spurs, sousaphones and leather-bound books with spray-on dust.

On their first Friday, a third executive producer wandered into the break room. "You guys need invitations?"

"To what?"

"Cast party. I got extra."

"But we're not cast."

"Doesn't matter." The producer gave them an envelope. "Need coke with that?"

"What?"

"Call me if you do." He handed out business cards. *Dallas Reel.*

The producer was right: All night long, nobody cared they weren't cast. And what a party it was!

Actually, it was a whole bunch of them. Ford and Mark quickly learned that a single invitation was like an all-day pass to an underground social network connecting the entire L.A. scene in a fluid movement of strangers who came together in brief alliances to locate the next party, where they promptly dissolved to re-form new permutations and so on. The buddies didn't recognize any stars for the first two hours, then just a bit actor who played a series of O.D. victims during three seasons of *ER.* For the most part, everyone was like them, bottom-feeders on an insatiable quest. But what was that quest? A young gofer from New Line told them: to get a limo. Studio brass were always losing track of them, and you had to be ready.

"Been watching this one for an hour." The gofer nodded toward the white stretch Hummer in front of a Bauhaus manse on Laurel Canyon.

"Who's it belong to?" asked Ford.

"That guy."

A third executive producer trotted down the front steps with a bottle of champagne and a bottle blonde. They hopped in a black Ferrari and zoomed down the canyon.

"To the limo!"

Three young men dove in the backseat. The suspicious chauffeur turned around. "You with the studio?"

"Yeah."

The driver handed back a pile of stapled pages. "My screenplay. Coming-of-age story about rival chauffeurs . . ." They sped off.

That was several months ago. Killer parties every weekend. Ford picked up material for his scripts. Mark picked up a hobby. He began collecting phone numbers of actresses and actress-types that he stored in the directory of his cell phone until most of the alphabet was represented. Then Ford got fired. It's a long story, and we'll get to that. But right now: Skybar.

The Glicks basked. Supermodels posed. Mark and Ford made their way around the pool to a tiny, tin-roofed bar. Mark ordered an apple martini. Ford asked for a Coke.

"You should get something to drink," said Mark. "Help you relax."

"I'm getting something to drink."

"You know what I mean."

The pair leaned against a wall outside the women's room so Mark could lurk. A waiter came by. Ford grabbed two flutes of Dom Pérignon from the passing tray.

"Ford," said Mark. "You're drinking."

On the far edge of the patio, a melancholy young woman stood alone at the railing, gazing out over the City of Angels, her long, wispy hair fluttering in the breeze. Each time she turned around, another blinding burst from paparazzi. So she didn't turn around much. Ally Street, the newly cast star of *All That Glitters*.

Street was soon joined by another attractive but older woman, her agent/publicist Tori Gersh, the primary reason for Street's success. The actress had literally come out of nowhere to land the big role, following the heavily reported dismissal of Naomi Passious for creative differences, which meant drugs. The casting of a complete unknown in such a high-profile part triggered an avalanche of media requests and forced Gersh to rapidly compose the fake biography: Born during a West Virginia blizzard that killed her parents and raised by gypsies who sold counterfeit Bon Jovi beach towels in midways along the Atlantic seaboard before escaping to join a breakaway convent in New Hampshire that had rejected Vatican II and was later indicted for an Internet Ponzi scam involving "miracle" wrinkle gel, then three missing years in the Pacific Northwest that she refused to talk about before resurfacing as Guinevere in a renaissance troupe out of Bakersfield, where Gersh's Volvo just happened to break down. The trades consistently described Street's rise to fame as meteoric, even though meteors actually fall.

And that's how she didn't come to be in Skybar tonight, standing next to Tori at the railing. They looked out over the city and saw a shooting star.

"I hate these parties," said Ally.

"Just a few more minutes," said Tori. "For appearances."

Two people came toward them. One was another publicist. He shook their hands. "Ms. Street, a pleasure. I'm a big admirer of your work. I'd like you to meet my client, Jason Geddy."

Jason shook Ally's hand. "Yo, word."

Paparazzi cameras flashed.

A brief period of very small talk. The other publicist shook their hands again and left.

"That was nice of them," said Ally.

"Nice, nothing," said Tori. "It was just to generate rumors about you two in the press. Jason's career's been racing south ever since the breakup of Boyz II Synched XS."

On the other side of the patio, Mark pestered a babe exiting the women's room.

"Excuse me, you're a model, aren't you?"

She raised her chin in umbrage. "*Spokes*model."

Mark tapped a spot on the side of his face. "You got throw-up."

Ford slumped against the wall and grabbed two more glasses from a passing tray.

Mark opened his cell phone and looked up at the woman. "Maybe I can call you sometime?"

"Uh, sure . . ."

Ford killed the glass in his left hand, then his right. The woman hurried away. Mark turned to Ford and held up his open cell phone. "Just got another number."

Ford read the blue liquid display: 555-1234.

Mark closed the phone. "That was a good one, too. I was low on *H*'s."

"Do you ever call them?"

"Constantly."

"And?"

"They've all been wrong numbers. I think something's the matter with my phone."

Ford scanned the patio with double vision. "Haven't seen any stars yet."

"There's Ally Street," said Mark.

"Where?"

"Against the railing."

Ten minutes later, the rest of the gang from props clustered around Ford. They stared at his cell phone in astonishment.

"I can't believe you got Ally Street's number!"

"I just walked up to her," said Ford. "I guess everyone else is too intimidated."

"When are you going to call her?"

"Tonight," said Ford. "She wants to meet later."

"Probably a fake number," said Mark. "That's what they do."

Ford flipped open his cell and hit the last number entered. A phone rang on the other side of the pool.

"Hello?"

Midnight.

The props guys sipped Long Island iced teas and gazed out an upstairs picture window overlooking Wilshire Boulevard. Novelty ice cubes blinked in their drinks. New tote bags hung from their shoulders.

The music was loud and industrial, the dark room behind them jammed and sweaty with people dancing by the light of a hundred blinking cocktails. A record label release party for the new anarchist punk band Plastic Corporate Man Massacre, whose name was embroidered on the promotional tote bags.

"When are you supposed to call Ally?" asked Mark.

Ford held his watch to his drink. "Half hour."

"Let's get something to eat."

They took the elevator to the ground floor. The party was being held above a high-end department store, and the Otis doors opened to the bright, jarring light of the bedroom section. Ushers in bow ties were waiting to take the next group upstairs; others escorted the props guys back through the cologne atrium to the front entrance.

A daisy-yellow Malibu convertible headed north on Vine. Normally, Ford would have been behind the wheel. He was the gang's permanent designated driver, because he never drank, until now. So they reverted to their previous rotation: whoever was currently shit-scared onto the temporary wagon. Tonight that would be Pedro, still trying to shake off being awakened naked in a Topanga Dumpster by a bunch of transients poking him with sticks.

They turned left on Sunset, the radio cranked. Ford's head lolled, chin to his chest.

". . . All right now, baby, it's all riiiiiight now! . . ."

Five more blocks. The Malibu entered a drive-through. Pedro shook Ford. "Wake up!"

Ford looked around. "Where are we?"

"The In-N-Out."

"May I take your order?"

"What do they have?" asked Ford.

"Just burgers, fries, soda. It's the In-N-Out."

Mark was trying to make calls on his cell but only getting out-of-service messages.

"Hey, Ford," said Pedro. "What time were you supposed to call Ally?"

"Oh, shit!" Ford flipped open his own cell.

A hand reached over the passenger door and snatched it away. The gang turned.

Two guys with ski masks and guns.

"Give it up! That other phone! Now!"

Mark held out a quivering arm.

"Wallets and watches!" demanded the second robber.

The guys were suddenly sober, fishing out billfolds and undoing wristbands.

"Hurry the fuck up!"

"May I take your order?"

A police car with two hungry officers pulled in.

"Damn!" The jackers took off across the parking lot and disappeared through a hole in the fence with the Days Inn.

Five hearts pounded in the convertible, five frozen guys holding wallets and watches.

"Hello? Anyone there? Can I take your order?"

They began snapping out of it.

"That was close," said Pedro. "We almost lost our wallets."

"They got my cell phone!" said Mark. "All my numbers!"

"They got mine!" said Ford. "How am I going to call Ally?"

A yellow Malibu sat in the rear of the parking lot behind the In-N-Out.

"This is insane!" Pedro grabbed into the backseat. "Give me back my phone!"

Mark jerked it out of reach.

"Come on, give it!" said Pedro. "I never would have lent it to you if I'd known—"

"I have to get my cell phone back!" said Mark, punching in numbers.

"I have to call Ally!" said Ford.

"You're both drunk!"

"Shhhh! It's ringing!" said Mark. "Uh, hello? . . . Yeah, it's us . . . We just met . . . The guys you robbed . . . Sorry, should have figured there were several . . . At the In-N-Out . . . That's right. I want to make a deal. I want my phone back . . . No, this isn't a joke. We'll pay . . . because I got a bunch of stuff stored in it I need . . . Look, it's not worth anything to you anyway. We'll have the police trace your calls and then you go to jail . . . No, I wasn't threatening you. I was trying to make a point— . . . You just found my personal info in the phone? You're going to hunt me down and kill me? . . ."

Ford waved drunkenly in Mark's face. "Gimme, gimme, gimme. Let me talk to him . . ."

"Hold on. Someone else wants to talk to you . . ."

"Hi, Ford Oelman here . . . Right, another fuck-head. Listen, we'll give you two hundred dollars for the— . . . Because I met this really hot actress tonight and her number's in the phone . . . Ally Street . . . I did so meet her! . . . Skybar . . . Me neither, but I got on the list this time . . . I *know* she's really hot—I just told you that . . . Can we speed this up? I was supposed to call her twenty minutes ago . . . You found her number? . . . Great! Why don't you just read it off to me and then we don't have to meet? . . . What do you mean, you're going to call her yourself? . . . No, *I'm* supposed to call her. You can't—"

"What happened?" said Mark.

"He hung up."

Mark grabbed the phone and dialed again.

"Is it ringing?" said Ford.

"Busy signal." Mark hit redial. "Still busy."

"Gimme that." Ford hit redial. On the fifth try, he gave Mark a thumbs-up. ". . . Hello. It's me again . . . The guy who knows Ally Street . . . You just talked to her? . . . You set up a meeting? . . . But how— . . . You said you were my driver? . . . Could you repeat that last part? . . . I see . . . Hold on . . ." Ford covered the phone and turned to Mark. "The price is now five hundred."

"Five hundred!"

"Says they'll give us both phones as well as the location where I'm supposed to meet Ally."

Mark winced at the cost, then nodded reluctantly. "Split it fifty-fifty?"

"Deal." Ford uncovered the phone. "Five hundred it is . . . Yeah, I know the place . . . Fifteen minutes in front of the Pig 'N Whistle. You got it . . . Hey, when you talked to her did she say anything about me, you know, if she thought I was cute or—"

"What happened?"

"He hung up."

Fifteen minutes later.

A yellow Malibu sat in the shadows of a dark side street off Hollywood Boulevard, a half-block down from the Pig N' Whistle.

"What are you doing?" said Ford, pointing up the street with a five-hundred-dollar wad from an ATM. "We're supposed to meet over there!"

"Not a chance," said Pedro, stretching his neck to see if anyone was lying in wait near the pub. "I should have my head examined just for being *here*. This is the most dumbass stunt I ever—"

Pedro felt something cold and metal in his ear.

"Gimme your wallets," said a man in a ski mask.

"And your watches," said his accomplice.

The money was plucked from Ford's hand. The robbers collected the rest of their loot and ran off.

Ford turned to Mark. "They lied."

The next morning.

Ford lifted his head off the pillow and checked the alarm clock. Actually afternoon. His head fell back down with a groan.

Mark was already up, frying ham and eggs in the kitchen of their modest third-floor unit at the Alto Nido Apartments. It was the quiet north end of Ivar Avenue, Jackson Browne playing softly on a small stereo from the Home Shopping Club mounted under a cabinet next to the stove.

Ford stumbled into the kitchen rubbing his eyes.

". . . *Running on empty . . . Running bliiiiiiiiiind! . . .*"

He filled a glass under the faucet and plopped two Alka-Seltzers, waiting on the fizzing action by staring out the window over the sink: light freeway traffic, partial glimpse of the Capitol Records tower . . . Hold it. Something out of place. He turned to Mark at the kitchen table, sawing ham and dipping in yolk. "Why is it so quiet?"

Mark flipped a page of the *Los Angeles Times* sports section and pointed toward the living room with his fork. Three guys watching TV. "The silent treatment."

"Why are they giving you the silent treatment?"

"My guess is you're going to get it, too."

"What did I do?"

"Still sore about the robbery."

"*I* didn't steal anything."

Mark turned the page. "They won't listen."

Ford grabbed the edge of the sink. "Whoa . . ." He felt a momentary wooziness and the sensation something was pushing on his eyeballs from the inside. "I think I need to go back to bed."

He started walking away. Pedro ran into the kitchen and grabbed his arm.

"Look," said Ford. "I'm sorry as hell about last night, but Jesus!"

Pedro's face wasn't angry. It was white.

Soon, they were all gathered around the TV in the living room. A publicity photo of Ally Street filled the screen. The image switched to a reporter on the sidewalk in front of a trendy restaurant.

"*. . . Tinseltown remains stunned by last night's brazen abduction of Ally Street, who witnesses said was standing on this very spot along famous Sunset Boulevard when she was forced inside a dark van by masked gunmen . . .*"

Mark turned up the volume.

"*. . . Ms. Street's dining party reported that shortly before the kidnapping, the actress received a mysterious call on her cell phone and excused herself . . .*"

The roommates exchanged looks.

"*. . . Authorities aren't officially commenting, but inside sources at the police department say they've been able to trace that final call to another cell phone and are seeking to interview this man, described only as a 'person of interest' . . .*"

A blown-up paparazzi photo from Skybar appeared on the tube.

"It's Ford!" said Pedro. "When he was talking to Ally last night by the pool!"

"... *Meanwhile, a Vistamax spokesman said the studio is saddened by the news and will do all in its power to ensure Ms. Street's safe return and maintain the shooting schedule for a holiday release* ..."

Loud banging on the apartment door.

"Open up! Police!"

1

NINE MONTHS EARLIER

Serge sat in a grimy motel room along Tampa's Nebraska Avenue, banging away on a manual Underwood typewriter.

Coleman chugged a Budweiser and stared out the window at prostitutes and a bearded man pushing a rusty shopping cart full of curled phone books. There was no middle ground—the section of town where motels rent by the hour or the month. Disagreements and unidentifiable thumps through thin walls.

Coleman tossed his empty aluminum can in the wastebasket, but it bounced out because the basket was already full of crumpled pages with "Scene One" at the top.

Serge ripped another sheet from the typewriter's spool, wadded it up and threw it in the corner.

Coleman popped another beer. "How's your screenplay coming?"

Serge inserted a fresh page. "Great. Almost finished. Guaranteed to make my movie career. All I need is the opening hook." He began typing again.

Coleman stopped chugging and lowered his beer. "How do you write a movie, anyway?"

Serge sighed and stopped typing. "Well, you begin by just letting your mind float. After a while, if you don't have any *distractions*, you enter an astral-plane dream state, where the scene you're writing becomes as real as this desk." He slapped the top of the table.

Coleman killed the rest of the beer and tossed it in the corner. "Can I come with you?"

"Sure." Serge resumed typing. "But first you'll have to loosen all the bolts on your imagination."

"No problem." Coleman snatched a fat spliff from over his ear and fired it up. He blew a large cloud toward the ceiling. "Okay, I'm ready." He leaned over Serge's shoulder for a peek at the typewriter. "Where are we going? . . ."

SCENE ONE
Nine Months Earlier

```
Klieg lights sweep the night sky. A
bustling city street in black-and-
white. Vintage automobiles from the
'40s drive past the exterior of a
popular bar in Morocco. A neon
sign: SERGE'S. The perspective segues
inside. People drinking, gambling,
singing along with the piano
player. The camera zooms. A tall,
debonair man in an immaculate white
tuxedo appears from a back room. He
moves through the crowd with
panache and approaches the source
of the music.
```

Coleman glances up from his stool: "Hey, Serge, look at me, I can play the piano!"

Serge fits an unlit cigarette between his lips and lets it droop.

Coleman, noticing his hands on the keyboard: "And I'm black!"

Suddenly, a commotion toward the front of the club. SS uniforms fill the entrance. Serge turns toward them with a penetrating gaze.

Coleman: "What is it, boss?"

Serge: "I don't like Nazis."

"Why's that, boss?"

"Goose-stepping never preceded any big laughs."

"What are you going to do, boss?"

Serge faces the door and grabs his crotch. "Master race this!"

The platoon draws its sidearms and charges. Serge and Coleman begin running but are quickly pinned down in the back of the club.

German captain: "Shoot them."

Soldiers raise their Lugers.

Coleman: "What do we do now, boss?"

Serge: "Damn. I wrote us into a
corner."

A crumpled ball of paper bounced off the top of the
wastebasket. Serge inserted a new sheet.

"That was a rush," said Coleman, looking at the joint in
his hand. "I thought we were dead for sure."

Serge ignored him. Internal dialogue chattering in his
head. He tapped furiously on his trusty Underwood, the kind
Mickey Spillane would have used. Warm memories of the
Old Florida washed over him like something that is warm
and also washes over you.

Coleman popped another beer. "You mentioned something about a movie career?"

Serge was on a roll, typing like a machine. "I'm following the Sly Stallone formula—write myself into a killer
script, star in the movie, then get overpaid for hack work the
rest of my life . . . I'm almost done."

Coleman walked up and looked over Serge's shoulder
again. "But you're back on page one."

"It's all about the opening hook. After that, the rest writes
itself."

"You got an opening hook?"

Serge ripped out the page and crumpled it.

Coleman fit the end of his joint into a roach clip. "Maybe
you're hung up on location."

"Maybe you're right." Serge inserted another sheet.

"Wait for me," said Coleman. He began hitting the roach . . .

SCENE ONE
Nine Months Earlier, the Lunar Surface

A rocket ship lands. The horn section of a Stanley Kubrick soundtrack builds in the background as
the spacecraft's hatch opens dra-
matically.

Serge steps out, hands on hips.
Coleman stands next to him with a
Budweiser in the new ZX9 micro-
atmospheric delivery system.

Serge surveys the horizon with
thermogoggles. The orchestral music
swells; kettle drums signal an
epiphany.

Coleman stops sucking on the beer
tube extending through the self-
sealing port in the side of his
space helmet: "See an opening hook
out there?"

"Just an old black monolith." A
crumpled ball of paper falls slow-
motion into a crater.

Coleman clutches the tube in his
mouth again: "What about a different time frame?"

SCENE ONE
A Hundred and Nineteen Years Earlier

Horses' hooves thunder across the
Wild West. A large posse seals off
all escape.

Two outlaws squirm along the edge
of a cliff.

Serge: "Who <u>are</u> those guys?"

Coleman peeks over the cliff at the
water hundreds of feet below: "I
can't swim."

Serge: "I have to go to the bathroom." He steps off the cliff

and into a seedy motel room.

Coleman sat down at the foot of a bed. "Why are we staying at this crappy place, anyway?"

"Inspiration," Serge yelled from around the corner. A toilet flushed. He came back out. "I thought some stuff might
happen that would give me ideas . . ." He wandered to the
window and stared outside at Nebraska Avenue. A car
crashed. Gunshots echoed from an alley. A streetwalker in a
cheerleading uniform pulled a switchblade on a pimp. Serge
went back to his typewriter and sat down in front of an
empty page. "Why can't I think of anything?"

A knock at the door. Coleman answered. A man with
strands of aluminum foil in a long beard stood next to a shopping cart. He wanted to know if they had any phone books.
Coleman gave him two thick ones from the nightstand.

Serge started typing again. "Who was that?"

Coleman closed the door. "I don't know."

"What did he want?"

"Our phone books."

"Another sign of The End Times."

Coleman sat down again and picked at his toes. "So when did movies become your latest obsession?"

"What do you mean *latest*? I've always been into movies."

"You know what I'm talking about. Every couple months you get on some kick, and we have to drive all over the place and completely change the way we live. Then something new comes along and you forget all about the last thing."

"Like when?"

"Are you kidding?" Coleman switched the foot he was scratching. "There was the space program, then politics, railroads, the Keys, the history of some Florida shit, then the space program Part Two—remember that? When the shuttle crashed? You cried for like two weeks."

Serge pointed at Coleman. "You didn't tell anyone!"

"Of course not. I'm just saying I didn't realize you'd switched again. I thought you were still writing your book. Whatever happened to that?"

"I finished it," said Serge. "But all the rejection letters claimed there wasn't a market, like they know everything."

"What was the title?"

"*Chicken Soup for the Fucked-up Chicken-Soup Book Buyer.*"

Coleman scratched his toes harder.

Serge crumpled the latest sheet into a tight ball. "If only I could find the opening hook . . ."

A loud banging sound.

Serge looked around. "What was that?"

Coleman pointed across the room. "That guy in the closet you tied up and gagged. I think he's come to."

Bang, bang, bang.

"Interruptions!" Serge got up and grabbed a pistol by the barrel. He headed across the room.

Bang, bang, bang.

Serge opened the closet door and cracked the man in the skull with the butt of the gun. He closed the door.

Coleman looked up at Serge as he came back across the room. "Is he okay?"

"He's resting." Serge sat down and stared at the typewriter. "Nothing interesting ever happens."

Coleman pointed at the closet again. "Serge, what about the guy—"

"Shhhh!"

"But that's a really fascinating—"

"I'm trying to concentrate!"

Coleman shrugged. Minutes passed. Serge finally stood and shook his head. "I don't know what the problem is. I can't get the hook."

"What about sex?" said Coleman. "That always works."

"Too gratuitous."

Another knock at the front door.

"What now!" Serge walked over and turned the knob.

Standing outside was a stunning brunette in a conservative business suit. High cheekbones, full lips, almost six feet tall. A high-priced trial attorney on lunch break.

"Serge, you never called me back."

He returned to his typewriter and sat. "I'm in lockdown. Have to finish my screenplay."

"Can't you take a *little* break?"

"Not until I find the hook."

The attorney walked up behind Serge and began running her hands down his chest. Serge stared at the typewriter. Her hands reached his stomach and began undoing buttons. "It's been two weeks since the charity ball. Didn't you have a good time?"

"Yes"—eyes straight on the page.

It *had* been a good time. The attorney was precisely Serge's type—a woman in full bloom. She would have been a stunning thirty-five-year-old, but was unreal considering she was actually forty-eight. Still, most guys would have preferred the alternative of a tittering twentysomething. Not Serge. A bimbo package still meant a bimbo mind, and the first inane comment always collapsed his sexual house of cards. After enough flaccid evenings, Serge began giving pop quizzes. The fastest litmus test, he found, was vice-presidential running mates on losing tickets. The mandatory minimum was Sargent Shriver, but anything before Edmund Muskie lit the afterburners.

The feeling was mutual among a certain segment of professional women in Tampa Bay. Bimbos come in two flavors, after all. They usually met Serge because of the enormous time he spent in museums and art galleries. Besides looking spiffy in a tux, he could hold his own in dinner conversation with any *Jeopardy!* finalist. Sure, the women knew he was nuts. But that was the thing about Serge: It could take hours to figure that out. Over the short course of a cocktail reception, he merely appeared effervescent and charismatic. Only much later in the evening did it become evident that Serge was wired out of his gourd. But by then it was the sex time, when this turned into a plus. More than one date had seen the origins of the universe.

The attorney now undoing Serge's shirt was his third chamber of commerce member in as many months. "Let's play." She reached for his belt buckle. "I don't have to be back until two."

Serge pushed her hands aside. "Even if I wanted to, you

know how I am when I'm trying to concentrate. I've got twenty planes circling in my head waiting to land."

The attorney understood Serge inside out, weaknesses. She nuzzled and whispered in his ear with a raspy voice. "I'll go to one of your special places. My sleeping bag's in the car."

Serge's breathing shallowed. His face reddened. "Anyplace I want?"

She ran her tongue along his neck. "Mmmm, hmmmm . . ."

He stood up and wrote an address on a scrap of paper. "Tomorrow at noon."

She initially pouted over the delay, then gave him a wicked grin and strolled out the door. "Don't be late."

Serge's attention was already back at the typewriter. "Uh, right . . ."

The door closed on one side of the room and banging started on the other.

Serge jumped up and grabbed his gun again. "This place is nonstop bullshit!"

"But, Serge," said Coleman, pointing toward the closet, "I still think you should write about—"

"Can you please be quiet? I got too much coming at me at the same time."

Bang, bang, bang.

"But, Serge, it's a really exciting—"

"Not now!" Serge opened the closet. Crack. He closed it.

Sixteen Hours Later, Far Away

A Greyhound bus arrived in the dark. The empty street glistened and smelled from a recent rain.

No bus station, just a roadside shelter a block from the town square with an obelisk of engraved names from World

War II. There wasn't anyone waiting for the 331, but the driver was required to stop anyway. A police cruiser went by. One of the few left with the old *Car 54* bubble-top lights.

Mark was using bunched-up clothes as a pillow, trying to sleep against the window. His eyes fluttered when the Greyhound lurched away from the curb and continued west.

Ford was completely awake in the next seat.

Mark sat up and stretched. "How long was I out?"

"Two hours."

Mark's watch said four A.M. They passed a barbershop and went through a blinking yellow light.

"Where are we?"

"Kansas," said Ford. "Wamego."

Mark yawned and ran a hand through uncombed hair. "Can these towns get any smaller?"

Yes.

There'd been a transfer in St. Louis, but then back roads again. Higginsville, Salina, Russell, Hays. And what was with all the junctions? Ellsworth Junction, Quinter Junction, Grand Junction, Junction City.

Twenty hours since leaving Zanesville. Stripped their lives to a duffel bag each. Stuffed the rest in plastic garbage sacks and left them on the porch for Salvation Army. Got the deposit from the landlord and bought $99 one-way tickets to L.A.

Mark was alert now as the bus picked up speed in the emptiness between towns. He got out a homemade sandwich. "I'll never travel by bus again." Tuna, soggy.

"I kind of like it," said Ford. "See things you never do otherwise. Gives me ideas."

"You been writing?"

Ford jotted something in a composition book. "It's quiet at night. Just the bus sound. I've gotten a lot done."

The book rested in Ford's lap on top of a zippered cloth

bag full of spare pens and rubber-banded packs of typewritten pages and more notebooks crammed with tiny print. One of the pockets bulged with the odd receipts and napkins Ford had used when a book wasn't handy.

"Why'd you get rid of your typewriter?" asked Mark.

"Too much hassle to take. I'll buy one in a pawnshop when we get there."

Mark turned to the window. "I'd like to paint."

Ford jotted something. "Then do it."

"Don't know how. I think I'd be bad at it."

Sunrise in Colorado. Sunset in Utah. In between, vast, lifeless panoramas that adjusted the young men's scale of things. And the other passengers, who put it in perspective. The bandanna guy who sat down behind them in Aurora and asked if they had anything to get high. The screaming child who locked himself in the restroom outside Beaver and forced the driver to pull over. The gaunt man in a personal aroma envelope of sour wine.

Hour fifty-two. Ford's neck was starting to hurt, but hope came in a welcome sign with a golden bear. The California line. Interstate 15, making good time. Mark watched the Mojave go by. Ford wrote. Baker and Barstow.

"You're lucky you have a dream," said Mark. "Wish I had one."

"I'm not fooling myself. The odds are astronomical."

"The way you work so hard? No, you're definitely going to make it."

"I'd do it anyway. The best life is when your dreams come true. The second best is when they don't, but you never stop chasing."

"I've always wanted to take up an instrument," said Mark. "Except I'm not crazy about music. Is that important?"

Ford gazed out the window. "This is the way they all came."

"Who?"

"The dreamers." Ford closed his book and stuck it in the zippered bag. "Free ranch land, then Sutter's Mill and the gold rush. And when the gold ran out, they struck oil."

"Talk about your luck."

"Finally, Hollywood. An entire generation fantasizing about being discovered at a soda fountain in Schwab's."

"I heard that story wasn't true."

"It's not. But kids from small towns all over America still kept arriving by bus with a single beat-up suitcase, not knowing what they were going to do next. We're on the same journey."

"Look. The skyline."

"I feel like I'm in the forties."

"I thought there'd be more buildings."

"The city's spread out."

The bus headed into the sprawl. The going became slow, red light after red, countless stops dropping off passengers. The road began grading up. "The Hollywood sign!"

They finally arrived at the Cahuenga Boulevard stop. The driver yanked two duffel bags from the luggage compartment and set them on two gold stars in the sidewalk. Ford and Mark slung them over their shoulders and began hiking up the street, reading names under their feet. Will Rogers, Andy Griffith, Carol Burnett . . . Someone selling celebrity maps was playing the Kinks on a tape deck . . . James Cagney, Dean Martin, Betty Grable . . . past the Kodak Theater, approaching another movie house with dirty impressions in the concrete.

". . . *You can see all the stars as you walk down Hollywood Boulevard . . .*"

"Ford, I think that's Grauman's Chinese."

"I'm getting photos." He set his duffel down and pulled out a camera.

"Check the hand prints," said Mark. "Crosby, Harlow, Elizabeth Taylor . . ."

"Look this way," said Ford. "I'll take your picture."

A female voice: "Would you like to be in the picture, too?"

The guys turned. It was like a Beach Boys song, a California vision from a travel brochure. Long, straight, sun-bleached blond hair. More sun bringing out the freckles in her perfect tan. A smile from a teeth-whitening ad. Cutoff shorts and a Dodgers jersey tied in a knot above the navel.

"Sure," said Ford, handing her the camera. "It's all set. Just press this."

"This?"

"No, the other button."

"Okay."

The two buddies stood on Taylor's prints and put their arms around each other's shoulders.

"Say 'cheese'!"

"Cheese!"

Ford took his arm off Mark's shoulder. "What's she doing?"

"I think that's called running away with your camera."

2

TAMPA

A toilet flushed in a grimy motel room along Tampa's Nebraska Avenue. Serge emerged from the bathroom.

Coleman was sitting cross-legged on the bed, scratching his feet.

"Serge. I think I have athlete's foot."

Serge walked over to the TV set. "Then stop scratching. It only makes it worse."

"I know. But you can't help it. And if you're toasted—they really got you."

Serge inserted a DVD in the personal player that he always took with him on the road.

"Serge, it itches."

The DVD started. The night skyline of Tampa appeared over water. "Use foot cream."

"Don't have any." Scratch.

"Then go pee on your feet."

"What!"

"Pee on your feet," said Serge. "Kills athlete's foot."

"Like hell," said Coleman, holding the flame of a Bic lighter near his toes. "You're just trying to trick me into doing something stupid."

"If you don't believe me, look it up on the Internet. Human urine has natural enzymes that knock out athlete's foot like that!"—he slapped his hands together—"Also works on jellyfish stings. You have to know these things if you're going to live here. I have to go to the bathroom." Serge paused the movie and went around the corner.

Coleman scratched. A toilet flushed. Serge came back.

"Serge . . ."

"What?"

"I don't think I can pee."

"Give it time." Serge reached in a suitcase and began fiddling with a small electronic gadget.

"But you can go anytime you want," said Coleman. "Matter of fact you've been going all the time lately."

Serge punched buttons on the gadget. "I'm on a new regimen. Drinking ninety-six glasses of water a day."

"Why?"

"Purify my body. It's a temple." Serge pressed more buttons.

"But don't they just say to drink eight glasses a day?"

"That's why I drink ninety-six. It's how you get ahead in this world."

"Can't you make yourself sick?"

"Don't worry. I'm also taking diuretics."

"What for?"

"I was getting sick." He activated the gadget's backlight.

Coleman looked at the device in Serge's hands. "Your new iPod?"

"This thing's amazing. Holds ten thousand songs. But I'm only up to eight hundred. I can't stop thinking about it. The next thing I know, I've spent ten hours rearranging playlists and downloading show tunes." Serge got up and headed for the bathroom, pressing buttons and working the patented click-wheel.

Coleman sat down in front of the paused picture on the TV set. "So what's this movie?"

"The Punisher," Serge yelled from the bathroom.

"What's it about?"

"My favorite," said Serge, coming back into the room. "Lots of punishment."

He sat down on the bed next to Coleman, restarted the movie with the remote and went back to his iPod.

Coleman gestured at the skyline on TV. "I didn't know Tampa looked so cool."

Serge pressed buttons and nodded. *"The Punisher* finally showcased our fine city in the light we so richly deserve. I was first in line opening night. I figured, this is it! Tampa's on its way now! Then, the ultimate injustice."

"What was that?"

"Nobody went to see the fucking thing."

"Why not?"

"Beats me. It had Travolta after all, plus a killer script. We really lucked out there."

"Why do you say that?"

"Hollywood's completely out of ideas. They could have easily stuck us with an unoriginal script, but fortunately we got the thirty-seventh movie about a comic-book hero."

"Weren't you an extra in that thing?"

Serge nodded. "Stood in line a whole day when they were taking applications. Even wore my best tropical shirt, which is why they selected me. Said I had the right look. That's the way their culture works, lots of flattery right up until those guards dragged me off the set."

"What happened?"

"Artistic differences. They were filming the climactic

scene with Travolta, and I yelled, 'You call *that* punishment?' "

There was a metal box on the wall behind the bed. It had a slot. Coleman stuck a quarter in it. The quarter was on a string. He pulled it back out. The bed began to vibrate. Coleman reclined on a pillow, fired up a joint and began watching the movie. Serge played with his iPod.

"Serge . . ."

"What?"

"Why do you like old motels so much?"

"Florida history."

"Why do you like Florida history so much?"

"Because it's in short supply. We're such a young state, it makes every piece extra special. Unfortunately, that's also the problem. Too many carpetbagging developers from up north think something sixty years old isn't important. But what else have we got? That's another objective of my screenplay, to motivate preservation, like *Miami Vice* did for South Beach. If we don't start right now, what will our grandchildren have?"

"We're having grandchildren?"

"Universal grandchildren, like the president talks about in his weekly radio address."

Coleman hit his joint. "I don't get that station."

"Nobody does. The most powerful man on the planet has the worst-rated program."

"That's embarrassing."

"The shame is, it doesn't have to be," said Serge. "A few months ago I mailed the White House some suggestions to pump up the show."

"Like what?"

"Prank calls. He's already got the red phone. He could dial other world leaders and disguise his voice. It would be a scream! I also suggested he do like that guy on Howard

Stern and play the piano with his penis. He doesn't even need to know the piano; he could team up with the vice president and learn 'Chopsticks.' People would *definitely* start tuning in. Then, right after the song, he could pitch another tax break for his buddies and who'd complain?" Serge walked over to the window and peeked through the blinds. "Did you notice the bottom of our motel sign? Says: COLOR TV, with each letter a different color. It's like we're at the pyramids."

Coleman's voice warbled: "I like beds with the Magic Fingers."

"Another barometer of historic excellence." Serge left the window and sat back down at his typewriter. "Okay. Focus. You can do it! . . ."

"I'm bored," said Coleman. "Let's go do something."

"Can't," said Serge. "I'm way behind deadline on this script. I've already lost two weeks playing with my iPod and peeing."

Coleman went back to hitting his joint.

Serge suddenly jumped up. "I have to get the hell out of here."

"I thought you were behind deadline."

"I am. But I've been in the same place too long. I can't breathe—the walls . . ." He grabbed a suitcase. "Besides, the police are looking for us. The room's gotten too hot."

Serge was cramming socks in his luggage when he heard a liquid trickling sound on the carpet. He turned around. "Coleman! What the fuck are you doing?"

"Peeing on my feet. Like you said."

"In the shower!"

"Ohhhh," said Coleman, nodding. "That makes a lot more sense. I was beginning to wonder because usually your ideas are pretty good."

Serge threw up his arms in exasperation, then unplugged

his DVD player. A regular broadcast came on the set. Local news. A reporter stood in front of an upscale ranch house swarming with detectives. *"Police are still investigating yesterday's apparent abduction of a nursing home mogul from his driveway in this exclusive north Tampa enclave. Shocked neighbors said they saw nothing but heard tires squeal just after dawn . . ."*

The camera zoomed in on a set of dropped car keys with an evidence flag next to a late-model Escalade. *"Authorities have no leads. However, the victim was recently in the news in an unrelated matter after evicting dozens of Medicare residents to make way for more profitable private payers. Despite numerous complaints against the owner, state regulators said the facility complied with all current law and their hands were tied . . ."*

Loud banging from the closet again.

Serge glanced in the direction of the noise. "What's his fucking problem?"

"Maybe his arm's asleep."

Serge went over to the closet. He opened the door. A man lay tied up on the floor. His mouth had been duct-taped shut, blood trickling from his nostrils. Serge reached in his pocket and pulled out a Polaroid photo. The picture was of the same man lying in the same closet with tape across his mouth. Written on the bottom of the photo: *Dodd.*

Serge leaned down and tore the tape off the man's mouth. "Who did this to you?"

The man looked baffled. "Uh . . . you did."

Serge pressed the tape back on the hostage's mouth and closed the door.

"Serge," said Coleman. "Don't you remember doing that? It was just the other morning. We jumped him in his driveway. Then you took that photo after shoving him in the closet . . . And you've been pistol-whipping him for two days."

"Oh, I didn't forget," said Serge. "I was doing a scene from the movie *Memento*. One of my all-time favorites!"

"I saw that one," said Coleman. "But I could never figure out what was going on. Kept jumping around in time."

"Which is why it was such a pleasant surprise," said Serge. "I usually hate it when some show-off wrecks a perfectly good linear story by jumbling the chronology."

Coleman looked toward the closet door. "So what's the plan? Robbery? Ransom?"

"Punishment," said Serge. "Hand me my tools . . ."

ZANESVILLE, OHIO

Two men in dark suits and thin, dark ties rummaged through garbage bags on the porch of a two-story brick duplex. Their matching fedoras made similarities in height and weight seem closer.

"Wonder where they went to," said the man on the left. He reached in one of the sacks and pulled out a shower caddy with suction cups.

"Anywhere," said the other, studying a clock radio in the shape of a football. "Who would have thought they'd come here?"

A group of kids in down vests rode by on bikes. One wore the orange sash of a school crossing guard. The unit on the other side of the duplex had an American flag in a brass holder and a dead wreath on the door.

"They did it in reverse," said the first man, tossing aside a liberated ant farm. "People from Ohio usually flee to Florida. Think they might head back?"

"Doubt it."

The door on the other side of the duplex opened, but the

outside screen door stayed latched. An old woman in curlers had a cordless phone in her hand and a Pall Mall in her mouth. "What are you doing out there? I'm calling the police!"

The man on the left set down a plastic stadium cup and walked up to the screen. He opened a gold badge. "Ma'am, would you mind answering a few questions?"

She hung up the phone. "I didn't do anything."

"No, ma'am. The two gentlemen who lived next door. Did you know them?"

"Not really. They were quiet, always paid on time."

"So you were their landlord?"

"What did they do?"

"Nothing, ma'am. We're just trying to locate next of kin."

"Did something bad happen?"

"We'll ask the questions," said the other, joining his partner and flipping open a notebook. "Did they say where they might have gone?"

"No." She grabbed a ceramic frog from a table near the door and flicked an ash in its mouth. "They were such nice boys."

"You know where they worked?"

"I just know the mall."

"Which one?"

"Colony Square's the only one in Zanesville . . ." She flicked in the frog again, then stopped and squinted at them. "Thought you said you were with the local police."

"No, ma'am," said the one on the left.

"Know what they did at the mall?" asked the other.

"Not really. I think they worked at the food court. I'd see them coming back late in their uniforms . . ." She touched a spot on the side of her chest. "They had these little designs. Choo-choo trains, except instead of smoke coming out of the stacks, there were pretzels."

The men looked at each other and nodded. "Pretzel Depot."

The woman snapped her fingers. "That's the place!"

"Remember anything else that might be helpful?"

"Not really."

They tipped their hats. "Appreciate your help, ma'am."

The men trotted down the porch steps.

"Oh, I do remember something," the woman called after them.

The men stopped and turned. "What's that, ma'am?"

"Funny little thing. I asked them about it once . . ."

"Yes? . . ."

"Come to find out, they hated pretzels. Can you beat that?"

"No, ma'am."

3

A n itinerant burglar with a methamphetamine hobby walked briskly past a grimy motel room on Nebraska Avenue, confidently gesturing to an invisible audience and continuing his thirty-hour filibuster of incorrect conclusions.

Inside the room, Serge unscrewed the thermostat cover and threw it over his shoulder. He dissected the exposed innards, canting his head back at the closet: "Another rule-breaker. Can't tell you how tired I'm getting of their migration." Serge carefully extracted the coiled metal thermal strip and glass bulb of mercury. "Nearly blew a gasket when I first read about that nursing home closing for renovations . . ."

The Magic Fingers started again. Coleman reclined and set a beer on his stomach. "What's wrong with renovating a nursing home? Makes it nicer for the old people."

"Another Florida scam to exploit our seniors, and they keep getting away with it! The state always says its hands are tied . . ." He turned and smiled at Coleman. ". . . But mine aren't."

Coleman drained the can and crumpled it. "Scam?"

Serge rummaged in his suitcase. "Ruthless, out-of-state investors look for old Florida nursing homes full of Medicare patients. They get them super cheap because Medicare doesn't pay much. Then they float some bullshit why they have to close the place for six months—improvements, asbestos, whatever. They just turn all these old people out on the street, granny-dumping on a mass scale . . ." Serge rooted deeper in his luggage. "Where's that darn thing? . . . Then, once investors have emptied the place and made the ostensible repairs, they reopen—exclusively for private payers. Triples the home's book value, and they immediately sell to a conglomerate . . . I found it!" Serge set a sleep timer on the TV and commenced another suitcase search. "Some of the residents are ninety years old, confused, confined to bed, suddenly finding themselves shuttled on stretchers from one temporary shelter to another until they find a new home . . ." More stuff came out of the suitcase: metal hooks, fasteners. ". . . Very traumatic, like repotting temperamental houseplants. Some die within weeks, or even in transit, but the investors don't care . . ."

"What are those hook things?" asked Coleman.

"Marital aids. Got them at a porn store." Serge sorted the hardware on the nightstand. "Was having chronic problems tying people down spread-eagle. The beds in economy motels are usually pretty plain without anything convenient to attach restraints."

The bed stopped vibrating. Coleman put the quarter in the slot again. The bed began humming. "But, Serge, I didn't know you were the kind of person who shopped at porn stores. You're always making fun of my adult videos."

"Because they *are* funny. A housewife answers the door for a plumber, and five minutes later she's wearing nothing but leather riding chaps and blowing a referee's whistle."

Serge unplugged the cord to the bed vibrator.

"Hey!" said Coleman. "I was jiggling here!"

"You need to get off the bed anyway." Serge grabbed the sleep timer and plugged the Magic Fingers cord into it, then plugged the timer back in the wall. He twisted the dial to one hour. It began ticking. "Now it's time to meet our special guest!"

Serge fetched his trusty .45 automatic from the suitcase. He threw open the closet door and violently jerked the man to his feet. The gun went between his eyes. "First funny move and your brains are Martha's pick-of-the-month wallpaper. We understand each other?" The man nodded hard. "Good! To the bed! Lie on your back!" Serge began tying an ankle. "So one day I was in the Pink Pussycat. I always feel gooey when I'm in those places, like I have to take three hot showers as soon as I get out, but I make the sacrifice to chronicle the decay of civilization. I'm walking down the S-and-M aisle with trapezes and water-sports tubing, and as soon as I saw these things, I said, 'Hot damn! That's exactly what I've been looking for!' A lot of people must have been having the same problem, because this company in Hallandale started marketing clamps that cup under the corners of box springs to provide universal mounts for handcuffs and ropes and shit." Serge tossed the empty box to Coleman, who read the product's motto: NO BEDPOSTS? NO PROBLEM!

Serge finished tying knots on the man's limbs. He handed the pistol to Coleman. "Keep an eye on him. I have to get something from the trunk." Serge opened the door a crack and peeked outside. He darted into the parking lot, then dashed back a minute later with two heavy-looking pieces of machinery.

Coleman scratched his head with the gun barrel. "What are those things?"

Serge raised each hand respectively. "Compressor, pneumatic nail gun."

"They look expensive."

"Only forty bucks at the pawnshop."

"That's all?"

"Another cool thing about Florida. You can always depend on construction workers to encounter problems with their portfolios, like drug debts. The savings get passed on to us."

Serge flicked open a Swiss army knife and began stripping the compressor's power cord.

"What are you planning?"

A chuck of insulation flew off Serge's blade. "Science project."

"You mean like in school?"

"My favorite part of education. I'd work on my project all year long, even through summer vacation. The effort finally paid off in seventh grade."

"Which project did you do?"

"All of them, combined into one giant extravaganza—magnetism, optics, kinetic energy, steam engine, photosynthesis, electric generator . . ."—Serge was now stripping wires on thermostat components—". . . model rocketry, a papier-mâché volcano that really worked, and finally a climactic series of violent chemical reactions in a maze of glass pipes and vapor traps—head and shoulders the best science project you ever saw, and definitely better than that kid who beat me germinating those fucking beans."

"You didn't win?"

"The first hint that life wasn't going to be totally fair. I turned my project on, and everything's going perfect, getting bigger, faster, louder, ten different things happening at once. The other kids loved it, but the teacher demanded that I turn it off immediately. I said, 'What do you mean?' She said,

'Shut it down right now!' I said, 'I can't. You're a science teacher and you don't understand basic thermodynamics? Once in motion, this thing's got a mind all its own.' "

"And that's how you lost to the bean kid?"

"They evacuated the school." Serge began twisting bare wires together. "Then it turned out they didn't have enough insurance."

The hostage panicked and started screaming under his mouth tape.

Serge looked up. "What? . . . Oh, I know what you're thinking. Bare wires—fire hazard. Don't worry." Serge began wrapping the naked copper with black electric tape. "Wouldn't dream of not meeting code."

The man squirmed desperately as Serge removed a panel on the side of the nail gun and switched the positive wire to another post. He grabbed the hostage's collar with both hands, ripping open his shirt. The man wept quietly as the nail gun was duct-taped to his chest. Serge used practically the whole roll—"Don't want this thing falling over and causing an accident."

Finally, he was done. Serge stepped back and beamed proudly at the man. "What do you think?"

Two big white eyes.

Serge walked to the foot of the bed and pointed down at the cannibalized temperature control on the edge of the mattress. "Pay attention because I'm only going to explain once. I patched the mercury switch from the thermostat into the power cord of the compressor, which runs the nail gun taped over your heart. I also took the liberty of modifying the gun's wiring to bypass the trigger, so it's fully automatic, like a machine gun. But I digress—back to the thermostat. Did you know they can be used in a pinch to detonate bombs? True. Works on vibration principle. Extremely sensitive. When a temperature change expands or contracts the

metal coil, it tips the bulb full of mercury, a conductive liquid, which flows to the other end, completing the circuit
with the electric contact sticking through the glass here . . ."

Coleman exhaled a cloud of smoke. "What's the ticking
thing plugged into the wall?"

"The part I'm really jazzed about." Serge pulled a quarter from his pocket and stuck it in the Magic Fingers. "A di-
rect connection to Florida motel nostalgia."

"What's wrong?" said Coleman. "The bed's not moving."

"That's what the timer's for. When it gets to zero, it'll
start the bed vibrator, sloshing the mercury, tripping the
compressor and activating the gun . . . Wonder if I have
enough nails in the magazine strip?"

"How many?" asked Coleman.

"Only fifty, but they're the big galvanized ones for
pressure-treated four-by-fours."

"That should be plenty."

More screaming under the mouth tape.

"Don't be such a baby!" said Serge. "It's not as bad as it
sounds. After the first twenty or so, you won't feel a thing.
Besides, there's a tiny chance you can untie yourself and get
that thing off your chest if you don't make any sudden
moves." He rubbed his chin. "Actually, that mercury switch
is pretty sensitive, so I'm probably wrong. On the other
hand, who knows? The key is to keep a chipper outlook.
You've still got at least twenty minutes on the timer."

Coleman leaned toward the socket. "More like fifteen."

"How time flies when you're having fun!" Serge fed the
bandolier of nails into the side of the gun. He couldn't get it
to catch. He tried again. He struggled. "Something's
wrong." He stopped and held the strip to his face. "Shit!
They're the wrong size! My science project is completely
fucked!" He threw the nails against the dresser. "Dammit!
Dammit! Dammit!"

Coleman got up and put a hand on his pal's shoulder. "Easy. It'll be okay."

"The whole day's ruined! And it's the beginning of the week, so the wrong tone has been set. Which means the entire year's shot to bloody hell!" Serge began punching a wall. "Why even go on living? Why! Why! Why! . . ." Serge suddenly stopped and smiled at Coleman. "We're going to have some fun."

"Thought you didn't want to go on living."

"I do my best work under pressure. That's why I create unnecessary alarm." Serge ran out the door and quickly returned with a roll of aluminum foil and a big blue container of salt. He handed Coleman his .45 pistol. "Keep him covered while I turn him over."

Coleman aimed the gun with his right hand and drank a beer with his left. "What are you doing?"

"You'll see . . ." Serge untied the man's left hand and foot and rolled him up on his right side. "No funny business! Coleman's not the best shot when he's drinking, so he might hit something you care about . . ." He tore off three long sheets of foil and spread them across the bed. Then he rolled the man back onto the crinkly sheets and retied his limbs.

Coleman scrunched his face. "I still don't get it."

"Keep watching." Serge reached in the trash for a jumbo convenience-store soda cup. He filled it with water, dumped in a bunch of salt and stirred with a screwdriver, then liberally splashed the man head to foot. He filled the cup a second time, more salt, splashing the man again, a third time. "Lather, rinse, repeat . . ." He cut the power cord to the nail gun, stripped the wires and crinkled foil around the bare ends, holding them in place with more electrical tape.

"Get it now?" said Serge.

Coleman shrugged.

"Salt water is an electrolyte, conducting the foil. Full

body electrocution. The worst! . . ." He closed his eyes and shook at the thought. ". . . Lots of writhing and foaming. Glad we won't be here because only a sicko would want to watch."

"You sure you want to do this?" said Coleman. "I'm not criticizing, but we'll have to lay low again. Last time on TV, they called you a serial killer."

Serge gritted his teeth. "The media!"

"But you did do all that stuff they said. I was there."

"I know, but 'serial' means you get some kind of perverse satisfaction and intend to keep picking out more innocent victims."

"You don't?"

"Of course not!" said Serge. "I always tell myself: This is absolutely the last one. But it's the fucking state we live in! I just keep coming across people who need killing."

Coleman pointed at the bed. "Where'd you find the foil and salt so fast?"

"Same place as the duct tape," said Serge. "Three Boy Scout items you should always keep in your trunk. Duct tape and foil can fix anything."

"Salt?"

"For my food. They never put in enough. I douse everything."

"Isn't too much salt bad?" said Coleman. "Heard it makes you hyper."

"Hyper*tension*," corrected Serge. "But people say that like it's something undesirable. Personally, I want hypertension. Sounds positive. Like in the movies: 'Hang on to your seats for a new level of suspense beyond Hitchcock! It's never-ending hypertension!' . . . How long now?"

Coleman bent down to the timer. "Eight minutes."

Serge crammed a few last items in his suitcase and snapped it shut. "Got all your stuff?"

Coleman picked up a gym bag. "Why didn't you just wire the foil straight to the sleep timer instead of that mercury thing?"

"Because the Magic Fingers wouldn't come into play. Why kill someone if it isn't culturally relevant?"

"It would be less work."

"This isn't about work. It's about enjoying yourself." Serge leaned over the bed. "Have you learned your lesson? Are you going to fuck with old people again?"

The man shook his head hard.

Serge smiled and nodded. "I've got some good news."

The man raised his head expectantly.

"I just saved a bunch of money on my car insurance." He walked out the door with Coleman.

FORT LAUDERDALE

Wooden stakes propped up immature palm trees recently planted in small, grassy islands scattered uniformly across the parking lot of the Broward Mall.

The shopping center was ten miles inland, part of the lush, manicured creep advancing on the Everglades. No industry, just residences, retail and car care. The mall was a medium-size one, as South Florida malls went, but the parking lot appeared especially large when it was empty at times like this, which was ten A.M. on a Tuesday.

A senior citizens' bus pulled up to the curb in front of JCPenney. Retirees climbed out and headed into the store at a velocity that was the opposite of staying out of the way. A few shuffled slightly faster to get dibs on the complimentary electric scooters. The familiarity of the department store made them comfortable. They liked to shop weekday mornings when there weren't a bunch of other customers rushing around them in the aisles. Then they all crammed the cafeterias for lunch.

Among them were three lifelong friends. Used to be six, before the funerals started. Like many aging residents of Miami-Dade, they were forced out of their retirement home when it stopped taking Medicare and had to migrate north across the county line to one of the newer, cookie-cutter facilities. They were not happy about it. They wore untucked guayaberas.

The oldest grabbed an electric scooter and rode alongside his two friends, who walked with canes up the aisle toward men's socks. They picked out sheer, dark ones that would rise to their shins. The man on the scooter tossed a pair in his handlebar basket and hit the chair's accelerator. It took off at a high rate of speed. In reverse. The man's head disappeared under a row of sport coats hanging along the wall. "Son of a bitch!"

Salespeople came running. All they could see were two white legs below a rack of thrashing blazers. They pulled the scooter out.

"Sir, are you all right?"

"No, he's not all right," said one of his companions. "He's an idiot!"

"It wasn't me!" said the man on the scooter. "The damn thing malfunctioned!"

"Every scooter you get on malfunctions!"

"They need a recall."

"Guys," said the third member of the trio. "Let's not get into this again. We have the day to enjoy."

They headed up another aisle. "I need to look at shoes." The scooter veered off.

"We'll be over at the watches."

Two hunched men in guayaberas approached a display case. They leaned their canes against the glass. The woman behind the counter was tall, with cropped brunette hair and sophistication. Her smile had a touch of pity, but in a good way. Memories of her late grandfather. "What can I show you today?"

The taller one wore a Scottish golf cap. "I've had cheap watches my whole life. I've decided to treat myself."

"How much were you thinking of spending?"

"The hell does it matter?" said the shorter one, adjusting his flat-brimmed straw hat and chewing a toothpick. "I'll be dead soon."

The woman maintained poise. "I have some nice ones I think you'll like."

She laid a pair of five-hundred-dollar jobs side by side on the counter. Pearl inlays, sterling bands.

"Is this a joke?" said the one in the straw hat.

"What do you mean?"

"There aren't any numbers. Not even little markers. How am I supposed to tell time?"

"Sir, the plain face is very stylish."

"Right. I'll be walking around very stylish—and late." He nudged his buddy. "Did you get that? This is the new style. They give you less and charge more."

The saleswoman began removing the watches.

"No," said the one in the golf cap. "Leave those out. I kind of like 'em."

"I want numbers," said the straw hat.

The woman reached back inside the case again with an unflappable smile. "I think you might prefer these. Sleek, very thin. Hardly know you have it on." She laid two more watches next to the first pair. Gold with black cowhide bands.

"Roman numerals? Do I look Roman?" He turned to his friend. "You know any buses that arrive at X?"

"Leave those out," said the golf cap. "They're growing on me."

"I have some with American numbers," said the saleswoman. Two more watches on the counter.

"I don't know." He turned to his friend. "What do you think?"

"I think I like that one down there." He pointed toward the far end of the case.

"Sir, that's an excellent choice. But I have to warn you it's a little up there."

"Let me see it."

She retrieved the watch and set it beside the others—except she placed this one on a velvet pad. "One of our finest. Swiss, self-winding. Twenty-four carat."

"Are those real diamonds marking the hours?"

She nodded.

"Doesn't have a price tag."

"Thirty-eight hundred," said the woman.

The man in the golf cap whistled at the figure. "That's a lot!"

The saleswoman reached for the timepiece. "If it's too much—"

"I didn't say that. Leave it. What about that other one there that was next to it in the case?"

"Same manufacturer, slightly different style. The first is for day. The other's night."

"People do that?"

"They do that."

"Can I see them side by side?"

She fetched the other watch.

The golf cap picked it up and turned to his friend. "What do you think?"

"I don't know. Now I'm confused."

An electric scooter zipped by in the background.

"I'll take this one," said the golf cap. "Do you have gift wrap?"

"I thought it was for you," said the woman.

"I might forget by the time I get home. It'll be a nice surprise."

A tremendous crash.

Everyone in the vicinity jumped and spun around. An electric scooter was imbedded sideways in what used to be a tower of glass shelves displaying last-second Father's Day gifts. It was one of those long crashes where loosened shelving continued to fall and shatter. An old man lay on the ground, covered with broken glass. Panicked employees ran over. One got the first-aid kit. They carefully picked the biggest, sharpest pieces off the man's chest and helped him up into a sitting position.

"Sir! Are you okay? Does anything hurt?"

"That goddam thing tried to kill me!"

"But you're okay, right? Do you want an ambulance?"

"Don't touch me!" He stood and brushed glass dust from his pink trousers. "I'm hungry."

The staff held its breath as the man hobbled off. Their eyes followed him all the way across the store until he was safely out the door to the parking lot, providing a modicum of liability defense.

The floor manager's heart was pounding. He looked at the other salespeople and wiped his forehead. "I think we just dodged a lawsuit." The employees headed back to their respective departments. A tall brunette returned to her sales counter.

The watches and men were gone.

MEANWHILE, BACK IN TAMPA

A '71 Buick sat outside an antique mall in Palma Ceia. A sign announced an autographing event: TODAY ONLY!

Serge and Coleman stood in the back of a long line. It was moving, but not fast enough.

"What's taking so long?" said Serge, standing on tiptoes and stretching his neck. "I'll bet someone's gabbing up there."

"Serge, I think I need to sit down."

"You're hammered, aren't you?"

Coleman giggled. "You are correct, trivia breath!"

"I hate it when you get like this. Just don't touch anything."

Coleman picked up a rare figurine of a sad clown with a crumpled hat.

"Gimme that!" Serge set it back on a shelf. "We have to pay for anything we break. This isn't like one of those big stores where we can run away again."

Coleman swayed and latched on to a china cabinet. Plates rattled.

"Watch it!" Serge grabbed Coleman by the shoulders and carefully balanced him on the vertical axis. He slowly removed his hands. "There. Don't move."

"Was this always an antique place?" asked Coleman. "From the outside it looked like it used to be a restaurant or something."

"It was," said Serge. "Old neighborhood bar and grill called Dino's. The kind of place with live honky-tonk musicians in the corner. True story: Forty years ago, some customer was in here drinking and it begins getting late and suddenly the guy gets up and starts playing a guitar left on the stage by one of the musicians on break. I mean like a crazy man, attacking the instrument, distressed noise. They thought he was having a seizure."

"Was he?"

"Naw, it was just Jimi Hendrix. Knocking back a few after playing Curtis Hixon or some other torn-down arena." Serge began jamming on an air guitar behind his head: ". . . *Wah-wah-wah-wah-wowoooowah-wah-wah!* . . . *Purple Haze inside my veins!* . . ."

The man in line in front of them turned around. Serge was playing with his teeth now. ". . . *Waahhhoooo-wah-wah-zowoozoo-wahhhhhh!* . . ."

"Sir!" said the man. "Do you mind?"

Serge stopped and looked up. "Oh, excuse me . . ."

The man turned back around.

". . . *While I kiss the sky!*"

The man turned back again with disdain.

Serge grinned.

"Serge," said Coleman. "This line is taking a lot longer than you said. Let's get out of here."

"Hang on," said Serge. "I hate lines, too. But sometimes it's worth it. This may be our last chance to meet the great Karl Slover."

"Karl?"

"You're joking, right? I told you about him in the car."

"Must have been doing something. Who is he?"

"Just one of the last living Munchkins is who. And Tampa has him! Lives just up the street. But I decided to wait until a public appearance instead of knocking on his door because I'm not familiar with Munchkin lifestyle and didn't want to barge in on anything freaky."

"Is this part of your current Florida movie kick?" Coleman picked up a ceramic German boy playing the accordion.

Serge grabbed the figurine and replaced it on the shelf. "Nothing *current* about it. This is different from every previous obsession. Movies are my life now."

"If you say so."

"No, really. I've dedicated my existence to absorbing the entire film history of Florida so I can find out what the problem is."

"I didn't know there was a problem."

"Oh, there's a problem all right." Serge snatched a sleeping cherub from Coleman's hands. "Why should California get all the glory? Every movie filmed out there has that same shot, aimed up at tall rows of palm trees running down both sides of the street like we should all genuflect. Shit, the *bad* parts of Fort Myers have that."

"Doesn't seem fair."

"Here's the thing that really makes me want to kill. A movie is supposed to depict Florida, and they don't even pay us the common courtesy of shooting it here. Remember *Some Like It Hot*? Filmed at the Hotel del Coronado in San Diego. And don't even get me started on the Miami Beach scenes in *Get Shorty*."

"That wasn't Miami Beach?"

"Santa Monica," said Serge. "I want answers."

"But, Serge, what can one person do?"

"That's what they said back in the 2000 election. Then Katherine Harris ends up in Congress. But not this time. Did you know there used to be studios all over this state competing with Hollywood? During the silent era, one was almost as big. Jacksonville."

"What happened?"

"Shortsighted civic leaders and residents complaining about disruptions. The last straw was when they used a bunch of extras to film a riot, and it became a real riot." Serge tilted his head to see around the line. "Then, to add insult, the latest blow from California. They're making a move on our cash crop."

"What's that?"

"You say Florida, and people think oranges and tourism. But our biggest export is weirdness. Remember a few years ago with those fugitives and chads and Elian and that guy who slept with his pet alligator under suspicious circumstances and had all those bite marks? Everyone you talked to: 'Man, you people in Florida are crazy!' Then California elects a robot and puts a bunch of losers on trial. They stole our weirdness crown. I mean to take it back."

The line grew shorter until Coleman could see someone sitting behind a desk signing movie stills. "He's short."

"Tall for a Munchkin," said Serge. "Did you know he played six different parts?"

"Which?"

"One of the trumpeters, a female Munchkin in a bonnet, and who can forget those eggs where the cute little baby Munchkins popped out?"

Coleman pointed. "Looks like we're up."

An assistant at the desk asked which movie photos they'd like to purchase.

"Just a second," said Serge. "I need to do something first." He turned to the people in line behind him. "Could you please step back . . . That's right, a little more . . ."

Serge faced the desk again. "Karl, this is going to bring back memories . . ." He placed his hands on his hips and began thrusting his pelvis: "We represent the lollipop *guild*! . . . the lollipop *guild*! . . . the lollipop *guild*! . . . We represent . . ."

The assistant stood up. "Sir, please . . ."

"Wait, there's another verse."

"We have a long line."

"All right," said Serge. "Hey, Karl, bet you haven't heard that in a long time. But don't get all misty on me . . ."

"Sir, which photograph?"

"Right, which picture? Let's see . . . the one with the good witch? No . . . Here's one with Dorothy and Toto . . . Karl, you knew Garland. What was she like? Did she keep in touch or just climb over the Munchkins on her way up? Any red flags of the drug abuse yet to come? . . ."

"Sir!"

"Of course. That would be out of school. And you're a class act . . . Did you get to see the flying monkeys? They scared the shit out of me when I was a kid! What about you?

I mean, you were an adult and knew they were fake. Still, the concept—minding your own business walking along the yellow brick road. Did you realize they have these giant condors in the Pacific Northwest that can pick up a full-grown Munchkin? Then you're sitting two hundred feet up a tree in a big nest with the hatchlings. What kind of life is that? My advice: Stay clear of Portland . . ."

"Sir, I'm afraid we're going to have to ask you to leave."

"Leave? . . . Oh, I see what this is about. Moving product, making him sign his little hand off. Well, your days of exploiting him are over! . . . Karl, I got your back . . ."

"We're calling the police."

"Good. Call the press, too. Let's see what *they* think about this Munchkin sweat farm."

Crash.

A rack of figurines went over.

"Coleman! Run! . . ."

THE FOOD COURT OF A NONDESCRIPT MALL IN BURBANK

A man in a paper hat swept the floor behind the counter. "I hate pretzels!"

"Shhhh!" said Ford. "The customers."

"What customers?" said Mark, a choo-choo over his right breast.

"Some might come in," said Ford.

Mark set his broom against the wall. "Didn't you tell them we didn't want to be closers?"

"It's all they had." Ford looked down at a stack of type-written pages that he kept behind the register.

"I hate closing," said Mark. He glanced up at the clock, fifteen till ten. "You get everything put away, all ready to split, and some idiots come in with a minute to go and can't make up their minds. Then they finally order something complex."

Ford crossed out a verb with his pen, making it active. "Looks like we're in luck tonight."

Mark pointed at the pages. "Where'd you learn this screenwriting stuff, anyway?"

"Wannabe screenwriting magazines full of ads saying they'll get your script produced and then request five hundred dollars for copying and postage every few weeks as long as you're stupid enough. But if you stick to the articles, you're okay."

Mark read the current page over Ford's shoulder. "It's just talking."

"That's how it's done. All dialogue. Once you're familiar with your characters, it flows. Most of mine are people I know." He marked through a nonagreeing pronoun. "A minute of talking, a page. Hundred pages, you got a movie. You need a setting, just give it a label and the movie people figure the rest."

"Label?"

"Say you need a busy city street at night? Just type: 'busy city street at night.' They'll come up with the honking Checker cabs and neon cocktail glasses and Latin kids in white tank tops and Saint Christopher medals spilling out of a pizzeria. All that detail stuff is for books. I just need a label."

"What about a space station?" asked Mark.

"Or a space station," said Ford. "Or the food court of a nondescript mall in Burbank."

"What are these abbreviations, O.S.? P.O.V.?"

"Off stage, point of view. Like, 'Character reacts to noise O.S.,' or 'Switch to killer's P.O.V.' "

"Can I see?"

Ford handed the stack to Mark, who slowly became engrossed. "Say, this ain't bad. Like I'm not even reading, just turning pages."

"Based on true events. Wrote most of it since I got here and bought that cheap typewriter at the pawnshop."

"What are all these dollar signs?"

"The capital *S* doesn't work."

"You put me in here. You changed my name to Mark."

"For legal reasons . . ."

"You made me stupid."

". . . In case you sued."

A group of blue-collar young men strolled through the food court, trying to decide.

"Oh, no," said Mark. A minute till ten, said the clock.

"They'll probably eat somewhere else," said Ford.

"Go to the Magic Wok," said Mark. "*Please* go to the Magic Wok."

"See?" said Ford. "They're heading somewhere else."

"They're turning around!" said Mark. "They're looking at our sign. Fuck, fuck, fuck! . . ."

The young men approached the counter. Ford stepped up to the register and smiled. "Can I take your order?"

"Just a sec." Their eyes angled up at the menu board. "Okay, wait." They read some more. They talked it over among themselves. They came to a decision. They decided against it. The first customer pointed up over Ford's head. "What's the Orient Express?"

"Slightly tangy. Comes with Chinese mustard."

"Can I get extra packets?"

"Sure."

"What about the Rock Island Line?"

"Rock salt," said Ford. "Not really rock salt, but they tell us to say that. It's just big salt."

"Is it salty?"

"Pretty salty."

Background: ". . . *Fuck, fuck, fuck* . . ."

Ford briefly turned his head: "Shhhh!"

"The Grand Central Station?" asked the customer.

"Our largest," said Ford. "Feeds two."

"I don't know." The customer looked at his friends. "What do you think, guys?"

"... *Fuck!* ..."

The customer quickly spun back to the counter.

Ford smiled nervously.

"What was that?"

"I didn't say anything," said Ford.

"Not you. That guy back there."

"I didn't hear anything," said Ford. He noticed a blue Navy anchor on the man's forearm.

"Yeah, he said something all right. Was he talking to us?"

"I'm sorry," said Ford. "He's had a hard day."

"*I've* had a hard day. And now all I want to do is eat a pretzel, but somebody's got a *fucking attitude*!"

"You ever work retail?" snapped Mark. He tapped the face on his wristwatch. "It's four after closing now. But no, we can't go home 'cause you can't pick a snack!"

Mark thought his eyes were playing tricks the way the man vaulted the counter from a standing start. Ford jumped in front of the enraged customer and put his hands up in surrender. "Free pretzels! Your friends, too! Anything you want! We're just going to throw them out anyway!"

The customer was still breathing fast. "If he apologizes."

"What!" said Mark.

"Mark! Shut up!" said Ford, then to himself: "Dammit, all I wanted to do was go home and watch *Training Day*."

"*Training Day*?"

"Yeah, I saw *Bad Lieutenant* last night so I was going to follow up."

"Can't believe you fuckin' said that!"

Ford hopped back and raised his hands again. "Don't hit me!"

But the man was smiling now. "Those are two of my all-time favorite films!"

"It's the same movie," said Ford.

"What do you mean?"

"Watch 'em back-to-back. *Lieutenant* was a little-known character study. The *Training Day* people must have recognized revenue potential and added the missing commercial pieces."

The customer looked up at thin air, visualizing. He nodded. "You know, you're right." The customer put out his hand. "Pedro Jimenez."

Ford shook it. "Ford Oelman."

"I love movies," said Pedro.

"Me, too," said Ford.

"Come on!" Mark nagged. "What's taking so long?"

"Shut the hell up!" yelled Pedro. "I haven't decided about you yet!"

Mark raised his broom as a defensive weapon.

Pedro turned back to Ford. "So why aren't you in them?"

"In what?"

"The movies. Why are you working here?"

"What are you talking about?" said Ford. "You don't just *decide* to be in movies."

"Not lead actor," Pedro said with a laugh. "There's a million other jobs. I mean, you love movies, and you're in the film capital of the universe. But you're working in a pretzel shop? Shoot, *I'm* in movies."

"You are? What do you do?"

"Props department at Vistamax across the street," said Pedro. "But I've been there long enough that sometimes I get to be a standby carpenter. That's what I used to do, hammering studs under the hot sun, but now I build movie sets in air-conditioning. Pays a hell of a lot better, too. And I'm that much closer to my dream."

"What's your dream?"

"To act. Ever since seeing *The Wild One*. First I wanted to be a *serious* actor, so I moved to New York and started auditioning off Broadway. Three or four days a week for six months, memorizing lines, rehearsing in a cramped apartment with my roommate, but the closest thing to a real part was when I got hired as a toy soldier at FAO Schwarz. And I even lost *that* role."

"What happened?"

"The whole time I'm working there, I'm thinking, Don't be an ingrate. You came to New York to act, so act. I kept repeating in my head, 'You're a soldier, you're a soldier . . .' One day I hear these security guards yelling: 'Stop! Stop! Shoplifter!' This guy goes running past, and I think, Hey, I'm a soldier, so I run out the door and chase him up Fifth Avenue in my uniform and those big rosy circles on my cheeks."

"That got you fired?"

"No. But then I caught the guy. Can you believe it? Who would have thought, running in that big hat with the chin strap? Tackled him on the corner of Fifty-seventh."

"So *that* got you fired?"

"No. But I was Method acting."

"And?"

"I bayoneted him. It was just a rubber bayonet, but the tabloids couldn't resist running the photos those tourists took. The store said it wasn't exactly the image they were going for. That's when I came out here and took the job in props, which led to the standby carpenter gig."

"What's a standby carpenter do?"

"Say some spoiled director changes his mind and wants a door where there's a window. You got thirty minutes."

"See any stars?"

"All the time. They're called The Talent. We're The Crew. The people who put deals together over lunch are The Suits. On the set, The Crew isn't allowed to speak to The Talent. In fact, it's better you don't even look at them. Who knows what'll tick them off? One word from Cameron and there's a new carpenter the next day."

"Sounds like a nasty place to work."

"Actually it's not. The Talent gets mobbed all the time on the street—they just want to work in peace. What you do if you're The Crew is act like they don't exist. The breaks between shoots can get pretty long. They're people, too. Sometimes they just want someone to talk to. They strike up a conversation with you, and you go 'uh-huh,' and keep on working, like *they're* the pests."

"So in a way," said Ford, "when you're on the set, you're an actor, too."

"I never thought of it that way."

"Could I get into props?" asked Ford.

"Definitely. Right now there's a couple temp openings, but with the turnover, you'd be full-time before you know it."

"Maybe I can show someone my script?"

Pedro laughed again.

"What's so funny?"

"Everyone in this town's carrying a script around with him."

"Really?"

Pedro reached in his back pocket and pulled out a stack of pages folded lengthwise. "Here's mine."

Ford took it and began reading.

"Just don't be pushy," said Pedro. "When you're in the right place, act like you're reading something really fantastic and make them curious. When they ask, tell them they can't see it. That's how this business works."

"I have a lot to learn," said Ford, flipping Pedro's script back to the cover and looking at the title in big, bold letters: *Nailed!* "What's it about?"

"This good-looking standby carpenter is drafted to act in a key scene by a desperate director after one of the stars has a fatal accident on the set. And he steals the show! Sounds far-fetched, but that's how Harrison Ford got his break, ex-

THE BIG BAMBOO ❋ 73

cept the fatal part. But here's my big twist in the climax that puts it over the top: Turns out the carpenter is the one who sabotaged the drawbridge that fell on the other actor in the first place!"

"I like the title."

"Works on multiple levels," said Pedro. "There's the obvious carpentry meaning, then it refers to the first actor getting killed, and finally the stand-in *nails* his role. Think it's too intellectual?"

"Audiences want to grow."

"That's what I thought."

Ford handed the script back. "Any interest?"

"Oh, sure. All the people at the parties say they're in love with it. But I'm not releasing the option unless I get to play myself. It's going to be my *Good Will Hunting*."

"Sounds great."

"Really think so? And you're a writer, too, so that means a lot more. Everyone who reads it at the parties can't believe it hasn't already been scooped up. Actually, they don't read it. They just look at the first couple pages like you did, and I tell them the rest while they eat finger food. That's those grease spots. Everyone's absolutely crazy about it!"

"Only one thing . . ." said Ford.

"You hate it. I knew it! Just like the people at the parties. They *said* they loved it, but then talk filtered back to me later. This fucking town . . ."

"No. You got me wrong. It's—"

"It's what?"

"The carpenter needs to be sympathetic."

"What do you mean?"

"Right now he's just an asshole. The audience will side with the dead actor, no matter how good the carpenter performs. Word of mouth will kill the second weekend receipts."

"How do I fix it?"

"Backstory the first actor as a jerk, so the audience already hates him. Then they'll cheer the sabotage, which is revenge for something the actor did to the carpenter in a flashback. But it has to be a really big screwing-over to justify murder. Like something involving his family."

"Or a smaller screwing-over, and I just have him sprain his ankle falling in the moat?"

"Or that."

Pedro finished taking notes on a Pretzel Depot napkin. "Gee, thanks."

"Can I ask a favor?" said Ford.

"Go for it."

"You mentioned part-time positions. Plural. You think maybe my friend Mark . . ."

"I knew you were going to ask that," said Pedro, folding the napkin and sliding it into his pocket. "Oh, why not? You helped me with my script."

Two men in dark suits and thin, dark ties sat in row 34. Most of the other passengers were asleep. The jet was over water.

An arm reached up and clicked on a reading light. The men stared again at a long-range surveillance photo of two young men with no forwarding address from Ohio.

"Where could they have gone?"

6

FORT LAUDERDALE

three retirees sported guayaberas and super moods as they bopped jauntily up the sidewalk. The trio crossed Las Olas at the light and turned in a doorway. The bar had all its windows open to the bright Atlantic Ocean on the other side of A1A.

The Elbo Room.

It was barely after noon on a Tuesday, so all the stools were available except the one under another old-timer with a thick crop of white hair and a barber shirt.

The guys headed his way with broad smiles. "Roy!"

Roy. The Pawn King. Ran a Collins Avenue shop back in the day, the most dependable fence on the beach. Now he cut hair at the Deauville. Except the scene at that end of the strip had long since dried up and there were no customers. Roy didn't mind. He spent his shifts sitting in one of the barber chairs, reading the *Herald* beneath faded photos of the celebrities getting trims fifty years ago. Or, like today, when he got a call from the old gang and closed up early for a little side action.

Roy hopped off his stool with his own smile and they all hugged. "Sergio! Chi-Chi! Coltrane! Great to see you! Been too long!"

"Roy! You look great!"

"Thanks." He sat back down. "But why'd you have us meet up here? It's more of a drive."

"Ask Mr. Movie History."

"Sergio . . ." Roy nodded. "Should have known."

Sergio swiveled on his stool, lost in time. "The good ol' Elbo Room, established 1938."

"It's changed too much," said Roy.

"Not for me," said Sergio. "It's the spirit that counts. Can you feel it?"

Chi-Chi leaned to Roy. "He had an espresso."

"When I close my eyes, I'm right back in that movie." Sergio pointed at the old publicity photos on the north wall. "Instead of Hollywood, they held the premiere at the landmark Gateway Theater up on Sunrise. Made the newsreels."

The bartender came over. "What'll it be, fellas?"

Sergio pointed toward a corner. "Isn't that where the Basil Demetomos Dialectic Jazz Quintet played?"

"We don't have jazz here. Just rock."

"No, in the movie. *Where the Boys Are*."

"Movie?"

"Paula Prentiss, George Hamilton. Travis McGee's marina was in the aerial shot over the opening credits. Just got finished studying the anniversary DVD. In the subtitles, they misspelled the Elbo Room through the whole damn thing. Added a *w*. Bet that burns your ass with all your obvious pride working here."

"You been drinking?"

"No," said Chi-Chi. "But we need to start. Round of Jack, neat."

"You got it."

Roy looked around. "Who's missing? Where's Moondog?"

Chi-Chi removed his toothpick and shook his head. "Two months ago."

"Didn't hear," said Roy.

"It was quick," said Coltrane. "Nobody expected."

"What's happening to us?" said Roy. "We used to run this place."

"Time," said Chi-Chi. "The old guard's almost all gone. First Greek Tommy, then Mort the Undertaker, now Moondog. Soon, no one will be left to tell these kids how it was."

"To happier topics," said Roy. "You mentioned on the phone about some swag?"

Chi-Chi placed a shaving bag on the bar. "Good score." He began removing watches. "Most are low-end but we got two beauts."

Roy stuck a jeweler's loupe in his eye and held the watches to his face. "These *are* nice." He picked up another. "Who'd you hit?"

"JCPenney."

"You're joking."

Chi-Chi took the toothpick out again. "Candy from a baby."

Roy grabbed another watch. "What game did you use?"

"Electric scooter."

"That's a good game," said Roy.

"Should have been there," said Coltrane. "It was priceless. Sergio was just supposed to create a diversion, but he kind of overdid it."

"Never seen so much broken glass," said Chi-Chi. "Thought he wasn't going to be able to get up, and we'd have to abort."

"You have to remember how suppressed the times were," said Sergio. "They slipped all kinds of secret stuff into that movie. Like when Timothy Hutton's dad, Jim, is hitchhiking, and the convertible full of spring-breaking coeds pulls up, and the driver asks, 'What size are your feet?' He says, 'Thirteen.' And she says, 'Get in!' . . ."

Roy took the jeweler's loupe out of his eye. "I can give you three."

"Sounds fair."

The bartender arrived with shots.

"The studio was going to use Hollywood heavies for the score," said Sergio. "But then newcomer Connie Francis said she only worked with a friend from Brooklyn. They thought she was crazy until they heard the demo. That young composer? Neil Sedaka!"

"Don't mind me asking," said Roy. "But why do you still do it? You don't need the money."

"Same reason as you," said Chi-Chi. "Feel alive."

"Here's to that," said Coltrane.

Roy set his empty glass down. "Speaking of trivia, Sergio, you seen that grandson of yours lately? The police came around again."

"Little Serge? Who knows? Hadn't heard from him for six months. Then he's banging on my window at three in the morning with a crazy story about figuring out the mystery of how that hermit pioneer moved twenty-ton boulders to build the Coral Castle south of Miami. Says he's off to build an even bigger one and runs away. That was July."

"Takes after you," said Chi-Chi.

"Where you going for lunch?" asked Roy.

"Cafeteria," said Coltrane. "Want to join us?"

"Not the cafeteria again!" said Sergio.

"What's wrong with the cafeteria?"

"Old people eat there."

"We're old."

"That's the point," said Sergio. "The Big Clock's ticking.

Whenever I'm in a cafeteria line, all I can think about is death breathing down my neck, and I'm stuck behind some slow-motion putz who can't decide whether he wants the bowl of Jell-O cubes."

"We're leaving for the cafeteria now," said Chi-Chi. "Come or don't."

"Wait up!" yelled Sergio.

TAMPA

Farther south on Nebraska Avenue, the hooker motels thin out. Traffic becomes lighter, then none at all as the road reaches an abandoned stretch of downtown so lifeless it appears radioactive. Not even bums or roaches. The only thing open is the historic Union Station, recently restored and used by Amtrak to service a skeleton clientele.

A '71 Buick Riviera rumbled across the train tracks and pulled around behind a boarded-up brick warehouse. A Lexus was already there.

"Why are we stopping here?" asked Coleman, pulling a sixer from a paper sack.

"I have to have sex with that woman."

"But we were going to do stuff."

"I know, but I gave her my word." Serge opened the door. "This won't take long."

"If you don't want to be here, why don't we split? People blow off appointments all the time."

"That's the problem with society," said Serge. "No premium on being dependable. Like when I drop off one-hour photos, I'm back in fifty-nine minutes and fifty-nine seconds. But are they ready? Oh, no. They're shorthanded today or got an overflow of Christmas orders. But if my coupon is *one day* past expiration—sorry, they have rules."

"What does all that have to do with coming here?"

"I believe in personal responsibility," said Serge. "If you want to change society, start with yourself and hope for karma. So now I'm forced to have sex if I want my photos on time."

A piece of plywood had already been crowbarred off a ground-floor window on the back of the building. They climbed inside. Serge headed up a rickety staircase. Coleman stayed on the bottom step, keeping lookout through a knothole.

Fifteen minutes passed in silence. Coleman was completing his third Schlitz when he began to detect a rhythmic creaking in the overhead joists. He pulled another can off the plastic ring and looked up toward the closed door at the top of the stairs.

Behind the door was a loft—the one film crews had used as *The Punisher*'s hideout in the fictitious Railroad Hotel. All evidence of that was now gone, just two people and a sleeping bag.

"They shot the Puerto Rico scenes at Fort DeSoto and Honeymoon Island," said Serge, thrusting hard. "The restaurant with the Memphis assassin was the venerable Goody Goody, 119 North Florida Avenue . . ."

"*Ohhhh! Ohhhh! My God! Ohhhh! I'm almost there! Don't stop! Faster, you maniac, faster! . . .*"

"Saints and Sinners nightclub was the Bank of America, Kennedy and Cass . . ."

At the foot of the stairs, Coleman picked at a chip of paint, trying to ignore the female shrieks.

"*Yesss! Yesss! Yesss! Yesss! Punish me! . . .*"

"Adlai Stevenson's running mate in fifty-six?"

"*Estes Kefauver! . . .*"

Serge gasped and quivered at the apex. His eyelids fluttered, a montage of nanosecond images from a half-century of Florida celluloid flashed across his mind's eye. *Hell Har-*

bor, *A Guy Named Joe, Tarzan's Secret Treasure, 30 Seconds Over Tokyo, Mr. Peabody and the Mermaid, Follow That Dream, Absence of Malice, The Creature from the Black Lagoon, Black Sunday, Ace Ventura, There's Something About Mary* . . .

"*Don't stop!* . . ."

He stopped. His eyes flew wide. "I've got it! I've got the opening hook!"

Coleman saw the loft's door fly open. Serge raced down the stairs, zipping his pants. "I've got the hook!"

A woman's voice screamed through the open door behind them. "*You son of a bitch! Come back here!* . . ."

7

HOLLYWOOD

A man floated facedown in a swimming pool.

"Is he dead?"

"Definitely."

"But how can he be dead?" asked Mark. "You said the movie's about him."

"It starts at the end and then goes back."

"Shhhh!" said Ford. "The scene with our apartment is coming up."

On TV: a black-and-white Hollywood street sloping down into the city. A sign at the corner: ALTO NIDO. The picture panned up to an open third-story window with gauzy curtains blowing out.

"*. . . I was living in an apartment house above Ivar and Franklin . . .*"

The camera zoomed through the curtains to a man in a bathrobe hunting and pecking on a manual typewriter. A pencil was clutched sideways in his teeth.

"Is that the guy from the pool?" asked Mark.

"I can't believe you've never seen *Sunset Boulevard*," said Pedro.

It had been two weeks since a pair of full-time slots opened up in the props department, and Ford and Mark had turned in their food court uniforms for good. They were assigned the same shift as Pedro, who introduced them to the rest of the gang in the hernia belts: Tino Carbella and Ray "Butter Fingers" Koch, who regularly had his pay docked.

"They're also aspiring actors," said Pedro. "Even had a few small speaking parts. A line here and there, but their characters are never fleshed out."

These were the good times. They worked together, and they played together.

They zipped set to set in golf carts. They talked "the industry" while tagging Westminster mantel clocks with red reservation slips. They brown-bagged it together in "Central Park," the all-purpose New York sliver of backlot behind the Sphinx and the all-purpose jungle lagoon. There was chemistry.

"I hate props," said Mark.

Then, a FOR RENT sign went up. Pedro placed a security deposit on a third-floor unit at the Alto Nido, and they all moved in together. Ford kept polishing his script and kept arriving early for work. He ignored Pedro's subtlety advice, instead delivering copies of his screenplay to the offices of every Vistamax exec remotely near the decision chain to green-light a project.

"You're being too pushy," said Pedro.

"Can't help it," said Ford. "I just have this feeling, like something big is about to happen."

VISTAMAX STUDIOS

Guards in a glass booth checked IDs and waved luxury vehicles through the antique iron front gates, which had been used as props in a recent send-up of Paramount Pictures.

Golf carts whizzed between soundstages. Two workers carried a plastic mountain range. At the very rear of the compound was the administration building. Twin silver Rolls-Royces flanked the entrance, twin names stenciled on cement curbs: M. GLICK, I. GLICK.

Mel and Ian sat at identical mahogany desks, side by side, in their spacious office overlooking Warner Bros. Studios in beautiful downtown Burbank. Behind their desks was a giant, scowling portrait of their grandfather and studio founder Horatio "Lockjaw" Glickschitz.

Horatio had originally launched his new studio as Screen Gems, until the lawsuit from the first Screen Gems, and it became Screen Jewelry for a brief period from 1931 until 1933, when it was finally and fatefully rechristened Olympus Films, a name that would grow in stature for five decades until the studio was acquired in an extremely hostile takeover by the Japanese generic VCR giant Vistamax. The brothers were out. But the new owners had bet heavily on the Beta format and, after the manufacturing division tanked in Osaka, they brought the Glicks back on board with a controlling interest of voting shares and a mandate to cut costs to the bone.

Accidentally, it worked.

A Vistamax production rarely cracked the top ten, but the budgets were so farcically low it didn't matter. The big main-street theaters had long since been replaced by mall-plex-o-ramas with twenty-odd screens that all needed to be filled. Multiplied by thousands of malls across America and, by default, a *bad* Vistamax film paid for itself the first weekend.

The Japanese said: More.

The Glicks were up to it, cranking out a preposterous volume with three-week shooting schedules and zero production values. An assembly line of eighty films a year, just like in the old days when everyone was under contract. This is how Vistamax became known as a "throwback" studio. That, and they fucked everyone. The highest-paid department was legal.

The Japanese were thrilled. They pumped dividends back into the studio, which the Glicks invested in a series of extremely profitable teen slasher flicks and personal cocaine habits that lasted to this day. Which was a Monday. . . . A secretary knocked on the door.

"Come in."

"Your nine o'clock," said Betty.

The Glicks wiped their noses and slid coke drawers shut.

Three unsure young men entered and stood in the center of the room. They all had spiked, gelled hair like the Glicks did—last week. They stared at the brothers' shaved heads and suffered a loss of nerve.

The Glicks simultaneously checked appointment books, then leaned back in padded European upholstery and folded hands in their laps.

"So, you want us to back your independent film," said Ian.

"Indies used to be hot," said Mel.

"But now they're ice-cold," said Ian.

"Which means they're just about to get hot again," said Mel. "Your timing's perfect."

"Tell us about it," said Ian.

The young man in the middle timidly stepped forward. "It's the story of a—"

"No," said Mel. "How much can we make it for?"

The young man was off balance. "Uh, depends on what you want . . ."

"We want shit," said Ian.

The young man glanced at his partners, then back at the brothers. "Do you know what the story's about?"

"No," said Mel.

"But we've heard good things," said Ian.

"How much?" asked Mel.

"It's hard to say because the story—"

"Does the story have a beginning and an end?" asked Ian.

The young man nodded.

"Then you're way ahead of the game," said Mel.

"You wouldn't believe some of the people we get in here," said Ian.

"It's got a beginning and an end," said Mel. "So there's your movie. Any problems in between, our indie department will hammer it out."

"Indie department?"

"All the big studios have them now," said Ian. "They've got that indie feel down to a science."

"Produce movies that look ten times more indie than any independent studio," said Mel.

"They can even make a movie look like it was shot on a credit card," said Ian.

"In fact, that would be better," said Mel. "Less expensive. We can make a fifty-thousand-dollar credit-card movie for under three million."

"That's our specialty," said Ian. "Costs the other studios at least five."

"It's settled," said Mel. "Credit-card movie. What else?"

"Well, because of the tone and texture of the period, we envisioned black-and-white—"

"Black-and-white's cheaper," said Ian. "Good thinking."

"Looks like you got yourself a picture," said Mel.

"We start shooting Thursday," said Ian.

"Fourth floor," said Mel, standing up to shake hands. "They'll have your contracts."

"But . . ."

"But what?" asked Ian.

"We just wanted financing. We were going to make the movie ourselves."

The Glicks looked at each other and laughed.

"Tell you what," said Mel. "We'll make you fourth assistant directors. Won't that be a hoot?"

Ian smiled at the young men. "Of course, we can't pay you extra for the directing jobs."

"In fact, we'd rather you didn't go near the set," said Mel. "Insurance reasons. You understand."

"But . . ."

"But what?" asked Ian.

"Me and my friends worked on this script for years. All through college. It's very personal."

"Don't worry," said Mel. "You won't even recognize it."

"But . . ."

"You want to be in films or not?"

"Yes, sir, Mr. Glick."

"Fourth floor."

The young men shook the brothers' hands and hurried out the door.

The Glicks opened their cocaine drawers.

"You try to help these kids," said Ian. Sniffle.

"Everyone wants to start at the top," said Mel. Sniffle. "Nobody wants to pay the dues like we did."

"Actually, *we* started at the top," said Mel.

"Right. The dues were much higher up there."

A knock at the door. The drawers closed.

"Come in."

Betty: "Your nine-thirty . . ."

The brothers checked their appointment books. Joey Bucks. Theatrical agent. Shit.

A fiftyish man in a tennis outfit entered. Trim, fit, salt-and-pepper hair combed like Hoffman. He was one of those people who *looked* like he looked ten years younger. Superconfident stride and an even cockier smile. The Glicks hated his guts.

"Great to see you!" said Ian, standing and shaking hands.

"Missed you at the club," said Joey.

"It's this nutty business. All the egos. Like running a pre-school."

"Tell me about it," said Joey.

They all sat at the same time.

"I hear you're doing good," said Mel. "That client of yours, Grant? See his face everywhere, on so many maga-zines, I despise him."

"Yeah, he's way too overexposed," said Joey. "We just convinced *People* to do a cover piece on his overexposure."

"What can we do for you today?" asked Ian.

"More like what *I'm* going to do for *you*," said Joey. He reached in the tennis bag next to his chair, and tossed a pair of eight-by-ten airbrushed casting photos at the brothers' desks. Both pictures fell on the floor and the brothers had to stoop. Joey leaned back in his chair and crossed his legs. "You'll owe me big time for this one."

The brothers studied the head shot: an actress in a soft light with long, sandy hair streaming behind her. It had been taken in front of an exhaust fan. The brothers read the name on the bottom. Natalie Schaaf.

Ian put his photo down. "Thanks for bringing her to us."

"But right now we don't have any parts," said Mel.

"Yes, you do," said Joey.

"We really don't," said Ian. "I'm serious."

"So am I," said Joey. "You might want to take another look at that photo."

The brothers did. Big deal.

"Okay, we looked again," said Ian. "We still don't have anything."

"You don't recognize her?" asked Joey.

The brothers shook their heads.

"The party Friday in Bel Air?" said Joey. "Heard she put on quite an audition."

Mel still didn't recognize the photo. "Ian, was this yours?"

Joey sprayed Binaca in his mouth. "And she's also got a fascinating background. Long family history in law enforcement."

Ian began nodding in defeat. "I forgot. We have a small role that just opened up this morning."

Joey stood and grabbed his tennis bag. "Always a pleasure doing business with you."

Mel got up and shook hands again. "Don't be a stranger."

A final stabbing grin. "I have a funny feeling I won't."

He left and closed the door.

"God, I hate that prick!" said Mel, opening a drawer.

"He's had work done," said Ian, opening his own drawer. "You can tell. Around the eyes."

Knock-knock. Betty. "Your ten o'clock."

"Work, work, work." Drawers closed. Their appointment books said: *Development*.

A young man in jeans entered. Brad. He had a clipboard. "Not much to report. Regular mixture of big and small screen. Mostly rehash. Feisty mom brings corporation to knees, feisty amputee loses the Olympics but wins our hearts, an adult has to go back to grade school for some reason, a dramatic comedy based on *The South Beach Diet* . . ."

"Tell us about it," said Ian.

"But it's just a diet book . . ." said Brad.

". . . That sold millions," added Mel.

"Couple of treatments," said Brad. "The first one opens with the reading of a baron's will. Jack Black forced to complete diet or forfeit estate to Ivy League half brother. Courteney Cox as the improbable love interest who inspires him to conquer all. Or straight-to-video with the Olsens stealing diet formula from bumbling foreign agents."

"What else?"

"A Victoria's Secret movie. A *Sports Illustrated* swimsuit movie. 'A very special Botox Christmas.' "

"That's it?"

"Well, there is one other thing. I hesitated to bring it up because it still has a lot of problems. But I've got this feeling . . ."

"What is it?"

He told them.

"I love it!" said Mel.

"You do?"

"The plot's a bit of a stretch," said Ian. "I mean, nothing like that could ever happen in real life."

"So we'll cover it up with sex," said Mel. "Who's the writer?"

"That's the best part," said Brad. "Already on staff."

"One of our own writers?" said Ian.

"Better," said Brad. "Works in props."

"Props?"

"He stuck it in my mailbox." Brad checked his clipboard. "Ford Oelman. I've had legal take a peek. Looks like we might already own it."

"How's that?" said Mel.

"Not ethically," said Brad. "But we'd win in court. Checked the security cameras. He was making notes and corrections on the clock, so we got him on intellectual property."

"Brad!" said Mel. "You're a genius!"

"We should give you a big bonus," said Ian.

"But we're not going to," said Mel. "Would fuck up the most-favored-nation clauses in everyone's contracts. You understand."

"Is this Ford guy working today?" asked Ian.

"Just saw him," said Brad. "Wheeling a guillotine to the Potemkin set."

Mel leaned to his intercom and pressed a button. "Betty . . ."

8

ST. PETERSBURG

A gold '71 Buick Riviera raced over Tampa Bay on the Gandy Bridge. Pelicans glided alongside the car at window level. Others dive-bombed the water for fish. The Buick reached the causeway on the west end of the span, featuring a coliform beach popular among shitkickers and sub-shitkickers genetically predisposed to Golden Flake chips, lapsed insurance, bottle rockets and Trans Ams with unrepaired fender damage.

The Buick kept going: bait stores, radio towers, Goodwill, a Crab Shack, batting cages and finally what Serge had come for. He made a skidding left into a parking lot on the south side of the road. Old signs with red neon from the Eisenhower years.

Serge jumped out and spread his arms. "There she is!"

"But it's just an old dog track," said Coleman.

"How can you say that about Derby Lane?" He began trotting toward the entrance. "Established 1925 . . ."

"Wait up." Coleman stopped and panted as Serge bought

tickets. "You've been going a million miles an hour, driving all over the place."

"I'm on a research roll." Serge handed Coleman his ticket. "Ever since I found my hook."

"I still don't understand the hook."

"I told you. It's a movie about *making* movies. Works every time. It's like crack in Hollywood."

"Sounds vague."

"The key to my hook is its vagueness. I've left room for the studio people to piss on it with their changes. Then it's *their* idea and they fall in love with it."

"I got a movie idea," said Coleman.

"Go for it."

"Remember *Planet of the Apes*?"

"A seventies high-water mark."

" '*Get your hands off me, you damn dirty ape!*' "

"And?"

"That's it."

They went inside.

"The only way to research is complete immersion," said Serge, heading up the grandstands. "That's why we have to visit as many Florida movie sites as possible: Ocala, home of *The Creature from the Black Lagoon*. Levy County, Elvis's destination in the hillbilly tour-de-force *Follow That Dream*. And don't forget Tarpon Springs, which gave us 1953's *Beneath the Twelve-Mile Reef*, the often-copied-but-never-duplicated tale of a Greek sponge-diving love triangle complicated by a giant killer octopus."

Coleman stopped climbing and grabbed his knees. "Serge. I need a break."

Serge looked around. "This should be high enough anyway." He took a seat and propped his feet up on the empty chair in front of him. "But sometimes studying Florida's film legacy is like searching for a lost city that's been covered by the dust of history. Like the studio that used to be over there."

Coleman sat in the next seat. "Where?"

"Right there." Serge waved an arm over the top of the scoreboard. "See all those mangroves on the edge of the water?"

"Yeah?"

"Thousands of years ago, the original Floridians lived there and piled up a shell mound. Then, during Prohibition, someone built a speakeasy called the San Remo Club, because the site was so remote. The building was later converted into the headquarters of Sun Haven Studios. It didn't last either."

"Why not?"

"Movies like *Hired Wife* and *Chloe, Love Is Calling*. Don't look for them on DVD."

Coleman pointed down at the track and giggled. "One of the dogs just went to the bathroom."

"Isn't it soothing?" said Serge. "This is what it's about, nothing but Old Florida: venerable race track circling the lagoon, palm trees, freshly mowed infield. But nobody appreciates it anymore . . ." He gestured at the people across the aisle. "Just a few triple-A personality types wired to their own doomsday clocks with disaster-filled day planners and family dynamics involving case workers." The people across the aisle turned and looked at Serge. He smiled. "I didn't mean you specifically. Or maybe I did. I haven't had enough time to chart your demise. Guess what? Babe Ruth and Dizzy Dean posed right down there for advertising photos in 1934, holding the number cards they used before the odds board went electric . . ."

The people got up and began walking down the stairs.

"Oh, I get it!" Serge shouted after them. "Go ahead! Run from the past!"

"I think you hurt their feelings," said Coleman.

"That was one of my mini-interventions." Serge placed his hands behind his head and leaned back. "Let's just relax and take this in."

Serge jumped up from his seat and moved down to the next one. Coleman got up and scooted over with him.

Serge put his feet up again. "It was the golden era when pari-mutuels ruled. Horses, dogs, jai alai, celebrities, elegance. I love coming here."

"I didn't know you gambled."

"I don't. I hate gambling."

"Why?"

"Because I'm good at math." Serge got up and moved over another seat.

Coleman moved with him. "But Serge, if you're in such a hurry to visit all these movie places, why are we wasting time here?"

"Because this grandstand is one of them." Serge moved over again. "It's where they shot Carl Reiner's intro in the remake of *Ocean's 11*. Except I don't know his exact seat, so I have to sit in all of them. Otherwise, I'm just living a lie."

Coleman stood. "I'm going to place a bet." Serge handed him a quarter. "Get me a newspaper."

Coleman came back a few minutes later, *Tribune* under his arm, walking extra slow not to spill the brimming cups of beer in each hand. He stopped and looked around.

"Up here!" Serge waved from the top row.

Coleman carefully climbed the stairs and set the cups on the ground. Serge took the newspaper and opened it. "What dog did you finally pick?"

Coleman took a seat and picked up one of the cups. "I only had a few bucks left so I bet on beer."

"It's a sure thing." Serge flipped his paper to the metro

section and folded it over. "Here we go. The Geriatric Rage Roundup."

Coleman had a beer-foam mustache. "What's that?"

"You know how the rest of the country is worried about the rage phenomenon? Aggressive driving, predatory kids, people going bonkers on airplanes?"

"Yeah?"

"So in Florida, it's senior citizens. Everyone makes fun like they're a bunch of doddering old farts, but nothing's further from the truth. I don't know the cause, but they retire to the Sunshine State and turn into killer bees. Super-irritable, attacking everything that moves. They scare the hell out of me."

Coleman took another big sip and wiped his mouth with his shirt. "But they seem so nice."

"Right up until shit's on," said Serge. "I see an old person, I cross the street."

"I haven't had any problems," said Coleman.

"That's because they mostly just fuck with each other. There's been such an explosion in gray-on-gray crime that Florida newspapers need special roundup boxes to fit it all in. Like this item from West Palm Beach: chairs flying again at a condo meeting. And Sarasota: Police had to clear the shuffleboard courts with tear gas. And Fort Lauderdale: the daily cafeteria meltdown. . . . Oooo, this was a big one. Forty people involved. Half the retirees ran screaming, the rest jumped in the pile. Broken hips, heart attacks. They triaged in the dining room and took them to five different hospitals . . ."

"How'd it start?"

"Cops say some guy in the cafeteria line couldn't make up his mind and got a bowl of Jell-O cubes mashed in his face. Here are the names and conditions and . . . Oh, my God!" Serge dropped the newspaper and took off down the stairs.

Coleman chased after him. "What is it?"

They ran across the parking lot and jumped in the Buick. "Serge, what's going on?"

Serge was busy screeching back onto the causeway and grabbing a cell phone from the glove compartment. He called information, then other numbers. "Room 23? Are you sure?" He hung up and floored the gas.

9

VISTAMAX STUDIOS

A knock at the door. Betty stuck her head inside. "Murray's here."

The brothers were finishing a late lunch. Ian chewed calamari. "Send him in."

A balding, middle-aged man with a pencil over his ear approached their desks. He wore a brown tie and a white dress shirt with the sleeves rolled up. He read from a computer printout with sprocket holes.

"Eight forty-two. White tiger escapes . . ."

"Tiger?"

"Morning rewrite," said Murray. "New African scene. Zebras, too."

The brothers were already feeling ill. The worst part of their day. Updates from the set of *All That Glitters*.

Everything would be right in the Vistamax garden if it wasn't for that one film.

While the Glicks ground out chum the rest of the year, the publicity side of the business necessitated they belly up to the high-roller table and produce at least one flagship picture a year. The movie didn't have to make much money. It could even lose a little money—a little. Just as long as it received half-decent reviews that kept Vistamax from slipping into the B-studio swamp militantly ignored by the entertainment press. It was a gray distinction, and one that was worth eight or nine figures.

This year's outing had looked better than ever when Vistamax landed the services of Werner B. Potemkin, the director's director, darling of the critics. It couldn't miss, guaranteed to vault Vistamax into unfamiliar realms of respectability. While the other studios threw gobs of cash at Potemkin, Vistamax was able to snare the legendary filmmaker with something much more valuable. Total creative control. Just think of all the money they'd save!

That was twenty rewrites and even more missed deadlines ago. The Glicks wondered what they'd been thinking. So did the Vistamax board, when red ink began washing ashore on the other side of the Pacific. So did the Asian crime bosses, who were using the former electronics manufacturer as their leap into legitimacy.

When news of the deal first broke, Hollywood was atwitter. Marquee director. Epic film. And the star would be their town! Then shooting began, and Potemkin's temperament turned the production into nothing less than kryptonite. Withered everything in range. Firings, resignations, rehab. The Japanese pressured the Glicks, who pressured Potemkin, who responded with tantrums in French and lawyers in Lamborghinis.

For a rare moment in their lives, the Glicks were helpless, forced to sit on their hands while an asshole flew their studio into the side of a mountain. All they could do was torture themselves with daily updates from the set, which meant Murray.

". . . Eight fifty-seven. Central Casting midgets arrive . . ."

Ian got up and poured a stiff drink at the office wet bar.

". . . Nine-sixteen. Delay from tiger escape causes stage lights to melt deadly iceberg . . . Nine thirty-six. Voice coaches arrive. The midgets are now singing midgets . . ."

Mel joined his brother at the bar.

". . . Ten-eighteen. Water from iceberg shorts out all power . . . Ten thirty-nine. Search begins for missing midget."

The Glicks brought bottles and glasses back to their desks.

". . . Eleven twenty-one, emergency generators and standby ice sculptors arrive . . . Twelve twenty-eight, midgets written out of script . . ."

Mel began banging his forehead on his desk.

". . . Twelve forty-five. Filming indefinitely suspended again when tiger and missing midget are found." Murray lowered his clipboard. "I've already taken care of flowers."

"Murray," said Ian. "Just kill me."

"You're welcome." Murray left.

The brothers pulled out coke drawers. Two extra-long lines in stereo. Then two more . . .

Knock-knock. Betty. "Ford Oelman to see you."

A young man took a bashful step into the office. "You called for me?"

Two drawers closed.

"You must be Ford!" said Ian.

Mel made a big waving motion with his arm. "Come on in, kid!"

"Have a seat!"

"We've been dying to meet you," said Mel.

"W-why?"

"Your screenplay, that's why!"

"He's so modest," said Ian.

"You're too modest," said Mel. "Take credit when credit's due!"

"We take credit," said Ian. "Even when it's not ours."

"Never seen such writing!"

"So fresh! So now!"

"Reminded me of *The Grifters*," said Mel. "Except you've done that whole new thing with it."

Ford was stunned. "You read it?"

"Not a word," said Mel.

"But we've heard great things."

"That's why we're going to make an exception this time and not be mad at you."

"Mad?" said Ford.

"Personal work on company time."

"It's a firing offense."

"But we've grown to like you."

"We just met," said Ford.

"That's right," said Ian. "You don't have any baggage."

"It's your most likable quality."

"Why don't you have a seat?" said Ian.

"He's already sitting," said Mel.

"Or you can stand," said Ian. "You're the writer."

"Love how he's dressed," said Mel, "downplaying the writer look."

"Got that whole props thing happening," said Ian.

Ford's eyes went back and forth.

"Writers can dress any way they want," explained Mel.

"So they usually dress weird," said Ian.

"The worst-dressed people in this town are directors."

"Especially a female director if she's attractive."

"Wears baggy shit to show crew she's not stuck-up."

"But you're the writer! You can dress any way you want."

"And the fact that you didn't says something."

"I'll bet my studio you have a lot to say."

"Don't know if you've heard," said Mel. "But the writer can do no wrong here at Vistamax."

"That's why we wanted to lay down some rules so you don't fuck up again."

"We won't fire you this time."

"Nobody told you the rules."

"What are you, a mind reader?"

"Of course not!" said Mel. "You're the writer!"

Ford became dizzy.

"We understand the artistic process," said Ian.

"Actually, we don't, or we'd be artists," said Mel.

"That's why we're going to cut you some slack this time."

Mel opened a drawer and produced scraps of paper with handwritten notes.

"Where'd you get those?" said Ford.

"Your personal locker in props."

"You worked on this during company time."

"Which makes it our intellectual property."

Ford jumped up from his chair. "But I've been working on that for years. Long before I got here. I only made a few notes at work."

"Only a few notes?" said Mel. "You can't pee in a pool and say, 'I just went in this one spot.' Fucks up the whole pool."

"Children swim in pools!" said Ian. "Did you ever stop to consider them?"

"Besides, we're not going to use the script anyway."

"It isn't that good."

Ford looked at one brother, then the other. "You said you loved it."

"We were trying to be encouraging," said Ian.

"You've got initiative, kid."

"Just leave it at home."

"Hey!" said Mel. "We got a surprise for you! Tell him, Ian. He's going to be tickled."

"On the way out, see Betty. We've told her to hook you up with gift certificates for the studio store."

"Just got in some great sweatshirts."

"Probably do all your Christmas shopping."

Mel stood and walked over to the door.

"But . . ." said Ford.

"He doesn't know how to thank us," Mel told his brother.

"Just keep doing that Ford magic," said Ian.

Mel opened the door. "That'll be thanks enough."

FORT LAUDERDALE

Serge burst through the hospital entrance and ran past the front desk.

"Sir!" yelled a nurse, jumping up from her chair. "You have to sign in!"

Serge kept running, checking room numbers on the way. The hall had speckled green floor tiles, bright ceiling lights and a background odor medley of disinfectant and unwellness.

The nurse was coming out from behind the front desk when Coleman ran by.

"Sir! . . ."

By the time she caught up with them, Serge was frozen in the doorway of room 23. Two visitors were already inside.

"Serge!" said Chi-Chi. "Thank God you made it. We tried to reach you but didn't know where—"

"Saw it in the paper." Serge took an anxious step forward. "Is he . . . ?"

"Just sleeping."

"Sir . . ." said the nurse in the hallway, holding a pen tethered to a clipboard with an ad hoc chain of rubber bands.

Chi-Chi stepped outside. "Can it wait a minute?"

Serge slowly entered the room and sat down on the front edge of a chair next to the bed. An old man was hooked up to a matrix of monitors and IV tubes. Serge nervously rocked back and forth.

The old man opened his eyes. "You never could sit still."

"Granddad!"

"Hi, Little Serge."

"You had a heart attack!"

"Thanks. I almost forgot."

"Are you okay?"

The old man looked around at all the wires and tubes. "No."

Serge grabbed his granddad's hand and leaned close. "You need anything? Name it."

The old man eased his head back on the pillow and closed his eyes. "I need to rest."

Serge rejoined the group in the doorway.

"Sorry about your granddad," said Coltrane.

"Got here as fast as I could. I was afraid . . ." Serge's voice trailed off as he signed his name on the visitors' list, dispatching the nurse.

"Coltrane and I followed the ambulance from the cafeteria. We were worried we wouldn't be able to get hold of you."

Serge looked around. "Does Lou know? Is she coming?"

Coltrane grabbed him by the hand. "Serge . . ."

"Not Louisiana."

"Nobody knows where you've been," said Chi-Chi. "A lot's happened. Lou went in her sleep four months ago. Her family plot is up in Orlando . . ."

"They were together forty-two years," said Serge. "He must have been devastated."

"He was," said Chi-Chi. "After the funeral, he just stayed up there, going by her grave every day with flowers. We finally convinced him it wasn't healthy and drove him back down. Great for a while. Even started working again. We thought it was going to be a whole new beginning."

"*Thought?*"

"Been talking to the doctors. Minor heart attack, but it seriously weakened him, on top of all the emotional strain with Lou. You know what they say: Once one goes . . . He's only alive because they're keeping his blood pressure up with the medicine."

"I . . . don't . . ."

"This is it," said Chi-Chi. "He's not leaving the hospital."

Serge stumbled back into the doorframe. "How long?"

"Nothing critical now, but the vitals will fade. A week or two."

Serge's face resolved. "I'm not leaving this room."

Coltrane got out car keys. "You'll change your mind."

"You have to rest sometime," said Chi-Chi, handing Serge a magnetic card. "We found a motel up the road to be close."

"We've been staying here in shifts," said Coltrane. "Sleep there whenever you want."

"There's something else," said Chi-Chi. "Don't be thrown if he starts talking nonsense. Alzheimer's. The doctors said it probably started a few years ago, but who could tell with all the crazy shit that came out of him?"

Sergio opened his eyes again. "I can hear every word you're saying."

"Sorry," said Chi-Chi.

"Just pretend I'm not here," said Sergio. "Why don't you tell him I have to wear diapers while you're at it?"

"He's had some accidents," said Coltrane.

"That was sarcasm," said Sergio. "Who's got the dementia around here?"

Chi-Chi pulled up a chair. "I'll take the next shift."

10

Two men in dark suits and thin, dark ties sat in a dim office with the blinds closed.

"Zanesville turned out to be a dead end. They only beat us by a couple of days, but it might as well have been a year. Trail went cold as death."

They were outranked by the older man on the other side of the desk. He folded his hands in thought. "No idea at all?"

A head shook. "They could be anywhere."

"What about known associates?"

"Back to the airport?"

The older man nodded.

HOLLYWOOD

A gritty coral sun turned reddish-brown as it dipped into the horizon and fought its way through the Los Angeles atmosphere. The view was down Ivar Street, sloping toward the skyline.

On the corner sat a four-story Mediterranean apartment house with a vintage green-and-yellow sign out front. ALTO NIDO.

A third-floor window was open. Sheer white curtains flut-tered out. Inside, a young man sat in a bathrobe and tapped on a typewriter. A pencil was clutched sideways in his teeth.

His four roommates from the Vistamax props department were moving in all directions.

Mark had one foot on a chair, lacing a shoe. "Ford, aren't you coming?"

"Just give me a minute."

Pedro came out of the bathroom, rubbing wet hair with a towel. "You better get moving. We have to leave soon."

Ford took the pencil out of his mouth. "Do we even know where this party is yet?"

"No."

"Then why the rush?" Tap, tap, tap . . .

"Because Dallas is going to call any second with the lo-cation and we'll have to leave immediately."

"I don't understand how we're getting into these parties," said Ford, standing up from his typewriter. "They're the most exclusive in town. Some *actors* can't get in."

"Dallas likes us," said Ray.

"Dallas Reel?" said Ford. "I still haven't figured out what that guy does."

"He's important is what he does," said Mark.

"But he just seems to be hanging around props like he doesn't have a job."

"Don't let that fool you," said Pedro. "He's huge. One of the biggest third executive producers in this town."

"Been in the credits of at least sixty films," added Mark.

"What for?"

"Gets the Glicks their coke."

Rrrrrrrrriiiiiinnnnnngggggggg!

"That's Dallas . . . Hello? . . . Right . . . I know the way . . . See you in ten . . ."

"Where is it?" asked Mark.

"Melrose and La Brea," said Pedro. "Launch party for a new fragrance by that chick who sings. They used cyclone fence to seal the alley behind an Afghan restaurant. We enter through the head shop next door. The password is *mellifluous*."

Two husky men with thick, folded arms stood in front of a head shop on Melrose. Limos and luxury cars cycled up the curb. Skinny models and older men with ponytails got out. The bouncers parted.

A group of young men walked down the sidewalk. The bouncers closed ranks. Pedro stepped up.

"*Mellifluous.*"

The guards remained stone.

"I said, *mellifluous.*"

Nothing.

Pedro looked back at the rest of the gang. "I don't know what's going on."

A cell phone rang. "Hello? . . . Oh, hi, Dallas . . . Yeah, we're out front. That's the problem. We can't— . . . I see, thanks . . ." He closed the phone and turned to the gang. "They changed the password. The first one was to throw off uninvited riffraff."

Pedro stepped up to the bouncers again.

"*Pandemic.*"

They parted. The guys went inside and walked down a long aisle of floor-standing hookahs, hand-blown bongs, and the new enviro-friendly California hybrids that plugged into the wall and vaporized instead of burned. The service corridor in the back of the shop connected to the Kebab-A-Go-Go. An usher in a bow tie opened a door. The alley behind the restaurant was filled with laser beams, flavored oxygen dispensers and a curry funk. Models smoked green-and-purple cigarettes. The gang spotted Dallas and waved. Dallas waved back. He was wearing a cranberry silk jogging suit, and he slowly worked his way through the crowd, pulling tiny glassine envelopes from his fanny pack and pressing them into the palms of his many friends.

"Hey, Dallas," said Pedro. "Great party. Thanks!"

"It's over. We have to get out of here."

"But they're barely getting started."

Dallas shook his head. "Peaked a half hour before it opened. The *In Crowd*'s heading straight to the second address."

They piled back in the Malibu and followed Dallas's Ferrari on a treacherous, winding road up Laurel Canyon. Magnificent valley glimpses between the houses.

"Whose place are we going to?" asked Ford.

"Professional voice," said Pedro.

"That deep, gravely narrator who does previews in the theaters for scary movies," said Mark. "You know: 'From the master of horror, a supernatural tale that'll freak your shit!' "

"The Voice of God?" asked Ford.

"No. The number two guy who gets his leftovers," said Pedro. "Television, too."

They parked in a swarm of valets and went inside. Ford moved room to room on tentative legs. Strange music, stranger people. Caterers circulated with trays. Ford turned down a flute of champagne, but accepted the ostrich-meat canapé with water chestnut surprise. The postmodern living room had brushed steel surfaces and metal guy-wires.

Pedro was on a sofa, talking to an old man with a ponytail. ". . . But the carpenter is sympathetic. The actor mowed down his family gangland-style."

"I'm married to it! Don't change a comma!"

Ford needed air. He strolled onto the spacious balcony.

Mark was at the railing talking to an aspiring actress whose unsymmetric mouth reminded him of Ellen Barkin. His cell phone was open. "Go ahead."

"Uh, 555-1234."

"I'll call."

She fled as Ford arrived at the railing and stared out over the luminous L.A. basin. "Feel like I've been here before."

"This same view's in practically every movie set here," said Mark. "To flag location."

Ford leaned over the rail and looked down. He straightened fast and took a queasy step back. "Whoa!"

"Pretty high, eh?" said Mark.

"We're sticking off the side of the mountain. What's holding us up?"

"Tall poles."

Ford looked side to side at the neighboring residences. "Don't they ever fall down?"

"All the time. Mud slides or weight overload from too many people at a party."

They turned around and looked back through the balcony's open sliding doors. A barrel-chested man leaned suavely against a baby grand, swirling a snifter of cognac. He had thick gray hair and a black blazer over a black turtleneck. Women in strapless evening gowns surrounded the piano and applauded quietly.

"Who's that?" asked Ford.

"Our host."

"What's he doing?"

"Requests."

". . . *The season finale of* Law and Order *you won't want to miss!* . . ."

Dallas came out on the balcony. "Just got the new address."

They collected the gang and headed for the front door,

past two old men with ponytails. "Just heard the stupidest script about a carpenter . . ."

Back to the car. Farther and faster up the mountain. Ford hit his blinker for a left on Mulholland. "Whose place now?"

"Former child star," said Pedro. "But not a big one. You know by the fourth season how the original kids aren't cute anymore and they bring in a younger relative?"

"Like cousin Oliver on *Brady Bunch*?"

"Right, but not him."

They swung through a circular drive.

"Holy cow!" Ford stared up at the mansion. "If he wasn't big, how can he afford a place like this?"

"Wrote a tell-all on the other child stars," said Pedro. "Got nasty. A kid who played a dork in suspenders took a shot at him outside the Staples Center, so he was in demand again. Did the talk shows and some celebrity boxing, then another book on the shooting incident and spending the first book's advance free-basing."

They went inside. This one was much, much louder. The Guess Who.

Ford found himself talking to a man in a safari vest.

"No kidding?" said Ford. "A real paparazzo?"

The man nodded and popped the ceramic stopper off a Grolsch.

". . . *American woman, get away from me-heeeee! . . .*"

"So how come you're not taking pictures?" asked Ford. "The place is crawling with stars."

The photographer took a swig. "People don't realize it, but we all specialize."

"Like what?"

"Actors leaving rehab, bandaged stars after nose jobs, telephoto work of celebs making out on yachts, stars who've let themselves go. One guy just did Brando. Had to sell his house."

"What's your specialty?"

"Getting Alec Baldwin to punch me for the out-of-court money." He showed Ford his Rolex. "At least it's steady."

"I got a question," said Ford. "The former child star standing over there who owns this place. Why does he have so many bodyguards?"

"They're not bodyguards. They're trainers. He pays them to keep him off drugs."

"You're kidding."

The photographer shook his head. "He's always trying to give them the slip. The main thing is for them not to let him go upstairs under any circumstances."

"Why not?"

"That's where everyone's doing drugs."

"How do you know?"

"Everyone knows. Every party in this town has a designated drug floor. Like a smoking section. Out of respect. Half of Hollywood is on a health jag; the other half is old school."

Pedro ran into the kitchen. "Ford, quick! Follow me!"

Ford was halfway up to the second floor. "But I don't want to do any drugs."

"We're not getting drugs," said Pedro. "We're getting a limo."

He opened a bathroom door. Two naked women in an oversize Jacuzzi smoking opium. He closed the door. On to the den. He opened the door. Oak library shelves and a parchment globe of the neoclassical world containing crystal decanters. Someone was screaming down on the Persian throw rug. Six people restrained a thrashing man trying to take bites out of his own shoulders. *The spiders!*

"Bad acid," said Pedro.

"They're chewing my eyes!"

He closed the door. Tino came over. "Limo yet?"

"Not yet . . . Wait. Hold everything . . ." Pedro pointed down the hall. "That looks like a promising lead."

Dallas was knocking on the last door at the end of the hall. The guys walked up behind him. Dallas knocked again, harder.

An impatient voice from the other side: "Who is it!"

"Doctor Feelgood."

Locks unbolted. The door opened three inches. The props guys caught a brief glimpse as Dallas passed a Baggie through the slit: Mel in undershorts with something attached to his nipples; Ian wearing nothing but white powder on his upper lip; an unconscious young woman on the bed, panties around one ankle. The door slammed shut.

"That girl looked like she was in trouble," said Ford.

"Just partied too much," said Dallas. "Or they put something in her drink. That's the rumor going around."

"What are they going to do to her?" asked Ford.

"Anything they want."

"Shouldn't we do something?"

"Somewhere else, yes, we should," said Dallas. "But I'm sure she gave her consent before passing out."

"What?"

"Every woman in this party would kill to trade places with her," said Dallas. "She's going to get a part out of this. A *speaking* part." A beeper went off. Dallas looked down. "Gotta run."

"I don't know," said Ford, looking at his friends. "I still think we should do something."

"We are," said Tino, knocking on the door.

"Who the fuck is it?"

"Mr. Glick, we work for you. The Vistamax limo. Do you still need it, because some other executives from the studio—"

"Take it! Jesus! Just leave us the fuck alone!"

"Yes, sir, Mr. Glick. Thank you, sir."

"We're on!" said Ray. They ran back down the hall.

"I can't stop thinking about that girl," said Ford. "I have a bad feeling."

They scampered down the stairs. A former child star dashed past them going up. He was tackled on the landing by a trainer. "Oh, no, you don't! . . ."

Ford followed Pedro and the others to the front door. He heard something in passing. He turned around.

Two guys with highball glasses were shmoozing up a casting agent.

". . . Started shooting today. Like *The Grifters*, but different. Probably the first decent script they've done all year."

"Must have been a slip-up," said the agent.

They laughed.

"Excuse me," said Ford. "Are you talking about Vistamax?"

"Yeah. Unless you're with them."

More laughs.

"Where's this movie set?"

"I don't know," said one of the highball guys. "Some place down south. Arkansas?"

"Alabama," said Ford.

"As a matter of fact, you're right. It is Alabama . . . Hey, how'd you know?"

FORT LAUDERDALE

Six A.M. Patient room 23. The sky started getting light outside.

Chi-Chi was snoring in his chair by the door. Coleman had gone back to crash at the Howard Johnson with Coltrane.

Serge was still sitting next to his granddad's bed. Hadn't slept a wink. Bloodshot eyes, head occasionally bobbing down, then jerking up, then slowly bobbing down again.

His granddad began coughing. "Little Serge, you still there?"

Serge scooted closer. "Yes."

"I don't feel so hot."

"Want me to get a nurse?"

"I don't know. I feel strange." He began hacking again, then stopped and fixed his eyes on the ceiling. "What's happening? Did someone turn off the lights? It's so dark. I'm floating out of my body . . ."

Serge leaned forward and clutched his grandfather's hand. "I'm here."

". . . There's a tunnel, a bright light at the end . . ."

Serge gulped and squeezed the hand harder. "There's nothing to be afraid of."

"I . . . I'm walking toward the light now . . . It's getting brighter. I hear beautiful music. I—"

The old man's eyes closed, and his head fell to the side.

"Grandpa!" yelled Serge. "Nooooooo!"

The old man opened his eyes and grabbed the TV remote. "I was just fuckin' with you."

The TV changed channels. "Oh, good. A *Miami Vice* rerun. This is my favorite episode. Ted Nugent guest stars."

Serge looked up at the set mounted on the wall. "Grandpa, that's *60 Minutes.*"

"The series was never the same after they blew up Crockett's Daytona. And don't even get me started on the Sheena Easton story line . . ."

"Grandpa—"

"You read where they're planning to build a Disney World around here? Just like the one in California . . ."

"Grandpa—"

"Little Serge. Hurry up and finish your breakfast." He tried raising his head, IV tubes stretching. "We have to get hopping if we're going to catch some fish."

"Take it easy and rest," said Serge. He adjusted his granddad's pillows.

"Did I tell you about the big Alabama score?"

"What Alabama score?"

"I didn't tell you? I thought I told you. You sure I didn't tell you?"

"When were you in Alabama?" asked Serge.

"Biggest score yet. My finest piece of work. I was president of an oil company! Can you believe that? Your ol' granddad . . ." He looked up at the TV. "Ooooo, this is a good part. Crockett and Tubbs have another buddy talk on

the nature of women. Everything you need to know about re-
lationships is in this series . . ."

"Grandpa," said Serge. "What about Alabama?"

"Alabama? What are you talking about?" Cough.

Serge sighed.

"Lean closer, Little Serge . . ."

He did.

"You have to go to L.A."

"What?"

Sergio began snoring.

Chi-Chi woke up and came over from his chair by the
door. "How's he doing?"

"Sleeping."

"Did you talk?"

"Yeah, but he was rambling at the end."

"At least you got to talk."

Serge's butt was numb. He shifted weight in the chair.
Chi-Chi put a hand on his back. "Serge, you look like shit.
Why don't you get some sleep?"

"No. I have to stay."

"I talked to the doctors," said Chi-Chi. "Completely sta-
ble. But he needs his rest. So do you."

Serge shook his head. "What if something happens?
He'll be alone . . . I can't imagine anything worse."

"Nothing's going to happen," said Chi-Chi. "I'm heading
back to the HoJo. Why don't you come with me, just for a
few hours?"

Noon. A rejuvenated Serge walked briskly down the
hospital hallway, breaking into a trot. He reached the door of
room 23. "What the—?"

A nurse walked by with patient files. Serge grabbed her by

THE BIG BAMBOO ✳ 119

the arm. "Who's that woman? What's she doing in my grand-father's bed?"

The nurse checked the chart on the door. "That's her room."

"Where's my grandfather?"

Another nurse heard them and came over. "Were you re-lated to Mr. Storms?"

"Were?"

VISTAMAX STUDIOS

A secretary's voice in the lobby: "What do you think you're doing? You can't just barge in there! . . ."

The door flew open.

Ian looked up from a desk drawer. "Who are you?"

"Ford Oelman."

"Who?"

"I was just in here the other day."

Mel squinted at Ford's face. "Uh, sure, right . . ."

"You don't remember me?"

"Of course we do," said Ian.

"But we see a lot of people."

"What were we talking about again?"

"My screenplay," said Ford. "The oil scam in Alabama."

"Did we like it?" asked Ian.

"No. You said you couldn't use it."

"I see," said Mel. "Well, don't get discouraged. It's a crazy business. Just keep up the good work."

"But right now we have some other matters . . ." said Ian.

". . . So if you don't mind," said Mel.

"You started shooting it," said Ford.

"We have to—. . . What?"

"You're filming my movie," said Ford. "I just came from the soundstage."

"I'm sure you're mistaken."

"They got the oil derrick and the limo and the old guys, just like I wrote."

"Which stage?"

"Fourteen."

Ian leaned and pressed a button on the intercom. "Betty, could you bring in the shooting schedule for Fourteen."

"We'll straighten this out," said Mel.

Betty came in and handed Ian a pack of stapled pages with grids. He flipped through and stopped near the end. "Here we are. Yeah, you're right. Oil scam movie. But says here it was written by this guy over in Warsaw. You know, the one who did that Altmanesque comedy on Pol Pot. Very dark. Didn't do well here." Ian turned the page around to show Ford. "See? There's the writing credit."

"That's so like this business," Mel added with a chuckle. "Ten thousand screenwriters in this town and we have to go to Poland—"

"He didn't write it," said Ford.

"I just showed you the page. Weren't you paying attention?"

"You're shooting my fucking movie over there!" yelled Ford. "That was my big break and you just stole it!"

Mel picked up the phone. "I'm calling security."

"Wait a second," Ian told his brother. "I think I can handle this." He got up and walked over to Ford, putting an arm around his shoulders. "I understand how you feel. A totally normal reaction. But I've seen this same kind of thing a million times."

Mel joined them and put an arm around Ford's shoulders from the other side. "He's right. It's not your fault. I'd be angry, too, until I understood what was going on."

"There are only so many ideas out there," said Ian. "And only so many variations on those ideas. Virtually everything bears at least a vague resemblance to something else."

"It isn't vague," said Ford. "It's my exact script."

"Look, I don't want to say you're imagining things," said Ian.

"I'm not," said Ford. "It was based on a true story. That's how I know."

"True story?" said Mel. "Were you involved?"

Ford was suddenly flustered. "W-w-what do you mean?"

"Look at that treacherous peach face," said Ian. "Definitely a con man. Probably originally wrote the script for the real oil scam."

Ford lost color.

The brothers broke up laughing. Ian made a dismissive wave. "Must have read it in the papers."

"Uh . . . yeah," said Ford. "That's right. I read it in the newspaper."

"There you go," said Ian. "Someone else must have read the same articles."

"You don't have a copyright on the papers, do you?" said Mel, laughing again.

"People are always complaining that we've ripped off their stories," said Mel.

"Normally we sic our lawyers on them," said Ian.

"But you're family," said Mel, squeezing Ford's shoulder. "We've heard great things about what you're doing in props."

"You have?"

"I'm speaking hypothetically."

"But it really is my movie," said Ford. "You have to believe me."

"I believe you wrote a great screenplay. But you have to start accepting that it's just a coincidence. I know it's hard for a writer. In your mind, remote similarities become huge, overarching plot duplications."

"Someone just retyped it," said Ford.

"That's exactly what they all say."

"But we like you, kid," said Mel. "So we're going to forget your little outburst. A harmless misunderstanding."

"You'll forget?"

Ian squeezed his shoulder again. "That's right, we forgive you."

"No need to thank us," said Mel. "It's just the kind of guys we are."

Ian began walking him to the door. "Now, we really do need to be going. Get back over to props and keep doing that special Ford thing that we haven't been hearing much about."

Ford left the office in a daze. The door closed.

Desk drawers opened.

"You'd think he'd be happy seeing his work on the big screen," said Mel.

Another commotion in the lobby. The secretary's voice again: "What do you think you're doing? You can't just go in there! . . ."

"Shit, he's back!" Ian closed his drawer.

The door opened. Six bulky Japanese men entered.

"Oh, it's you," said Mel.

Betty came in behind. "I tried to stop them."

"It's okay," said Ian. "You can go now."

Betty closed the door. The brothers were already rushing around their desks to pull chairs over from the wall.

"I didn't hear anything about you coming for a visit," said Mel. "You should have called."

"We were in the neighborhood."

The brothers dragged the last chairs into place. Some of the men had digits missing. Ian and Mel went back behind their desks. Everyone sat. Except one. He remained standing by the door. The more Ian and Mel tried not to look at his face, the more they found themselves looking. That was the desired effect.

Ian's eyes returned to their leader, sitting in the closest chair. "What do we owe the pleasure?"

The leader had heavy acne scarring. He lit a filterless cigarette and pinched it between his thumb and index finger. "Should we be worried?"

"About what?" asked Mel.

The man answered by using the floor as an ashtray.

"Oh, *All That Glitters*?" said Ian. "No, everything's under control."

The Glicks tried to hide their trembling. They'd been introduced a couple of times in Japan: the leader, Mr. Yokamura, and his lieutenants, Mr. Takita, Mr. Bushijo and Mr. Komodo. But inside the Glicks' heads, the names sounded like this: "Blah, blah, blah." The quartet was usually in the background when they met the top Vistamax executives in Osaka. The executives said the men were investors. And they made the executives nervous, too. Then there was the guy by the door. A whole different level. And dammit if the Glicks weren't looking at his face again! But how could you not? It wasn't just the full facial tattoo, but the design. A life-size human skull. When the brothers were in Japan, they'd heard the whispers. Torture, execution, soulless. One story had a five-man hit team sent to take him out, and the next morning a rival gangster found five severed heads on his hat rack. No more hit teams were sent. They called him "The Tat." But not to that face.

Mr. Yokamura flicked his cigarette on the floor again and cleared his throat.

The brothers were staring at the tattoo again. Shit.

"Uh, yeah," said Mel, shifting his eyes. "As a matter of fact, the movie couldn't be doing better."

"You should see the rushes," said Ian.

The man stood and crushed out his cigarette with a pointy shoe. "Then I must be speaking to people who are mistaken." He headed for the door, and the others followed. "Please keep me informed."

"Absolutely," Ian yelled after him. "What about lunch? You already got a hotel? If you need anything . . ."

But they were already gone.

ORLANDO

Late morning. Already too hot.

A large rectangular hole was cut in the manicured lawn. A priest stood at one end. Thirty folding chairs at the other. The chairs were empty except for four people in the front row.

"I wasn't there," said Serge.

"You can't keep beating yourself up," said Chi-Chi.

Altamonte Springs Memorial Gardens was wedged in the newly developed, high-traffic retail district on Semoran Boulevard. The dew burning off the grass made it extra humid.

"I don't like this cemetery," said Serge.

"What's not to like?" said Coltrane, wiping his forehead with an already drenched handkerchief. "It's practically new."

"Shhhh!" whispered Chi-Chi. "The priest is starting."

"Dearly beloved . . ."

"New is the problem," said Serge. "No headstones. Just brass plaques flush to the ground, plastic flowers. I was going to get a big monument."

"This is what he wanted," whispered Coltrane. "Picked it out himself when he was visiting Lou. Her grave's right over there."

"God is with us . . ."

Serge looked to the side. "We're next to an ABC store."

"You're distracting the priest," snipped Chi-Chi.

". . . Although Sergio may not have been a great man . . ."

"Did I just hear right?" said Serge.

"He was the priest on call," said Chi-Chi. "We did our best."

". . . I understand from his friends that he was far from a failure . . ."

"What the hell?"

"Quiet," said Chi-Chi. "He'll hear you."

". . . He did his best trying to help raise his grandson, who I understand is with us here today"—the priest glanced down at a piece of paper—*"Sare-gay . . ."*

Serge's face fell in his hands.

"Easy," said Chi-Chi. "A lot of people mispronounce that."

The priest left. The four men continued sitting silently.

Chi-Chi finally turned. "You going to be okay?"

Serge nodded.

"You took a big chance coming here today," said Chi-Chi. "Lots of warrants out."

"There's no way I wasn't coming."

"He'd be proud of you."

Across the street from the cemetery, a white sedan sat at the curb. Extra antennas, blackwall tires. Two men in dark suits and thin, dark ties held binoculars.

"He took a big chance coming here today."

"I knew he'd come. There's no way he'd miss it."

"We ready to move?"

"Not yet. Wait till the civilians leave, in case there's trouble . . . How's our backup?"

The second man grabbed a microphone. "Unit two. Status."

On the far side of the cemetery, two workers in green overalls raked leaves. They had flesh-colored wires running into their left ears. One furtively raised a wrist to his mouth.

The man in the white sedan put down the mike. "Backup's ready."

"Okay, this might be it," said his partner. "The two old guys are getting up . . . Stand by . . ."

Binoculars focused on a pair of hunched, white-haired men slowly making their way with canes. "Tell unit two: Wait for my command. I want to make sure they're clear of any fire lines."

The binoculars followed the old men down a footpath and out the cemetery's western gate. The binoculars swung back to the grave. Two guys in bright floral shirts started getting up.

"Now!"

Men in green overalls dropped their rakes and sprinted across the grass. The sedan's doors flew open, its passengers converging from the opposite directions with guns drawn.

"Freeze!"

They did.

The men in the suits ran to the gravesite. The first one pulled up short. "What the hell's going on?" His partner yanked dark wigs off Chi-Chi and Coltrane.

A '71 Buick Riviera raced past the Sea World exit on I-4. Coleman threw his cane and white wig in the backseat, on top of Serge's. "Where'd Chi-Chi say to meet for the reception?"

"The Boo."

Coleman cracked a Schlitz. "I love the Boo."

HOLLYWOOD, ALTO NIDO APARTMENTS

Ford was at his kitchen table with the yellow pages, alphabetically crossing off names in the bulging local section for entertainment attorneys. Twenty calls already and no luck. The conversations always started out promisingly enough, lawyers asking identical questions. Yes, friends had seen the script. Yes, he could verify it was long before production started. Yes, he could prove he submitted it to the studio. Then he mentioned Vistamax or the Glicks and that was it. Most strongly advised him to drop it; others just hung up.

Ford was about to call it quits when he dialed the number for a one-man firm with an address at the dicey end of Sunset.

"The Glick brothers!" screamed the lawyer. Ford braced for a dial tone that didn't come. Instead, the attorney went on a tear. "They've got to be stopped! They've been screwing people for years, but everyone's too intimidated by their legal department! Not me! . . ."

Sure, he'd take the case. When could they meet? An hour?

Ford took a cab. The road hooked right, centering the L.A. skyline in the distance. He began checking addresses. Liquor store, bail bond, auto detailing. They came to the number he'd jotted down, and the taxi pulled up beside a decapitated parking meter. Ford looked at the building. There had to be a mistake. He checked the address in his hand. Yep, same number as the Mexican restaurant with the big rooster on the window and hand-painted signs in Spanish. Then he noticed a small doorway next to the restaurant. Same address, but with a *B* at the end.

Ford tipped the driver and went inside. Just a staircase. He climbed it. There was a door at the top with a translucent window and a name in chipped gold letters: Rodney Demopolis.

He knocked and saw a form move on the other side of the textured glass. "Come in!"

Ford opened the door. The man behind the desk stood. Receding hair and the right weight for his medium height, except it was distributed wrong. One of those thin guys with a gut. A paper napkin was tucked in the collar of his short-sleeved dress shirt.

"You must be Ford! Great to meet you! Call me Rod! Give me a second to clean this up . . ."

The desktop was a landfill. Random legal papers and loose notes around a bed of wax paper streaked with guacamole and sour cream. Ford looked in the corner at the only other chair, supporting a stack of filing boxes. The walls were empty except for two crooked diplomas. A ceiling fan rotated with an unbalanced clicking. The windows were open. Cars, yelling, a radio beyond the fidelity of its speakers. Rod chewed quickly. Balled-up wax paper went in the wastebasket, followed by the collar napkin. He ran around the desk to shake hands.

"So, we're going to take on the infamous Glick brothers! Hope you know what you're in for, but it will all be worth it in the end . . ." He hunted for something on the desk. "And not just money—justice has cried out too long! Here we are. My notes from our call. No, that's something else. Where are they?" He resumed the search. "This is why I got into law in the first place. But don't pooh-pooh the money either. We could be talking class action, and as the named plaintiff to give standing, you get extra. Could this be it?" He reached under a per curiam opinion. "Nope." More digging. "Ever eat at the joint downstairs? Probably not 'cause only Mexicans go there. Killer tacos, totally different from the American kind. None of the pig goes to waste. There's a language barrier. You speak Spanish? I just point. Ordered *orejas* and didn't even know I was eating ears. Know any other writers they've done this to?"

"I'm sort of new here."

"That's okay. I'll put an ad in the trades. It'll have to be small, probably one column by a half inch because . . ."—he gestured around the office—". . . well, this ain't exactly *L.A. Law*. Ever watch that show? That's also why I got in this racket. I know the actor who had a ten-episode arc as Brackman's evil brother. Real nice guy in person. People confuse personas. So, we start with some ads. Have to shake the tree. Who knows what will fall out?" He found a video-game controller under an amicus brief and stuck it in a bottom drawer. "Know what? To heck with my notes! It was just an hour ago . . ."

Ford thinking: I've made a big mistake.

Rod walked around to the front of the desk again and leaned on a corner. "Here's what we're going to do. I'll take your statement. You don't mind if I record it, do you? Start from the beginning and don't leave anything out. Then I'll style the suit, file it first thing tomorrow and we're off to the races. Where's that tape recorder? . . ."

FLORIDA

A '71 Buick Riviera was stuck in a sea of traffic on U.S. 192. A hundred cars moving a few blocks at a time, traffic light to traffic light, all red.

Greetings from Kissimmee, Florida. A thin, long strip city of cheap motels, go-cart tracks, bungee towers, family buffets and knockoff souvenir boutiques for budget tourists commuting to Disney on the other side of I-4. Rows of giant, screaming marquees lit up at night like Vegas, except 3-for-$10 T-shirts instead of Wayne Newton.

The light turned green. A minute later, the Riviera began moving slowly. The same light turned red again.

Serge smacked the steering wheel. "I can't tell you how crazy this kind of traffic makes me. Why are all these people going this way?"

Coleman drained a beer and crumpled the can. "We're going this way, too."

"But they're making lifestyle mistakes. We're driving for truth."

The Riviera continued east, businesses slamming up

against each other for miles, then an uncharacteristic break in the new construction where an old establishment had refused to sell out. The small, weather-beaten shack sat far back from the road in an overgrown field. During the early '70s, it was the only thing to the horizon in every direction, a place where the first performers and other Disney employees could retreat from the manufactured glee and kick back. Now it was under siege.

The Riviera turned off the highway and onto a dirt road that wound through the field. It would be generous to call them potholes—more like the road had been carpet bombed to prevent Panzers from reaching Dunkirk. The Buick bounced on its springs, passing a rusty, nonrunning ambulance from the TV series *M*A*S*H*. Serge pulled around back and parked in a shaded spot behind the Big Bamboo Lounge & Package.

The Boo.

Chi-Chi and Coltrane were already on stools when Serge's black silhouette appeared in the bright, open doorway at the rear of the saloon.

"Serge!" Coltrane waved him over. "We saved seats."

Serge moped across the room and eased himself onto a stool at the south end of the bar. Coleman hopped on the one next to him.

"We need to improve your mood," said Coltrane.

"So, what have you been doing with yourself these days?" asked Chi-Chi.

"He's bringing the movies back to Florida," said Coleman. "Just finished a screenplay."

"That's great!" said Chi-Chi. "How long is it?"

"One page," said Coleman.

The bartender arrived with two Mason jars. Draft for Coleman, OJ for Serge. He placed each of the drinks on the bar's trademark "coasters," three folded squares of toilet paper.

Serge picked up his jar. "Thanks, Jayson."

"Sorry about your granddad. Anything you need."

Serge pursed his lips and nodded.

Chi-Chi got the bartender's attention. "Serge is a movie buff. Didn't they film *Monster* around here?"

"The Aileen Wuornos thing with Charlize Theron?" asked the bartender.

"That's the one."

The bartender pointed at a wall. "Right up Orange Blossom Trail. The Little Diamond Motel stood in for that Daytona place where she holed up."

"Hear that, Serge? They shot a movie about a serial killer nearby," said Coltrane. "Doesn't that make you happy?"

Serge took a deep breath, his eyes wandering around the interior of the tropical cave, plastered solid with memories tacked up by long-gone theme park employees. Badges, photos, felt pennants, ride tickets, driver's licenses, bras. Big band on the juke. Crusty patrons began swinging by the end of the bar, paying condolences.

"Your granddad loved this place," said Chi-Chi, looking down at Serge's stool. "He was sitting right there when he got the famous Disney artist Ralph Kent to sketch Pinocchio on a paper plate. His favorite seat, so he could be next to the drawings."

Serge turned and put his hand out to the wall, touching framed original illustrations of the Seven Dwarfs. Above them was a new framed item, memorial photo of a smiling Sergio Storms, 1918–2006.

"I know you miss him," said Chi-Chi. "But he lived a long, full life. You need to remember the good times."

"I remember I wasn't there that last morning."

"Stop it," said Chi-Chi. "Everyone finds something to regret at this point. It's part of the process."

"At least you got to see him," added Coltrane. "Imagine if you didn't notice that article in the paper."

Serge showed a trace of a smile. "He loved this old joint."

Chi-Chi raised his jar. "That he did. Said the name reminded him of pulp paperbacks. *The Big Sleep. The Big Nowhere . . .*"

". . . *The Big Bamboo*," said Serge. A memory flickered and his smile grew larger. "I cracked up when he first mentioned the JCPenney job. He forgot he'd told me, and repeated it four or five more times, but it just kept getting funnier."

"That was nothing compared to the Alabama score," said Chi-Chi.

"Alabama?" said Serge. "When was my granddad up there?"

"Nine months ago. Something else you missed while you've been gone."

"The perfect game," said Coltrane. "Started in Panama City and ended over the state line west of Dothan."

"He was trying to tell me something about Alabama," said Serge. "Just thought it was more nonsense. Claimed he ran an oil company."

"That wasn't drifting," said Coltrane. "He really did, at least in the script."

"Script?"

Chi-Chi nodded. "The whole thing was written out. Very intricate. A hundred pages. That's what made the score so incredible."

Coltrane pulled wet toilet paper off the bottom of his drink. "We just assumed you knew about Alabama."

"I didn't."

"Then settle in and get ready," said Chi-Chi. "Have we got a story to tell . . . *bartender! . . .*"

VISTAMAX STUDIOS

The regular gang from the props department gathered around Ford as he emptied his locker into a cardboard box.

"I can't believe they fired you," said Ray.

"Of course they fired him," said Pedro. "He sued."

"It's just not right."

"What are you going to do?"

"I'm going to get them," said Ford. "I'm going to get them so good!"

"Who?"

"The Glick brothers. I'm going to get this whole studio!" Ford closed up the box and turned to the four humorless security guards waiting to escort him off the property.

A man in a suit walked up. "Is there a Ford Oelman here?"

"That's me."

The man handed him an envelope. "You've been served." He walked away.

Ford tore open the envelope.

"What is it?" asked Tino.

"I don't believe it," said Ford.

"What?"

"They're suing *me*."

"Ford!"

Ford turned. Mark was across the room, holding up the receiver of a phone on the inventory manager's desk. "You got a call."

"Who is it?"

"Rodney something."

A half hour later, Ford was standing in a loft over a Mexican restaurant.

"I don't know how to say this," said Rod. "I feel just terrible."

Ford waited.

Rod put his hands together like he was praying. "Okay, I'm just going to say it. I have to withdraw from the case."

"But—"

Rod waved him off. "I know it's a shitty thing to do. But I don't have a choice." He lifted a hefty stack of documents off his desk. "They've buried us in motions. And they're suing me personally."

"You said I had a strong case."

"You do. Doesn't matter . . ." Rod continued, more to himself than Ford: "I heard they did stuff like this, but I never thought it could get this bad. No wonder everyone's scared."

"What's happening?" said Ford. "What kind of motions?"

"The meritless kind. Just like their suit. But you have to answer every single one or they win by default. I was up past eleven last night responding to yesterday's filings only to get hit with another wave this morning. It's either shut down my practice to handle the paperwork or they win and take every-thing. Either way I'm burned."

"They sued me, too."

"I heard about that. SLAPP."

"What?"

"SLAPP. Strategic Lawsuits Against Public Participation. Unethical but legal tactic of big corporations. Usually used against everyday citizens protesting big polluters, develop-ers, lobbyists and such, but it works here as well. A moun-tain of torts. Defamation, interfering with potential economic gain. It never flies in court, but they don't care. The real objective is to wear down the little guys—that's us—financially and physically."

"What am I supposed to do?"

"Tell you what. Since I encouraged you, I'll go to talk to

the studio. Pro bono. If you drop the case, I can probably reason with them."

"But I don't want to drop the case. I think I can still beat them."

"Son, you don't understand. They've already won."

14

THE BIG BAMBOO

Mason jars were topped off. Chi-Chi adjusted
himself on the stool like he was getting ready
for a long drive.

Serge leaned forward on his elbows.

"Alabama," said Chi-Chi, raising his jar. "Damn."

"I want to know more about this script business," said
Serge.

"For a short game like JCPenney, you can just bullshit it
out over breakfast," said Chi-Chi. "In a long game like Alabama, you need a script. We couldn't believe it was so
good, especially for such a young crew."

"Other guys?" asked Serge.

"Will you let me tell the story?" said Chi-Chi. "That's
why they needed to team up with an older gang. Great script,
but not enough character in some of those peach faces to sell
it. That's the thing about the long game: You're working
against other con men."

"Criminals?" asked Coleman.

"Not exactly," said Chi-Chi. "But the kind of people who

can read other people. Businessmen who've built fortunes exploiting others in the gray edges of the law. The long game turns their greed against them and clouds judgment."

"Tell him about the hotel in Panama City," said Coltrane.

"Classy crew," said Chi-Chi. "Respected their elders, which isn't exactly a trend these days. They put us up in nice suites overlooking the Gulf of Mexico, one of those Panhandle resorts with the staircase architecture. We were there three weeks, a regular vacation like they promised. Topshelf room service kept coming while we sat around rehearsing. They even had tailors drop by and fit us. Finally, we were ready. The teams split up. Us old guys go to the country club."

"Were you members?" asked Serge.

"Doesn't matter at our age," said Chi-Chi. "Act like you belong and have the right clothes. They won't dare insult you. That's where the wardrobe came in. Expensive navyblue blazers with big brass buttons and yellow silk hankies poking out breast pockets. Plaid pants, white shoes. Normally I wouldn't be caught dead. Each afternoon we set up camp in the men's-only bar overlooking the eighteenth pin. Dark paneling, cigar smoke. You know the kind of place: Talk always ends up about money. And did we have a story! This particular club was big with bank types, presidents, board members. A bunch were from Alabama, since it was so close to the state line. Second homes on the Redneck Riviera. Fish in a barrel. We'd grab a private cocktail table in the corner each day, the ones with the big cushy chairs you sink into, which were hell on my knees. It was Sergio's finest hour. Underplayed his role to the nines. He's obviously the most important because the rest of us are acting like loud fools, and he's the quiet one handing out big checks. I don't just mean the amounts. We ordered a set of the largest business checks we could find, then casually left a couple on the table, catching guys at the other tables trying to read the dollar figures upside down, which were five and six digits. What did we care? We weren't going to cash them. After our Rémy Martin comes, all of us make a big show of whipping out our own leather books and writing a pile of checks back to Sergio. The mojo started. Club members begin trying to strike up conversations, but we'd quickly put our stuff away and act coy. The more secretive we were, the more curious they got. It was killing them! Went like this two whole weeks. Finally, one day, we pretend we're drunker than usual. On cue, Sergio goes to the restroom, and we spill the beans to the next table. Then we see Sergio returning and act all guilty: 'Don't say anything! We weren't supposed to tell you.' . . ."

"And that's when we started drilling for oil," said Coltrane.

"You want to tell the story?" said Chi-Chi.

"No, I want another drink."

"Then don't interrupt. Where was I?"

"But you can't drill in Florida," said Serge.

"That's why we had to go to Alabama," said Coltrane. "Shit, they don't care. They take money from other states to bury garbage that makes the hills glow at night like a black-light poster."

"Will you two shut up?" said Chi-Chi. "Now I lost my place."

"Bartender! . . ."

"I remember," said Chi-Chi. "We baited the trap; time to spring it. And this is where the young kids really impressed us, because you always hear how this generation wants everything handed to them. Not these guys. They didn't just grab the easy money—to them it was as much about tradition. They read their history, and they did their homework. That's why it worked. The game was so preposterous, not even other con men would suspect. But these kids showed us the old court photostats. It really happened before: Louisville, Kentucky, in 1958, and again the next year outside Lubbock. The last case popped up in Oklahoma during the OPEC embargo. And that's how we came to own an oil well."

"Where on earth do you buy an oil well?" asked Serge.

"Oil *derrick,* actually," said Chi-Chi. "The whole thing is the well. You lease them, for less than you'd think. There's dozens of companies—ship anywhere as long as you pay."

"But you don't have an oil field."

"They don't care," said Chi-Chi. "They're in the derrick-renting business. As long as your check clears, you can sink it in your living room and pump champagne."

Serge was skeptical. "But bankers check out everything. Weren't they bound to find—"

"Covered," said Chi-Chi. "There are very specific paper-work rules for this kind of thing. You follow them. Find a farmer in bib overalls willing to be an accomplice. Offer a few grand for six months' mineral rights, which is a windfall to him 'cause there ain't no oil. It's a standard contract—the people in those country clubs know all about them. Farmer gets front money and an eighth of whatever you strike. Split the rest in sixteen shares. File all the proper documents with the county and state, incorporate. Then, when those bankers from the country club start snooping around, it's all in order. Only thing left is to strike oil."

"But if there's no oil," said Coleman, "how'd you strike it?"

"We didn't strike it," said Chi-Chi. "We bought it."

"Bought it?"

"Five gallons of crude to be exact," said Chi-Chi. "Splashed it over the derrick that we never turned on. All set for the big day. After blabbing to our new friends at the club, they wouldn't leave us alone. Begged to meet the next time we went out to the well. The following Tuesday this long line of big-ass luxury cars heads north on U.S. 331 and crosses the state line at Florala. They drive deep into Covington County: spooky, unmaintained roads through moonshine country with a bunch of scraggly oaks making canopies."

Coleman waved for the bartender. "You'd think they'd get lost. Or scared."

"Turns out they knew the area better than we did. Foreclosed on properties all over the place. One of them even knew the last turn, which was through this broken cattle gate and up a bluff until they came to the most surreal sight: a giant wedding tent surrounded by grazing cows. They met us and shook hands. Then they asked the pink-elephant-in-the-room question: What's the tent for? And why wasn't the derrick running? We explained that a quick strike is good-news, bad-news. Good: less investment in exploratory drilling. Bad: the closer to the surface, the smaller the pocket, nothing remotely compared to the vast reserves farther down. We told them we didn't have the problem of a quick strike."

"Yeah, but why the tent?" asked Serge.

"I'm getting to that," said Chi-Chi. "We told them we had so many tanker trucks coming and going on these back roads that talk was starting. Sergio only had the one lease. He was forced to shut down and hide everything in the tent so he could go around buying more rights before too many people got wise. After that, those bankers couldn't whip out their checkbooks fast enough. We told them: Hold on, we weren't out to screw anyone, but we're the guys who had to sweat it out a month paying for pipes and bits going down a dry hole, no guarantee we'd ever hit anything. They couldn't just come in at the end. They'd have to spend backward up the well and amortize our risk. They said it was more than fair."

"And that's when you took them?" said Serge.

"No, that's when Sergio drove up and kicked everyone out," said Chi-Chi.

"Now I'm confused," said Coleman.

"Thing of beauty," said Chi-Chi. "Giant limo comes barreling across the field kicking up a giant dust cloud. Parks next to the tent and Sergio gets out with this terrific-looking blonde. She was in her mid-forties, but Sergio was eighty-six at the time. For the bankers, that math confirmed the oil strike more than any geologist ever could. They run over to him with big smiles and outstretched hands, but he just starts cursing at the rest of us about not being able to keep a secret. Tells everyone to get the fuck off the property. Then he jumps back in the limo and speeds away. We rush over to apologize. Promise to talk to Sergio and smooth everything. Then we make plans to meet them back at the club in a few days."

"And *that's* when you took them?" asked Coleman.

"No," said Chi-Chi. "We never went back to the club."

"So what happened?" said Serge.

"Exactly what we knew would happen," said Chi-Chi. "They bought up the mineral rights on all the surrounding property—and a whole lot more. We'd been by to see the farmers in advance and cut deals. Everyone made out. But here's the cherry on the sundae. After we cleared town, the bankers came back to that first field and found no hole. They ran to the police demanding charges be pressed, except there was no crime."

"Of course there was a crime," said Coleman.

Serge smiled. "No, there wasn't."

"Yes, there was," said Coleman. "When they . . . well, but when they . . . definitely when they . . . shoot, you're right."

Chi-Chi signaled the bartender for another beer.

The smile on Serge's face got bigger. "An interesting coincidence of geography?"

"Don't know what you mean," said Chi-Chi, starting to smile himself.

"Where did these young kids grow up?"

"Not sure," said Chi-Chi. "Might have been that same county."

"Where those bankers did a bunch of foreclosures?"

Chi-Chi nodded.

"Any of those foreclosures happen to be these kids' parents?"

"Now that you mention it . . ."

Serge raised his orange juice for a toast. "Sweet."

Chi-Chi clinked it with his jar. "Your granddad's finest hour."

"What was the take?"

"Over a million, almost two. But the best part is, except for expenses, the kids didn't keep any. Let the community divide it up. Told you they were class."

Serge set his OJ back on the bar. "But how did you meet them in the first place?"

Chi-Chi laughed, then his face went dead serious. "You don't know?"

"Know what?"

"Oh, my God! I thought he told you!"

"Told me what? What's going on?"

"It never dawned on me," said Chi-Chi. "I must have been drinking too much telling the story. Oh, man, Serge. You have to go to L.A.!"

"Did you say L.A.?"

"Can't believe nobody told—I guess with the heart attack and all our excitement . . ."

"Grandpa mentioned something about L.A., but I just thought it was just more ranting."

"He wasn't ranting," said Chi-Chi, climbing off his stool. "Okay, I'm going to do this right. I'm going to let your granddad tell you."

"Now, *you're* ranting."

"Wait here." Chi-Chi walked quickly out the front door to the parking lot.

Serge hit the bar with his fist. "Will somebody tell me what's going on?"

Chi-Chi retrieved an envelope from his glove compartment and headed back to the lounge. Behind him, a white sedan with blackwall tires drove by on highway 192.

A man in a dark suit and a thin, dark tie turned around in the passenger seat. "Just passed the place."

"I did?"

"You can make a U at the next light."

The sedan pulled into the left lane and stopped at a red. "Think he might be in there?"

"Not after that close call at the cemetery. But we can lean on his friends."

Chi-Chi hurried back into the bar, catching his breath. "Here." He handed Serge the envelope.

Serge took it and began tearing the flap, giving Chi-Chi a wary expression. "You sure you're okay?"

Chi-Chi nodded, still panting. "Your grandfather gave me that a few months ago. All happened in the last year. With you off to who knows where, he was afraid he wouldn't see you again. Made me promise to deliver that if anything happened to him."

Serge was still giving Chi-Chi an odd look as he pulled the letter from the envelope. He began reading.

A white sedan pulled up in front of The Big Bamboo. Two men in dark suits and thin, dark ties opened the doors.

Serge's eyes were almost out of his head as he finished the letter's first page and frantically flipped to the second. "Holy shit!"

"Something, eh?" said Chi-Chi.

Serge suddenly jumped up. "Come on!" He yanked Coleman off his stool. A jar of beer went flying. They ran out the back of the bar as two men in dark suits came in the front.

The men walked up to the counter and leaned against the end with a half-full jar of orange juice. The bartender grabbed the jar and dumped it in the sink. He set out fresh squares of toilet paper. "What can I get you fellas?"

One of the men showed the bartender a black-and-white photo. "Know this guy?"

The bartender leaned and pretended to study the picture, then stood up. "Nope, never seen him."

He turned to Chi-Chi, about to show the photo again when he realized the previously noisy lounge had gone silent. Everyone staring into their drinks.

The man shot his partner a knowing glance. He began walking behind the row of stools. "So this is how it's going to be? Well, just from where I'm standing I can see at least a dozen fire violations . . ."

His partner bent down. "What's this?" He picked a piece of paper off the floor. "Looks like a letter." He turned it over to the empty back side. "It's just the second page."

Chi-Chi smacked himself in the forehead.

"Let me see that," said his partner. His lips moved as he read. He reached the end of the letter and looked up in puzzlement. "Los Angeles?"

15

LOS ANGELES

Another Friday evening sunset on Ivar Street. Shadows grew tall. A green-and-yellow neon sign came on outside the Alto Nido apartments.

In a third-floor unit, four roommates worked combs, cologne and a hair dryer. The fifth tapped typewriter keys. He was starting to grow his first beard.

"Ford, this isn't good," said Pedro. "You haven't left the apartment since you were fired."

"Why don't you go out with us tonight?" said Ray.

"You have to snap out of it," said Mark.

Tino slipped into a sports shirt. "All the signs of depression—"

"Actually, I'm doing my best work," said Ford. Tap, tap, tap. "At first I only wanted to occupy my mind. Then it just started coming."

"What started coming?" asked Mark.

"New script." Ford twisted the roller, removing the sheet. He set it neatly on a stack of pages next to the typewriter. "And now it's done."

"That means you can go out with us?"

Ford stood. "Okay."

Pedro capped a Speed Stick. "That's more like it."

Ford turned on an electric razor with turbo-cut action. "Just give me a minute."

Tampa International Airport

Runway Niner. Seat 42B. Middle seat. Serge adjusted the overhead vents and reading lights. He pulled out the reading material in the pocket in front of him, unfolded the laminated safety guide, put it back. He rested his hands in his lap and smiled. He looked down. His knees were slightly touching the seat in front of him. Serge frowned. He shifted his weight and stretched his legs. No good. He shifted the other way. He grabbed both armrests and pushed himself back as far as he could. His knees still touched.

Seat 42A. Window seat. The older man in a business suit made notes in an organizer. His gray hair was leaving, but he was comfortable with it. The organizer began shaking; his Montblanc pen skidded into the margin. He looked at the passenger to his left, fiercely twisting his legs. Serge stopped and smiled. The man smiled back and returned to his work.

Seat 42C. Aisle. Coleman tapped Serge on the shoulder. "When do they start serving alcohol?"

"Not now. I'm having configuration problems." Serge bent down and reached under the seat in front of him, retrieving his carry-on. "There. My feet have more room. Knees clear."

"But now the carry-on is in your lap," said Coleman. "The rule says—"

"I know the rules," snapped Serge. "And the overhead bins are full. It's like a Rubik's Cube." Serge dumped the bag's contents in his lap. "Coleman, start stuffing this shit in your seat pocket." He turned to the businessman. "You using that pocket?"

"Huh?"

"Thanks."

When it was all stowed, Serge flattened his carry-on and crammed it next to the gym bag at Coleman's feet. "There." He successfully stretched out his legs and smiled. He folded his hands in his lap again. A moment passed. Serge glanced at the man next to him, then Coleman.

"Could have sworn I requested a window seat."

"What's the matter with that one?" asked Coleman.

"I can't see America. It's a five-hour flight, and two centuries of eminent-domain history will be just out of view. The Louisiana Purchase, Davey Crockett, the Sooners, the Gadsden Purchase—everybody forgets that one—the gold rush, and finally the Pacific Ocean, sea to shining sea! I'll tell you what: If I was doing business work and not looking outside, I'd give up my seat. That's what I'd do. Yes, sir, I sure wish someone would trade me their window seat. But you can't expect people to be psychic—they don't know how much I'd love to look out the window! Because if they did, they sure would offer to trade . . ."

"Excuse me," said the businessman. "I'd be happy to trade seats with you."

"Oh, no, no, no, no, no, no! Absolutely not!" said Serge. "Wouldn't hear of it! Don't want to inconvenience . . . Okay." Serge jumped up, and they awkwardly squeezed by each other.

The man opened his organizer and began writing again.

The jet taxied across the airfield and pivoted at the end of a long runway. The engines started revving. Serge tapped the businessman on the shoulder. "Know what I like to do on takeoff? Pretend to be a couple of guys from way back in history. You know, people who've never even *seen* an airplane. And when the wheels leave the ground, you talk like they would . . ." The jetliner began rolling down the tarmac, slowly at first, then rapidly picking up speed, eighty, ninety, a hundred miles an hour. "You be Thomas Jefferson. I'm Aaron Burr." The nose of the airplane angled up as they left the ground. "Tom! Tom! What the fuck's going on? Why is this happening? We're in the stomach of a big bird! . . . Okay, they just retracted the landing gear. You don't have to be Jefferson anymore."

The man tried to appear occupied with his work.

"So, you're a businessman," said Serge. "But you're sitting back here in coach. Good for you. To hell with people thinking you're not successful. I hate the snobs in first class. They think they're better, but they're just hurting themselves, lounging in those big seats while attendants tong out hot towels in a manner that makes the rest of us want to vote for Democrats. What do you do for a living? Okay, I'll go first. I'm in the movies. Well, not yet, but that's just a formality. I'm going to bring the film industry to Florida. Why, you ask? I'll tell you. Guess what the biggest-grossing film in Florida history is. Are you trying to guess? Tick-tock, tick-tock, time's up! *Deep Throat*. Four hundred million dollars and climbing. Right! I agree with you completely! Are blow jobs the first thing we want people to picture when we mention Florida?" Serge punched the seat in front of him, knocking the passenger forward. "Absolutely not! I mean, you're from this fine state. I know that because I peeked at your stuff there. No, we definitely don't want blow jobs! No cornholing, no around-the-worlds, no tittie-fucks, pearl necklaces, muff diving or golden showers. No brown ones either—yuck. I say, 'All of that—off the table!' Coleman disagrees with me, of course, but that's why it's a free country. Disney had it right before he died and they turned his dream into hell with long lines. Yes, good, clean entertainment for the whole family. That's my vision for America. But since porn has surfaced in the conversation, I want to talk about the movie *Wonderland*. You've heard of John Holmes, right? The adult film legend? Had a shlong the size of a Wiffle bat. Something like two thousand X-rated films on his résumé. But there's more to the story. Much more . . ."

"Sir . . ."

Serge looked up. A flight attendant was standing in the aisle. "Yes?"

"We've had some complaints. There are small children . . ."

"Children!" Serge jumped to his feet. "What's happened to them? How can I help?"

"Off-color language. Some passengers found it offensive—"

"*I* find it offensive," said Serge, jerking his head around. "Who's doing this?"

"Uh . . . you are."

"What? . . . Oh *that*. It's okay. The words were used self-referentially. I needed to establish the paradigm in order to smash it."

"Please try to be more careful."

"I just told you—I'm already on the team."

The flight attendant walked away. Serge sat down and leaned to the businessman. "She's having trouble getting her arms around the paradigm. Where were we? Right, John Holmes. Ever hear of the Wonderland Massacre? Most people haven't. But that case is to the eighties what Manson was to the sixties. More than grisly crime scenes, they were metaphors for their times. Half of L.A. was coked out of its skull. Crazy parties at the Starwood Club and all over the Hollywood Hills, including this little home on Wonderland Avenue. Then they found four dead bodies, savagely attacked like they'd scratched Ryan O'Neal's car. A chain reaction of drug rip-offs, and Holmes was involved. So he fled. Where to? You guessed it! Florida! Holed up in the Fountainhead Motel at 16001 Collins Avenue. I've stayed in the room, for spiritual reasons. Can't tell you how excited I was when I heard they were making a big movie starring Val Kilmer. Then I watched the thing and know where it ends? Holmes fleeing east on a California highway. No Florida at all, just chopped off that part of the story like they couldn't bear to share the spotlight. Jealousy is an ugly thing."

The businessman forced a grin and opened his laptop. He plugged it in to the telephone receptacle on the back of the seat in front of him.

Serge leaned for a closer look. "Wow, they have AeroLink on this flight! Costs like a million bucks a minute, doesn't it? . . . Oh, you're trying to do work, aren't you? I'll leave you alone."

Serge reached in his seat pocket and pulled out a sleek white gadget. He stuck it between the man's face and his laptop screen. "It's an iPod." Serge pulled it back and began pressing buttons. "Holds ten thousand songs. I'm only up to nine hundred. I can't stop thinking about it . . . Sorry, forgot. You're working . . ."

Serge sat back and pressed buttons, rearranging his L.A. playlist. He leaned to his left: "Listen. I know you're busy but could you do me a favor . . ."

A minute later, the businessman's head hung in surrender. His laptop sat on Serge's knees, plugged into the iPod.

"Thanks! I'll just be a second. Need to download some music. Don't worry—you won't be charged. Unless they find out your account was used to steal music; then it could get steep. But how else do they expect me to ever get to ten thousand? . . . Oh, no. Hold everything. They're asking for a user name and PIN number. What's happening to the world? Our whole lives are now user names and PIN numbers! How do you remember all yours? I sure can't! I started using the same ones every time, but I decided that was just an invitation for identity fraud and then . . ."—Serge patted the wallet in his side pocket—". . . you're forced to use other people's credit cards. So I began coming up with a bunch of arcane stuff that I can never recall, and then I have to hit the 'Forget your password?' button, which retrieves the 'hint question' I set up my account with. For extra security, I use trick questions that even I can't guess, in case I'm interrogated. Okay, what should my user name be? I'll try this . . . Shit. Has to be at least eight characters. How about this . . . Damn. Must be letters *and* numbers . . ."

Coleman leaned across the businessman. "Try 'Booty-call69.' "

Serge typed it in. "Already taken . . ."

The businessman stuck a tiny pillow behind his head. "I'm going to take a nap."

"Good thinking," said Serge, continuing to type. "Three-hour time difference. Jet lag will screw up your circadian rhythms every time. Except mine are naturally three hours ahead. Lucky genes. So don't worry about a thing. I'll stand watch. If anything important happens, you'll be the first to know."

The man snuggled his head into the pillow and closed his eyes.

A minute passed. The man felt someone shaking his shoulder. He opened his eyes.

"I have to go to the bathroom."

HOLLYWOOD

A yellow Malibu sped east on Santa Monica.

"Where are we going?" asked Ford, changing lanes to pass traffic backing up outside the Formosa Café.

"Redondo Beach," said Pedro. "Incredible party. Second best in L.A. tonight."

"What's the first?"

"Will's place."

"Will who?"

"Don't know," said Pedro, keeping his for-the-road cocktail below window level. "We were there last week. Asked the bouncer, but he would only smile and say, 'Will.' Incredible spread, like the Hearst mansion in San Simeon. Courtyard full of bizarre zoo animals wandering around Greek statues."

"It was off the hook," said Mark. "All these hot chicks passed out by the guitar-shaped pool and in the giant maze of shrubs. The basement had a panic room where everyone was smoking dope."

Ford stopped at a red light. "If that's the top party tonight, why aren't we going there?"

"Because of what happened last week," said Mark.

"We ended up in the library," said Pedro. "Everyone was completely wrecked. I tried to score with some babes by standing on a Louis the Fourteenth chair to do an Astaire dance move. You know, where Fred puts his foot up on the back and gently tips the chair over and steps down into a pirouette. Except the back snapped off and I crashed into an antique chess set. Some of the pieces broke, too. I was afraid they were going to try to make me pay, so I gathered the evidence in my shirt and found a balcony and began throwing chair parts and bishops over the side. Then someone started screaming down below: 'My chair!' Guess that was Will. Time to leave. That's when I tumbled down the big curved marble staircase. We couldn't find Ray, because he'd lost consciousness out back in a pile of emu shit. So we split in a limo, and Mark said something that pissed off the chauffeur, and he gets put out of the car on the side of the Ventura freeway and falls asleep in weeds below an overpass and wakes up with that rash on his face. Tino was the only one who made it home with me but doesn't remember about the welts or how one of his ears got packed with food. It was starting to get light out when Dallas showed up with some speed, and then we're driving to Mexico and found a pharmacy with chickens running around and an old lady behind the counter who looked like Lee Trevino and would sell us anything, and we took so much Darvon we went deaf."

"Deaf?" said Ford.

"Little fibers in the hearing canal get paralyzed, like Rush Limbaugh," said Pedro. "There's already a language barrier at the border, and on top of that I'm shouting at the Mexican customs cop: 'What? I can't hear you! What?' So now we can't get back in the country. Had to stay until the effects wore off and lost two days' pay. Then it turns out my spill down the stairs was worse than I thought, and I have to wear this wrist brace for six weeks, but they gave me more Darvon. Which reminds me, Ford, how come you don't party?"

Thirty-six Thousand Feet

The businessman in seat 42B opened his eyes. Someone was shaking his shoulder again.

"Wake up! Wake up! Wake up! . . ."

The man's head turned in alarm. "What is it?"

"I found *SkyMall* magazine in my seat pocket!" said Serge. "I love *SkyMall*! Isn't it the weirdest? Like this item: 'The last flashlight you will ever need!' How can they make such a bold claim? I must have one. Wait. Here's a personal executive submarine . . . Oooo! Look! Look! Look! There's the shore of Texas! Just made it across the Gulf of Mexico, so the flotation devices can't help us now. Ever seen the Alamo? Big, big disappointment. Right in the middle of downtown, much smaller than you'd think. I'd given up looking for it and pulled into a Taco Bell and hit this statue that some jokers had stuck in the middle of the drive-through. That's right—it was the Alamo. Then I had to drive away fast . . . Cool! They're about to show the movie! Here they come with the five-dollar headsets." Serge reached in his seat pocket and put on the headset he'd brought with him, then winked at the businessman. "They think they're dealing with children. Wonder what the movie's going to be. Hope it's a good one. Please, please, please! . . . Damn, it's *How to Lose a Guy in 10 Days*. I tell you how: Take him to movies like this." Serge removed his headset. "Know why I love cinema? Because it connects people—total strangers who would otherwise wind up strangling each other. But we all share these common moments. Like in *Five Easy Pieces* when Nicholson is having that sandwich argument with the waitress and tells her to stick it between her knees."

The man's expression changed. "That's one of my favorite scenes of all time!"

"Mine, too!" said Serge. "I loved it so much I tried it the very next time I went to a diner, and you know what? I got the same reaction! That's a sign of good writing."

The businessman was chuckling now. "What'd you think of his performance in *Cuckoo's Nest*?"

"Randall Patrick McMurphy. RPM. Revolutions Per Minute."

"Never realized that," said the businessman. "I'll bet we like a lot of the same films."

"See? We're bonding through the magic of cinema!" said Serge. "We just met and it's like we're old friends! Can I come over to your house and grill?"

The man's smile drooped.

"You're right again," said Serge. "I'm rushing things.

Here, I want you to read something extremely personal."
He reached in his shirt pocket and pulled out a letter. "It's
from my dead granddad. Hey, where'd page two go? Must
have dropped it. You'll still get the gist." He handed it to
the businessman, who began reading. Halfway down, his
jaw fell. He finished and handed it back to Serge. "Wow.
That's quite a story. I don't know how I'd react if I was in
your place."

Serge took the letter back. "It's all I've been able to think
about. Well, not all. Stuff just jumps around in my head.
Sometimes I can't turn it off. You fly a lot? What do you
think of the new security?"

"Makes me feel safer."

"Me, too," said Serge. "But it really put the pressure on
last night."

"Why's that?"

"Figuring out how to get all my makeshift weapons
through X-ray." Serge leaned and whispered. "I'm armed to
the teeth."

The man's eyes grew large.

"No, you got the wrong idea. I'm not some kind of nut.
It's for the terrorists." Serge leaned again and lowered his
voice. "We have to start thinking like they do. I mean, box
cutters! Next time they'll come up with something even
more unexpected, so we have to depend on our imaginations
to stay ahead." Serge patted something inside his shirt. "Did
you know you can kill someone instantly with a standard
pocket comb? Very unpleasant. You don't want to know. Just
take comfort that if anyone starts lighting his shoe, row
forty-two is covered."

The businessman reached up and pressed a button on the
overhead console.

Serge stretched his neck and looked around the passenger
compartment. "I wonder who the air marshal is. It could be

anyone . . ." Serge stopped and looked at the man. "Is it you?"

"Oh, no."

"Because they'd never suspect with that stomach. You'd be perfect. And of course if it really was you, you'd have to say no, so I understand perfectly. I won't make you uncomfortable by pressing the issue." He grinned at the man.

The man nervously grinned back.

"So," said Serge. "Is it you?"

A flight attendant arrived. She turned off the "assistance" light over the middle seat. "How can I help you?"

"We're three fairly big guys," said the businessman. "I was wondering if any other seats might be available."

"I'm sorry, sir. The flight is completely full."

The attendant walked away. Serge shook his head. "I'm surprised at you."

"But I was just thinking that—"

Serge held a hand up for him to stop. "No need to explain. I guess I misjudged." He reached in his shirt pocket and slowly removed a comb.

The businessman shielded his face with the leather organizer. "No! Please! Dear God! . . ."

Serge began combing his hair. "You are a very, very considerate human being. You saw me having trouble adjusting my legs. How thoughtful."

The man cautiously lowered his organizer and peeked over the top.

"I really lucked out with my seat assignment, getting you and all," said Serge. "These coast-to-coast flights are a regular weirdo sweepstakes." Serge reached in the seat pocket and pulled out a tiny digital camcorder. He pointed it out the window and whispered from the side of his mouth: "Keep a lookout."

"What for?" asked the businessman.

"This is an unapproved electronic device . . . Fuck 'em . . ."

REDONDO BEACH

A convertible Malibu drove along the coast in a light evening breeze.

"There's the place," said Pedro.

Ford turned off South Catalina Avenue and pulled up to a ten-thousand-square-foot beach house. Cars were being valeted by men in white robes. The gang found themselves in the kitchen. Candles everywhere. More white robes. A loud whirring noise: blender on puree, people tossing in organic vegetables and LSD.

Ford walked over to Pedro. "How come all these guys are wearing robes?"

"This is the headquarters for that cult. The one waiting for the seven-planet alignment."

"Then why'd they let us in?"

"Rush week."

Ford wandered conversation to conversation until he was out back, leaning against the railing of a sun-bleached observation deck. To his left, a man in a white robe chanted and played the sitar. To his right, another robed man pumped a keg. The man skimmed the foam off the top of a plastic cup and handed it to Ford. "Have you ever given any thought to joining a fraternal organization with strong community ties?"

"I'm not joining any cult," said Ford.

"Oh, no. We're not a cult."

"I read about you guys in the paper. Mind control . . ."

"Catholic Church started those rumors. They play hardball with upstarts. You want to talk about a *cult*."

"What about the castration?"

The man began pumping the keg again. "Press always

gets hung up on that, like it's the only thing we do. Ever read about the stretch of highway we clean up every summer?"

"No."

"That's my point. You need to enroll in our trial plan. Two weeks, no strings. Judge for yourself."

"How far in is the castration?"

"You're fixating," said the man. "Open your mind . . ."

Pedro walked by with his own cup of draft, talking to someone else in a white robe. ". . . so the carpenter files down the bolts on the drawbridge . . ."

Ford looked over the brochures he'd just been handed. The robed man began pumping the keg again. "It's a tiered payment structure. You live in the house and get the meal plan, but there's a discount if you don't want breakfast. Some of the guys like to sleep in . . ."

Mark ran over with a cell phone. "Dallas just called. We gotta go."

Holmby Hills.

"What's wrong with everyone at this party?" asked Ford.

"What do you mean?" said Pedro.

"They're all gloomy."

"That's because the host doesn't let anyone do drugs in his house."

"Why's that?"

"He's a dealer."

Wonderland Avenue.

Ford stuck his head through the twin front doors. "Holy cow. Who lives here?"

"Professional stage parents," said Pedro. "Two kids in prime time."

The place was the most jammin' yet. Competing stereos on full volume in every room: Gwen Stefani bleeding into Chili Peppers. Open drug use. Casualties everywhere. A gun discharged into the ceiling.

"What's the party for?" asked Ford.

"She's pregnant again. Baby shower."

Ford noticed something across the room: Mel Glick heading up the stairs with a blonde over his shoulders in a fireman's carry. Ian was right behind, toting a medical bag and Polaroid camera.

"Why doesn't anyone do anything?"

"Because they know what's going on," said Pedro.

"What's going on?"

"A transaction."

They went out on the balcony. Ford was struck again by the view.

"*. . . The City of Angels, lonely as I am . . .*"

He repeated his mistake of looking down over the railing. He stumbled back.

"What's the matter?" asked Pedro.

Ford blinked a few times. "I can't believe they build 'em like this. Each one's higher and scarier."

"You should see the Chemosphere House around the corner. Not even attached to the mountain. On top of a single pole."

"There was a place like that in *Body Double*," said Ford. "Craig Wasson peeped on Melanie Griffith with a tele-scope."

"That's the same house."

A loud rumble shook the building.

Ford looked up at a blinking red light. The belly of a giant jetliner roared directly overhead on its final descent into LAX.

Two Thousand Feet over Los Angeles

Serge was glued to the window. Singing.

"*Comin' into Los Angel-eeeeeez . . . bringin' in a couple of keeeeeez . . .*"

He turned to the businessman. "Don't worry. The only keys I carry fit in doorknobs."

The businessman tried to read a magazine.

Serge leaned over his tray table. A map of the United States lay across it. The map had a dotted red line across the country from Tampa to the Arizona-California border. Serge uncapped a Magic Marker and made sound effects as he added five more dashes to the coast. "Almost there." He capped the pen. "Remember me telling you over New Mexico about the wings that sheared off that cargo jet from rivet stress? I think we'll make it."

Coleman tapped the businessman on his left arm and held out a miniature bottle of vodka. "Want some?"

"No thanks."

Serge tapped the businessman on the right arm. "Just remembered: Most crashes occur within five minutes of take-off and landing, so we're not out of the woods yet. Best thing to do is get your mind off the smell of jet fuel. Remember that amateur video of the fiery, pinwheel crash down the runway in Sioux City? Don't picture it. That's how I cope. Just keep telling myself: 'Think happy thoughts. Teddy bears, fairies, gumdrops' . . ."

The businessman felt a tap on his left arm. Coleman pointed at a half-full vodka on the middle tray. "Are you gonna finish yours?"

"Take it."

"Thanks."

A tap on his right arm.

"I can see the control tower! We just have to clear this last freeway . . . Three hundred feet, two hundred . . . You be Mozart. I'm Joan of Arc . . . 'Holy shit, Mozart! Get me out of this fucking thing!' . . ."

The jet touched down and taxied to the gate. Passengers

got up en masse, unlatching overhead bins. Serge refilled his carry-on from the seat pockets.

The businessman wasn't moving.

"Smart call," said Serge. "Why compete with the insanity? Just relax till everyone's off and stroll out at your leisure. I would, but we have appointments . . ."

The businessman remained still as the rest of the passengers emptied out the front of the plane, Serge and Coleman bringing up the rear. A receiving line of cheerful pilots and flight attendants thanked each of them. Coleman tripped over the lip of the pressure door and tumbled into the accordion arm. The staff winced. Then Serge came by, shaking hands hard, profusely thanking them for heroics in the face of the unthinkable.

Finally, they were gone.

The businessman flipped open a cell phone and hit some numbers. "Hello? . . . Yes, we just landed . . . No, don't intercept. Fall back to loose surveillance . . . Because I saw the first page of the letter . . . Hold on to your hat—you're not going to believe this . . ."

RAMBOO

16

Avis rental lot. Recent coat of shiny black tar and highly reflective orange markings. Just after two A.M. Inside: a single reservationist with no work and someone mopping outside the restrooms.

A courtesy bus pulled up. Two red-eye clients went inside. The empty bus headed back to the terminal.

It was dead again. The lot was in the landing pattern. These were the strange hours that were totally silent or deafening. Serge unfolded the first page of his grandfather's letter. There were ten digits in a different-color ink across the bottom. He placed the page on top of a pay phone next to the bus shelter.

Across the street sat a Ramada Inn. Each floor above the first had a balcony. On the top floor, a tall woman in a blue windbreaker stood at a railing with high-power binoculars, overlooking rental car row. She observed someone in a bright tropical shirt next to the Avis shelter, sticking coins in a pay phone.

Serge held the receiver to his head and punched numbers.

He watched the two people at the reservation counter, an exhausted business traveler who couldn't get an upgrade and some idiot with a surfboard. The phone began ringing. Serge covered one ear as a 747 roared overhead.

On the Ramada balcony, a cell phone began ringing. The woman with binoculars answered. "Hello? . . . Serge? . . . Yeah, we're still on. A half hour . . . You got something to write with? . . . Nineteen-eleven West Olive . . . There'll be a message waiting for you at the counter . . ."

Turbine thrust drowned out the conversation. Serge covered his ear again and looked up at a DC-9 clearing the lot and touching down on the other side of the fence. ". . . See you there."

The woman hung up and raised her binoculars again, following Serge across the parking lot to rental slot 28.

Serge threw his bags in the trunk of a red Chrysler Sebring convertible with fifty-two miles on the odometer. Coleman was already in the passenger seat. Another roar overhead.

The woman on the Ramada balcony followed the Chrysler as it drove across the lot.

Another balcony two floors below, another set of binoculars. They belonged to a man in a dark suit and thin, dark tie. He was on the phone. "Unit two, you're on . . ."

"We're rolling."

The balcony man watched the convertible race out the Avis gate and into traffic. His binoculars panned back to the rental lot, picking up a black Grand Marquis going the same direction. The Marquis made a left and caught the Chrysler at a red light.

The woman on the top floor of the Ramada dialed her phone again. "Just spotted a black Grand Marquis. Looks like they brought backup. . . . That's right, a double cross . . . Go to Plan B."

A balmy wind blew through Serge's hair as he turned east on Manchester Avenue. Coleman was bent down, trying to light a joint. Serge bent down with him, sticking his iPod in a special cradle to transmit through the car radio.

One block back, the Grand Marquis followed in the same lane at the same speed. "What the hell's he doing?" said the driver. "They're all over the road."

Serge's head popped back up. "And now the moment we've waited for all our lives!"

Coleman exhaled a big hit. "What?"

"My Los Angeles soundtrack." Serge turned the iPod's click-wheel to the desired position. "Spent weeks selecting the perfect tunes to give us special powers." He hit play and maxed out the volume. The Chrysler turned left on Osage.

"*. . . I wonder why in L.A. . . .*"

The Grand Marquis followed. The passenger keyed his microphone. ". . . Still got him . . . We're making another left on Eighty-third . . ."

The Chrysler's occupants bobbed their heads to the music. "I haven't heard this song in forever," said Coleman.

"It's what we're all about," said Serge.

"*. . . To Live and Die in L.A.! . . .*"

The passenger in the Grand Marquis raised his microphone again. "Just made another left on Handley. It doesn't make sense. We're heading back to the airport."

"*Countersurveillance shake, checking for tails,*" said the radio. "*Fall back. This guy's a pro . . .*"

"Where are we going?" asked Coleman.

"I don't know. I think I just made a bunch of wrong turns . . . Wait. Here's Manchester again . . ."

They turned east for the freeway. Serge pointed out the left side of the car. "Landmark alert. Randy's Doughnuts. Featured prominently as Jeff Goldblum drives to the airport at the beginning of *Into the Night.*"

Coleman held a big hit. "There's a giant doughnut on top of the building."

"It's Randy's."

"That's fucked up."

The Chrysler approached a red light. At the last second, Serge cut over to the turn lane.

"What is it?" asked Coleman.

"There's a twenty-four-hour Home Warehouse." The light turned green. Serge drove a block and pulled into the parking lot. "I'll be right back."

Ten minutes later he trotted out of the store with a clear gallon jug. It had a red warning label, skull and crossbones. "Pop the front hood."

Coleman reached under the dash and pulled a lever. The trunk sprang open.

"Hang tight with that joint," said Serge. He came around and reached in the car for another lever.

A black Grand Marquis sat on the other side of the parking lot. "What's he doing?"

The driver shrugged and kept watching with binoculars.

"What are you doing?" asked Coleman.

Serge uncapped a plastic tank near the Chrysler's battery and began topping it off with his jug. "Serge's Super Washer Fluid."

"What's that?"

Serge capped the plastic tank and slammed the hood. He climbed back in the car and showed Coleman the jug.

"Muriatic acid?"

"To clean the windshield," said Serge. "I have to have perfect visibility."

Coleman toked his roach. "Looks fine to me. What's the matter with regular washer fluid?"

"Leaves a film," said Serge. "Barely perceptible fog that most people can't detect. But I pick it up with my polarized fishing glasses. And once I see it, it's all I see. Not to mention bugs. If they get baked on, forget it. You can spray a whole tank of the regular blue shit and there'll still be specks, which always show up on the photos I take while driving."

Coleman leaned forward. "You're right. I see specks."

"Fuck specks." Serge activated the windshield washer. Twin jets squirted the glass, wipers sweeping.

"The specks are gone," said Coleman.

"This stuff's incredible. They usually use it to dissolve concrete. That's why I have to be careful with the ratio to water or it'll etch the glass."

"There's a whole page of warnings here on this jug."

"That's just for morons. Like the people who spray Lemon Pledge on food."

"Ow," said Coleman, rubbing his arm. "A drop splashed on me. It's burning!"

"Don't rub it," said Serge, turning off the jets. "It'll make it worse. And definitely don't spit. Apply some vinegar to neutralize the pH."

"I don't have any vinegar."

"I know. I hope you weren't fond of that spot on your arm."

"Is it going to leave a permanent mark?"

"Unfortunately."

"Serge!"

"I hear long sleeves are coming back." They began driving again, and Serge slipped on his polarized fishing glasses. "There we go."

"Serge, it's night."

"It's L.A. Everyone wears sunglasses at night."

The Chrysler made a pair of lefts. The black Grand Marquis remained a half-dozen lengths back. Serge raced up an entrance ramp to the freeway. He slammed to a stop.

Coleman grabbed the dash. "What happened?"

Serge pointed up beside the car. "Ramps in California have traffic lights."

"Far out."

"It's a completely different culture. Their freeways have stoplights, ours have dye-pack stains."

"Stains?"

The light turned green. Serge accelerated. "Everywhere you drive in Florida, interstate ramps have all these splatter marks that look like people were throwing balloons filled with powder-blue paint. Except they're really the mess chucked out the window after dye packs exploded in bank robbers' getaway cars."

"You're pulling my leg."

"Shit you not. Statistics show bandits prefer branch offices near highway interchanges for quick escape. Like other Floridians, I'd been seeing these blue skid marks for years and never knew what they were. But after the first time you figure it out, you start seeing them everywhere—Miami to Jacksonville to Pensacola—so many you begin wondering, 'What the heck's going on out here when I'm not around? Is it just pure chance we're not crossing paths?' The answer, of course, is yes."

"It's creepy knowing those people are sharing our roads," said Coleman. "Maybe we should move to a safer place."

"Like where?"

Back at the entrance ramp, the light turned green again. A Grand Marquis pulled onto the freeway.

"I don't know," said Coleman. "Maybe move here. The weather's nice. Kind of pretty . . ."

"You nuts?" said Serge. "Our crime might be unnerving, but in California everything else is insane. Earthquakes, mud slides, forest fires, primal scream, laws requiring signs that say everything will kill you, rogue sea lions taking over coastal towns, attack dogs bred to the size of bison, strip malls with designer enemas, a power grid that makes my train set look like Con Edison, and a governor and first lady who've had all the moisture sucked out of their heads."

"But at least there's no crime."

"Oh, there's crime all right," said Serge. "It's just more glamorous. Sure, celebrities *say* they're liberal and want peace. Then they crash their cars drunk and slap each other stupid at the spa. If that's not enough, come to find out, they all secretly have guns! Which you'd misguidedly think is a contradiction because they're *for* gun control, except they explain they have additional safety concerns that regular people don't face. They're right: other stars."

"Remember when Grace Slick pointed a shotgun at those deputies?"

"Exactly what I'm talking about," said Serge. "All the newspeople were reporting how high she was, and I'm thinking, So? That's her job. My big question was, what's Grace Slick doing with a gauge in her crib? Have I been listening to 'Surrealistic Pillow' on the wrong speed all these years?"

Coleman was turned around in his seat. "Serge . . ."

"What?"

"I think we're being followed."

"You're paranoid."

"No, really. That Grand Marquis. See how he's weaving through traffic trying to catch up?"

Serge glanced in the rearview. "I see him. Probably another lunatic left-coast driver. I'll speed up and try to lose him."

He stomped on the gas. Eighty, ninety . . .

The passenger in the Marquis pointed with his radio mike. "They've made us."

"No they haven't."

"Look. That one guy's staring back here. And now they're speeding up."

"Then we'll speed up."

"Won't that make them more suspicious?"

"No. On freeways, what you want to do is get over in the next lane and pass them. Then they just think you're a speeder and drop their guard. After a while, you slow down and let them pass, and you're back in the chase."

Serge continued accelerating. "Have I lost them?" The needle hit an even hundred.

"No, but they're getting over in the next lane. They're going to pass." Coleman turned back around. "Guess you were right. Just speeders."

Serge looked up at the rearview again with a glint in his eye. "God, I hate speeders! Families drive on these streets . . . I got an idea."

"What?"

"You'll see," said Serge. "First I need to slow back down to the speed limit."

The Marquis's passenger pointed again. "You were right. They're slowing down. They don't suspect us."

"I told you."

Serge switched his gaze to the side mirror. "You might want to buckle your seatbelt. This could get a little bouncy."

"Oh, shit."

Serge reached into the overnight bag under his legs. "Coleman, take this."

"Video camera?"

"You know that destabilizing maneuver they teach on the driving course at police academies?" said Serge. "They steer the nose of the patrol car into one of the rear fenders, putting the suspect's vehicle into an uncontrollable spin. Then it crashes and the driver is easy to beat up."

"I've seen that on the news," said Coleman. "The cops capture it with the automatic dashboard camera."

"That's why I want you to film," said Serge. "We might make CNN."

Coleman turned on the camcorder and squinted into the viewfinder. "You going to do the destabilizing maneuver?"

"No. I'm going to unveil Serge's *Super* Destabilizing Maneuver." He checked the mirror again. Two hundred yards and closing. "Coleman, I need you to check the rental documents. They're in the glove compartment."

"I'm holding the video camera."

"You see what I'm doing over here?" said Serge. "You have two hands."

Coleman reached in the glove box and grabbed the rental packet. "What am I looking for?"

"See if the collision coverage box is checked."

"Jesus," said Coleman. "Did you notice what they can charge for a gallon of gas if we don't bring the tank back full?"

"Come on!"

"Okay, wait, there's a lot of shit here. That box is checked, that one isn't . . . here it is, collision. Yes, it's checked!"

"We're go!" Serge's eyes stayed on the side mirror. Four car lengths, three, two . . . "That's it, just a little more, come to papa . . ."

One car length. A half. "Now!" Serge cut the steering wheel at the last second, slaloming into the next lane in front of the Marquis. He deftly worked the pedals in tandem with both feet, briefly slamming the brakes with his left, then punching the gas with his right.

Alarm in the Grand Marquis: "What the hell's he—"

They tapped bumpers. The Chrysler accelerated away.

"Are you filming it?" asked Serge.

"Yep," said Coleman, aiming back with the camera. "They're having trouble doing eighty with the airbags deployed and . . . Man! They sailed right through that guardrail!"

"Make sure you get the fireball."

"I'm getting it."

Coleman finally turned around and shut off the camera. "Those poor guys."

"Speed kills."

Coleman was looking at the rental agreement again. "Serge, this collision box that's checked. What's *waiver* mean?"

"Why didn't you tell me it said *waiver*?"

"You just asked if the collision box was checked."

"That means we turned *down* coverage. Now we'll have to report the car stolen. On the other hand, I get to push it off a cliff."

Hollywood Tattletale

FILM BUDGET TO BREAK RECORD

HOLLYWOOD—According to a leaked copy of the secret shooting script for *All That Glitters*, legendary director Werner B. Potemkin is planning the most elaborate, expensive and dangerous movie climax ever attempted.

No one dared hazard an estimate on the final cost of the scene, but all agree it will easily push the overall budget into record territory.

An insider, who spoke on the condition of being paid, described a massive production that merges memorable scenes from numerous Academy Award–winning classics, including *Casablanca*,

Lawrence of Arabia, On the Waterfront, North by Northwest and *Oklahoma!*

But most ambitious are the technical challenges of combining the attack on the Death Star with the parting of the Red Sea, further complicated by Potemkin's refusal to use scale models or computer manipulation.

"We're going to flood the two-million-gallon concrete basin on Soundstage 19 that we built for that pirate movie," said the insider. "And we're going to use real stuntmen with concealed scuba gear."

Olive Avenue bends north through Burbank. Then it becomes wide and straight, a corridor of tall palms, abrupt mountains at the end. Serge reached the 1600 block, checking stores for addresses. He spotted the retro sign three blocks ahead.

"Coleman, there it is! I've got chills!"

"That motel?"

Serge whipped the convertible through the entrance of the Safari Inn. "This is where Jim Lovell's wife lost her wedding ring down the shower drain in *Apollo 13.* Christian Slater and Patricia Arquette also stayed here in *True Romance.*"

Serge jumped out of the car and ran inside to the front desk. "Serge Storms. Secret message for me?"

The manager stared at Serge a moment, then went looking through the wooden slots on the wall behind the desk. He found a slip of paper and handed it across the counter.

Serge ran out the door.

The Chrysler was waiting outside. Empty. Serge's eyes swept the parking lot. "Coleman!"

A horn honked. Tires screeched. "Watch it!"

"Sorry." Coleman stopped and stood on the centerline of the highway. He drank a freshly popped beer while cars whizzed by on both sides. Finally, a break. Coleman trotting the rest of the way back to the car. "Hi, Serge."

"Coleman, what are you doing?"

"Store over there. I was thirsty."

"We've got work to do." Serge unfolded the note and read. He stuck it back in his pocket and walked quickly through the parking lot, checking doors for room numbers. He came to the end. He opened the note again. "This can't be right."

"What is it?"

Serge pointed up at the second floor. "Room 109."

"So."

"That's where Slater and Arquette stayed. She got the stuffing beat out of her in there by James Gandolfini, still unknown before *The Sopranos.*"

"Rooms all look alike."

"I'm positive."

"You know the number?"

"No, but I freeze-framed the DVD a bunch of times. Last room upstairs on the left that forms an acute angle with the south wing."

Coleman chugged the rest of his tall boy. "I'm thirsty again."

"This is too much of a coincidence." Serge reached in the convertible for his .45 automatic. "What are we dealing with here?"

"Let's leave."

"The note said the door would be unlocked. Go inside and wait for the meeting." He checked the Colt to make sure the magazine was full, then stuck it in his waistband and covered it with the untucked floral shirt. "My street sense tells me it's a trap. We've already been marked for death."

"And you're still going?"

"I make a lot of stuff up. I don't know why."

Coleman was playing with the front of his pants. "My belt's too tight. I'm out of notches again."

"Or maybe I'm not making it up. I could be giving myself a test." Serge reached in the car for his video camera. "Coleman, stay here and keep watch."

"Why the camera?"

"I loved *True Romance*," said Serge, checking the battery. "There's no way I'm not going to film this."

"You need me to do anything?"

"Yes! Stand watch!" said Serge. "Stay in the car and honk three times if anyone approaches the room. No, wait. They'll recognize that. It's the standard warning honk. Okay, I got it. First, *don't* honk. *Then* honk three times. It'll confuse them."

Before Coleman could respond, Serge was bounding up the stairs three steps at a time. He made the second floor and flattened himself against a wall in the breezeway. He peeked around the corner. So far so good. He began creeping along the landing like a cheetah. Room 112, 111, 110 . . . 109! Serge coiled and leaped to the other side of the door. He silently reached for the knob. Unlocked.

Coleman leaned against the rental car. He watched Serge turn the knob the rest of the way and slip inside. Coleman forgot his beer was empty and raised it to his lips. "Hmmm." He looked inside the hole.

Serge moved through 109 on tiptoes. Nobody home. He looked under the bed and made the standard sweep, closet, shower, all clear. He set the video camera on the dresser and glanced at his watch. Two minutes till the meet. He sat down on the edge of the bed and began to relax. A car honked three times.

Serge sprang and pulled his pistol. He crept across the room and slowly reached for the knob. Careful . . . Quiet . . .

He jerked the door open and lunged with the gun. An empty landing. Three more honks. He looked down at the parking lot.

Coleman was looking back. He held a beer can upside down and shook it to show it was empty. He pointed at the store across the street.

Serge shook his head hard and threw up his arms. He went back in the room.

Before he could close the door all the way, a muscle-bound man with dreadlocks darted out of the next room and kicked it in. He decked Serge with a right hook. Serge jumped up, but the man was already aiming a gun. Like a cobra, Serge struck and knocked the pistol out of his grip, sending it clattering across the tile floor. Serge was off balance from the follow-through, and the man kneed him in the groin. He doubled over; the same knee came up again and caught him in the chin. He tumbled toward the bathroom.

Serge groaned on the floor, trying to clear his head. The man had at least fifty pounds on him, and it wasn't fat. He reached down for a two-handed grip, picked Serge up and flung him through the glass shower door.

Coleman tossed his empty beer in a garbage can and walked back to the car. He looked up at room 109. Nothing happening. He reached into the convertible and fiddled with the radio until he found a groove. He hit a roach secretly cupped in his hand.

"... Hollywood's swingin' ..."

Crash.

Serge slammed into a full-length wall mirror, crumpling to the floor with the jagged pieces.

The attacker found his pistol in the corner. He walked up to Serge and aimed at his forehead. "This is it. Moment of truth." He cocked the hammer.

A woozy Serge struggled to push himself up to his knees.

Dazed, bloody. He reached in his shirt pocket and slowly removed a comb. He pointed it with an unsteady arm.

The man chuckled. "Got a lot of heart, kid, you know
that?" He stuck the pistol back in its shoulder holster. "You
want to play? I'll give you one shot."

Serge was having trouble holding his arm up. He wiped
blood from his eyes with the other hand.

The man leaned forward, toying with Serge. "Come on.
Do your worst."

Serge lunged with the comb. The man reeled backward in
agony—"*Aaaauuhhhhh!*"

He flashed with rage and charged Serge, catching him in
the gut and driving him across the room until they both went
sprawling in a tangle of limbs. They wrestled across the
floor. They grabbed each other by the throat and choked.
Both beyond exhaustion. Serge wearily drew his right hand
back, delivering a listless punch to the jaw. The man's head
bobbed and he pulled his own fist back, returning the half-
hearted jab. Serge swung an off-the-mark roundhouse; the
man missed with an uppercut. Back, forth, over and over,
until they were completely spent, panting hard, unable to do
anything but prop themselves up next to each other against
the side of the bed. A minute later, Serge jabbed his arm out
sideways.

"Ow," said the man.

A minute later a jab hit Serge in the cheek. "Ow."

"Let's take a break."

"Okay," said Serge.

"I'm still going to kill you . . ."

"In a minute . . ."

The man felt a slight pain in his thigh. He realized he was
sitting on the gun. He retrieved it and summoned the
strength to press the barrel against Serge's temple.
"Minute's up . . ."

"Dammit!" said Serge. "I told myself this was a trap!"

"You should have listened."

"Just hold on," said Serge. "Before you shoot, would you at least tell me why?"

"Why what?"

"I came here in a pretty good mood. We could have had some laughs, but instead you have to kill me."

"The double cross. Pretending to be Serge . . ."

"But I *am* Serge."

"You think we're stupid? Like we weren't watching the rental lot when you left with your backup?"

"What backup?"

"The black Grand Marquis."

"I didn't have a backup."

"I know we fucked you over, but you can drop the act now."

"Wait a second," said Serge. "*Black* Grand Marquis?"

"This is getting old." The man cocked the pistol again.

"I swear!" said Serge. "I can prove that wasn't our backup. Just let me get my video camera."

"It's a trick. Forget it."

"What if I am Serge? Think of the mistake you'll be making."

The man paused. "I should have my head examined. Okay, make it quick. But the first wrong move . . ." He pushed Serge's head with the end of the gun.

Serge got up and grabbed his camera off the dresser. He rewound the tape and began playing the footage from the freeway. "See?"

The man grabbed the camera and pointed the gun. "Step back." Serge did. The man brought the tiny LCD screen to his face for a closer look. "That's the car, all right, and . . . Whoa. Nice footwork on the pedals." He turned the camera off. "Okay, that definitely wasn't your backup. But it still doesn't mean you're Serge."

Serge reached in his pocket.

"Freeze!"

"I'm just getting a piece of paper." He pulled out the first page of the letter and handed it over. The man's expression evolved as his eyes moved down the paper. He reached the bottom and looked up. "Oh, my God! You really are Serge! I can't believe I almost shot you!"

The motel room door opened. Two more men marched Coleman inside at gunpoint.

"I don't know how they got the drop on me," said Coleman. "They were invisible, like they had some kind of cloaking device."

"We walked right up to him," said the man with the gun. "He was in the car smoking a joint under the dashboard."

"Serge," said the one with the dreadlocks, "I'm awfully sorry." He picked up the room's phone. "I'll straighten this out. We'll meet again tomorrow at noon. And this time there won't be any surprises."

"Where?"

"Pat and Lorraine's."

"Pat and Lorraine's!" said Serge. "I've always wanted to eat there! I hear they have great coffee."

The man smiled. "The last thing you need is another cup of coffee."

17

VISTAMAX STUDIOS

Guards checked IDs. Golf carts zipped between sets.

Upstairs in the administration building, copies of the *Hollywood Tattletale* lay on both brothers' desks, folded over to the latest Potemkin article.

"He's lost it," said Ian.

"We have to shut him down," said Mel.

"But how?"

Shouting in the lobby: "What do you think you're doing? You can't just barge—"

The door flew open. Mel closed a drawer and sighed. "Nobody knocks anymore."

In stormed a female theatrical agent with clenched fists. "You motherfuckers!"

"I tried to stop her," said Betty.

"You raped her!" yelled the woman.

"Uh, Betty," said Ian. "You can go."

The door closed.

"Now just calm down," said Mel.

The woman breathed fire. She had a tangerine scarf and a vague resemblance to Penny Marshall, but lighter hair. "You won't get away with this! I'll have you arrested!"

"Take it easy," said Mel. "Let's talk about this."

"*Rape* is such an overused word," said Ian.

The woman grabbed an abstract sculpture off a pedestal near the door. Ian ducked. It hit the wall, shattering into countless abstract pieces.

"You're obviously upset," said Mel.

"You think *this* is upset? You have no idea!"

"Back up," said Ian. "Who got raped?"

"You know damn well who!"

The brothers looked confused. It was sincere. There were so many.

"That baby shower for the stage parents up on Wonderland!" yelled the agent. "Ally Street!"

"Ohhhh," said Ian. "*Her.*"

"I think we can clear this up," said Mel. "Just a big misunderstanding."

"Nothing happened," said Ian.

"And it was consensual," said Mel.

"Ally came on to us. She was really drunk."

"We helped her into bed before she could fall down the stairs and hurt herself."

"Bullshit!" said the woman. "You put something in her drink. I've heard the stories about you two!"

"How about this," said Ian. "We give her a part. She'll even get a few lines, a nice credit for her résumé. We're still not admitting anything, but we have a lot of respect for you."

"Your name's big in this town," said Mel.

"What is it again?" said Ian.

"Gersh!" she snapped. "Tori Gersh!"

"That's right." Mel turned to his brother. "I always told you I liked Tori. Very reasonable person to deal with."

"We could have a big future," said Ian. "Why don't you head on up to legal." He grabbed his phone. "I'll call ahead and have them start typing the contract."

"Is that how you want to play?" said Tori. "Fine! Here's the deal. Not a small little part with a few lines. A leading role."

The brothers laughed.

"We can't do that," said Ian. "What's she ever been in?"

"Be sensible," said Mel. "A small speaking part is the going rate for this kind of thing. Ask around."

"Not this time," said Tori. She reached into her purse and threw something. A pile of Polaroid photos scattered across Mel's desk: the brothers, naked, unconscious in a variety of compromising positions. Accessories, too.

Mel became queasy. "Where'd you get these?"

"Ally wasn't as smashed as you thought," said Tori. "You blew it and didn't put enough in her drink. She woke up first. Not too bad with a camera, eh?"

"Look at this one," Ian told his brother. "I'd never do that. It's obviously posed!"

"And this one," said Mel. "Why would I do *that*?"

"She staged these pictures!" said Ian.

"Took advantage of us while we were passed out!" said Mel.

"What's it going to be?" said Tori. "Leading role or copies of those start turning up in newsrooms?"

The brothers bit their lips. "Okay, okay," Ian finally said. "Don't go and do anything crazy."

"Say it!" yelled Tori.

They cringed.

"Say it!"

Mel forced his mouth to form the words: ". . . A . . . leading . . . role."

Ian picked up the phone. "Legal's on fourth. I'll make the call."

Tori hoisted a purse strap over her shoulder. "Nice doing business with you."

"Don't be a stranger," said Ian.

Tori went out and Betty came in. "Line three."

"Who is it?" asked Ian.

"Wouldn't say. Sounded Japanese. And mad."

"Damn," said Mel. "Tell him we're not here."

"We better take it," said Ian. "He'll just show up again in person and it'll be a lot worse."

"Betty, put him through," said Mel. He reached for the receiver. "Mr. Yokamura, what a pleasant— . . . I can't understand— . . . You're yelling too loud . . . You saw the article on Potemkin? . . . I was just picking up the phone to call about that. Another false report. This town's full of liars . . . No, we've got everything completely under control . . ."

HALF HOUR OUT OF HOLLYWOOD, JUST WEST OF GLENDALE

A rented Chrysler Sebring headed north on Eagle Rock Boulevard. Serge counted addresses out loud. "Forty-five hundred . . . forty-six hundred . . . There it is! Forty-seven twenty!"

"Where?"

"The corner of Ridgeview. That big sign with the mariachi chicken special after eleven . . ."

"Pat and Lorraine's?"

Serge parked on the street. Coleman chugged the rest of his Schlitz and stepped onto the sidewalk. "Looks dumpy."

"Show some respect," said Serge, grabbing his video camera and iPod. "You're on holy ground, like Lourdes or the Presley crèche in Tupelo."

They opened the front door. A group of people at a corner table saw them and waved. Serge lit up with recognition and waved back. "Coleman, best behavior. These are future friends."

"Serge!"

"Grab a seat!"

"We've heard a lot about you!"

Serge pulled out a chair. He stopped and looked around. "Where is he?"

"Not here yet, but any minute."

Serge began videotaping the restaurant's interior. "Can't tell you how excited I am to finally meet him. It's the only thing I've been able to think about since I got the letter. Well, not the only thing. My mind tends to jump around. The U.S. mint just released the Nevada state quarter. Photos from the Cassini probe have top NASA scientists scratching their heads. You'll always be disappointed by shampoo from a convenience store. The Dutch are now the tallest people in the world. I haven't been bowling in years." Serge aimed his camera down at a place mat. "So, you got *the table*."

"We got *the table*," said the man with dreadlocks. "Knew you'd insist."

Serge turned off the video. "The table was pulled out from the wall."

"What?"

"In the movie," said Serge. "It was out from the wall. Remember that famous circular panning shot? They laid tracks around the table for the camera dolly."

"Everything they said about you is true," said the woman sitting to his right.

"Let's pull it out from the wall," said Serge.

"Please," said the dreadlocks. "Just relax."

"You're right," said Serge. "I'm the guest. Besides, I have all these new friends. That's the most important thing in life. I should count my blessings. I'll bet we could scoot it out just a tiny—"

"Serge!"

"I'm good."

"You sure?" said the ponytail. "Because something big is about to happen in the next few days. We wanted to see if you might be interested— . . . What are you doing?"

Serge quickly folded his hands on the place mat. "Nothing."

"You were nudging the table out from the wall."

"No, I wasn't."

"Serge, this is important. We're putting this thing together and could really use the help. We need to know if you're in . . ."

Serge placed his iPod on the table and connected it to tiny external speakers. He started the L.A. soundtrack.

"Serge?"

"What?"

"Are you listening?"

"Sure. You were saying something."

". . . *'Clowns to the left of me, jokers to the right'* . . ."

"Is that 'Steeler's Wheel'?" asked the woman next to him. "I loved that song in junior high."

"Me, too," said Serge. "The perfect track for the movie . . ."—Serge turned to the man across from him— ". . . that had the table out from the wall."

Five minutes and a ten-dollar tip to the waitress later, Serge was smiling at a table pulled out from the wall.

"Happy now?" asked the dreadlocks.

"You're the one who's tense," said Serge. "Go ahead. What were you saying? . . ."

"Coordination and timing are crucial . . ."

Serge reached in his pocket and unfolded a square of paper on the table.

"What's that?" asked the woman.

"Screen capture from the movie. Printer quality wasn't

too good, but still works for historic comparison. The clock
up there's different, but those two planters next to it—who'd
have thought they'd still be here? Some of the chairs are also
the same, like the red jobs we're sitting on. They got new
curtains . . ."

Someone on the sidewalk walked by the restaurant's
windows.

"Serge . . ."

"Hold on. See up there on the wall?" He tapped his printout. "The spot was right over Joe Capa's left shoulder when
he asks Mr. Pink why he didn't tip. It's the only thing that
would ever tell you the classic scene was shot here . . ."

"Serge . . ."

"You have to look hard. There are two little black-and-
white movie cards over the cinnamon roll sign. The bottom
one's from *Reservoir Dogs*, and the top is the 1947 noir
thriller *Born to Kill*. That completely makes it for me. Eso-
teric homage to Lawrence Tierney, may he rest in peace . . ."

"Serge . . ."

Bells jingled. The front door opened. The man with the
dreadlocks pointed. "There he is."

Serge grabbed his video camera and turned around.

VISTAMAX STUDIOS

Soundstage 23. A man with a long, untrimmed beard sat in a director's chair. Stitched on the back: *Potemkin.*

A younger man entered the set through a side door. He shook out an umbrella and hung up a dripping raincoat. He came over and sat in the first assistant director's chair. "Thought we were shooting outside this afternoon."

"Had to scrap it because of the rain," said Potemkin.

"But it was a rain scene," said the assistant.

"We can't use the rain machine in the rain."

"Why don't we just use the regular rain?"

"Doesn't look as real."

A crew member with a clapboard stood in front of a camera. At great expense, the movie set had been made up to look like a movie set.

"Scene four hundred and twelve. Take sixty-seven." Clap.

Potemkin raised a megaphone. "Annnnnnnnnnnd . . . action!"

On stage, an actor sat in another director's chair. *"Annnnnnnnnnd . . . action!"*

Ally Street threw her arms around the male lead's neck and tried to kiss him. He pushed her away. *"It's over. Has been for a long time, but I was too blind . . ."*

"You don't mean that. Not after everything."

The actor picked up an old brown suitcase. *"I'm taking the train back to New York. There's a war on."* He began walking toward a non-opening door painted on plywood.

"Put down the suitcase!"

"Where'd you get that gun?"

"I can't live without you . . ."

"Cut! Cut! Goddammit!" Potemkin was out of his chair. He slammed the script to the ground. "What's the matter with you? Can't you act? How did you ever get in my movie!"

"What did I do?"

"You were supposed to blow your line and start arguing with the coldhearted director. If there's one scene I thought you could handle, it's where you're supposed to act *badly*!"

"Sir," said the first assistant director. "That's the hardest kind of acting."

"Shut up! . . . I think we can save it till she pulls the gun. Cut in with camera two. Places everyone . . ."

Tori Gersh stood by the craft service table, mumbling under her breath: "Come on, Ally, you can do it . . ."

"Annnnnnnnnnnd . . . action!"

"Where'd you get that gun?"

"I can't live with you, uh, I mean . . ."

"Cut! Cut!" yelled the actor playing the director on the set. *"What are you, stupid? Can't you remember a simple goddam line?"*

"I'm doing the best I can!"

"Cut! Cut!" Potemkin was out of his chair again. "You call that emotion?"

"I was full of emotion," said Street.

"But you're supposed to be so overcome with emotion that you don't know how to feel. I'm not getting that! Instead I'm getting emotion!"

"I'm supposed to cry?"

"You're not listening! This is about how the old studio system mistreated everyone! It's the climax where all your frustrations come to a boil and you finally snap. You have to convince the audience that an otherwise sweet girl could be driven to murder. Then you raise the blank gun from props and fire it at the director. Except you secretly loaded it with real bullets between takes because you've had it with his insults, you stupid moron!"

Ally raised the gun and fired a blank at Potemkin, then dropped the pistol and ran off crying.

Potemkin looked in astonishment at the crew. "Did she just fucking shoot me? Has the whole world gone insane!" His lip began to quiver. Tears rolled down the director's cheeks, and he fled in the other direction.

The set was stone silent. Potemkin and Street weeping in opposite corners.

Tori Gersh closed her eyes and felt a headache coming on.

The first assistant director eventually stood up. "Okay, everybody, I think that's a wrap for today."

All That Glitters used to be behind schedule. Now, there wasn't one. Set 23 had been booked for the next day to rehearse a reality show reunion, so the crew was dislocated to 17, where they jumped to another scene earlier in the movie that Potemkin had since rewritten.

The cast began taking their places. Tori stood off to the

side, holding Ally by the shoulders. "You're a great actress. Just remember, he yells at everyone. Now go knock 'em dead."

A clapboard clapped. A megaphone rose.

"Annnnnnnd . . . action!"

Ally was in an ultra-snug vinyl jumpsuit. She tossed a grappling hook aside and pulled a spy-tool off her utility belt. Soon, the cover was off the nuclear bomb. A digital display ticked down . . . *1:01, 1:00, :59, :58* . . . Ally held snippers to the green wire, then the red, the yellow, the blue, the green again.

"You don't have to stay," she told the male lead. *"This only takes one person."*

"You know I'd never leave. My love for you is eternal."

"You're just saying that because you can't outrun the blast radius in less than a minute."

"That, too. Which wire do you think it is?".

"I feel lucky today. Red's my favorite color. Kiss me!"

They embraced passionately. The camera trucked around the couple as Ally got her right breast groped. Their mouths slowly parted. Ally looked out the corner of her eye at the amber digits. Eight seconds, seven, six . . . *"I guess it's time to save the world."* Ally placed her snippers around a wire.

And she snipped the yellow one.

"Cut! Cut!" shouted Potemkin. "You fucking idiot! You cut the wrong wire!"

"I forgot which one," said Ally.

"You just said *red*!"

"The kiss threw me off."

The first assistant director leaned sideways from his chair. "Maybe the sound guys can dub the mix."

"No! No! No!" shouted Potemkin. "It has to be red because of the metaphorical reference to the McCarthy hearings. Where's the standby electrician?"

The crew stood around the coffee urn while the wire was replaced.

They were ready again.

"Feed her the line," barked Potemkin.

An assistant read stiffly from a script. "I guess it's time to save the world."

"Annnnnnnd . . . action!"

"*I guess it's time to save the world.*" Ally placed her snippers around the red wire. "Shit—".

The snippers fell inside the bomb, causing a short. The digital display went black. A tiny puff of smoke.

"Cut! Cut! . . . What the hell just happened?"

"I broke a nail," said Ally.

"I'm not fucking believing this! Did you use to ride the short bus to school?"

Standby electricians began soldering a new digital display. Three makeup people buzzed around Ally, attaching a false nail with theatrical glue.

"Places," said the assistant director.

The electricians and makeup people dashed off.

Clapboard man: "Take fifty-nine."

"Forget the lines!" yelled Potemkin. "Pick it up with cutting the wire . . . Ally! Can your brain handle that? In case you were wondering, it's the *red* one!"

"Don't talk to me that way."

"I'll talk to you any way I want, you no-talent tramp!"

Ally and her co-star took their positions.

"Annnnnnnd . . . action!"

Ally reached in the bomb, ripping out all the wiring.

"Cut! Cut! Have you lost your mind?"

Ally grabbed the lightweight plastic prop and raised it over her head.

"What the hell are you doing?"

It smashed to the ground, spraying pieces.

"My nuclear bomb!"

The set was a tomb. A lonely plastic cog rolled across the floor.

Ally in one corner, Potemkin in another. Tori's mouth hung open. She took a deep, resigned breath and walked out a side door into the bright California sun.

A rented Chrysler Sebring drove west on Hollywood Boulevard, leaving behind the Walk of Fame tourist frenzy. The road entered an established residential neighborhood with a scattering of old-growth motels. The car turned up a driveway in the lush hillside.

Highland Gardens.

Serge checked the address against his notes. 7047.

They registered without incident at the front desk. Serge carried suitcases down a hallway that needed paint.

"What do we do now?" asked Coleman, lugging paper bags from grocery and liquor stores.

"Just what they told us at the restaurant," said Serge. "Stay out of sight until it's time. Like Martin Sheen waiting for a mission in that Saigon hotel."

"Now you're talking."

"Coleman! You have taste! I didn't know you liked *Apocalypse Now*."

"Oh, yeah. Sheen goes on a bender and gets really wasted and breaks shit. Great movie."

They came to room 105. Serge stuck a key in the door.

Division of labor: Serge rapidly assembled his reference headquarters of books and music. Coleman cleared the bathroom counter and threw the soap in the wastebasket. Serge plugged the iPod into external speakers and cranked up his L.A. chore tunes. Coleman unwrapped all the plastic cups that came with the room and stacked them behind the faucet.

Serge rewired the TV to his video equipment. Coleman put iced beverages in the sink and arranged munchies in a convenient semicircle for impaired access. Serge precisely stowed film and ammo in dresser drawers. Coleman made joints and rum drinks.

Serge grabbed his camera for contingency photos and snapped pictures of his buddy at work. "I've never seen you move so fast."

"Time's limited." Coleman sliced lime wedges in advance. "Everything will soon become tricky. What's that music?"

"Posthumous album 'Pearl.' Kris Kristofferson cover track. Next question."

"Why'd you pay extra for this room?"

"Because they're gouging history buffs." Serge closed the sock drawer. "Room 105, Highland Gardens, formerly the Landmark."

Coleman torched a mombo spliff. Serge pointed at the floor. "She hit face-first right where you're standing. October third, twenty-six years ago."

"Who did?" Coleman held the joint between his middle fingers and cupped his hands to his mouth like he was doing bird calls.

"You pulling my leg?" said Serge. "This is Joplin's room."

Coleman blew out an enormous amount of smoke. "I don't know this old stuff like you."

"That's okay. I don't know how to interlace my hands like that to smoke dope."

"You mean a carburetor? It's the first thing they teach you."

". . . *Freedom's just another word for nothing left to lose . . .*"

Coleman exhaled another cloud and stared down at the

spot on the floor. "Whoa! . . . Death is trippy when you're ripped. How'd it happen?"

"Heroin. Shot up enough scag to drop a charging rhino. Then went out to the lobby for cigarettes and came back in here and—wham! The junkie's belly flop. Facial bones shattered like a skeet-shooting disk. The maid found her the next morning in a blood slick. I'm guessing there were flies by then." Serge looked around the room, smiling and nodding. "I'm in a happy place."

"Serge?"

"What?"

"I'm bored."

"I thought the pot would make this really entertaining."

"If it was a little entertaining," said Coleman. "But instead, if it's a little boring, then it makes it really boring."

"Now I'm bored, too."

Coleman pressed the TV's power button.

Serge opened a suitcase. "What's on the tube?"

"Not sure yet. It's in the middle of another commercial for boner pills."

"I never understand those ads," said Serge, pulling a stack of celebrity magazines from his luggage. "They always warn about erections lasting longer than four hours. I mean, when *don't* they?"

Coleman's head jerked back. "Four hours!"

"What? Don't yours . . . ?"

"I wish."

"Really?" said Serge, handing Coleman half the magazines.

"Trust me. I've tried." Coleman flipped open a recent issue of *In Touch.* "You never struck me as the kind of guy with chicks on the brain so much."

"Oh, it's not just women. I could be in a new museum for the first time."

"Is that why you wear those long, untucked shirts?"

"Avoids questions."

Coleman turned a page. "What are we looking for?"

"Clues," said Serge, folding over a copy of *Us.* "If we're going to operate in this city, we have to find the pulse of the stars or we'll be eaten alive . . . Here we go: *Laverne and Shirley*'s Squiggy is now a pro basketball scout. So that's what he's been up to . . ."

"I found an article," said Coleman. *"Is the* American Idol *voting fair? Take our poll!"*

"Angelina takes her toddler on a play date . . ." Serge flipped the page. *"Diane Sawyer has an age-defying secret!"*

"This story blames a star's incoherent Letterman appearance on 'professional exhaustion,' " said Coleman. "What's that mean?"

"Let me put it this way," said Serge. "You suffer from amateur exhaustion."

"Oh, I get it."

Serge threw his magazines aside. "I have the pulse now. It's stupid."

Coleman closed his own magazine. "I'm bored again."

"I know, I know. I'm trying to think. . . ."

A knock at the door.

Serge whipped out a gun. "Who's that!"

He crept across the room and peeked out the peephole. A tall man in a silver running suit glanced nervously up and down the hall from behind dark sunglasses. His dyed blond hair was slicked straight back.

Serge opened the door a crack. "Yes?"

"Are you Coleman?"

"No."

"It's okay," Coleman yelled from back in the room. "You can let him in."

Serge opened the door the rest of the way, and the man

quickly brushed past him. Serge shook the confusion out of his head and followed.

Coleman and the stranger gathered in a corner. Money changed hands. Baggies came out of the man's fanny pack.

"Coleman," said Serge. "You've never been to California. How'd you find a connection so fast?"

"Guess it's a gift."

A business card snapped crisply out of the fanny pack. The stranger placed it in Serge's hand.

Serge looked up from the card. "Not *the* Dallas Reel."

The man smiled.

"Oh, my God!" said Serge. "I love your work. What? Sixty films now?"

"I'm impressed," said Dallas. "Most people only know four or five."

"Not me," said Serge. "I stay and memorize all the credits. Can't leave the theater until I at least get to Glenn Glenn Sound. So what's a third executive producer do?"

Dallas zipped the fanny pack closed. "Pretty much this." A beeper went off. He looked down. "That's mine. Gotta run."

Serge closed the door behind him and walked back into the room. "Imagine that."

Coleman was spreading Baggies on a nightstand. Pills, grass, powder. "But we're bored again."

Serge pointed at the drugs. "Wait, I got it! We'll do a historical reenactment!"

"What's that?"

Serge moved a chair out of the way. "Watch 'em all the time on the Discovery Channel. They investigate to see if a famous celebrity's death might have actually been murder." Serge walked to the motel room door, turned around and began counting off steps. "They did this one on Marilyn. Her death bungalow had since been demolished, so they used forensic photos to build a new one, replicating every last detail: lamps, ashtrays, color of the walls. Then they conducted tissue-absorption analysis for all the pills on her nightstand. You be Joplin."

"What do I do?"

"Simulate an OD." Serge handed him the Baggies. "I want you to do as many drugs as you can in the next thirty minutes. And be sure to wash it all down with lots of liquor."

"But you always yell at me when I get that way."

"Except this is research. If we can prove Joplin was murdered, we might be talking a grant."

Coleman filled a plastic cup with rum and grabbed a sack of striped capsules.

A half hour later Serge helped him off the bed. "Here's the room key. I want you to go out to the lobby. The cigarette machine's gone, so just tag the front desk and return." Serge began timing with his wristwatch. "The first test is to see if you can make it back here by yourself . . . No, Coleman, the other way . . ."

Serge walked him out into the hall. "I'll be waiting . . ." He closed the door.

Serge's new group of friends was meeting again for lunch at Pat & Lorraine's. Without Serge and Coleman.

"How do we know we can count on him?"

"I have complete trust. He's Sergio's grandson, after all."

"I don't mean trust. I mean *depend*."

"What are you talking about?"

Serge leaned close to the television. His *Midnight Cowboy* DVD. Serge only watched the end, where Ratso's bus rolls down the Miracle Mile in Coral Gables. He looked at his watch. "What's taking him so long?"

Serge opened the door and stuck his head out in the hall. "Where could that idiot have—"

Moaning at his feet.

"What are you doing down there? Stop fooling around!" He grabbed Coleman under the armpits and dragged him backward into the room. "It's starting to look like Joplin was murdered. This is getting exciting."

Serge left Coleman on the carpet and cued up "Piece of My Heart." He crouched down and lightly slapped his pal on the cheeks. "Coleman! Wake up! I think we're about to crack the case!"

Coleman slowly came around. "Where am I?"

"In the middle of an investigation that'll blow the lid off!" Serge pulled him to his feet. "This is the crucial part. I need you to stand right here."

Serge stepped back and looked Coleman up and down, rough calculations of height and weight. He took a baby step forward and put out his arms. "I'm ready. I want you to close your eyes and put your arms by your side."

Coleman complied.

"Good. Now, fall forward."

Coleman's eyes opened. "I'm not doing that."

"I'll catch you. I promise."

"What if you don't?"

"Are you religious? Because this is about faith. Put your faith in your best friend and nothing will happen. You just have to let go. Release your doubts and fall into it like a big, cozy pillow."

Coleman closed his eyes again. "Okay, but you better catch me . . ."

* * *

Pat and Lorraine's.

"I'm still not a hundred percent on those guys. Something's not kosher."

"Like what?"

"Are you nuts? The fat guy's a fuck-up and the other's—
. . . I have no idea what that is."

"You liked Sergio, right?"

"Of course."

"We owe him big time. This is his grandson. It's the least we can do."

"But . . ."

"But what? Sergio was odd too, and it all worked out in the end."

"I hope you're right."

Serge knelt over Coleman on the motel carpet. "Keep your head tilted back or you'll bleed everywhere."

"You said you'd catch me!"

"You didn't wait for my signal."

"You didn't say anything about a signal."

"I don't have to. There's always a signal."

Coleman lightly touched tender spots on his face. "What do you think?"

"It's beginning to look like Joplin wasn't murdered after all."

"I mean my nose. It feels broken."

"That's just the pain. You hit pretty hard. But your contribution to the historical record has been duly noted."

"You said to have faith."

"Yeah, but there's a lot of bad religions going around. You have to be more skeptical."

19

ALTO NIDO APARTMENTS

F riday evening. Third floor.
   A room full of bachelors, splashed cologne and
   brushed teeth.

Except one. He was in bed.

Pedro popped his head through the neck-hole of a polo shirt. "Ford, why don't you join us?"

Ford just stared at the ceiling.

"This isn't healthy," said Mark. "We thought you'd snapped out of it working on that new script . . ."

"But now you're back to staying in bed sixteen hours a day," said Tino.

"And you've stopped writing," said Ray.

"We know you're going through a lot," said Pedro. "But you need to get out. Have some fun."

"I scored an extra invitation from Dallas," said Tino.

Ford rolled over on his side and faced the wall. "They're not going to let me in the party. They fired me. And threw me off the property. Remember?"

Mark looked at the others. "Do it."

They grabbed Ford by the arms and dragged him out of the sheets.

"Let go of me."

"It's for your own good."

Five guys in a Malibu cruised down Sunset Strip and pulled up in front of Skybar.

The midpoint cast party for *All That Glitters*.

Mark and Ford took up positions outside the ladies' room. A waiter walked by and Ford lifted two flutes of champagne off his tray.

"Ford, you're drinking," said Mark.

Ford knocked one of the glasses back.

Mark reached for the second one. "Thanks . . ."

"They're both for me." Ford knocked the other one back.

The party was effective. More champagne. Pedro walked up. "Can you believe this place? It's like the women aren't real."

"Ford's drinking," said Mark.

"You are?" said Pedro.

Ford nodded with glazed eyes and grabbed two more passing flutes.

"Must be the firing," said Pedro. "Good for you!"

Tino arrived. "Isn't that Ally Street over there?"

"Where?"

"By the railing. With that older woman."

"Think it's her agent."

"I'm going to go talk to her," said Pedro.

"She's a big star," said Tino. "You don't stand a chance."

"That's what everyone thinks," said Pedro. "So nobody approaches. Then we see them in star magazines with total losers and wonder, How did *that* happen?"

"You've convinced me. *I'm* going to hit on her."

"But she's mine," said Pedro.

Ray came over. "What's happening?"

"We're going to hit on Ally Street," said Tino.

"Who is?"

"We're still arguing."

"You don't stand a chance," said Ray.

"Pedro was just explaining his theory," said Tino.

A burst of paparazzi flashes lit up the other side of the patio. "Crap." Pedro's shoulders slumped. "Jason Geddy's hitting on her."

"Told you we didn't stand a chance."

"It was fun while it lasted."

"Wait, he's leaving with his manager," said Tino. "We're back in the hunt."

They gaped across the patio at Ally, alone again, gazing off into the night. The wind lifted that stunning blond mane streaming out behind her.

"Watch this," said Pedro. He took a step and stopped.

"So what are you waiting for?"

Pedro took a step back. "I'm nervous."

"Then I'm going to try," said Mark. "Here goes."

"Why aren't you moving?"

"I'm scared."

"I'm going," said Ray. "It's all about projecting confidence." He took two steps and came back.

"What's the matter, Mr. Confidence?"

"I went farther than you!"

"You guys are chickenshit," said Tino. "Watch this . . ."
They watched.

"What's the matter?"

"Shut up."

Another waiter came by. Ford grabbed two more glasses of champagne and headed across the patio.

"Where's *he* going?" said Pedro.

The guys couldn't believe their eyes. First, that Ford ac-

tually had the guts to go over there. And again, when Ally
accepted his champagne. Paparazzi cameras flashed.

"Now I've seen everything," said Tino.

No, he hadn't. Ally was soon laughing at something Ford
had said.

"Did you see that?" said Mark. "She touched his arm.
That meant something."

Ford trotted back to his buddies, holding up an open cell
phone. "She wants to meet later."

The night wore on, party after party. They headed east on
Wilshire, Ford the big topic of conversation in the car. They
wanted all the juicy details.

"She's really down to earth. Not stuck-up like they say in
the magazines."

"What's the deal with this mysterious romantic ren-
dezvous you're supposed to go to later?" asked Tino.

"Has a few places she needs to hit first for public rela-
tions. Her agent set them up. But after that, she wants to get
together."

"Aren't you glad you came out with us now?" said Ray.

"Looks like your luck has finally changed," said Tino.

Pedro pulled into a fast-food drive-through.

"May I take your order?"

"Hey, Ford," said Pedro. "What time were you supposed
to call Ally?"

"Oh, shit!" Ford flipped open his phone.

"Give it up!"

The guys turned around.

The morning after.

Roommates scrambled inside a third-floor unit of the
Alto Nido apartments. Pedro ransacked the top drawer of
Ford's dresser. "Where's that number for his attorney?"

"It has to be here somewhere!" said Ray.

"I can't believe they arrested him," said Tino, rifling papers next to a typewriter.

"I think they just took him into custody for questioning," said Pedro.

"Same thing."

"Here it is," said Mark. "Rodney Demopolis."

Police headquarters. Interrogation Room C.

"And that's the whole story," said Ford. "You have to believe me."

"I do," said Detective Babcock. "Want another soda?"

Ford shook his head.

"Sounds like you just had a rough night. But you have to understand how this looks from our side. I need to fill in some blanks."

"Like what?"

"You said you were recently fired. Our officers talked to some people at the studio this morning. They said you made threats and security had to throw you off the property."

"I was just excited. They didn't need those guards. I would have left anyway."

Babcock wrote something. "Tell me again about when you phoned the guys who robbed you. Sorry for saying this, but it sounds really, well, stupid. Why would anyone do that?"

"I was drunk. I wanted to get laid."

The division's lieutenant watched from behind the two-way mirror. A speaker on the wall piped in the conversation. A corporal with a handful of documents opened the door. "Lieutenant, some of the suspect's co-workers voluntarily showed up and signed affidavits that they witnessed the robbery of his cell phone."

"Let me see those."

Another corporal opened the door. "Lieutenant. Just heard from the mobile company. Story checks out about the stolen phone. Several calls have been made on that number since we took him into custody."

"Thank you."

"Sir . . ."

"What?"

"His attorney's here."

"He hasn't asked for one."

The corporal shrugged. "He's outside. Demands to talk to his client. Says file charges or release him."

Ford folded his hands on top of the table to keep them from shaking. "Can I go now?"

"Not just yet," said the detective. "We're almost done. How would you feel about a polygraph?"

"But you said you believed me."

"I do. That's why I want a polygraph, to eliminate you as a suspect."

"I'm pretty nervous. Won't that throw it off?"

"We ask some baseline questions that take it into account. Don't worry; it's not admissible."

"Okay," said Ford. "I'll do it."

Detective Reamsnyder came in the room. "That asshole confess yet?"

"Will you take it easy? He's a good kid."

Reamsnyder sat on the corner of the desk. "Got some news. Cellular company said his phone's been used since we've had him here."

"There you go," said Babcock. "It was stolen, just like he said."

"Only means he has an accomplice."

"He's going to take a polygraph."

"No, he's not," said Reamsnyder.

"What do you mean?"

"His lawyer's here. Lieutenant says release him."

Babcock pursed his lips in frustration and pushed his chair back from the table. "Looks like you're free to go."

"Really? Cool!" Ford jumped up and headed for the door.

"Hey, shithead," Reamsnyder called after him. "Don't leave town."

20

Hollywood Tattletale

SHOOTING SCHEDULE DELAYED BY KIDNAPPING

HOLLYWOOD—The nation remains stunned by this weekend's abduction of Vistamax actress Ally Street from a crowded Sunset Boulevard sidewalk.

Despite the brazen nature of the crime in front of dozens of witnesses, police have only partial and conflicting descriptions of the assailants, which they attribute to high substance levels and general chaos at that hour on the strip.

"We thought they were filming a movie," said one tourist from St. Paul. "It almost seemed real."

"The screaming and desperate cries for help are what got my attention," said another visitor from Akron. "But it turned out to be something else."

The motive for the kidnapping remains a mystery, and investigators report receiving no ransom demands or other communication from the abductors. However, sources close to the actress maintain they have every reason to believe Street is still alive and are hoping for the best.

"We're hoping for the best," said Tori Gersh, Street's agent and publicist. Gersh made the comments during her fifth press conference since the incident, where she also thanked well-wishers for the thousands of cards and stuffed animals before breaking into sobs again and handing the microphone to Vistamax co-owner Mel Glick, who refused to take questions and read a brief statement:

"While the importance of movies cannot be overstated, this type of tragedy puts everything in perspective. The studio's employees and shareholders continue to pray for the safe return of a beloved member of the Vistamax family. Meanwhile, what can the public do? If Ally was here, I know she'd want all of us to keep going to the theaters. Otherwise, the kidnappers win."

The producers and publicist were then rushed to a waiting limo while police escorts cleared a path through the crush of reporters, fans and unemployed onlookers who remain encamped outside the studio gates, where the scene has taken on a virtual circus-like atmosphere, because of the sword-swallowers and cotton-candy carts. Meanwhile, distraught celebrities have been seen coming and going through the gates at all hours, including boy-band heartthrob Jason Geddy, who almost dated Street and is reported to be in seclusion at the Viper Room.

In a separate development, already rampant rumors spiked yesterday when police briefly took into custody an unnamed low-level employee from the studio's props department, who was reportedly stalking Street and observed harassing her at Sky-bar just hours before the abduction. Police later released the suspect, who was immediately swarmed by reporters outside police headquarters.

"I don't know what's going on. Please, leave me alone," said the young man, whom the entertainment press has been able to identify as The Stalker Ford Oelman.

In light of the actress's disappearance, filming of *All That Glitters* has been indefinitely suspended again.

"We were going to shoot around her," said a Potemkin spokesperson. "But we decided it would send the wrong message."

THAT AFTERNOON

Vistamax Studios, office of the Glick brothers.

Mel paced and waved his arms. "Of all the crazy things!"

Ian stared up at the wall, whining to the giant oil portrait of his grandfather. "What are we going to do?"

Tori Gersh sat quietly in a chair across from their desks. "Get a grip."

Mel opened a drawer. "How can you be so calm?"

"Because there's nothing else we can do. Falling apart won't solve anything." She checked the time. "Did you tell your secretary?"

Ian nodded. "The call comes directly in here. She's not supposed to answer it under any circumstances."

"Why doesn't the phone ring?" said Mel.

The phone rang. The brothers jumped.

"Let me handle this," said Tori.

Ian looked at the caller ID. "Ford Oelman? Where have I heard that name?"

"Shhhh!" said Tori. She picked up the phone. "Hello? . . ."

"I remember," said Mel. "That kid from props with the screenplay. He was on the news."

"That's right," said Ian. "The Stalker Ford Oelman."

Tori waved for them to be quiet. "Yes, I'm still here . . . No, we haven't called the police . . . That was the Glicks you heard . . ."

Mel pointed. "But what's his name doing on our caller ID?"

Tori covered the phone. "Shut up or you're going to fuck this!" She uncovered the phone. "I'm back . . . Nothing's wrong . . . I have the hundred thousand right here . . ."—she glanced down at the briefcase by her feet—". . . I understand . . . Yes, I have a pen . . . Uh-huh, uh-huh . . . Got it. I'm on my way."

She hung up. The brothers were leaning forward. "So?"

"So, I have to hurry. Only got thirty minutes." She reached down and grabbed the briefcase handle.

"What's the plan?"

"I pay."

"That's the plan?" said Mel.

"This isn't one of your stupid movies!" She got up and headed across the room.

"It's our money!"

"I have to go." Tori opened the door. Betty was standing there. With two detectives. "I was just about to knock," said the secretary. "These two gentlemen . . ."

They entered the room without invitation. "You have a minute?" asked Babcock.

"Why? I mean sure," said Ian.

Tori headed out into the lobby.

"You, too," said Reamsnyder.

She turned around. "Me?"

"Just a few questions."

"But I'm late . . ."—glancing at her watch—". . . an appointment."

"Only take a minute," said Babcock.

"What's in the briefcase?" asked Reamsnyder.

"Papers."

"You're gripping the handle pretty hard."

Tori exhaled and came back to the office. "This kidnapping business has me on edge."

"Understandable . . . Have a seat."

Tori sat. So did the brothers. The detectives stayed standing, for the edge.

"How can we help?" asked Ian.

Babcock walked across the room and stared out the window. "You haven't gotten a call from the kidnappers, have you?"

Mel opened his mouth.

"No," Tori said quickly.

Reamsnyder walked to the other side of the room and stared up at the oil painting. "You'd tell us if you did?"

"Why wouldn't we?" said Ian.

"Because kidnappers always say, 'No police.' "

"And that's always a mistake," said Babcock, surreptitiously pressing the caller ID button on Ian's message machine. FORD OELMAN. "Friends and relatives think it's less risky if the authorities aren't involved."

"But they're wrong," said Reamsnyder. "They don't understand the kind of people they're dealing with. Going it alone is very dangerous."

"Costs lives," said Babcock. "Seen it over and over."

"Would you object to us wiring your office?" asked Reamsnyder.

"Yes," said Mel. "I mean no. I mean sure. Go ahead."

Tori shot him a look. Mel shrugged at her behind the detectives' backs.

"Excuse me," said Tori. "I read somewhere they now have devices that can detect that kind of thing. We don't want to endanger Ally."

"Our new equipment is more advanced."

"Put in whatever you want," said Mel.

Tori glared again.

"Great," said Babcock. "I'll call the audio guys."

SUNSET AND VINE

A shiny black Porsche 911 Cabriolet sat at a red light.

Tori was wearing a bright red scarf, like the phone call had instructed. Curved, smoky sunglasses. The call didn't mention that.

She looked down at her own shorthand note: Sunset, west. Alone. *Cell phone. Roof open. Briefcase, passenger floor.*

The light turned green. Tori accelerated through Cahuenga and Highland, precisely the speed limit. Out the top of the car: towering palm trees and towering billboards for the new Hanks movie, the new Zellweger movie, the old Affleck movie coming to a video store near you. Through a yellow light at Fairfax, Tori growing worried. She checked the phone in her lap to make sure it was on.

The Porsche took the left bend in the road at the Marmont. Okay, something was clearly wrong. What spooked them? A police tail? Maybe the detectives knew more than they were letting on. She checked her rearview.

The 8000 block, hills getting steeper. Swank canyon homes peeked down into the car. So did the man with binoculars on the top floor of the "Riot" Hyatt, where Zeppelin raced motorcycles through the halls. He was dialing a cell phone.

This is definitely a bust, thought Tori. She was looking

over her shoulder for a U-turn when the phone rang. She fumbled it in her hands and it almost went out the window. ". . . Hello?"

Tori listened. "La Cienega? . . ." She looked up at the street sign of the intersection she was just about to cross: *La Cienega*. Brakes squealed. The Porsche skidded up the sidewalk, tires rubbing the curb. A startled pack of tourists jumped back. Except one. He vaulted the closed door on the right side of the Porsche and landed in the passenger seat.

"Drive."

A rattled Tori threw the sports car back in gear and nearly sideswiped a Gray Line bus. The man grabbed the briefcase on the floor next to his feet. "Is this for me?"

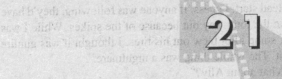

21

MEANWHILE, BACK AT VISTAMAX

What's taking her so long?" said Ian.

The door opened.

"Tori!"

"Did you give them the money?"

"Where's Ally?"

Tori plopped down in a chair. "He scared the hell out of me."

"What happened?" said Ian.

"Jumped in my car."

"Jumped in your car?"

"Dressed like a tourist," said Tori. "Made me drive all over the place to make sure there wasn't a tail. We ended up in the Hertz lot by the airport."

"Hertz?"

"Final precaution," said Tori. "Told me to turn in the entrance with those fold-down spikes where the signs say 'severe tire damage.' Leaped out with the briefcase, climbed a fence and took off in a car he'd planted earlier on a side street."

"What for?"

"Head start, I guess. If anyone was following, they'd have to take the long way out because of the spikes. While I was there, some idiot blew out his tires. I thought it was gunfire at first. The whole thing was a nightmare."

"What about Ally?"

"Said he'd call once he was safe."

"That wasn't the deal," said Mel.

"He said the deal had changed."

"I got a bad feeling."

The phone rang.

Everyone froze. They looked down at the caller ID. FORD OELMAN.

Tori took a deep breath and picked it up. "Hello?"

Silence on the other end.

"Hello?" she repeated.

Finally, a voice that had been altered with an electronic synthesizer. "You fucked up."

"What do you mean?" said Tori.

"We told you no police! You got a tap on the line."

"We do not!"

"Yes, you do. We have one of those special devices. And an undercover unit followed you to the rental lot."

"What are you talking about?"

"Looks like you just killed off your female lead."

"But we gave you the money!"

Click.

Tori's head snapped toward the brothers. "Did the police come by already?"

"Yeah, they just left," said Ian.

"What'd they do?"

"Put in a tracer," said Mel. "And a recorder . . ."

The office door opened.

". . . And a bug," said Detective Babcock. "We heard everything you just said."

"You bugged this office!" yelled Tori.

"You lied to us!" yelled Reamsnyder.

"Because of what just happened!" Tori yelled back. "I told you!"

"Everyone calm down," said Babcock. "This won't get us anywhere. What's done is done. The important thing is that we work together from now on."

Tori gritted her teeth. "If anything happens to Ally—"

"They'll call back," said Babcock.

"How do you know?"

"Because that's what they do. Probably want more money since the first was so easy."

"Meanwhile, every second counts," said Reamsnyder. "We're already processing the Hertz lot. The undercover unit that was following you took some pictures before he jumped the fence, but they don't show much."

"Was that the guy who blew out his tires?" asked Tori.

Babcock nodded. "Forgot about the spikes."

Tori sat back and folded her arms. "A crack team you got."

"We need your help," said Reamsnyder.

"Did you get a good look at him?" said Babcock.

"What the hell do you think?" said Tori. "We rode around town together."

"No, I mean did it look like he was wearing a disguise? Mustache, wig?"

Tori shook her head.

"Okay then. A sketch artist is on the way over. And we'd like to put some other people in here around the clock in case you get another call. They'll stay out of the way. Can you think of anything else?"

"Yeah," said Tori. "You're assholes."

ONE HOUR LATER

A ten-foot grizzly stood on its hind legs, all teeth, ready to attack. The bear was surrounded by dozens of other taxidermied animals in the big-game trophy room of the Vistamax props department. Tigers, leopards, moose, an ibex. The walls were covered with antler heads on wooden plaques. There was a closet at the end of the room. Muffled noises and whispers inside.

The closet was as dark as a photo lab, even after eyes adjusted. Someone found the light switch; a naked bulb came on. Gasps.

The tiny room had a matrix of metal storage shelves for the smaller game: squirrels, badgers, bats, snakes, three butterfly collections and fifty jars with things pickling inside, for mad scientist scenes. So much stuff there was barely enough room for Tori, Ian and Mel to squeeze together.

"What are we going to do?" asked Mel.

"This is a disaster!" said Ian.

"Keep your voices down!" said Tori.

"They're on to us," said Mel. "Did you see how that one detective was looking at me?"

"We'll go to jail!" said Ian.

"They'll rape me!" said Mel.

"Nobody's getting raped," said Tori. "As long as we all stay calm and stick to the plan."

"It's a dumb plan," said Ian. "We never should have agreed—"

"It's a perfect plan," said Tori. "In fact, the police will actually help."

"How can they possibly help?"

"Credence," said Tori. "We'll invite them to the press conferences. More publicity. That was one of the objectives."

"But now we're neck-deep in felonies," said Mel.

"We didn't bargain for that," said Ian.

"No crimes have been committed," said Tori.

"Of course crimes have been committed," said Mel. "What do you call giving the police a false kidnapping report?"

"We never did that," said Tori. "In fact, we *denied* there was a kidnapping. Remember? All they have is the rehearsed stuff we said for the benefit of the bugs planted in your office. I told you: It's all been carefully planned out."

"I don't know," said Ian.

"I do," said Tori. "Everything's falling into place. As long as none of us goes and does anything stupid."

"I can't take the pressure," said Mel.

"Look, you told me Potemkin was out of control, but his contract wouldn't let you halt production."

"So?"

"So I found a way. Fake the abduction of his star actress and let public opinion shut it down. Potemkin may be crazy, but even *he* isn't stupid enough to continue filming with that kind of media or he'd become the biggest leper . . ."

". . . In a town full of lepers," said Mel.

Ian began to nod. "He won't be able to get a good table."

"But what about when she shows back up?" said Mel. "He'll just start shooting again."

"Time's on our side," said Tori. "No production can stay down forever. People have to eat. He'll start losing crew and talent, probably begin another project himself."

"You really believe that?" asked Mel.

"We can't lose," said Tori. "I've already gotten twenty offers for the exclusive story, dead or alive. More on the dead side."

"That can't hurt at the box office," said Ian.

"I've already talked to editing," said Tori. "We have

enough in the can to piece together a couple hours. It still won't make any sense, so we'll call it an art film."

"It just might work," said Mel. "Bank on one big weekend before word of mouth starts."

"Then position the DVD as a cult classic," said Mel.

"And we recoup the rest from France and Scandinavia," said Ian. "They're big on films that don't hold your interest."

"But our biggest ace in the hole is when Ally makes the daring escape from her sadistic captors," said Tori. "Imagine *that* news conference."

"Are you sure she's solid?" asked Ian.

"Hundred percent," said Tori. "She *hates* Potemkin. Barely had to convince her to be kidnapped."

"What about her career?" asked Ian. "That movie's not going to help."

"She's through after this."

"What do you mean?"

"I can parlay the abduction into six months of articles and a book deal. Then she's last month's flavor. After that, I'll leak a scandal story on her to the tabloids in exchange for positive coverage of my up-and-coming clients."

"But I thought you were her friend," said Ian. "Remember how you shouted at us over the . . . misunderstanding?"

"That was before I went to the set and found out she couldn't act," said Tori. "Fuck her."

"Tori! That's terrible!" said Mel. "You're our kind of people!"

"But who are these guys you hired?" asked Ian. "That's the part that worries me. What do you really know about them?"

"Relax," said Tori. "They're pros, absolutely the best."

"How'd you get them?" asked Mel. "I'd have no idea where to start looking."

"Friends of mine put me in contact. Vouched for them up and down."

"A hundred thousand dollars still sounds steep," said Ian. "Seems like we could have gotten by with a lot less—"

"What do you think this is, hiring college kids to deliver holiday mail?" said Tori. "That's what you have to pay if you want something like this done right."

"I'm just wondering if we can trust them with Ally's safety," said Ian. "If something goes wrong, we're all accomplices."

Tori laughed. "I'm more concerned about the kidnappers' well-being. Ally's so high maintenance she makes Paris Hilton look like a Navy SEAL."

SUNSET STRIP

The Standard Hotel. Room 222.

A knock at the door.

Coleman staggered over, holding a bottle of Beam by the neck. "Who is it?"

"It's me, Serge. Open up."

"Who?"

"Serge! Open up!"

A long pause. Coleman took a swig. "Serge isn't here."

"No, you idiot. *I'm* Serge. Open up!"

"Who?"

"Serge!"

Another pause. "Serge isn't here."

"We're not making a comedy album! Unbolt the door right now or I'll kill you!"

Coleman opened up. "Oh, hi, Serge." He stuck his head out in the hall. "Some guy was just here asking for you."

"Boob." Serge came inside with a briefcase and looked across the suite. "Holy mother!"

The curtains were drawn all the way open: Ally Street out on the balcony, leaning over the railing.

Serge made a mad dash, yanked her back inside and pulled the drapes shut. "What the hell's wrong with you? People can see up here!"

"I want to go down to the pool."

Serge was at a loss. "What part of kidnapping are you having trouble with?"

"I'm losing my tan."

Coleman tapped Serge's shoulder. "The sign on the front of our hotel is upside down."

"That's on purpose."

"What about the lobby?" asked Coleman. "There was this hot chick in lingerie living in a giant aquarium behind the reception desk."

"It's L.A."

"Did you get my water?" asked Ally.

"Forgot," said Serge, placing the briefcase on the dresser. "I was kind of busy. There's some bottles the hotel provided in the closet."

"It's not my brand."

"It's water," said Serge.

"I need my brand."

"Serge," said Coleman, holding up a foil strip. "They have rubbers in the courtesy bar." He held up his other hand. "And my dope is all wet."

"What?"

"I can't smoke it wet. I forgot it was in my pocket when I took a shower."

"Why were you wearing pants— . . . Forget it. Hair dryer's by the bathroom."

"Thanks."

Serge flipped the latches on the briefcase. He slowly lifted the lid with heart-flutter anticipation. Bingo. Jammed with packs of hundred-dollar bills that seemed to give off rays and make the room brighter. Wait, the room *was* brighter. Serge turned around. "Ahhhhh!" Curtains open again, Ally straying onto the balcony.

Serge sprinted and jerked her back inside.

There was a small bang; lights dimmed momentarily. "Everything's okay," said Coleman. "Just dropped the dryer in the sink."

Serge closed the briefcase. "Do I have to child-proof?"

Coleman came over with the charred dryer. "Did you get the money?"

"Yeah," said Serge. "But then I met this guy and traded it for some magic beans."

Coleman pitched the small appliance in the trash. "They gave us a broken dryer. And it blew my dope all over the rug."

Serge slid the briefcase under the bed. He reached in a suitcase and removed his portable DVD player.

Coleman got down on his hands and knees, picking through the carpet. "Found a place last night that you'd like."

"I was wondering where you went," said Serge, placing the DVD player on top of the television. "I woke up and your bed was empty."

"Can we get my water now?" asked Ally.

"After I passed out, I got up and it was still only midnight," said Coleman. "So I walked down the block to the Chateau Marmont."

"Good choice."

"Oh, yeah," said Coleman. "Belushi croaked there, so I figured it was *the* place to party. Had like ten drinks."

"Must have spent a fortune," said Serge, turning the TV sideways. "A beer is what? Ten dollars?"

"I don't know. I was drinking scotch."

"Wow. Your tab had to be over two hundred dollars . . ."

"Except it was eighteen-year-old scotch."

Serge extracted sets of RCA cables from his suitcase. ". . . Four hundred."

"And I was buying rounds for the bar."

"Jesus!" said Serge. "How much did you spend?"

"I don't know," said Coleman, getting out his wallet.

"Did you hear me?" said Ally.

Coleman opened the billfold to the currency section. "Hey, all my money's still here."

"You skipped out on your tab at the Marmont?"

"I don't remember," said Coleman. "I was pretty stoned, too. Near the end, the bartender had to keep wiping up my spills. Then I got the two-minute warning."

Serge unscrewed co-ax. "The what?"

"You know when that voice in your brain says you have to start heading for your bed right now or you won't make it?"

"Unreal. You drank all night at the Marmont for free."

Coleman stuck the wallet back in his pocket. "And I'd always heard it was expensive."

Serge attached the last of the wires and turned the TV back around. "There."

Coleman touched his forehead. "But I can't remember how I got this bump."

"That was my fault," said Serge, walking over to his suitcase. "You blacked out on the roll-away bed and started snoring like an elephant. Tried to turn you over, but you were too heavy, so I spun the bed around. At least you'd be snoring the other way . . ."

"Are you ignoring me?" said Ally.

". . . Then you got up in the middle of the night to go to the bathroom and walked the wrong way into the sliding glass door."

Coleman rubbed the knot. "I thought it was a force field."

"And I need my personal trainer," said Ally.

Serge set a tall stack of flat plastic cases on top of the television.

Coleman cracked a beer. "What's all that?"

"My L.A. collection." Serge opened one of the DVD cases and slipped a disk into the player. He pressed play. Val Kilmer came on the screen.

"What about my trainer?" said Ally.

"Quiet!" said Serge. "I'm studying."

Coleman began rolling a joint of Hawaiian red bud and turquoise Burlington. "What are we watching?"

"*Wonderland*," said Serge. "The John Holmes murders. Actual events as well as location shoots took place all around here."

The door opened. Serge hit pause. He ran out in the hall and dragged Ally back in.

"Let go of me!"

Serge grabbed the .45 from his suitcase and stuck it between her eyes. "Try that again and I'll . . ."

"You'll what!"

Serge tossed the gun aside. ". . . I'll . . . make you drink tap water."

"I want my trainer! I'm going to lose tone!"

"You're in luck," said Serge. "*I'm* a personal trainer."

"You are not!"

Serge nodded emphatically. "That's my main field. I just do this other on the side . . . Let's get started." He took Ally by the arm and walked her into the bathroom. "Begin jogging in place." Ally began jogging.

"Faster!" said Serge.

She went faster.

"Faster!"

She went even faster.

"That's great!" said Serge. "I've never had a student learn so fast!"

"Really?"

"Keep doing that and don't stop until I say."

"Okay."

Serge came back in the room and sat down on the foot of the bed. He restarted the movie and hit ultra-slo-mo. "Coleman, look!"

"What?"

"Our hotel is coming up. You think I chose room two-twenty-two by accident?"

A voice echoed out of the bathroom. "How long do I have to do this?"

"Until my movie's over," said Serge.

The sound of her footsteps dropped off. "Are you messing with me?"

"Don't slow down," said Serge. "An uneven pace actually makes you fatter."

Ally speeded back up.

Serge pointed with the remote. "This is the aerial montage of Kilmer leaving the Wonderland drug den and making a coke-crazed, pinball drive all over Hollywood . . . Steadyyyyy, steadyyyyy, *now!*" He froze the screen and zoomed in. "There's our room! There's our room! See?"

"Where?"

"Right here!" Serge grabbed a Magic Marker off the dresser and made a circle on the TV screen. "That's ours. Think about it! Like a hall of mirrors. Our room is in the movie . . . that's playing in our room . . . that's in the movie . . . that's playing in our room! . . . I try to dwell on it until it starts screwing with my head. Like the first time I grasped I was a self-aware organism, conscious of the universe, hurtling toward the black abyss of death, and then I had to go read a comic book." Serge rubbed the circle on the

TV with his palm. "It won't come off." He looked at his pen. "Whoops, used a permanent marker. . . . Oh, well. Inherent risks of being an innkeeper."

Another bathroom echo: "What's the name of the program you have me on?"

"The 'Stop Fucking with Serge Workout.' "

Coleman leaned toward the TV. "It *is* our room."

The door to the hall opened.

Serge dashed and pulled Ally back inside.

"You're no trainer!"

"What did I tell you about opening that door?"

She pooched out her lower lip. "I'm all smelly now. I have to take a shower."

"Knock yourself out."

"I'm not getting in that shower."

"Why not?"

"Your friend peed on his feet in there."

"How do you know?"

"I could hear it. He wasn't running the shower."

"Coleman! Run the shower!"

"I did after she told me. That's why my dope's wet."

Serge restarted his DVD. "If we weren't such good friends, I'd vote you off the island." He grabbed a notebook and began writing with a pencil. A tap on his shoulder.

"I need my water."

The pencil snapped.

22

VISTAMAX STUDIOS

Tori and the Glicks sat quietly in the brothers' spacious office. They smiled nervously at the detectives. The detectives smiled back.

Tori's cell phone rang. She smiled again and looked at the display. She got up, walked across the room and faced the corner. "Hello? . . ."

The detectives exchanged glances. They strained to hear but couldn't.

"Slow down," Tori whispered. "You're talking too fast . . . I know she's a piece of work . . . You're just going to have to be patient . . . Look, I can't really talk now . . ."

Ian's cell phone rang. He checked the display. International prefix from Japan. He went to another corner. "Hello? . . . I was just about to call . . . I'm whispering because the police are here . . . Oh, you already heard about that? . . . Yeah, I guess we had a little kidnapping . . . Listen, I can't talk now, but it's all part of this great plan . . ."

The detectives looked at each other again.

". . . No! Don't leave the room under any circumstances! . . ." said Tori.

". . . What was that? 'Don't pay a single dime in ransom'?" said Ian. "What do you mean, 'Or else'? . . . Oh, I see . . ."

Tori came back from one corner of the room. Ian returned from another. They sat down and smiled again.

"Anything the matter?" asked Detective Babcock.

"No," said Tori. "Why? Something look the matter?"

THE STANDARD HOTEL

A honeymooning couple in dripping bathing suits walked down a second-floor corridor. They heard yelling as they passed room 222.

"No!" screamed Ally. "I won't do it!"

Serge's right hand had her neck in a stranglehold. His left held a glass to her mouth.

"Drink the fuckin' tap water!"

"No! . . ."

Serge gripped her throat harder. Then gurgling. Fluid streamed down her chin. She spit the rest in Serge's face. "Fuck you!"

Coleman swayed against the balcony railing, staring down at the pool. "Everyone's skinny."

Serge wiped his face and grabbed the .45. He jammed it between her eyes.

"What are you going to do?" said Ally. "Shoot me?"

"If you keep pushing!"

"It'll make too much noise. And what would Tori think?"

Damn this woman. Always a valid comeback! Serge put the gun away, retreated to the foot of the bed and turned on the TV. Ally had been giving Serge the silent treatment until she realized that it helped him watch his movies. So she reversed field.

". . . This is ridiculous!" said Ally. "I can't take it anymore! . . ."

"Shut up!"

". . . We're living animals. No, animals have it better! . . ."

"Shut up!"

She stepped in front of the television. ". . . I will not shut up! I will not stop talking! . . ."

Coleman staggered across the room, spilling a tall glass of bourbon. He squeezed between Ally and the TV. "I think I'll take a shower."

". . . Maybe you're used to pigsties! . . ."

Serge rocked violently on the edge of the bed, covering his ears. "Shut up! Shut up! Shut up! . . ."

Ally turned around and pressed the TV's power button. The screen went black.

Serge dropped his hands from his head. "What just happened?"

"We haven't had a maid for three days!"

"You turned off the TV."

"I need new shoes!"

"You turned off the TV."

"Do I have your attention?"

The shower began running. Coleman: "I think I'll take a nap now."

"What are you doing?" shouted Ally. "Put me down! Put me down this instant!"

He did. She hit the bed and bounced two feet. "You're mean!"

"Just getting warmed up." He advanced like a panther.

Sniffles.

Serge pulled up short. "Don't you dare."

Trembling mouth, tears welling.

"No, not that! Anything else!"

Sobs began.

Serge sat on the side of the bed. "Please don't cry. . . .
Please stop . . ."

It only grew louder.

"C'mon, I can't take it," said Serge. "Women and children crying, it rips me up. Men crying, I kick 'em in the
balls, because I can't take that either, but in a different
way."

Full blubbering now. "I need my acting coach!"

"But the police are looking for us."

"My instrument will get rusty."

"Instrument? You've been in this town too long."

A protracted, pitiful wail.

"Okay, okay," said Serge. "I'll get you an acting
coach . . . Actually, *I'm* an acting coach."

"You are not."

"I swear."

"This is just like when you said you were a trainer."

"I've taught some of the best."

"Liar!"

"Honest." Serge narrowed his eyes and formed his mouth
into a straight line. "*'Go ahead. Make my day!'*"

Ally raised her head with streaked mascara. "Clint?"

"Confidentiality clauses prevent me."

"I don't know. I still think you're lying."

"Come on. You want your instrument to get rusty?"

"No."

"What were you working on with your regular coach?"

"Femme fatale."

"Perfect," said Serge. "We'll start with *Body Heat*. A
Florida classic."

"You're kidding, right?"

"What's the matter? It's a great movie."

"I know," said Ally. "I loved *Body Heat*! Especially Kathleen Turner. It's what got me into acting in the first place."

"My theory proven again," said Serge. "Movies connect people."

"Remember when she meets William Hurt by the bandshell."

"Remember it? I've *been* there! . . . *'You can stand with me but you'll have to agree not to talk about the heat!'*"

"*'You're not too smart, are you?'*" said Ally. "*'I like that in a man.'*"

"Then Hurt buys her a cherry snow cone that she drops on her chest, and he offers to get some paper towels . . . *'I'll even wipe it off for you.'*"

Ally's eyes beckoned. "*'You don't want to lick it?'*"

She and Serge slammed together in a sexual froth. Ally tore at his pants. He ripped her shirt. She bit his neck. He cracked his knuckles . . .

Panama City, Florida

A massive penthouse took up the entire top floor of a high-rise beachfront condo. It was paid for by a string of new car dealerships in Alabama and eastern Mississippi that led all their respective markets because of promotional tie-ins with college football.

The building's other units completed the stair-like architecture down to the beach and were filled with radiant sunlight from a cloudless view over the Gulf of Mexico.

Not the penthouse.

The living room had dark paneling, made even darker by the thick curtains that were drawn tight. A framed parchment certificate hung on the wall: HONORARY DEGREE. A big-screen TV was replaying the 1978 Crimson Tide championship game.

A diminutive man who looked like Rick Moranis sat on the couch, mouthing along with the play-by-play that he knew by heart. He was wearing a dark red football helmet that was too big for his head. He had wood.

The phone rang.

"Damn." The game was paused. "Hello? . . . You'll have to speak up . . . Louder . . . Because I'm wearing the helmet . . . Screw it! Hold on . . ." He took the helmet off. "This better be good. I was in the middle of the Sugar Bowl . . . What do you mean they're dead? . . . What kind of accident? . . . Flew through a guardrail? What the hell am I paying you for? . . . No, I will not calm down! You guaranteed they could handle anything, and they can't even drive! . . . You're damn right you're going to try again . . . I want you to send in The Fullback . . . I know he's the last resort . . . I know he gets messy. That's the whole point. This mess *needs* a mess . . . Okay, one more chance, but that's it. If you can't wrap this up soon, I want The Fullback!"

The phone slammed.

The helmet went back on. The game resumed. The man mouthed along with the announcers. He reached without looking for the petroleum jelly.

THE STANDARD HOTEL

Coleman felt warm water raining on his face. "Where am I?" He opened his eyes and struggled to pull himself up in the shower. "Whoa. That soap dish came right off."

Wet feet stepped on a bath mat. Coleman's brain was splitting. He reached inside the mini-fridge and grabbed a can of the dog that bit him. Down she went in one long, frosty guzzle. He adjusted his eyes. Natural light streamed from the bedroom, so it was still day. He smiled at his luck. Another double shift of partying. He opened the fridge again.

The rest of room 222 had a palpably cheery vibe when Coleman came around the corner. He walked to the dresser, where Serge was making some kind of list on a notepad.

Coleman pointed at the bed. "What's she doing?"

Serge glanced over his shoulder at Ally, cross-legged and humming. "Getting her chakras centered."

"What's the list for?"

Serge thought a second and wrote something else. "Since we had sex, I figured we could take the next step and go shopping together."

"I thought you said we couldn't leave the room."

"I know, but she was incredible—weakened me by using Florida movie lines. Besides, I've been going bonkers in here myself. We're surrounded by all these historic spots, and I haven't been able to hit a single one. Figured we'd alternate, her stores and my movie sites." Serge began talking to himself as he proofread the list: ". . . Tofu, mega-vitamins, dermal-abrasion body mud, herbal supplements frowned on by the FDA, iced tea brewed to support oppressed peoples, chemical strips that pull the shit out of your nose pores, pesticide-free vegetables where they instead disorient the insects with ultrasonic transmitters, two cases of Demi's Ambivalence Spring Water . . . Honey, am I forgetting anything?"

"Did you remember the ionizer?" said Ally.

"Why do we need an ionizer?"

"You have any idea what's in the air in this room?"

"No."

"For one thing, Coleman."

"Huh?"

"The studies. More than half of all dust and airborne particles is exfoliation."

"Dead skin?"

"You clean yourself pretty good, but your friend . . ." Ally glanced toward Coleman. "If I'm going to stay cooped up in this room, I can't be breathing him all the time."

"Coleman! Have you been molting in here?"

"Didn't mean to."

Ally unfolded her legs and got off the bed. "You share an apartment with him back in Florida, right?"

"Yeah?"

"I'll bet there's at least two pounds of him in the duct-work."

"Jesus!" said Serge. "Why did you have to say that? Now it's all I'll be able to think about the rest of my life." He added ionizer to the list and made an emphatic circle.

A terrible scream.

Serge and Ally jumped.

Coleman was looking in the bathroom mirror. "Something's wrong with the side of my face! It's fucked up! I think I have one of those flesh diseases where everything falls off the bone!"

"Coleman . . ."

"Look how it's already eaten away! Those little squares . . ."

"Coleman . . ."

"They'll have to scoop out half my face. Children will point! . . ."

"Coleman! It's just tile marks where you passed out in the shower."

Ally put her hair in a ponytail and tucked it through the back of a plain black baseball cap. She slipped on dark sunglasses.

"That's not much of a disguise," said Serge.

Ally picked up her purse. "It's the standard actress disguise. All my friends wear it when they want people to know they're actresses."

A team of ominous-looking men in hunting vests exited the Holiday Inn on Highland. They marched in rhythm across the parking lot and climbed on six identical yellow ninja bikes. The motorcycles blasted off down the street, popping wheelies.

*　　*　　*

A valet eased a Sebring convertible up to the entrance of the Standard Hotel. Serge climbed in and gunned it onto Sunset. He took the first right and drove fifty yards down a steep hill. An inbound jet roared overhead. Serge tapped the horn.

A fire door opened on the side of the hotel. Two heads poked out. One in a black baseball cap. The coast was clear except for a couple of residents on mountain bikes.

"Hurry up!" yelled Serge.

Coleman and Ally jumped in the car. The bicyclists stared as the rental raced by.

"Wasn't that Ally Street?"

Serge had done his map homework. He zipped around town with geographical efficiency, hitting stores and sights in quick succession, ripping through their mutual lists. Ally was up front, next to Serge, sipping her water. Coleman was in the backseat reading a tabloid.

"Serge, check out this story. 'OJ shocker: I want to be buried next to Nicole.' What do you think?"

"Only if we can do it now."

The Chrysler sped west on Hollywood. Serge suddenly hit the brakes and skidded up to the curb, next to a man sitting on the sidewalk under an umbrella. A hand-painted sign leaned against the chair: STAR MAPS—$10.

Serge opened his wallet and leaned across Ally. "One map, please. Ten dollars is a lot for a piece of paper, but I must have it. Sure wish they had these in Florida, but the guys on the corners down there just wash your windshield against your will."

The man stepped up to the car and held out a map. Serge pulled back his money. "Wait a second. Is this a legitimate map? Who regulates you guys? These are real stars, right? Not a bunch of has-beens and never-weres. I better not find Gene Rayburn, Totie Fields or Mason Reese. Nobody from

Love, American Style or *Here Come the Brides,* and definitely not the Hudson Brothers or any other secret square."
Serge held out the ten-spot again. The man grabbed the bill, but Serge wouldn't let go. Serge grabbed the map; the man wouldn't release. They struggled . . . The man finally stumbled backward with the ten. Serge recoiled into the driver's door with the map.

"Weirdo."

"I heard that," said Serge. "You'll never do lunch in this town again."

The man's face changed. "Wait. I recognize her. Don't tell me . . ." Snapping his fingers. ". . . That's Ally Street!"

"No, it's not."

"Sure, it is . . . Don't move." The man ran to the sidewalk and reached under his chair. He dashed back to the car and handed Ally a thick stack of paper. "A guy who sells maps witnesses the murder of a CIA research assistant and traces it back to the president . . ."

Serge blasted away from the curb. They rolled into Beverly Hills. A map was spread across the steering wheel. "Our first stop, the *Get Smart* house."

Coleman bent down and lit a joint. "Remember the cone of silence?"

"They also had a portable cone," said Serge. "That clear plastic dumbbell. . . . Dun-dun-naaaaaaa-*duh!* Dun-dun-naaaaaaa-*duh!* . . ."

Coleman joined in the humming of the theme song. They turned down a residential street.

Serge grabbed his heart as they approached the address on the map. "I can't believe our luck!"

"What?"

"That guy with the gray hair opening the mailbox. It's Don Adams!" They drove by, Serge pumping a fist in the air. "Wooooo! Tennessee Tuxedo motherfucker!"

A man with a handful of envelopes turned around as a rental car made a squealing left at the end of the block.

"Now we know where Don Adams lives," said Serge. "We own him."

"He's our bitch," said Coleman.

"Carson's next, bless his soul."

"They got Carson's house on that map?"

"Not exactly. His ex-wife's."

"Which one?"

"Number three."

Serge glared at the home as he drove by. "God, I hate her!"

"Why?"

"Because Johnny did. That's where I take my orders."

The Chrysler hooked south.

"Who's next?" asked Coleman.

Serge tapped the map. "Ed McMahon."

"In the same neighborhood? What a coincidence."

"Must have grown up together," said Serge. "Probably rode their bikes on this very street."

Coleman took another hit. He had mastered talking while holding his breath. "Ed would be cool to party with."

"You know it! Johnny was always ribbing him about getting tanked."

Coleman exhaled. "Think he smokes weed?"

"Well, he knows Doc, so he's already got a connection."

"What about *my* list?" said Ally. "We're supposed to alternate."

"We are."

"You just did Don Adams, Carson and now Ed. That's three in a row."

"They're near each other," said Serge.

"So are my stores. Come on!"

"When you're right, you're right." He turned at Pico.

It started in the organic-food palace. Ally turning heads. Two leotard people whispered by the alfalfa. At the skin-care salon, a seaweed-packed woman sat up. "Are you Ally Street?"

The same thing outside. Every few blocks, people on sidewalks pointing excitedly as the Chrysler drove by, trying to fish Instamatics from oversize purses with sequins spelling out the Hollywood sign. Then the ionizer store, where a woman from Baltimore ran up with an autograph book. "Could you sign below Hasselhoff?"

Ally smiled and accepted the pen.

"No! No! No!" yelled Serge, snatching the pen and pushing the book away. "You're thinking of someone else!"

The woman followed them to the car, picking up more autograph-seekers on the way. "We love you, Ally!" "We're praying for your safe return!" "Please sign!"

"It's not her!" Serge peeled out of the parking lot.

Three blocks later he checked the empty rearview and let off the gas. They passed through an intersection with six bright-yellow bullet bikes at the corner.

"That was close."

Suddenly, a mechanized thunder all around the car. The motorcycle formation split in two, a trio of bikes pulling along each side of the car. Serge punched the gas again, tearing out of the Hills and up to Bel Air. Fifty, sixty, seventy miles an hour. The ninja bikes stayed with him. Each had two riders—a driver and a passenger in back—all of them dressed in yellow riding suits with matching yellow helmets and opaque black visors. The passengers took aim at the Chrysler.

"Uh-oh," said Serge. "The worst-case scenario."

"Assassins?" said Coleman.

"Photographers."

Serge began weaving. The motorcycles backed off to

avoid collision, then accelerated and closed again. Serge activated the cruise control and cocked his .45. "Steer!"

Ally grabbed the wheel from the passenger side.

Serge turned around and knelt in the driver's seat, firing a full clip into the asphalt around the cyclists, who peeled off in retreat like a squadron of Spitfires.

24

Ten Miles South of Sylacauga, Alabama, Hometown of Jim Nabors

Seven camouflaged men marched single file up a steep trail in the part of the state where the convenience stores advertise shells, and they mean shotgun. The mountain was heavily forested. The men had olive-and-black face paint and carried rifles over their shoulders. Streams of tobacco juice flew with musical rhythm.

"Huge" didn't begin to capture the man at the front of the hunting column. He outscaled the others like a separate species. Every muscle group a caricature. Shoulders that looked like shoulder pads.

The Fullback.

He actually *had* been a fullback, too. Red-shirt freshman at a division II school. The kind of player coaches love. Mean. Knees were his specialty, but he also liked spearing, clothes-lining, helmet-to-helmet contact, leg whipping and breaking fingers at the bottom of a fumble pile. Once someone accidentally got a hand inside his face mask and he bit off the pinkie above the last knuckle. Only one problem: All this was against his own team in preseason scrimmage. The coaches hated to cut him, but he was like a prize thoroughbred you couldn't break. Championship speed but unridable. So he bounced around pumping gas before falling in with a mountain gang that ran moonshine, untaxed cigarettes and slot machines. Otherwise, they kept to themselves and were left alone because of the heavy lifting they occasionally did for the Redneck Mafia.

The Redneck Mafia wasn't really a mafia because it wasn't organized. They were less a single entity than a class of people, members of the boll-weevil power structure who handpicked politicians and cut sweetheart deals for state contracts in rural counties without news coverage. Their only continuous criminal enterprise was college football recruitment violations.

But they were still tough as nails—didn't cotton to people taking advantage of them the way they did others. Like making 'em look the fools in an oil scam.

The seven hunters continued up the mountain trail until it leveled. The Fullback stopped and raised a fist for them to be quiet. They crouched and unshouldered Remingtons. Silent breathing. Then, barely a rustle. Through a rifle scope, one of the gang sighted the neck and head of a mature buck. Six points, maybe eight—couldn't tell with the brush.

"Too far for me."

"Me, too. Not even a graze at this range—"

A rifle clap echoed off the mountainside.

The buck leaped with a slug high in his hindquarters, normally a worthless shot, only enough to make the deer limp. Except that was The Fullback's intention. He cleared his chamber and handed the weapon to the man behind him, then dove into the forest.

The man holding two rifles let another stream of brown juice fly from the incestuous gap in his teeth. "Now the fun begins."

The "fun" was nothing less than legend. A limping buck is slow for a deer but more than fast for any man. Most any.

The left-behind hunters sat on a pair of fallen logs and passed the Red Man. A cell phone rang. "Hello? . . . I see . . . I understand . . . We're leaving right now." He closed the phone.

"What is it?" asked the hunter next to him, digging tobacco.

"Me and Buford have to head back." He got up and shouldered his rifle. "Flight tonight from Birmingham."

"Where to?"

"L.A."

Two camouflaged men started down the mountain.

A half hour passed.

Something large in the brush. The remaining hunters stood.

The Fullback muscled his way through the last branches and back onto the trail. Blood all down himself. Over his shoulders, an eight-pointer with a broken neck that no two other men could have carried. He dropped the carcass at their feet.

The one holding two rifles shook his head. "Damnedest thing . . ." He handed a Remington to The Fullback and turned in the direction they'd come. "Every time I see it, I still don't believe—"

The hunter's words were silenced by a massive forearm wrapped under his chin from behind, crushing the windpipe. The Fullback lifted a teasing three inches, making him struggle to reach for the ground with his toes.

Another hunter walked up to the one turning blue. He spat and refilled his cheek: "Your mind must be pretty busy right now. I'll answer the biggest question first. We're going to show you mercy."

Glimmer of relief.

"Because the worst thing is dying without knowing why."
He leaned nose to nose. "Those slots you reported broken?
Counters were tampered. You been skimming."

The man desperately wanted to deny, but there wasn't air.
A loud snap echoed inside his head, and he found himself
looking in a completely different direction. His chin invol-
untarily raised toward the sky as every neck muscle seized
in total spasm. After five seconds, the muscles sagged all the
way for good, his head falling limp to his chest. Arms and
legs wouldn't respond, but his eyes still worked for the next
half minute before blood and oxygen ran out, long enough
to realize he was bounding back down the path, slung over
The Fullback's shoulders like a buck.

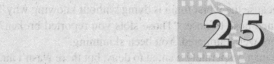

25

Delta Flight 1654

Two jowled men in dark suits sat in the back of a jet-liner connecting from Atlanta. They were reading Southeastern Conference football magazines bought in the Birmingham airport. The plane began circling for its approach to LAX. The man near the window looked down at the Sunset Strip.

Coleman chugged a Blue Ribbon on the balcony of room 222. The shadow of an inbound jet swept over the pool. He went back inside.

"We didn't get everything I needed," said Ally.

"I know," said Serge, pacing the carpet. "I can't believe how bad it got out there. Don't people have lives?"

"I'm bored," said Ally.

"I want to go party," said Coleman.

"We're *all* getting cabin fever," said Serge. "I want to go out as much as you. But leaving this room again is now out of the question. You saw what happened."

"What are we going to do?" asked Coleman.

"We need a rainy-day activity to occupy our minds." Serge reached in one of Ally's shopping bags.

"Hey!" yelled Ally. "Those are my panty hose."

"Take one for the team," said Serge, ripping the hose in half. He opened his suitcase and pulled out the digital camcorder.

"What are you doing?" asked Coleman.

"What do nuclear families usually do on vacation?"

"Get stoned?"

Serge dragged three chairs across the room and placed them in front of the balcony doors. "Make home movies of their trip."

"That's your stupidest idea yet," said Ally.

"Has the goodwill from our sex ended already?" asked Serge. "*Men's Journal* says I got at least twelve more hours before we have to go back on war footing."

Coleman was rooting around the mini-fridge again. "But how do we film our trip if we can't leave the room?"

"It won't be a traditional vacation movie." Serge yanked a white sheet off the bed and laid part of it across the dresser. He began writing with a fat Magic Marker. "In fact, it won't be a vacation movie at all because I hate them. Alleged friends invite you for dinner, then over dessert it's the Uncle Ferg Show, driving a Winnebago through Vermont. I usually call in a bomb threat."

The door to the hallway opened. Serge retrieved Ally. "Don't start that again."

"I'm out of water . . ."

Serge finished writing on the bedsheet and began fastening the top edge to the curtain rod in front of the balcony. "We're going to film a pilot. Then cross our fingers."

"A pilot?" said Coleman. "We don't stand a chance."

Serge finished hanging the backdrop sheet behind the

chairs and handed Coleman half of Ally's panty hose. "I'd have agreed with you before cable, but now it's wide open. If the networks don't pick us up, we can't miss in syndication."

Serge set his camcorder on the dresser and aimed it at the chairs. He hit record. A red light came on.

"We're rolling!"

Hollywood Tattletale

GEDDY INDIFFERENT AS KIDNAPPING TAKES TURN

HOLLYWOOD—In a phenomenon that is equal parts Elvis sighting and the Patti Hearst case, shanghaied starlet Ally Street has reportedly been spotted numerous times all over Los Angeles in the company of two suspected kidnappers.

Police spokesmen said the reports have yet to be verified, but they've issued a plea for the abductors or anyone else with information to call a special anonymous tip line, 1-800-GOT-ALLY?

The alleged sightings have been clustered in the West Hollywood area, but range as far away as Encino and Yorba Linda. Some eyewitnesses reported Ms. Street being shepherded around at gunpoint, while others said she appeared to be traveling voluntarily and was free to leave at any time. All described the starlet as upbeat.

"At first I wasn't sure it was her," said Arnie Snead of Brisbane. "But then I recognized the actress disguise and put two and two together."

"It was definitely Ally," said Claire Milken of Oshkosh. "I knew it the moment I saw her coming out of Just Ionizers."

Adding intrigue is one unconfirmed incident in which Ally is believed to have driven the getaway car while one of her presumed kidnappers fired on celebrity photographers during a midday chase through Bel Air. Reactions to the incident were mixed: Defenders insist that Ally must be suffering from the so-called Stockholm Syndrome, while an E! telephone poll registered high support for the shooting.

In a related development, boy-band heartthrob Jason Geddy, who almost dated Ms. Street, is facing a hail of criticism for nearly seeing someone else during the actress's hostage ordeal. The hunky singer was swarmed by the entertainment press when spotted leaving a trendy Laguna Beach clinic, where he wasn't allowed to visit cover-girl waif Elle Faux, who was resting comfortably and taking IV after falling below eighty pounds again.

Geddy refused comment as he rushed from the facility and hopped into his newly restored De-Lorean. However, heartthrob publicist Ruben Slice issued an official statement quoting his client: "That business with the shooting is not the same Ally I almost asked out. She's someone else now. It's time to move on."

VISTAMAX STUDIOS

A naked lightbulb came on inside a props closet.

"This is a disaster!" shouted Mel. "It's on every channel."

"The police are zeroing in!" said Ian. "We're going to jail!"

"Will you two relax?" said Tori.

"What the hell were they doing leaving the hideout in the first place?" said Mel. "You told us they were pros!"

"They are," said Tori. "I just got off the phone. They said they barely left the room for a second, and the press made up all that other stuff."

"I don't trust these guys," said Ian.

"They gave me their word," said Tori. "They swore they'd stay put until this is over."

"I got a bad feeling," said Mel.

"We were absolutely clear," said Tori. "Not a toe outside the room."

RODEO DRIVE

"Out of the way!" yelled Serge, sprinting down the sidewalk and crashing into people, purses and shopping bags flying.

"Watch it, asshole!"

"Should never have let you talk me into this," said Serge.

"I needed more stuff," said Ally, running alongside.

Serge looked back at the tour group that had been in pursuit since Frederick's. *"Ally! Don't give up hope! . . ."*

Serge looked ahead: A second screaming mob stampeded toward them from the other direction.

Serge and Ally hit the brakes. Nowhere to go. Both groups about to sandwich them.

Coleman whipped around the corner in a rented Chrysler. They dove in. A phone rang.

"Hello?" said Serge. ". . . Oh, hi, Tori . . . I was just about to—. . . Of course we're in the room right now. Where else would we be? . . . You've been calling all morning before you tried my cell? . . . I must have been on the Internet . . ."

The crowds chased the car down the street. Coleman ran a yellow and lost them. He eased up to a red light at Wilshire.

". . . The police came by again?" said Serge. "Well, they're paid to do that . . . Naturally they suspect you. A lot of these are inside jobs . . ."

A Yugo pulled up in the next lane, people hanging out windows with pens and autograph books; Ally signing and handing them back. *"You're the greatest!"*

". . . No, that's the television you hear . . ." said Serge. ". . . You explained that in your last call . . . Right, the room. Don't leave it. Couldn't be simpler . . ."

An Acura pulled up on the other side of the Chrysler, fans taking pictures. *"Ally! You're my hero!"*

". . . You don't have to keep repeating yourself," said Serge. "You have my personal guarantee: We're in like Flynn . . . Later . . ." He hung up.

The light turned green. Coleman patched out and left everyone at the line. "What was that phone call?"

"I wasn't paying attention . . . Turn here."

"Where are we going?"

Serge checked his star map. "Ed McMahon's."

"That's right. We never did get to see his place."

"I love Ed's place," said Serge. "One of the few celebrity homes where you're actually allowed to go up and knock on the door."

"Why's that?" asked Coleman.

"Because *he* does it. The sweepstakes van he drives around. Normally I'd respect his privacy, but that's a clear sign he's lonely . . . Turn here."

"Serge, I think people don't mind because he's giving away money."

Serge looked at Coleman a moment. "You think that makes a difference?"

"Definitely. If I'm vacuuming and have to answer the door, you better make it worth my while."

"Since when do you vacuum?"

"I'm talking about Ed. Must get a lot of foot traffic because of his popularity. Probably vacuuming right now."

"I want to do what's right," said Serge. "You're sure about this prize thing?"

"Pretty sure."

Serge opened his wallet. "I got eighteen dollars. What do you have?"

"Maybe ten."

"Slow down," said Serge. "That's his house right there."

Coleman came to a stop at the end of the driveway. "Looks like a jungle. I can't even see the building."

"Shoot. He's not home."

"How do you know?"

"The prize van's gone."

Coleman got ready to drive away. Serge grabbed his shoulder.

"What is it?" asked Coleman.

Serge was staring in the passenger-side mirror. He rubbed his eyes and looked again. "I think I've seen that car before."

Coleman looked in his own side mirror. "Which one?"

"That Crown Vic parked a block back. Two guys in dark suits."

"Lots of people have been following us," said Coleman. "Probably want autographs."

"One way to find out. Switch seats."

They climbed over each other.

A block back, two jowled men watched the Chrysler pull

away from Ed McMahon's place. The driver lowered his binoculars and started up the Crown Vic.

Coleman fiddled with the radio. "What are we doing now?"

Serge kept his eyes on the mirror. "Tailing them."

"But we're in front."

"I've fooled them into thinking they're following us." Serge hit his turn signal. "Nobody expects to be tailed from in front."

The Chrysler made a left on Sepulveda and pulled up in front of Left Coast Scuba. The trailing sedan parked across the street.

"Stay here," said Serge. He entered the store and came out fifteen minutes later with a large shopping bag that had the Hollywood sign across a dive flag. He handed it to Coleman and started the car.

Coleman reached inside and pulled a black rubber sleeve out the top of the bag. "Wet suits?"

"My favorite science project was always the field experiment."

The Chrysler swung around the side of the store and into the service alley.

A man with binoculars spit tobacco into a cup. "Should we follow?"

"Stay put. There's no way out of that alley."

The men in the sedan waited. Five minutes. Ten. One looked at the other. "What do you think?"

"Could have made us." He started the engine. "Ditched the car and fled on foot."

The men drove around the back of the store and rolled slowly down an alley of broken glass and sludge-filled pot-holes. The sedan approached the dead end.

"Where could they have gone?"

"Wait . . . what's that behind the box compactor?"

"It's the Chrysler."

"It's empty."

"So they did ditch and run."

"But where'd they go?"

A pistol cocked.

The men turned.

"Would you mind stepping out of the car?"

27

DOWNTOWN LOS ANGELES

An editor on the graveyard shift sat in a dim production room of the local NBC affiliate. He ripped open a brown parcel and pulled out a videocassette.

Moments later, the production room was filled with the entire news staff, crowded around the editor's chair as he restarted the tape on the main monitor. "You're not going to believe this . . ."

No one made a sound until the video ended.

The editor swiveled around to face them. "See what I mean?"

"We have to go on the air right away," said the news director. "Tell 'em to cut in. I'll call the police."

PACIFIC COAST HIGHWAY

Five A.M. the next morning, a Chrysler Sebring drove north along the rim of the Golden State. Ally was sleeping in the backseat. It started to get light.

"Can you believe these views?" said Serge.

"It's kind of pretty," said Coleman.

"I'm always bragging about A1A, but you have to give credit where it's due."

The banging and screaming from the trunk resumed.

"I really wish they wouldn't do that," said Serge. "It's such a peaceful time of day."

"Maybe they're uncomfortable."

"Of course they're uncomfortable," said Serge. "Not my fault. Detroit cutting corners again, this time trunk space. At a minimum, I want room enough for two bodies."

"You were able to get two bodies in this thing."

"But we had to sit on the lid to close it."

More banging. Ally sat up with tangled hair. "Dammit, they woke me again."

Coleman fired up his predawn joint. "Those guys are a long way from Alabama."

"And up to no good. Following us around, trying to get to my friends through me. If they thought that was going to fly, *they know nothing about Serge*! That's Eli Wallach."

"But why are we driving way up here? You could have taken care of them back in L.A."

"Considered it," said Serge. "But that's the whole problem with business travel. Always rushing, never any time to enjoy local color."

"I'm going back to sleep," said Ally.

The Chrysler entered a small fishing village above Santa Barbara. Steinbeck country. "This is my stop," said Serge. "They should have everything I need."

"Then why aren't we stopping?"

"Have to drive past to the staging area."

The Chrysler continued another mile until roadside vegetation thickened. Serge pulled off the highway and backed up to the brush. "Coleman, bring the wet suits."

They went around to the trunk.

"I don't know why they're still banging and screaming like that," said Serge. "They need to save their energy." He looked up and down the empty road and inserted the key.

The lid popped.

"You're dead!" shouted one of the hostages. "You are so fucking dead!"

"*I'm* dead," said Serge. "Look who's talking."

"You have no idea who you're dealing with!"

"Makes us even." Serge motioned with his pistol. "Get out and start walking . . . Ally, wake up . . . Ally!"

A sleepy head. "Wha—?"

"Out of the car. My science project's starting."

"You're a boob." She laid her head back down.

Serge reached in the car and grabbed a handful of hair. "Up you go."

"Ow! Okay, okay!"

Everyone marched down through the brush and out onto the beach, which wasn't really a beach but a rocky sand spit littered with driftwood. Serge grabbed the shopping bag from Coleman and threw it at the men's feet. "Put those on."

They didn't move.

"Now!" Serge aimed the pistol.

One of them slowly bent down and reached in the bag. "Wet suits?"

"Hope I got your size right. They're supposed to be snug anyway."

Ally lay down in the sand and used a smooth rock for a pillow. Serge handed Coleman the gun as the men reluctantly changed into scuba outfits. "Keep 'em covered. I won't be long."

Serge raced back to the village they had just passed. A light mist. He went in a fishing tackle store and came out with sealed buckets. Next: a rental shack at the end of the dock. Serge handed a stolen credit card to a man in an orange rain poncho.

The man ran the card through a manual carbon imprinter and handed it back. "You're just one guy. Sure you need an eighteen-footer?"

"I like to spread out."

Serge climbed down a wooden ladder with barnacles exposed at low tide. Soon a high-pitched, two-stroke whine erupted from the water. Puffs of smoke and carbon monoxide. An inflatable Zodiac boat raced away from the pier and out to sea.

Dawn approached, but the fog made it seem farther off.

Two potbellied Alabama boys stood on an isolated shoreline. The wet suits felt like girdles.

"But we just want to *see* the gun," said one of the men. "We'll give it right back."

"I don't think I'm supposed to," said Coleman.

A thirty-five-horsepower drone came up the coast. The sound grew louder until an eighteen-foot Zodiac soared around the bend and ripped a hole in the fog. Serge idled the engine and nosed the boat ashore. "All aboard!"

The boat took off north. Two nervous men in wet suits sat up front, eyes on nothing but the gun in Serge's right hand. Serge manned the tiller with his left, sealed buckets and a curled-up Ally at his feet. He nudged her with the gun. "You're going to miss this."

"Stop it," said Ally. "I was almost asleep again."

Serge shouted over the engine and waves. "Where you guys from?"

They didn't answer.

"Come on," yelled Serge. "This is going to be a long trip without conversation. What parts?"

"Opelika," said one.

"Selma," said the other.

"I'm actually very fond of Alabama," said Serge. "*Where the skies are so blue!* That should be the state song instead of whatever they've got. Georgia uses Ray Charles, so Skynyrd should be eligible now that they've cleaned up. Did you know that was their rebuke to Neil Young trashing the state on the *Harvest* album? I remember thinking, yeah, Neil was out of line, but if blue skies are all you can come up with, it's faint-praise damning. Until I got a whiff of the smog out here. That's why Neil's voice always sounds like he's bringing up another hairball. So you have nothing to apologize for. Pay no mind to the jokes. 'Alabama: We're first alphabetically!'"

The hostages looked at each other from the corners of their eyes.

"Yes, sir. I love the sea!" Serge filled his lungs with salt air. "Reminds me of one of my all-time favorite Florida movies, *The Day of the Dolphin*! Remember that? George C. Scott taught this dolphin rudimentary English. Its name was *Fa*, short for *Alpha*. And at the end, Scott had to run the dolphin off so evil forces couldn't use him to plant a bomb under the president's yacht. And the dolphin goes, 'Fa love Pa,' and Scott goes, 'Pa doesn't love Fa . . .'"

Serge couldn't continue. He hugged Coleman and bawled on his shoulder. "How could he do that? It was just an innocent animal! . . ."

Coleman patted him on the back. "Easy, buddy . . ."

Serge sniffled and raised his head. The two men were creeping down the boat toward him. Serge aimed his gun. "That's no way to build trust."

Ten minutes later Serge recognized an outcropping on the

coastline. He cut the engine three hundred yards from shore. The boat bobbed silently as the fog began to lift.

"This is what it's all about," said Serge. "I may be a fool for the city, but you gotta air out the ol' melon from time to time or you'll explode . . ." His ears perked up. "Listen . . . I think they're on the way."

"Who's on the way?" asked Coleman.

"This is a seal watch." Serge restarted the engine. "Did some online research with the Sierra Club to locate their colonies. They live right over there on those rocks."

"I don't see them," said Coleman.

"Morning feeding time. It's amazing how you can practically set your watch by nature."

"Is that them over there?" said Coleman.

"Way to be alert." Serge throttled over as quietly as he could, gauging a vector parallel to shore. He cut the engine again and stood up. "This is it, guys. End of the line." He motioned with his gun. "Into the water."

They looked over the side at the dark sea.

"Your call," said Serge. "There's the shore. I can shoot, or you can try to swim for it. You look pretty buoyant—"

Two big splashes before he could finish the sentence. But instead of swimming for land, the men faced the boat and treaded water, expecting maybe Serge would shoot them anyway.

Coleman pointed at the oncoming mass of seals. "What are they hunting for?"

"Little fish."

The two men kept dog-paddling, focused on the disturbance in the waves coming toward them. One of them called up to Serge: "Do they ever hurt people?"

"Never," said Serge. "Although they could. Some are over six feet and very agile underwater, while others prefer basketball and musical instruments."

"Look at 'em go," said Coleman. "They sure move fast when they're hunting."

"They're not hunting anymore. They're running."

"Running?"

"The magnificent balance of the food chain. They go out for breakfast, and bigger stuff comes looking for them. That would be those tall fins over there."

"Poor seals," said Coleman.

"Don't worry," said Serge, peeling the lid off his pails and dumping bloody chum over the side. "They're very fast and wily. Rarely get caught . . ." The two men suddenly began swimming as fast as they could for shore. ". . . Except once in a while, an injured seal falls behind the pack . . ."

Coleman popped a beer. "Or something mistaken for a seal?"

Terrible screams off the starboard side. The water boiled with thrashing.

Serge pull-started the engine. "That's why you never, ever swim at dawn with the seals. And *definitely* not in a black wet suit."

The screaming ended and the sea became still again. Serge began motoring south. Coleman lay back against the inflatable bow, admiring the sunrise. "I never realized nature was so beautiful."

"But she can also be a cruel mistress."

28

THE STANDARD HOTEL, ROOM 222

The phone was ringing when they came in the door.
Serge picked it up. "Hello? . . . Oh, hi, Tori. . . .
We were just talking about you . . ."

Coleman turned on the television, surfing for porn. A local channel caught his eye.

". . . Of course we're in the room. Where else would we be? . . . Ally's fine . . ."

Coleman pointed at the set. "Hey, Serge. There's something about us on TV."

Serge waved for him to be quiet. ". . . No, nothing unusual . . ."

Coleman turned up the volume. A reporter with a microphone stood on the Walk of Fame. ". . . *Ms. Street doesn't yet have her own star on this famous boulevard, but you wouldn't know it from the sidewalk vendors doing brisk business in Ally gear . . . Excuse me, sir . . .*" The reporter approached a kiosk next to the Roosevelt Hotel. "*What are your bestsellers?*"

"The RUN! ALLY! RUN! shirts and keychains."

"What does Ally mean to you personally?"

"She's my role model."

"Why is that?"

"Because of everything she represents."

Serge paced with the phone. ". . . Well, I'm glad you're checking to make sure we're in the room. Just shows you're responsible . . ."

Coleman tugged Serge's arm and pointed at the set. The reporter stopped two tourists walking down the sidewalk in matching Ally shirts: *You Shop, Girl!*

"And what do you think about the Ally Street case?"

"It's so exciting knowing she's out there. It's like she's doing this for all of us."

"She's such an inspiration," added her friend.

Serge paced in front of the set. ". . . No, I didn't take any offense. It's your job to check . . . In fact, I'm getting to like this room. I don't *want* to leave . . . You don't have to apologize—I didn't take it that way . . . Right . . . Right . . . Of course . . ."—Serge rolled his eyes—". . . Yep . . . Right . . . You got it . . . Peace. Out . . ."

Coleman cracked a beer and changed channels with the remote.

Serge slammed the phone down. "All the women in my life! You try to be polite, but they still talk to you."

"Hey, Serge. We're on this other channel, too."

"What do you mean 'too'?"

"Our vacation movie."

"I'll be," said Serge. "They picked up the pilot."

"You were right after all."

"Now we're in a serious jam."

"Why's that?"

"They're going to want at least thirteen episodes." Serge grabbed his video camera. "We have to get cracking."

The door to the hall opened.

Serge pulled Ally back inside. "Don't start again."

"I quit."

"What do you mean, you quit?"

"I'm not doing this anymore. Find someone else. I had no idea when Tori first asked me . . ."

Serge pursed his lips in distress and emitted a shrill whine. "I thought you'd decided to cooperate."

"But there's no end in sight. It just gets weirder and weirder. I'm out of here." She reached for the knob again.

"Get away from that door."

"You can't make me stay."

"Yes, I can."

VISTAMAX STUDIOS

Two men and a woman walked down the main corridor of the props warehouse.

"I just talked to them," said Tori. "You'll feel much better."

"What'd they say?" asked Ian.

"I'll tell you when we get in the closet . . ."

Two workers sprinted past them.

"They sure were going fast," said Tori.

"We keep them on their toes," said Mel.

Several more employees went flying by. Tori watched them dart into the break room. "Is it always like this around here?"

Before the brothers could answer, they noticed more and more people dashing in from all directions, converging on the break room.

"Wonder what's going on," said Ian.

"Let's find out."

The trio headed over and joined the crowd spilling out the break room's doorway.

"What going on?" Mel asked someone in back. The man pointed up at the wall-mounted TV on the other side of the room that everyone was watching.

Everywhere in metropolitan Los Angeles, the same scene: people surrounding TVs in bars, offices, the electronics sections of department stores, where walls of fifty sets were all on the same channel, playing the same tape over and over. CNN got the uplink and the nation began watching.

In a Fort Lauderdale retirement home, Coltrane grabbed Chi-Chi by the arm. "Come quick! They're on TV!"

"Who's on TV?"

The pair entered the dayroom. Twenty seniors were already crowded around an old Magnavox. A harried anchorwoman was talking offscreen. *"Are we ready with that again? . . . Okay . . ."* She turned to the camera. *"We have breaking news to report in the Ally Street abduction case. Within the last hour CNN has received shocking hostage video from our sister station in Los Angeles. A word of caution: The footage is being aired unedited and may upset certain viewers . . ."*

The image switched to two men sitting with panty hose on their heads. The thin one held index cards. The fat one had a foam circle over his mouth, where he'd been drinking beer through the nylon mesh. The backdrop was a white bedsheet with big, black letters: CRAZY ABOUT MOVIES!

"Good evening," said the thin one. "This is our first show and boy are we excited! *We're crazy about movies!*"

The fat one raised his beer. "Movies. *Wooooo!*"

"Since this is our debut, I thought we'd start at the top. *Citizen Kane.* We rented it from Blockbuster last month, and it gets better every time. Welles said so much with so little, like the ironic emptiness of that dinner with his wife in the third act, not to mention those exquisite gradations of black-and-white cinematography that we'd see explored further in *The Third Man.* An absolute masterpiece. What did you think?"

"Great film," said Coleman. "I was really fucked up. Started with Old English Eight-Hundred and switched to wine. Also got into these sticky buds from Gainesville with the furry orange fibers that tell you to get all your shit in one sack 'cause it's going to blow your eyeballs out! Then the wine made me sick, and I got wedged between the toilet and the wall. Later, I woke up and freed myself and rejoined you on the couch just before the credits. All in all, one of the best movies I've ever seen."

"I give it five stars."

"Four and a half," said Coleman. "Almost a five, but what was the deal with the fuckin' sled?"

"Next, the segment of our show called 'Mr. Peabody's Way-Back Machine.' The 1970s were an utter waste of ten years in virtually every respect: socially, musically, politically. Except for Hollywood, which gave us the Second Golden Age of Film: *Patton, The Godfather, The French Connection, Cabaret, The Sting, Rocky, Annie Hall, American Graffiti, The Exorcist.* I get dizzy just thinking about it . . . Your thoughts?"

"Couldn't agree more," said Coleman. "The seventies ruled! Mainly because there were no video stores. And each weekend all the heads would go to the midnight rock concert movie. *Gimme Shelter, Let It Be, The Song Remains the Same, Concert for Bangladesh, The Last Waltz.* Everyone in the whole theater was baked! Remember when you could get a four-finger bag for twenty bucks? The potency was lower, but at those prices! Then we'd kick back and watch

Jagger jump around in that Uncle Sam hat. He was baked, too. It was a special time."

"Thank you—"

"Almost forgot about the Pink Floyd laser show at the planetarium . . ."

"That's not a movie."

"I know, but we were baked."

"Which brings us to the special guest portion of our program." Serge dragged a third chair into view. "And tonight we have with us a *very* special guest, the star of the upcoming Vistamax release, *All That Glitters* . . ." He stood, turned offscreen and began applauding. "Ally Street! Come on out here! . . ."

Serge kept applauding. "Ally Street, folks! . . . Ally, come on, we're filming . . ." Serge's applause dwindled. Coleman leaned forward and looked to the side to see what was taking so long.

"Ally! Get out here right now! Don't make me come over there! . . . Okay if that's the way you want it . . ." Serge whipped a giant gun from his pants and marched off the right side of the screen. A moment later, Ally walked into the picture with an arm twisted behind her back.

"Let go! You're hurting me!"

Serge shoved her down in a chair and took the next seat. He stuck the gun back in his pants. "Ally, you look great! What have you been doing with yourself? I mean, besides making an incredible movie!"

Ally folded her arms in protest.

Serge took a deep breath. "Seeing anyone?"

Ally secretly slipped a piece of hotel stationery from her pocket. She unfolded it and held it up for the camera: HELP!

"Gimme that!" said Serge, balling up the piece of paper. "Always kidding around. So what's new in Ally World?"

Defiance.

Serge chuckled nervously at the camera and tapped an index card on his knee. "I understand you've had some excitement in your life. Want to tell us about it?"

Ally shot him a disgusted look. "What are you, some kind of idiot?"

"I just go by the cards," said Serge. "They mentioned something about a kidnapping. I'll bet our audience would love to hear about it."

"Screw you! Okay? Screw you and your stupid friend. I'm out of here!" Ally got up and walked off camera.

"That's not how Hepburn handled success!"

A woman's hand appeared from the edge of the screen and threw a beverage in Serge's face. He smiled at the camera as drops rolled onto his chest. "What do you know? Our first show and already something for the highlight reel."

Serge jumped up and ran offscreen.

"Get back out there!"

"Take your hands off me!"

"I can't believe I fucked you! You don't even know the *current* vice president!"

"Let go!"

"You owe it to your fans!—"

The tape went black.

29

THE STANDARD HOTEL

Serge grabbed the ringing phone in room 222.

"... Hi, Tori. Hey! You'll never guess! We were on— ... You already saw it? Wasn't it great! ... Oh ... But I thought you'd like— ... I see ... I see ... Stop shouting. I can't understand— ... But we didn't leave the room. We filmed the whole thing inside— ... But you didn't say that ... No, you never said that ... What do you mean, 'I shouldn't have to'? ... Look, if you can't speak the language with precision, you shouldn't go blaming— ... You're shouting again ..."

Coleman cracked his third beer of the morning and emptied half in his first guzzle. While waiting for the burp, he read the side of the can like a cereal box.

Serge hung up the phone.

"Serge, you ever read beer cans?"

"I already know the plot."

"Says they won gold medals in Helsinki, Munich and Amsterdam. The last was 1903." Coleman giggled.

"What's so funny?"

"What if they won the medals for, like, the javelin? You know: 'Whoops. Sorry about that!'"

Serge didn't answer.

"What's the matter?" asked Coleman. "You don't look happy."

"Tori's mad at me again."

Coleman took another chug. "What's new?"

"This time she might have a point. I mean, she has been really nice, giving us this job." He stood.

"What are you going to do?"

"I have to think of a way to make it up," said Serge. "Something special that lets her know how much we think of her."

"Like what?"

He slapped the top of the TV. "I've got it!" He grabbed a magazine and some scissors.

Coleman looked over his buddy's shoulder. "What are you doing?"

"Starting the ransom note."

"But we already got paid."

Snip, snip. "This isn't about getting paid. It's about showing Tori we care." Snip, snip.

"But doesn't she keep telling us not to draw attention to ourselves?"

"Exactly," said Serge. "That's the thing about rules. You have to look for the reason behind them. Tori doesn't want us to do anything because the police might suspect her more. So that's why we *have* to do something. The note will divert suspicion away from her. What do you think?"

"You're very thoughtful."

"She's going to be so surprised!" Snip, snip, snip . . .

Coleman settled in to watch some tube. The day wore on. Coleman was surfing through the low numbers when he caught a local station. "Serge, we're on again . . ."

Serge snipped through a glossy page. "A rerun?"

"No, the second episode."

"Told you we'd get a series." Snip, snip.

"Serge, I don't think it's a series. The anchorwoman just said they were showing it for people to phone in tips to the police."

Serge stopped cutting and stared at Coleman. "Why are you doing this?"

"Doing what?"

"Tearing me down."

"I'm not. That's what they said on TV."

"Listen, our show isn't about any one person. This doesn't need to get ugly like Simon and Garfunkel."

Coleman shrugged and fired up a fattie. "How's the note coming?"

"Try finding a *Q*."

On TV in the background, two men wearing panty hose: *". . . Our latest demands for the release of Ally Street . . . One: no more sports movies where during the climactic game someone connected to the team is cheering from a hospital bed . . . Two: 'Born to Be Wild' banned from soundtracks about dickless suburbanites . . . Three: no more 'Judge' shows. What's with the chick always dragging in her loud, fat-ass best friend to yell at the guy that the loan of a month's rent was really a gift? That's not in my Constitution . . . Four . . ."*

Coleman toked up and held it as long as he could, then a coughing fit.

Serge pressed his hands down on the bedspread. "Coleman! You're blowing my little letters around!"

"Sorry." He picked paper squares off the floor. "Looks like a lot of work."

"It is," said Serge, squeezing Elmer's onto the back of an ampersand. "I don't know how the other kidnappers do it."

"... Seven: congressional investigation of theater snack counters. I want to buy ju-ju beans, not a ju-ju bean mine ... Eight: retroactive death penalty for the guy behind me during Star Trek II who told his girlfriend: 'Spock dies at the end'... Nine: What the fuck was William Hurt doing in Lost in Space? Not a demand, just curious ... Ten ..."

Coleman pointed at the completed portion of Serge's work along the edge of the bed. "Are the notes usually ten pages long?"

"No idea," said Serge. "Haven't read any before."

Coleman took another hit. "I think it's just supposed to be a single paragraph."

"Maybe for the other guys. But I take pride."

"What's in the note?"

"Well," said Serge, reaching for the first page, "I'm new to this and wasn't sure how it was supposed to work, so I remembered some stuff from an article I once read about effective business communication. They said you first have to understand your letter's objective. Land a job, pitch a product, apologize for banging the big client's wife. Next, gauge your audience. In kidnappings, usually hostile, so I thought I would open with a joke. After that, tell a little about myself, but not too much, because you want them to keep reading. Another thing the article said is if there's bad news, you bury it a little, soften them up first by emphasizing the positive. Then, when they're all happy and off guard, you tuck in the bombshell and hope they don't notice. Like, 'Why don't we get together sometime for lunch, and, oh, by the way, could you bring a million dollars in unmarked, nonsequential bills?'"

"Sounds like you know what you're doing," said Coleman.

"The only thing the note still needs is Proof of Life."

Ally was sitting on the bed. She had just finished trimming her toenails and was now painting little daisies on them. She felt she was being watched. She looked up at Serge and Coleman. "What?"

"We need Proof of Life," said Serge.

"What's that?" said Ally. She noticed Coleman's right hand. "Why does he have those scissors?"

"Don't make this difficult," said Serge. "We just need a little of your hair . . ."

VISTAMAX STUDIOS

A naked lightbulb came on in a props closet.

"Jesus Christ! What's wrong with those guys!" said Mel.

"They're psychopaths!" said Ian.

"Calm down," said Tori. "I just talked to them again. It's all taken care of. Another minor misunderstanding. I wasn't clear with my instructions."

"Minor! They're making movies! . . ."

". . . And sending them to the networks!" said Ian. "They're clearly insane!"

"No," said Tori. "Just intense. That's what you get with people in this line who are good. But everything's okay now. I had a very frank talk with them. That room's now probably the most boring in the whole town."

THE STANDARD HOTEL, ROOM 222

Ally ran across the room and over the top of the bed. "Get the hell away from me!"

Serge was right behind, followed by Coleman, bouncing over the mattress. "Just a little hair."

"Go to hell!"

"Coleman. Get her! She's circling back your way!"

"She got by me! She's too fast . . ."

Another lap around the room and over the bed.

"Coleman, don't run with scissors!"

VISTAMAX STUDIOS

The office of the Glick brothers was full of police again.

Sound technicians unplugged audio cables and packed up equipment.

"Sorry," apologized Detective Babcock. "The lieutenant says we've been putting in too many man-hours since the trail went cold. You have to understand—we haven't had any contact since . . . shoot, when was that?"

"You've done everything you could," said Tori. "We really appreciate the concern."

The sound technicians left. The detectives followed and got ready to close the door. Tori and the Glicks exhaled with relief.

Babcock stopped and turned around in the doorway.

Tori and the Glicks tensed and smiled again.

"There's still hope," said the detective. "Never let go of that."

"We won't. Thanks!" They waved.

"Who knows?" said Reamsnyder. "Six months down the road, something could turn up. We've seen crazier stuff."

Three people grinning. "Sure thing."

"Don't hesitate to call if you think of anything," said Babcock.

"We won't."

The door started closing. It opened.

"You have our cards?"

"Several," said Ian.

"You know where they are?"

"Somewhere," said Mel.

"Here's a few extras," said Babcock.

"Thanks."

"Well, we'll be going now." They waved from the doorway.

Tori waved back, talking to herself through smiling, gritted teeth. "Come on, close the door, that's it . . ."

They closed the door.

"Whew! . . ."

"Glad that's over . . ."

Crash!

The giant picture window on the side of the office shattered. A heavy rock skipped across the floor.

The door opened quickly.

"What was that!" said Babcock.

"Look!" said Reamsnyder. "A rock."

"Something's tied to it," said Babcock, picking it up and pulling off the string. "It's a ransom note."

TOKYO

The view from the seventy-fifth-floor office suite was blinding, even though it was after midnight. Garish, multicolored advertising lights made the night air glow like Times Square and Vegas combined, except in Japanese characters, except for the yellow McDonald's *M*. The streets below were clean but noisy with cars, buses, motorcycles.

A large man with pocked skin stared out the window, not focusing on anything in particular. Mr. Yokamura. He smoked a filterless cigarette pinched between his thumb and index finger. In the distance, a jumbo jet flew by at eye level on its approach to the international airport. The range created the illusion it was flying too slow to stay aloft. Mr. Yokamura had a phone to his head. It was ringing.

Behind him, on the other side of the office, was a flat-screen plasma TV. The volume had been turned off. It replayed the same thing Mr. Yokamura had seen too many times already: a pair of men wearing panty hose on their heads, voiced over in translation. When Ally Street held up her sheet of paper, it was superimposed with the Japanese symbol for HELP.

On the carpet was an executive putting cup and an array of five golf balls left midplay. A putter stuck halfway out the smashed glass of a display case containing priceless antiquities.

Someone answered the phone at the other end.

"Get me The Tat," said Mr. Yokamura.

No answer was necessary. Mr. Yokamura hung up and stared out the window with hands behind his back, watching another jetliner going the other way, across the Pacific.

VISTAMAX STUDIOS

A naked bulb came on in a props closet.

"I swear to God, I'm going to have a heart attack!" said Mel.

"A ransom note on a rock!" said Ian. "Where did you find those madmen!"

"Just calm down," said Tori. "It's not as bad as it looks."

"How can you say that?"

"Because we've still got the advantage," said Tori. "Except for that note, the police have nothing. Nothing at all. And that's how it's going to stay."

"I can't go through with this," said Ian.

"You don't have a choice!" snapped Tori. "The note said

they're going to call us again in . . ."—she looked at her watch—". . . fifteen minutes."

"But the cops will be there again," said Mel.

"Of course they're going to be there," said Tori. "That's why you need to get ahold of yourself. All we have to do is make it through this one last meeting and we're in the clear."

"They're not going to buy it," said Ian. "I can feel them closing in."

"Will you relax?" said Tori. "The police don't know a thing. They're totally in the dark."

The closet suddenly got very bright. The startled trio turned toward the open door.

"We're ready to take the call," said Detective Babcock.

HOLLYWOOD

Serge loved *The Big Lebowski*. He was on the edge of the bed, repeating lines with Jeff Bridges and John Goodman. He hit the back button again, replaying the scene leading up to the ransom phone call.

"This isn't a fucking game!"

"Oh, but it is a game. She was involved in her own kidnapping. You said so yourself . . ."

The actors checked their watches in the movie. Serge checked his own watch. "Dammit! We were supposed to make the call ten minutes ago! . . . Ally, they're going to want to hear your voice to prove you're alive. . . . Ally? . . ."

Serge ran out onto the balcony, pulled her back inside and yanked the curtain shut. "Does everyone remember their lines?"

Ally sat on the side of the bed and looked away. "Fuck off."

"Coleman, you ready? . . . *Coleman!*"

Coleman was sprawled facedown on the carpet with limbs bent in unintended directions like a chalk outline. Serge grabbed him under the armpits and sat him up against a wall. He lightly slapped his cheeks. "Coleman! Wake up! We have to make the call!"

Coleman's head began bobbing. "Ooooo. Serge, what happened?"

"Your regular afternoon power pass-out. Remember our code names?"

"Code names?"

"The ones we rehearsed all morning!"

"Oh, those." Coleman got up and grabbed a beer.

"Okay, everybody. This is it. Take your places." He flipped open a cell phone. "And . . . *action!*"

The Glicks' office was at full, fire-marshal capacity. The brothers, Tori, detectives, electronics experts. A sound guy was wearing headphones, adjusting knobs. There was a distant whapping noise from the helicopter hovering over the Vistamax lot, waiting to triangulate microwave signals. Nobody talking. Anxious smiles from the movie people. A clock ticked. Trickles of sweat ran down Ian's forehead.

Detective Reamsnyder handed him a handkerchief. "You're sweating."

"Uh, because we're dealing with bloodthirsty kidnappers?"

"Now you're starting to understand," said Babcock. "You should have called us from the beginning."

Reamsnyder checked his watch, then the Xerox of the crammed, ten-page ransom letter. "They're late. The note says they were supposed to call ten minutes ago."

"Let me see that thing again." Babcock took the letter from his partner and put on reading glasses:

Dear Ian and Mel Glick,

First, let me say I'm your biggest fan—love all your movies. Yes, sir, best stuff coming out of Tinseltown today. Like the wacky-but-touching mob comedy about the dyslexic don who keeps getting the wrong people killed but leaves the life after winning the Scramble-Gram championship. Or that totally fresh idea turning a *Saturday Night Live* skit into a full-length feature—genius! You can't crank them out fast enough for me!

Hey, I got a movie joke for you. It's from the legendary screenwriter Terry Southern, who left us far too soon, but I don't want to dwell on that injustice because the business article said to keep this positive. The joke is about a terrible film being made. When you tell it at parties, you can substitute one of your competitors. Anyway, this film is really stinking up the set, and finally the lead actress says, "Who do I have to fuck to get *off* this movie?" Get it? See how she turned the whole thing around? I laugh every time!

In case you're wondering, you don't know me. But I'm very dependable and ambitious, so we should have no problem working together. Speaking of which, I have a number of treatments I'm working on. Are you ready? Think Farrelly brothers. Personally, I don't care for their stuff, but there's nothing wrong with making a little money, eh? It's a nutty-but-moving feel-good about unsymmetrical conjoined twins attached at the butt and the forehead who weather their classmates' cruel taunts to win heart or hearts on the cheerleading squad. Okay, forget that. It sounded better in my head before I saw it glued together here. This next one's a lot better. Designed to attract a handsome A-list star who's never won an Academy Award and looking for a surefire vehicle to overcome his pretty-boy image. So in his role, he has to gain thirty pounds, wear makeup to deform his face *and* he's a retard. Start clearing space on the mantel! What am I talking about? You must get thousands of annoying letters every day asking for stuff, and I don't want you to throw it in the trash with the others. Right now, our business is what *I* can do for *you*.

Please keep reminding yourself that this is a happy letter. I'm very content as I paste these words, and we're still on good terms. Okay? Here's goes: We're the guys who kidnapped Ally Street. I don't know how you usually handle these things, whether you require proof of life. *Proof of Life.* Did you see that one? What's up with Meg Ryan? I decided I don't like her anymore. I wanted to cut some of Ally's hair, but she wouldn't let us, so those are some toenail clippings taped to the bottom of the page . . .

Rrrrrrrrrring!

Heads turned. The technician checked modulation levels and the caller ID: FORD OELMAN. He gave detectives the thumbs-up.

"Okay, everybody," said Babcock. "This is it. Take your places." He silently signaled the room—one finger, two fingers, *three*! The detective and Ian simultaneously picked up receivers.

"This is Ian. Talk to me."

"A million dollars in unmarked bills. No sequential serial numbers."

"Sure, but you'll have to give us time."

"You're stalling. The police are there, aren't they?"

Babcock shook his head at Ian, then made a swirling motion with a finger: Keep him talking.

"Absolutely not," said Ian. "We'd never—"

"It's okay," said Serge. "That's what I'd do . . . Put me on the speakerphone so we can all talk."

Ian looked at Babcock. The detective thought a moment, then nodded. Ian pressed a button.

Serge's voice rattled out of a small box on Ian's desk. "Who's in charge there?"

"Detective Babcock. What's all that noise in the background?"

"You mean the ionizing?"

Babcock gave the sound tech a look that asked if they had a location yet. The tech shook his head. Babcock turned back to the speaker. "I thought ionizers were quiet."

"Yeah, but I got fifteen of 'em. Because my room-mate's— . . . You're not eating, are you?"

"Roommate? How many of you are there?"

"I can't say any more," said Serge. "No offense—it's kidnapping rules. Otherwise I'm a big supporter of the LAPD."

"We appreciate it."

"No, really. You take a lot of unfair criticism. The public just doesn't understand why twenty guys with batons have to beat the piss out of some drunk who can't even stand up by himself. He could have a grenade, right? Or a vial of anthrax. That's what would be going through *my* mind."

"Let me speak to Ally."

"This is the part where you want to make sure she's still alive?"

"This is the part."

"All right . . . Hey, Ally! Someone wants to talk to you . . . Come on, Ally, don't be like that . . . Just say a couple words . . . Jesus, when I'm trying to watch a movie, I can't get you to shut up! . . ."

"Is everything all right?" asked Babcock.

"She's mad at me again," said Serge. "Are you married?"

"Put her on the phone."

"We're having technical difficulties."

"She's not there, is she?"

"No, she's definitely here, unfortunately."

"Why can't I speak with her?"

"She wants her water."

"You're withholding food and water?"

"Long story," said Serge. "But I'll make it short: Never kidnap an actress. Probably won't come up in your line, but this is absolutely my last . . . Ally! Please! You're embarrassing me in front of people—I'm on the speaker . . . You're in trouble when I get off the phone . . . Uh, Babcock? You still there?"

"I'm here."

"I'll have to call you back."

"Wait, I—"

Click.

Babcock looked at the sound tech. He shook his head. "Almost had 'em."

The detective turned to the Glicks, drenched in sweat. "You recognize that voice?"

They began stuttering.

The phone rang.

The detective hit the speaker button. "Babcock."

"Is this Babcock?"

"Who's this?"

"Coleman. He's trying to talk to her now . . ."

Yelling in the background: "Code name!"

"Oh, shit," said Coleman. "What do I do now, Serge?"

"You did it again!"

"Wait, I can fix it . . ."

The desk speaker made the sound of a beer can popping open.

"Detective?"

"I'm here."

"Yes, this is the kidnapper code-named Coleman

Lantern, and me and my partner code-named Serge *Suppressor* want to assure you that Ally is perfectly fine."

Babcock looked toward the sound tech, who held up a single finger: one more minute.

"You have to be reasonable," said Babcock. "We're going to need some kind of proof."

"Proof?" said Coleman. "Let me see . . . I got it . . . Give me a second to get across the room." They heard a rustling sound.

"Okay," said Coleman. "I'm standing next to Ally holding up a copy of today's newspaper."

Serge: "Gimme that phone!"

"I'm doing good here. I think he likes me."

"Give it to me!"

"I'm part of this, too!"

"Give it!"

"No!"

"Yes!"

"Ow! My ear!—"

Click.

Babcock turned. The sound tech shook his head.

Rrrrrrringgggggggg.

"Babcock here. Everything okay?"

"Make another mental note," said Serge. "Never work with a special-needs kidnapper."

"If we can't talk to Ally, could you and I meet somewhere?"

"I don't think so," said Serge, sitting down in front of the TV. "You'd catch me."

"I promise I won't."

Serge became distracted by *The Big Lebowski*. He turned up the volume.

"Dude, are you fucking this up?"

"Who was that?" asked Babcock.

"John Goodman," said Serge.

"The actor?"

"Yeah."

Babcock gave the others in the room a confused look, then turned back to the speaker. "How's he involved?"

"The driver on the ransom run," said Serge.

"What was that noise?" asked Babcock. "Sounded like gunfire?"

"Automatic . . ." Serge's voice became trance-like as he drifted deeper into the movie.

"What's happening?"

"We fucked up! Now she's dead!"

"Who was that?" said Babcock.

"Jeff Bridges."

"What the hell's going on?"

Serge didn't answer. He leaned closer to the TV and slowly shut the phone.

An amplified dial tone filled the office of the Glick brothers. Babcock pressed a button and cut it off. Silence. An initial odd moment where nobody moved or spoke.

Babcock looked at Tori, then the Glicks. "This is way, way off the record. And I pray to God I'm wrong, but I want to prepare you . . ."

"For what?" asked Ian.

"No matter what they say on the phone, there's a reason why they're not letting you talk to the victim."

"What is it?" asked Tori.

Reamsnyder took a deep breath. "There's a very high likelihood she's already dead."

"As I said, I hope we're wrong," added Babcock. "But we've worked a number of these. Not once has the victim turned up alive after the kidnappers refused to offer proof this long past the abduction."

"Oh, my God!" yelled Tori. "Our poor Ally!" Her sobbing face fell in her hands. The brothers ran over to console. Ian looked up. "We through here?"

The detectives nodded with sympathy and walked out of the office.

Reamsnyder turned to his partner in the hall. "Still think they're in on it?"

"Until about fifteen minutes ago," said Babcock. "But there's no way those calls were a put-on."

JAPAN

A massive warehouse complex stood in the industrialized outskirts of Tokyo, serviced by trucks and rail lines connected to the port. The area was similar to the rest of Tokyo but different in slight ways that would be hard to describe by someone who had never been there.

In the middle of the compound was central headquarters, and in the middle of that was a pecking order of executive offices around a large-capacity conference room. From there to the outside gates were eight levels of security. The first seven currently had two or three bodies each, draped over guard desks or slumped in corridors, some with hands still on holsters they hadn't been able to unsnap in time.

A man dressed completely in black walked down the hallway to the last security post. The guards overcame their initial shock and jumped into action. The intruder was in his late twenties, not quite tall, but lean with a high center of gravity. A flat-brimmed Billy Jack hat sat low to his eyes.

But the guards didn't notice any of that. What grabbed their attention and didn't let go was the full facial tattoo.

As with many young men, getting a tattoo seemed like such a great idea at the time. It had been a big night on the town with his buds, the kind that turns into a competition, each tattoo getting more and more outrageous until The Tat topped them all. Having his entire face done would have been enough, but the life-size skull sealed the deal.

Congratulations: You win!

Then life wore on, friends went their way, and the full facial tattoo, as in most cultures, hindered employment in sectors that didn't pay badly. He worked the hard construction jobs and under the lifts of auto repair shops, days filled entirely with growing rage.

Five years later The Tat was spending most of his time alone in an apartment with all mirrors and reflective surfaces removed. He channeled frustrations into a workout regimen that emphasized upper-body strength and the ancient disciplines of karate, double karate and anti-karate. He became an empty machine with an all-consuming purpose: hurt something. His income changed. Way, way up. To the degree that facial art was a drawback behind a cash register, its value couldn't be underestimated in the intimidation industry. He'd found his calling. If you wanted the best, you knew where to look.

The Tat continued down the warehouse hallway, two more bodies behind him at the final guard station. He reached for the handle of the innermost door.

On the other side, a large oval table sat in the middle of the conference room. Five men in long-sleeved shirts filled briefcases with cash. More currency fluttered rapidly in a row of counting machines. One of the men had a green visor and a ledger. The others, guns.

The door opened. Everyone looked. Any other time, they would have said, "How did you get in here?"

Instead: "What the hell did you do to your face?"

The Tat was ice. "Mr. Yokamura wants his money."

Stunned silence gave way to laughter and derision.

The Tat never raised his voice. "Give me the money."

The counting machines were turned off. Men reached across their chests for pistol grips.

The Tat filled four briefcases with a methodical velocity, leaving behind cash that had too much blood on it. And five bodies. The official causes of death would be inconclusive because of overlapping gunshots, knife wounds and compound fractures.

The Tat snapped the last of the briefcases shut, grabbed two in each hand and headed for the door. He began hearing an electronic pulse. The theme from *The Good, the Bad and the Ugly*.

He put the briefcases down and pulled a cell phone from his pocket.

"Los Angeles? . . . I understand. . . . No, I won't need any help."

HOLLYWOOD BOULEVARD

Standing room only inside a cramped dive on the 6200 block. The Frolic Room. A juke was going. Drinks flowed, clamor of conversation, everyone ignoring the TV on the back wall and the live helicopter feed of another freeway chase. An anchorman cut in with breaking news.

"Hey, look!" One of the patrons pointed up at the set. "It's *Crazy About Movies!*"

If the bar was a boat, it would have capsized. Everyone stampeded to the end with the TV. Someone unplugged the juke. Two men in panty hose appeared on-screen in front of a marble wall. A boom box sat on the ground, playing the show's new intro music by Bob Seger.

"... *In those Hollywood nights! ... In those Hollywood hills!* ..."

Serge reached down and turned off the music.

"*We're here today at Westwood Memorial Cemetery, where billboards for the latest releases rise above the palms. But the real attractions are the historic stars buried everywhere. Billy Wilder, Natalie Wood, Dean Martin. They also have my favorite epitaph of all time* ..." Serge held up a charcoal rubbing of a nearby tombstone:

JACK LEMMON
IN . . .

"... *Which brings us to our first guest, Marilyn Monroe.*"

Two stockinged heads turned around and looked at the crypt behind them. They faced the camera again. "*That was great,*" said Serge. "*We'll be sure to have her back on* ... *And now some things we hate: new special-edition DVDs that come out right after I bought the first 'special edition.'*"

"*The price of weed,*" said Coleman.

"*The guy in the Jaguar car ads who pronounces it Jag-you-are.*"

Coleman: "*Yeah! Jag-you-are!*"

"*Kill that motherfucker!*"

The bar began cheering.

"*Celebs who are stuck-up* ..." Serge looked off camera. "... *like Ally Street.*"

"*Jennifer Aniston isn't stuck-up,*" said Coleman. "*She smokes weed.*"

"Russell Crowe's stuck-up, but Don Adams is a regular guy," said Serge. *"We caught up with him the other day."*

"He's our bitch."

"And now our next guest." Serge stood and began clapping. *"Let's hear it for Juror Number Five!"*

A chunky man in shorts and an untucked golf shirt walked on camera, talking into a cell phone.

Serge smiled.

The man sat down and continued talking on the phone.

Serge continued smiling.

The man finally finished his conversation and hung up. *"So, you wanted to get my take on that murder trial in Long Beach?"*

"No," said Serge. *"I just told you that to get you on the show. You have no take. You're an idiot."*

Coleman threw a coat over the juror's head from behind, and they began beating the crap out of him.

The Frolic Room went wild.

Three new people entered the dark, narrow pub and walked up behind the hooting crowd. "The best dive in L.A.," said Serge. "Opened in 1930 as Frank Fink's. The *F* on the sign is the same. Cozy, after-hours hangout of the early stars, who slipped over from the legendary Pantages Theater next door. That mural's a Hirschfeld of past customers. Groucho, Bette Davis." He put his hand on a stool. "And this is where Kevin Spacey sat in *L.A. Confidential.* The whole place oozes Chandler."

"That dude from *Friends*?" asked Coleman.

"Raymond. *The Big Sleep, Lady in the Lake.*"

Coleman shrugged.

"People think of him as the king of the noir mysteries, but he was really a great humorist. Wrote classic private eye lines like, 'I'm an occasional drinker, the kind of guy who goes out for a beer and wakes up in Singapore with a full beard.'"

"Who does that remind me of?" said Coleman.

"He did hard-boiled the way it was meant. Today there's way too much soft-boiled."

"What's the difference?"

"Like in a hard-boiled, people spike horse and get their jaws broken with brass knuckles. In soft-boiled, the mystery is solved by some lady's cat." Another cheer went up in the bar. Serge tapped the shoulder of the man in front of him. "What's all the excitement?"

The man pointed at the television. "*Crazy About Movies!* is on."

". . . *Things we dig: Mark V Limited, Dicker and Dicker of Beverly Hills, Spiegel Catalog, Chicago 60609 . . .*"

"I love that show," said Serge.

"Me, too." The man gave Serge a double-take. "Have we met?"

"Don't think so."

"No, you definitely look familiar . . ." The lack of panty hose threw him off, but then he noticed Coleman and Ally, and all the tumblers fell into place. "It's them! Hey, everybody! It's Ally and the *Crazy About Movies!* dudes!"

Ally glowed as she was mobbed for autographs. Serge and Coleman, too.

"We love you guys! . . ."

"You're the greatest! . . ."

Ten different people slipped Coleman drugs. The bartender offered free drinks and a stack of pages. "About a bartender with special powers from a plutonium leak . . ."

Serge hurriedly signed autographs. "Guys, we need to get out of here. We're attracting too much attention."

"Serge!"

"Dallas!"

Dallas pointed at the TV. "You didn't tell me you had a show."

"We just got picked up."

"So what are you doing here?"

"Trying to get out."

"I have a limo," said Dallas. "We're heading to a party. Very exclusive, discreet. You won't be bothered."

PANAMA CITY, FLORIDA

The curtains were drawn on a massive condo penthouse overlooking the Gulf of Mexico.

Inside, no light but the seventy-two-inch big-screen TV. Bone-rattling Dolby surround-sound, subwoofer under the couch. The quarterback took the snap.

"He's open! He's open! . . . Damn . . ."

The pasty man in a crimson bathrobe was right on the edge of the overstuffed sofa, like he hadn't already seen the '92 championship game five hundred times. "Pick up the strong safety! Pick up the strong safety! . . ."

The phone rang. He ignored it.

It kept ringing. He checked caller ID.

A red football helmet flew across the room. "You better be calling to tell me everything's fixed."

He listened.

"What do you mean they're dead, too? . . . What happened this time? . . . You trying to tell me they were killed by a bunch of seals? . . . Oh . . . Look, enough fucking around. I want The Fullback! . . . You already did? You should have said that in the first place!"

LOS ANGELES

Another *Hard Day's Night* chase, this one up Hollywood Boulevard from the Frolic Room. Serge, Coleman, Ally and Dallas dove in the back of a waiting limo and locked the doors. People beat on tinted windows as they took off.

Serge stared back out the opera window as the crowd grew small. He turned around. Coleman was snorting something off the back of Dallas's hand. The stretch took a skirting route along the hills until it passed through imposing iron gates and up a long sloping drive to an English estate. Women in bikinis pranced across the lawn. Others played volleyball on trucked-in beach sand. More antics in the lagoon.

Dallas got out. "What do you think?"

Serge froze and grabbed Coleman by the arm. "We've made it to the mountaintop."

"Where are we?"

"The Playboy Mansion."

"All right!"

Low-grade race-car drivers and tennis stars immediately glommed onto Ally. Servants issued them swim trunks at poolside cabanas.

"Coleman, over there!" said Serge. "I've wanted to see that my whole life!"

"What is it?"

They trotted past a large picture window in the back of the manse. Hef was sitting at an octagonal table in silk pajamas, playing gin with his regular gang from the old days.

One of the players lit a cigar. "I don't know why you're still so sore."

"I'm nobody's bitch."

"That's not what I heard on TV."

Serge splashed down a watery staircase until the pool level was up to his chest. Coleman and Ally followed. It grew dark.

Coleman looked around. "We're in a cave."

"The infamous grotto. Mere mortals can only hope."

"What do we do in the grotto?"

"Mingle." Serge splashed his way over to a bare-chested Miss September. She ignored him with an askance gaze that said he was plankton in her world.

Serge coughed on purpose.

She continued staring off, but this time the look said he was a nematode.

Serge tapped her on the shoulder.

She turned.

Serge waved energetically. "Howdy!"

"Uh . . . hi."

Serge took a seat on the boulder next to her. "So, you like to mingle?" He began idly kicking his feet in the water. "I love mingling. And hate it. Oh, I've got the start down pat. Just jump right in and go to it: 'Hey, Bill, golf handicap, the

Dow, will you look at the size of this honkin' kitchen! Blah, blah, blah . . .' And suddenly you find yourself at The Point. We all know The Point. Like when you're on the phone with someone you don't know very well, and you're both politely trying to end the call but can't get the timing right. And you become more and more self-conscious and finally say something really stupid: 'Listen, anyway, I got this thing. So, like, bye.' And you hang up and smack yourself: 'Jeez! I sounded like such an idiot!' Then you start resenting *them* because they have something on you. Know what I mean? Ever have that happen? Huh?"

"It's been nice," said the centerfold, "but I think I see someone I know—"

"I'm sure you do," said Serge. "So back to us: We're at one of those points now. Actually, way past it, if you want to split hairs. And there are two conversations going on: the one between me and you, and the other one inside my head: How the hell do I get out of this? What a mistake. I thought you might have something interesting to say, but you're just all tits and— . . . Wow! Now what does *that* shocked expression mean? . . . Anyway, for me, that's how mingling is all the time. So, like, bye."

Serge splashed his way over to two older men with gray hair and gold chains who looked like Peter Lawford and Joey Bishop, but weren't.

"Howdy! My handicap's down to fifteen, the Dow's killing me and every house I've ever owned could fit in that fucking kitchen." Serge grinned.

They smiled uncomfortably.

"I'm naturally insecure," said Serge, jerking a thumb over his shoulder. "When I was back there watching you guys talk, I started imagining all kinds of things, like you cats are hatching another plan to rape our retirement accounts, and I'm not on the CC: list . . ."

Dallas splashed into the grotto. "Serge. Found another party. But it's a tight window."

Serge smiled at the guys in the gold chains and pointed back out the entrance. "Anyway, like, I got this thing . . ."

34

VISTAMAX

A closet in the props department.

"Who are those lunatics?" yelled Ian. "I thought they were going to blow everything!"

"Could you believe those ransom calls?" said Mel. "Now the cops think she's dead and . . . Tori, why are you smiling?"

"Because of our incredible luck."

"Every time shit happens, you say something like that!"

"Don't you see?" said Tori. "Death sells. Imagine the coverage after my press release. Then, in a few weeks, an even bigger wave of publicity when she makes the harrowing escape. This is better than before!"

Mel grabbed his stomach. "Why doesn't it feel better?"

Tori opened her cell phone and punched numbers. "We just have to make sure she stays completely out of sight while she's supposed to be dead."

LAX

Serge's cell phone began ringing. He didn't hear it.

"Al-ly! Al-ly! Al-ly! . . ."

A chugging contest.

The cheering crowd formed a giant ring around her and Coleman. They were up in the Encounter Restaurant. Most people don't realize it's a restaurant, but almost everyone recognizes the futuristic building on spider legs that serves as the airport's architectural signature. The restaurant is so tall and distinct that you can spot it from any point at the airport, like through the long line of picture windows at the international gates, where spurts of incoming passengers filtered through Customs.

Officials inspected passports and immigration forms. In the background: armed military, German shepherds and a quarantine zone for potted plants that people still insisted on bringing into the country for some reason. Ten lines and ten long, flat tables covered with unpredictable suitcase contents revealing the infinite variety of life. A separate area off to the side for random body searches. Also: language problems, crying children and a fast-talking guy in a red silk shirt explaining the case of Kahlúa he'd failed to declare from Cabo San Lucas.

More passengers poured off the umbilical arm from a Boeing 747. A chorus of gasps. Everyone stared just a little too long at that skull-face tattoo, then quickly looked anywhere else. The Tat was pulled out of line for the full, high-risk search, just like every other time.

They tore through everything, felt luggage linings for secret compartments, patted him down, used wands, brought over the dogs, even unscrewed his stick deodorant to see if something was stashed below.

302 # TIM DORSEY

Whistle clean. They handed The Tat his documents and tried to smile.

The Tat didn't make the return effort. He exited the international air side and merged with a rushing river of foot traffic in the main terminal. A beeping cart came by with someone in a leg cast. He passed a gate pumping more passengers into the airport from a Birmingham flight connecting in Atlanta. An enormous man with pecs bulging out of a Roll Tide jacket came down the ramp. He checked an overhead sign and made a right turn for baggage claim.

Serge stared out a window of the Encounter Restaurant, watching an airbus with a sunburst foreign insignia thrust up at a sharp takeoff angle.

Ally was mobbed for autographs.

Coleman stumbled over to the window. "I've never come to an airport before when I wasn't flying."

"Most people don't," said Serge. "That's why I do it all the time. Absorb the energy. Lives in motion. Sometimes I come just to ride the monorails, the last great free entertainment value in America before they started asking for boarding passes."

Coleman looked down. Tiny people caught taxis, checked in curbside and smoked rapidly. "I think I've seen this building before. Like in a movie."

"One of L.A.'s most recognizable landmarks," said Serge. "Dozens of films set in this city have used it as background shots to bookmark the location."

Coleman pointed back at the dining room. "It's the weirdest restaurant I've ever seen, like the inside of some crazy spaceship."

"That's what it's supposed to look like," said Serge. "It's the Encounter Restaurant, as in alien encounter. Market research showed enough people wanted to simulate the experience of being abducted by extraterrestrials, getting beamed up to a flying saucer and having to pay a lot for dinner."

Dallas Reels worked his way across the room, slipping tiny envelopes into hands. "Hey, Serge, new party. You in?"

"Sure. Be with you in a minute." Serge stared out the window again. A man in a Roll Tide jacket got into a Hertz courtesy bus. "Look at all those people down there. Each with their own hopes, dreams, heartaches." He watched a man with a full facial tattoo climb in the back of a cab. "Sometimes I wonder what they're all up to."

35

REDONDO BEACH

A black stretch limo sat in the driveway of an expansive vacation retreat. A rented Taurus pulled up behind it. The driver didn't get out.

Inside the house:

"It's Ally Street!"

"It's the guys from TV!"

Another mob scene. The buzz swept the party. Coleman ended up on the back porch, surrounded by men in white robes.

"Love your work! . . ."

One of the men pumped a keg and handed Coleman a plastic cup of draft. "Have you ever given any serious thought to joining a fraternal organization?"

Serge and Ally were trapped in the kitchen. More autographs. A young man in a leather jacket shook Serge's hand. "You're my hero. You say everything that's on everyone's mind." He handed Serge a cassette. "Could you review my movie on your next show? Shot it with a friend's video camera. About a misunderstood genius trapped in the body of a loser . . ."

A robed man held the keg spigot over Coleman's cup. ". . . And if you like sports, we have a strong intramural program. Remember the solar temple cult up in Frisco? We beat them silly every year in flag football. Except last year they forfeited because of that cyanide business. Their note said Earth was about to take a meteor the size of Utah, but they really just didn't want to face us in the semifinals . . ."

More autographs. A young man in a trench coat piled on the praise. "I love you guys!"

"Thanks," said Serge, signing a napkin.

"Here's my business card. I have a wine and cheese showing next week. I'm a performance artist."

Serge handed the napkin back. "Performance artist?"

"I wanted to be a regular artist but didn't have any talent. The National Endowment doesn't understand."

"What's your medium?" asked Serge.

"Postmodern naturalism. I go to the landfill and collect everyday items that represent the entropy of civilization. Then I put them in my ass and take pictures."

Serge wormed his way through the packed living room and onto the porch. "Coleman? . . ." He went back inside and stuck his head in the den. "Ally, you seen Coleman?"

Ally looked up from the broken arm she was autographing. "Hasn't been in here."

"Where'd that idiot go? . . . Coleman! . . ." Serge walked down a hall, checking bedroom doors. Nothing but drugs and sex. He opened the last one. "Coleman!"

"Hi, Serge," said Coleman, wearing a long white robe. "Meet my new friends."

He was encircled by men in similar robes, holding candles.

"What the hell do you think you're doing?"

"Joining their club," said Coleman. "This is my initiation. Real nice guys . . ." They handed Coleman another beer and gave him a light for the joint in his mouth. "See what I mean? I've found a home."

Serge glanced at a table against the wall: stainless steel tray with surgical instruments. "Coleman! They're going to castrate you!"

"No, we're not," said one of the robed men.

"What are those tools?"

"There was a bris last night."

Serge grabbed Coleman and dashed from the room. The robed men watched the door close. "Damn."

They collected Ally from the kitchen and rushed out the front door. Dallas was waiting in the driveway. "There you are." He pointed at his beeper. "We have to hurry."

"Could you just take us back to our car?" asked Serge.

"No problem."

The limo headed inland a half hour and pulled up behind a rented Chrysler parked just down the street from the Frolic Room.

"Thanks for the lift."

"Sure you don't want to go with us?" said Dallas.

"Been a long day." Serge climbed out of the stretch and reached in his pocket for keys. Something up the street caught his eye. "Uh-oh." He leaned back in one of the limo's windows. "Decided to go to that party after all. We'll follow in our car."

"Cool."

They jumped in the convertible. Coleman turned on the radio. "What made you change your mind?"

"Can't go back to our hotel with that car following us."

"Which one?"

"*Don't look!* . . . The Taurus. It's just like with the Crown Vic."

"How long has he been there?"

"Since the cult house. Maybe the airport."

The Chrysler shadowed the limo, and the Taurus shadowed the Chrysler. They headed up the canyon, vehicles down-shifting, climbing higher and higher into the hills. Mansions rising straight up from the road. Serge followed Dallas's taillights another mile and parked behind the limo. He got out and turned around. Three houses back, a Taurus turned off its lights.

"I knew it."

Inside the house, the usual. "It's Ally!" "It's the TV guys!"

Except it was later in the evening, everyone deeper in the bag. The excitement took on its own life. Yelling, shoving fans yearning to touch them, feet stepped on. A uniformed man with a serving tray reached over several heads to hand Serge a stuffed mushroom and a stack of pages. "Caterer finds sixteenth-century recipe that just might take down the pope!"

There was a stir at the front entrance. People reflexively cleared a path when the giant in a crimson jacket ducked his head and came through the door. Serge noticed the ripple in the crowd. He traced it back to the meaty, sun-burned head sticking up above the rest, advancing toward him.

Coleman lost his beer in the jostling. "Where'd all these people come from?"

"I can't move," said Ally, fighting for elbow room to autograph stuff.

"To the balcony!" said Serge.

They wiggled their way outside, but it was only worse.

Then they couldn't wiggle back. Instead, the mass of fans and autograph collectors followed and forced them farther out onto the balcony, until they were trapped against the metal railing over a sheer drop.

"What are we going to do?" asked Coleman.

"I'm getting crushed again," said Ally.

Serge didn't hear them. He was looking back in the house, focused on that one large head bobbing above a whole living room of heads, working its way toward the balcony. Serge turned around: that great sparkling view of Los Angeles again. He looked down over the railing. Not an option.

There was a creaking sound. Ally latched on to the railing. "What the hell was that?"

A sizable lurch. People screamed and grabbed each other as they lost balance. But they didn't go back inside. If anything, they pressed closer to the railing in hysteria. More creaking and another lurch, another round of shrieks. Serge looked at the home next door, a good two feet higher than it had been a minute ago.

"Everyone, back in the house!" yelled Serge. "We have to get off the balcony!"

They were screaming too loud.

"Coleman! Ally! We have to get inside!"

"I can't move!"

"Neither can I!"

Another lurch. Then a gunshot.

The yelling stopped.

Serge raised his pistol in the air again and squeezed off two more rounds.

The yelling started again, but at least they were moving back inside. And how. It quickly became a panicked stampede into the living room. Glass shattering, coffee tables collapsing, doors ripped off hinges. Strong as he was, the giant in the crimson jacket couldn't fight the tide. His eyes momentarily met Serge's on the other side of the room. Distilled rage. Then Serge was off again, hugging close to a wall, skirting the crowd and leading his friends to a side exit in the split-level garage. The man watched helplessly, cursing and beating on the people carrying him backward out the front door.

Pandemonium in the street. The Fullback broke free of the mob and sprinted up the road toward a Chrysler Sebring parked at the curb. But the three passengers were already inside. Serge turned the ignition.

The Fullback was at max stride, ready to dive onto the trunk. Serge hit the gas. The giant took a desperate swipe at the back of the car with his right hand, coming up with a fistful of air. The convertible sped away.

The giant spun on the balls of his feet, running back to his own Taurus. He threw it in gear and took off after the Sebring . . . *Ker-thump, ker-thump, ker-thump.* A stiletto knife through the sidewall of a flat tire on the driver's side.

Serge checked the empty rearview and eased off the pedal. He reached the end of the street and gently tapped the brakes for an expertly controlled slide through the hairpin turn. He accelerated in the other direction on a switchback, the only way to traverse the steepest sections of the Hollywood Hills.

Suddenly, a high-rpm roar overwhelmed the convertible. "What can that—?"

A jet-black ninja motorcycle shot between Serge and the guardrail with no room to spare.

The cyclist spun out with a smoking back tire and stopped in the middle of the road, facing the Chrysler.

Serge slammed the brakes. The gang stared in disbelief as the cyclist dismounted: black cowboy boots, long black overcoat and black helmet with tinted visor. The helmet came off.

"Holy Jesus!" said Ally. "Look at his face!"

Serge grabbed the top of the windshield and stood up. "What were you thinking?"

The Tat answered by throwing open his overcoat, revealing an array of menacing weapons from local pawnshops. Daggers, throwing stars, pistols. He whipped out nunchucks and twirled them around his head with invisible speed. The demonstration went on for some time. Finally, he stopped and flicked a pair of switches on the sticks, clicking open razor points at each end. The twirling started again.

Serge looked up at the starry sky and sighed.

The Tat eventually stowed the sticks. He crossed his arms over his chest and drew a pair of .44 revolvers. He tossed the guns back and forth between his hands. He started twirling them.

Serge tapped his watch. "Get to the point!"

The Tat turned with his back to the car, pointed the pistols over his shoulders and fired. Mirrors on both sides of the convertible snapped off with sparks. The Tat faced them again and took three dramatic steps toward Serge, raising the revolvers. "Now you die . . ."

The sound of thunder. The Tat looked up.

A twenty-room house slid down the mountainside and crashed into the street.

"Oooooo." Coleman winced. "You can only see his feet sticking out."

"But no ruby slippers."

The road was completely blocked. So Serge made a five-point turn in the narrow cliffside street and started back the other way.

"What was that guy's problem?" said Ally.

"It's L.A.," said Serge. "Everyone craves attention."

To the left of his periphery, a dark figure in a crimson jacket bounded down the hillside with incredible speed and agility. By the time Serge noticed, the phantom had reached the edge of the road just ahead of the convertible, still running full clip.

A jarring thud. He landed on the Chrysler's hood, face and arms against the windshield.

Coleman pointed. "Who's *this* guy?"

"Kaiser Sosee." Serge turned on the windshield wipers.

The Fullback snapped them off. He punched through the windshield with his right fist, reaching for Serge's neck.

Serge leaned back. "Now we definitely have to report the car stolen."

The Sebring headed down the canyon. Fingers grasped for Serge's face, just out of reach. The Fullback tried pulling his arm back out.

"Looks like he's stuck," said Coleman.

"He is," said Serge, hitting a blinker and turning onto Hollywood Boulevard. "Mustn't know anything about safety glass. You can punch through, but the laminated epoxy layer holds it all together and you can't get your arm back out. Like Chinese finger cuffs."

With his free hand, The Fullback began ripping open the hole around his arm. Blood squirted everywhere.

"I think he figured it out," said Coleman.

Ally leaned forward from the backseat. "I don't like him up there."

"Gee. I'm sorry," said Serge. "I won't put him there next time."

"Get him off!"

"I'm working on it."

A hand came through the enlarged hole in the glass. Serge swerved. The hand went back out.

"Coleman, what would they do in the movies?"

"If we were in Italy, you could take him out with a vegetable cart."

"But it's America."

"Then you're supposed to drive down an alley with a bunch of boxes and trash."

"That's Jersey." The hand came through the window again. Serge viciously cut the wheel left and right. The hand went back out.

"He's still there!" yelled Ally.

"Not now!" said Serge.

The Fullback had just gotten to his knees, preparing to lunge over the top of the windshield. Serge tapped the brakes. The giant flattened to the hood.

Traffic thickened as they raced toward the intersection in front of Grauman's. Tourists snapped photos as the rental car whizzed by.

"Check it out," said Coleman. "One of those double-decker tour buses."

"I see it," said Serge. "They look cool, but so much depends on your driver, especially if they do the PA thing. I once got a Teamster *way* too into Tallulah Bankhead."

"Slow down," said Coleman. "I can't fire this joint."

"Light it under the dash like you usually do."

"Okay."

The Fullback's arm was through the windshield again, inches from Serge's face.

"He's still up there!" said Ally.

Serge leaned his head back as far as he could, The Fullback's fingertips brushing his Adam's apple. "Will you shut up back there!"

"Did you just tell me to shut up?" Ally grabbed Serge's head from behind.

"What the hell are you doing?"

The Fullback grabbed Serge's neck from in front.

Serge couldn't breathe. Couldn't move his head. He desperately reached for the dashboard, but it was just out of range. The grip on his throat grew tighter. He became faint. He tried calling for Coleman under the dash, but no voice would come out. With the last effort in his body, Serge threw an elbow over his shoulder, catching Ally in the jaw. She released her grip and fell back, allowing Serge to reach the dash. He pressed the washer button, squirting The Fullback in the eyes with Serge's Super Windshield Fluid. The Fullback screamed and clawed at his face. Serge swerved a final time, and the giant rolled off the Chrysler's hood into the street.

Coleman sat back up, puffing a fully involved joint. "Hey, where'd he go?"

"We came to his stop."

Behind them, a double-decker tour bus screeched to an emergency halt after a series of disgusting thumps. Passengers hung out the windows and looked down at the wheels.

Something hit Serge in the back of the head. "Ow! What was that for?"

"Pull over!" yelled Ally.

"What's the matter?"

"Pull over this second!"

Serge made a left onto a dark side street. He parked and turned around. "What now!"

"I'm getting out!"

"You're not going anywhere."

"You hit me!"

"That was a defensive blow," said Serge. "Technically, I'm guarding the plate."

Ally swung a leg over the side of the car.

Serge pulled his pistol. "Don't go any farther."

"You're not going to shoot."

"I'm warning you."

"Tori will find out."

"Try me."

"You're bluffing."

Hollywood Tattletale

VIGIL ATTENDANCE WAY UP

HOLLYWOOD—Abducted actress Ally Street is now presumed dead by police after ransom talks broke down during a series of bizarre telephone calls received at Vistamax Studios, according to an unofficial press release from a source close to the negotiations.

Hopes were high for the star of the indefinitely shelved *All That Glitters* when officials received a cheerful ransom note. But the mood quickly soured during jumbled conversations that indicated Ms. Street's kidnappers were either international terrorists or local drug abusers. The shocking and exclusive revelations of the terrorist angle came to light during one of the cryptic calls. While the captors made no political demands, they reportedly read a brief statement protesting a recent spate of police brutality before referring to a cache of grenades and anthrax.

In a related development, detectives were observed leaving the home of TV and movie personality John Goodman. Repeated knocks on Goodman's door went suspiciously unanswered, and police would only say it was "just a cordial visit." Caught outside a trendy Brentwood eatery, Goodman's publicist said he had no knowledge of the police visit, but was confident that all the facts would come out.

Although Goodman's name came up numerous times during the hostage talks, police theorize that the actor had only limited and incidental contact with the abductors, who were dropping his name to score points. When asked about their theory, an official police spokesman said, "That's not our theory."

By nightfall, hundreds of fans could be seen leaving flowers outside the Vistamax gates, where a well-attended candlelight vigil lasted past midnight and featured touching performances by many top musicians on the vigil circuit. While few of the mourners actually knew Street, most whom we spoke with said "we felt as though we knew her" or "we wished we had known her" or "how'd you like that notepad shoved up your ass?"

Meanwhile, Street's publicist and agent Tori Gersh called a hastily arranged press conference to demand an official inquiry into the source of the police leaks. "Each new detail is so painful," said a tearful Ms. Gersh. "Like the fact that they were withholding food and water."

Police had no response to Gersh's accusations, but word that the department had been accused of something prompted sporadic looting in several neighborhoods and tied up traffic leaving the Lakers game.

BEVERLY HILLS HOTEL, THE POLO LOUNGE

Lush leaves and primrose blooms filled the courtyard. Tori and the Glicks huddled around a small café table under the warm California sun. A folded-over copy of the *Hollywood Tattletale* lay between them. Tori's wine had a couple of sips missing, but the brothers' glasses were already empty, and they waved for the waiter as if they were marooned.

People at other tables leaned and whispered. ". . . *The Glicks . . .*" A snappy waiter arrived, towel over his arm, and poured Merlot with ceremony.

Mel grabbed his glass with both hands. "I can't take the stress."

Ian grabbed his chest. "I can't breathe."

"Drink your wine," said Tori. "It'll help you relax."

Ian guzzled and motioned the waiter for a refill. "How can you be so calm?"

"Because it's over," said Tori, reclining in her chair and savoring another sip. "A few loose ends, but the hard part is done. Instead of heart attacks, you should be celebrating."

Her confidence became contagious. "You really think so?"

"Absolutely," said Tori, swirling the wine under her nose. "I'll admit it got pretty hairy for a while. You wouldn't be human if you didn't feel it. But that's all done. You two have been worrying so long you've forgotten to stop."

"She's right," said Ian. "We're making ourselves crazy for nothing."

"That's more like it," said Tori.

Mel nodded. "What can possibly go wrong now?"

"Nothing," said Tori. "We're completely in the clear."

Excited yelling erupted from the hotel. All heads turned.

Two waiters blocked the doorway to the Polo Lounge. "Sirs! You're not dressed—"

"Get the fuck out of my way! Do you know who we are? I know the Glicks personally . . . Hey, Ian! Mel! Be right with you! . . ."

The brothers strained to see what was going on.

Two waiters stumbled backward. Serge and Coleman marched quickly toward the table. Tori covered her eyes. "Holy Jesus!"

"What's shakin'?" said Serge.

A flustered maître d' ran over and began apologizing to the Glicks. Two beefy security guards arrived seconds later, grabbing the intruders.

"Let me go!" yelled Serge. "You're making a big mistake! We know them!"

The maître d' looked at the brothers. "You know them?"

The stunned Glicks shook their heads.

One of the guards jerked Serge by the arm. "Okay, fella, get moving . . ."

"We're the kidnappers!"

Ian screamed. Mel dumped wine on himself. "We know them! We know them! . . ."

"Is everything all right?" asked the maître d'.

"Yes," said Mel.

"Just go away," said Ian.

The maître d' nodded for guards to release them. Then he backed away from the table, bowing.

Serge straightened out his shirt. "That's better. I'd heard good things about this place, but I was beginning to wonder . . ." He scooted a chair up between the brothers for a tight fit. "So, this is the inner sanctum."

"Tori!" Ian demanded. "What the hell are they doing here?"

"We were never supposed to meet them!" said Mel. "That was the understanding."

Tori turned to Serge. "What *are* you doing here?"

"Gellin' like a felon."

"Dammit," said Tori. "You were supposed to call me this morning!"

"Change in plans." Serge took a small canvas bag off his shoulder and set it in his lap. "I've learned that whenever there's a possibility for misunderstanding, it's better to take the time and meet face-to-face. Shows respect." Serge raised a finger to the waiter. "Your finest water." He pointed at Coleman. "Beer, right?"

Coleman nodded, digging a fist into the bowl of mixed nuts on the table.

"Tori!" whispered Ian. "We're not insulated anymore!"

"That's the only reason we agreed in the first place!" whispered Mel. "You guaranteed no contact with lowlifes!"

"Lowlifes?" said Serge, bolting up straight. "You must be thinking of other kidnappers. Me and my partner are all about culture." Serge surveyed the courtyard. "Like this place. We could get used to meeting you here."

"Serge!" said Tori. "You're scaring me. What's happened? What's wrong?"

"Give me a minute," said Serge. "I have to set up." He reached in the canvas bag and placed his iPod on the table, connecting it to portable speakers. "I can't believe I'm actually here! Wanted to come my whole life, but never thought I'd get the chance." Serge worked the click-wheel to his L.A. soundtrack. Music started. "Thousands of people have been made and destroyed in this very courtyard. I'll bet you two guys have all kinds of juicy stories! Were you here way back before cell phones? Did waiters really used to carry the old rotary jobs to your table when you got a call?" He leaned forward on his elbows and grinned. "I'm all ears!"

"We just have drinks."

". . . *Welcome to the Hotel California* . . ."

Serge sat up and frowned. "That's no fun." He pulled a hanging vine toward his face and sniffed a flower. "Did you know this used to be a wasteland of undesirable real estate? Until they opened this joint in 1912. They said they were crazy! Then Pickford and Fairbanks built nearby and the rest of Hollywood followed . . ."

"*. . . Such a lovely place . . .*"

"What really blows my mind is there's no traffic-light eyesore at the intersection out front. And it's a five-way fucker, too. Now *that's* class. If this was Miami, you'd be hosing glass and blood twenty-four seven. But out here you just take turns. Because you're civilized . . ."

The maître d' hovered nervously. "Sir, I'll have to ask you to turn off the music."

"It's my soundtrack."

"We don't want any trouble."

"You should have thought of that before you let the Eagles put a picture of this place on the album cover."

"Sir, please . . ."

"*Allllllllll* right." Serge reluctantly pressed the stop button. "There. You happy? Is it true you can check out anytime you like, but you can never leave?"

The maître d' backed away, bowing again.

Serge leaned to Ian. "Another fashionable Eagles-hater. Probably heard *The Long Run* a million times at his frat house, and it pushed him off the ledge."

The next table was staring. Serge turned and grinned. A sixtyish woman had dangling earrings that belonged on a chandelier. She sneered back.

Serge began singing to her: "*Woooo! Hoooo! Witchy Woman! See how high—*"

Tori grabbed his arm. "Will you stop that!"

"Has anyone been to the gift shop?" said Serge. "Went looking for a souvenir pin, but they just had a bunch of junk out of my price range like baseball caps with the hotel's name in diamonds . . . Oooo. I . . . spy . . . souvenir . . . *matches!*" He snatched the pack out of the ashtray, dropped them in his shirt pocket and threw his arms up. "He shoots! He scores!"

Mel shielded his face. "Everyone's looking!"

"Yes, sir," said Serge, looking up at trees draped in strands of white Christmas lights. "I could get used to noshing here with you on a regular basis."

"We're never meeting again!" said Mel. "If we had known—"

"You don't have a choice," said Serge, fiddling with his iPod. "The change in plans. It's pretty complex so we'll have to start seeing a lot of each other until it sorts out."

"Tori! Do something!"

"What's changed?" she asked.

"I don't quite know how to put this . . ." said Serge. He stuck the iPod in Ian's face and grinned. "Holds ten thousand songs"—he pulled it back and fiddled some more—"It's like the ransom note. Good news, bad news, so don't overreact until you've heard both parts . . ."

"Oh, Jesus!" Ian flagged down their waiter. "Bring the bottle!"

"Right away, sir."

"What the hell's happened?" snapped Mel.

"Don't rush me. I want to put this the right way . . ." Serge plugged a funky new speaker into the iPod. Except it wasn't a speaker; it was a microphone. He fiddled some more and activated the record function. "Which do you want first? Bad news or good?"

"Dammit!"

"Okay," said Serge. "I'm guessing you're a bad-news-first type. People fall distinctly into the two categories. They say potty training—"

"What the fuck's happened!"

"Promise you won't be mad?" said Serge.

"Son of a bitch!"

Serge looked at Tori. "I'm not going to tell if he doesn't promise."

"We promise!" said Tori. "What's happened?"

"Okay, here goes: Ally's dead."

"What!" yelled Ian. Every table turned.

"Tori!" whispered Mel. "Her death was just supposed to be a hoax!"

"It *was* supposed to be a hoax," said Tori. She turned to Serge. "This isn't funny anymore. Really, where is she?"

"I don't know," said Serge. "Depends whether you're religious or not. Heaven, hell, worm bellies."

"You're not joking," said Tori. "You're serious, aren't you?"

"I wouldn't kid about something like that."

"But what happened?"

"What do you think happened? I killed her."

"I know. I mean how?"

"My gun went off six times."

"But why?" asked Tori.

"She knew my buttons and kept pressing them like an epileptic in an arcade. If it's any consolation, I gave her fair warning."

"Oh, my God!" said Ian, hyperventilating. "She can't really be dead!"

Serge put a hand on his shoulder. "My experience is denial never solved anything. Right now, we need to band together like in the movies. I was thinking *The Seven Samurai,* if they only had five. Think I could get an office near yours? Something with a window if it's available. I get cranky without sunlight . . ."

Ian's head fell to his chest, shaking with sobs.

"Okay, forget the office," said Serge. "I'll work out of my car. I'm more productive there anyway."

"We'll get the gas chamber!" said Mel.

"You never asked me about the good news."

Tears streaked down Ian's face. "What can possibly be good about this?"

"I have a new plan!" Serge reclined and crossed his arms with self-satisfaction. "Aren't you proud of me? After the mishap, I could have gotten down in the dumps, but no! I climbed right back on that drawing-board horse. That's what you're paying us for . . ."

". . . We're professionals," said Coleman, a finger way back in his mouth scraping a tooth.

Both brothers weeping now.

"I thought you'd be happy," said Serge. "Don't you want to hear the plan?"

"Okay, I'll shoot myself later for asking," said Tori. "What's the plan?"

Serge rubbed his palms together. "First, you give us two million dollars—"

"Two million dollars!" said Ian.

"Why do you need two million?" asked Mel.

"There's two of us," said Serge. "Me and him."

They looked over at Coleman, the finger farther back. "Serge, I got a piece of nut stuck—"

"Coleman! I'm negotiating!"

"Sorry."

"We need the money to leave the country and start new lives."

Coleman examined a wet cashew chunk on the end of his finger, then flicked it.

"This is extortion!" said Mel. A nut chunk hit him in the eye.

"Think of it like spending on yourselves," said Serge. "It'll put us as far away from you as possible. But that's not all! For two mil, you get the ultra-lux job. Right after leaving here, I'll get to work making sure they never, ever pin this on you."

"How are you going to do that?" asked Ian.

"By pinning it on someone else." Serge motioned for all of them to huddle closer. "Here's what I had in mind . . ."

Ten minutes later Serge sat back and smiled again. "What do you think?"

"Never work," said Tori.

"Of course it'll work," said Serge. "I planned it down to the last detail."

"You know, I think it *will* work," said Ian.

Mel nodded. "It's worth a try."

"I can't believe you're siding with him now!" said Tori.

"Me neither," said Ian. "But it sounds like he's got all the bases covered."

"We see a lot of mystery scripts," said Mel. "Even the best had more holes."

"Great," said Serge. "Just one more thing. I was kind of saving it until I'd won you over. A final condition of my employment. It's nonnegotiable . . ."

ALTO NIDO APARTMENTS

Ford Oelman trotted down the stairs from his third-floor unit and opened the front door.

Police cars everywhere. Detectives waiting at the bottom of the steps.

"What's going on?"

"We have a search warrant," said Reamsnyder.

Babcock produced a pair of handcuffs. "And an arrest warrant."

"But you already questioned me," protested Ford, cuffs snapping behind his back. "You said you believed me."

"Please step out of the way."

An evidence team with crime-scene kits trotted up the stairs. The detectives stuck Ford in the back of a patrol car.

"What am I charged with?"

"Obstruction for now." The door slammed.

Ford watched forensic experts making continuous trips in and out of the building. Clear bags of fiber samples, strips of latent-print impression, cardboard boxes with unknown contents. His heart began to pound.

The detectives were upstairs, going room to room. Cameras flashed. They passed the guy shooting video in the hall. Babcock flipped his notepad to the number he had written down from the caller ID at Vistamax. He entered it in his cell phone and told everyone to be quiet. They listened. Nothing.

Neighbors and passersby filled the street behind police lines. Gestures, gossip. Satellite trucks arrived. News crews zoomed through the back window of a patrol car, where someone was hiding his face.

Babcock gave the cell phone a couple more tries in different parts of the apartment. No luck. He left the building and stood next to the patrol car. He opened his phone again to call headquarters. He hit redial.

A muted ringing sound from somewhere.

Nobody was answering at headquarters. Hmmm, that's weird. He hit redial again. The soft ringing started again. Where was that coming from? Babcock turned around and saw Ford's car. He looked at the display on his cell. Of course. Headquarters was usually on redial, but not this time.

"Reamsnyder, come here."

"What is it?"

Babcock didn't answer, just walked slowly toward Ford's car.

"Something's ringing," said Reamsnyder.

Babcock showed him the display on his phone. "Sounds like it's coming from the trunk."

"The car's not in the search warrant."

Babcock opened the back door of the police cruiser car and helped Ford get out. "Have any objection to us looking in your trunk?"

"I'm innocent. Look wherever you want."

The detectives slipped on latex gloves. "Keys?"

Ford turned sideways. "Right pocket."

Babcock hit redial again. The ringing started again. Reamsnyder unlocked the trunk. The sound got louder. The detective reached inside and gingerly picked up a ringing cell phone. "I thought you said it was stolen."

"It was. How'd that get there?"

"That's our question."

"Look at this," said Reamsnyder, holding up a pair of monogrammed women's panties. *A.S.* "Bet we get a DNA match."

Babcock put a hand on top of Ford's head and pushed him back into the patrol car. "We have some new charges."

The door slammed.

THE STANDARD HOTEL, ROOM 222

Serge had been sitting on the edge of the bed for fifteen minutes, staring at a half-empty prescription bottle with a faded, three-year-old label.

Coleman surfed the TV. "I thought you threw all that stuff out."

"I did. Found this in a drawer six months ago. Don't know why I kept it."

"You said you hated taking that stuff."

Serge nodded and unsnapped the cap.

"You're not thinking of going back on it?" asked Coleman. "We won't have any more fun."

"I've got a big appointment in the morning."

"That's right. Your final condition of employment with the Glicks."

"It's something I've dreamed about my whole life. Now that I have it, I don't want to screw up." Serge stared at the bottle another moment, then closed his eyes and tossed a handful of pills down his throat. He opened his eyes. "No going back now."

Hollywood Tattletale

STALKER FORD OELMAN ARRESTED AGAIN

HOLLYWOOD—A former low-level employee of the Vistamax props department has been arrested and charged with the murder of abducted movie icon Ally Street.

The apprehension of stalker-turned-killer Ford Oelman came during a coordinated raid on his Alto Nido hideout near Ivar and Franklin, where police intercepted the suspect just as he was attempting to flee the jurisdiction. He is being held without bail in the theatrical wing of the county jail.

Discovered during the raid was the cell phone used during ransom negotiations as well as an unidentified piece of apparel rumored to be of a sexual nature. The clothing item has since been scientifically linked to Ms. Street, according to LAPD Detectives G. Babcock and P. Reamsnyder, who spoke on the condition of anonymity.

Investigators are still unclear on motive, but studio sources describe a disgruntled employee who was fired for erratic behavior including bursting into the private office of Vistamax owners Ian and Mel Glick.

"He was insane," said Ian.

"I feared for my life," said Mel. "I hope he gets the help he needs."

After being terminated, Mr. Oelman was overheard making threats against the entire studio before having to be physically removed by security. Court records also show hundreds of civil filings against Vistamax by the former employee.

"That's a red flag," said an unnamed attorney at the studio. "He was clearly obsessed. We could barely keep up with all the paperwork he was generating."

Police initially suspected Mr. Oelman amid reports that he had been stalking the actress at Skybar just hours before her abduction. He was briefly taken into custody for questioning during early stages of the investigation, but was soon released based on what now appears to have been a bogus alibi.

"Would Ally still be alive if the police hadn't made a mistake?" asked Mel Glick. "Who knows? You can drive yourself insane with questions like that."

Second-guessing the police dominated all local newscasts. A handful of buildings burned to the ground.

"I don't blame the detectives," said Street's distraught agent Tori Gersh. "I blame the sick bastard who took Ally!"

Meanwhile, at the county jail, celebrity attorneys were lined up around the visiting room for a chance to take on the no-win case. In a late-breaking development, however, Mr. Oelman has made the highly questionable decision of retaining legal newcomer Rodney Demopolis, who has never been on a talk show.

Mr. Demopolis's first press conference is scheduled for noon.

Serge parked in front of a sleek professional building and took the elevator to the tenth floor. Vistamax Development Division. He entered an office. The walls were covered with autographed movie posters in expensive frames. Eastwood. Pitt. Gibson.

The receptionist was wearing a telephone headset. ". . . Have a seat, Mr. Storms."

Serge had just started picking up a magazine when a door flew open on the other side of the waiting room. Two men waved furiously. "Serge! Get in here, you maniac!" "We've been dying to meet you!"

Serge entered the largest office he'd ever seen, made even more spacious by the lack of furnishing. Just two swivel chairs facing a white leather couch. It helped showcase the view: The wall opposite the sofa was a single, giant floor-to-ceiling window overlooking the Hollywood Hills. Serge could see the sign.

They all sat at the same time, Serge on the couch, the two men in the chairs. The chairs were the retro kind that looked like carved-out eggs. The development guys had to swivel to see each other. Serge didn't have a problem confusing the two. The one on the left was muscle-bound with a shaved head, blue warmup pants and a sleeveless workout jersey. The other wore the traditional business shirt and tie in a slightly mussed fashion like the drummer for Cheap Trick. They had notepads and anticipating smiles, waiting for Serge to say something.

Serge sat, eyes moving back and forth between them.

A chair squeaked as the muscular one swiveled toward his colleague. "That's so cool. He's the writer and he isn't saying anything."

"You're the writer. You can say anything," said the drummer. "But the fact that you're not saying anything says a lot more."

"The Glicks are high on you. They absolutely insisted we take a meeting."

"Told us great things."

"They did?" said Serge.

"In theory. It's a thrill to meet!"

"We have huge plans for you!"

"You're the next big thing!"

"Which means we have to act fast, because the next big thing is tomorrow's yesterday's news."

"One day we love you, the next we can't take your calls."

"Sorry, those are the rules."

"Need anything? Espresso? Biscotti?"

"I'm fine," said Serge.

"Heard about your asymmetrical conjoined twins treatment."

"Love everything about it."

"Just a few tweaks for the market. But in strict fidelity to your vision."

"You're the writer."

"First, we make them symmetrical."

"Then they're not twins."

"Only one person."

"She's a secret agent."

"We're talking to Sandra Bullock."

"What else you got for us in that nutty head of yours?"
They leaned forward again.

"Uh . . ." Serge checked his notes. "I was thinking a sports movie that's also chick flick. Like *A League of Their Own*, only—"

"Gender crossover."

"Genius."

"The key is to limit the sports . . ."

". . . Then take it out."

"Just a hint of off-camera sports floating in the background."

"We've heard enough."

"You're our man."

The secretary brought in the contracts. Serge flipped page after long-form page of microscopic print. Section C, Part 2, paragraph vii . . .

Serge shook his head in disbelief. "So it's true."

"What's true?"

"I'd heard about these clauses, but I thought someone was pulling my chain. They really do exist."

"What are you talking about?"

"These right here," said Serge. "Where you reserve certain residuals *from the beginning to the end of time*."

"In case they make time machines . . ."

"*On this world or any other*," read Serge.

"In case we colonize Mars . . ."

"*In the known or unknown existence*."

"You never know."

"This really is serious?" said Serge. "You don't see the humor?"

"What do you mean?"

Serge began writing in the margins. "I need to make some changes . . ."

They read over Serge's new terms, then stood and shook hands. "You drive a hard bargain."

"Welcome aboard."

"Any questions?"

"Yeah." Serge pulled a prescription bottle from his pocket. "You got a wastebasket?"

FOX NEWS

"This is Greta Van Susteren and welcome back to On the Record, *where our distinguished panel continues its gavel-to-gavel coverage of the Ally Street murder case. Just before our break, we witnessed the defense's first news conference. Gloria Allred, your reaction?"*

"I'm still stunned. Is he working for the prosecution?"

"Geoffrey Fieger?"

"Sure, it's a shaky start. But at least he understands these things need to be tried in the media."

"Let's take another look at that tape."

Noon. Courthouse steps.

A head with receding hair poked up from behind a bank of fifty microphones. He tapped one. "Are these things on?"

"Go ahead!"

"As you know, I represent Ford Oelman, who has been viciously smeared by a police department attempting to try this case on the courthouse steps. Not only am I prepared to establish my client's innocence beyond all doubt, but in just a few days I will produce the real killers. We're look-ing for a devil-worshipping Indonesian heroin syndicate in a brown van walking a dog—"

"What about the panties?" yelled a reporter.

"What panties?"

"The ones found in your client's car."

"You sure?"

"They found them with his cell phone traced to the ransom calls."

"I'm going to have to ask him about that."

"What about the hundreds of court filings against the studio?"

"That's an easy one," said Rodney. "I filed those for him."

"He asked you to?"

"Well, yeah . . ."

"So it's true?"

"What is?"

"That he was bent on revenge."

"Who said that?"

"You did."

"Wow," said Rodney. "That doesn't sound good."

39

THE GLICKS' OFFICE

Mel was on the phone.

"You what!"

"Signed him to a contract! Isn't that great?" said the muscular development agent. "You'll love the terms. We were able to pay him less than our usual low in exchange for certain provisos he requested."

"You weren't supposed to sign him to shit!"

"Thought that's what you wanted. Said you were high on him."

"Favor for the in-laws. But now they can connect him to us!"

"The in-laws can connect him?—"

"Shut up! You have no idea what you've just done! . . . Hold a sec . . ."

Ian was whispering, motioning his brother to cover the phone. "This could actually help."

"How can it possibly help?"

"Remember we were trying to figure how to get two mil-

lion dollars out of the company without you-know-who in
Japan finding out? Said not to pay a dime?"

"So?"

"It's the perfect legit write-off, and the two bozos in development are our beards. We bury it deep in the books."

"Of course!" Mel uncovered the phone. "I've changed
my mind. You did a fantastic job landing this guy."

"What changed your mind?"

"Found out he was about to go to a competitor. As a matter of fact, I want you to increase the deal. Two million dollars. Nonrefundable advance for an exclusive five-picture
deal."

"Two million! No newcomer gets that."

"Do it." He hung up.

"Now we just have to make sure word of the deal doesn't
get out," said Ian.

"If you-know-who . . ."—Mel looked west—". . . It's
sayo-nara."

"I'll get ahold of publicity. Tell them none of the regular
releases to the trades."

"And tell development it's hush-hush—we're trying to
land Nicholson."

"We'll pay them cash. I'll go to the bank this afternoon
and fill the briefcase."

"Cash?"

"Shortens the paper trail. Fewer eyes in accounting the
better."

"And we definitely don't want those psychos coming by
the studio to pick up a check."

"No kidding."

"That about does it. There's no possible way this can
leak."

"Jesus! Can you imagine if it did?"

The brothers broke up laughing.

Hollywood Tattletale

VISTAMAX PAYS NEWCOMER $2 MILLION; JAPAN IN SHOCK

HOLLYWOOD—In a stunning announcement, Vistamax Studios has paid an unprecedented $2 million advance to an unknown screenwriter with no previous credits to his name.

Anonymous sources close to the negotiations say the contract was inked with Floridian Serge A. Storms based upon the strength of several plot synopses, including what is being described as a career vehicle for Sandra Bullock.

Publicists for the actress said they were unaware of the proposed role for their client but welcomed the publicity.

The normally frugal Vistamax (see related story, page 17) also made other unheard-of concessions to prevent Mr. Storms from signing with rival Warner Brothers, including distribution rights to several of the outer planets and certain periods of history.

"Yes, it's unusual, but this is a franchise player," said one studio insider. "We don't lightly hand over Neptune and the Dark Ages."

Reached in Japan, a Vistamax board member responded to the news with unintelligible shouting before the line went dead.

Observers say the otherwise reclusive Glick brothers had been seen personally courting Mr. Storms for some time, although the intense negotiations almost collapsed last week during a heated argument in the Polo Lounge at the Beverly Hills Hotel.

"I've never seen anyone talk to the Glicks that way," said one of the hotel's waiters. "We almost had to throw them out. And he took a bunch of our matchbooks."

Besides a volatile temper, little else is know about the mysterious newcomer. "I do remember one thing," added the waiter. "He seemed to be an Eagles fan."

Reached in San Simeon, the Eagles' publicist said he had never heard of Mr. Storms, but thanked Eagles fans in general, especially those who preorder the new box set.

RELATED STORY, PAGE 17

POTEMKIN DENIES SPECULATION

HOLLYWOOD—In light of recent developments in the Ally Street kidnapping case, acclaimed director Werner B. Potemkin has decided to resume shooting his ambitious epic *All That Glitters*.

A leaked copy of the shooting schedule shows the director now plans to go forward with the grand climax of the film and push the already record budget at least $25 million higher, not including settlements from pending wrongful-death actions.

The revelation drew strong charges of insensitivity from the entertainment press, who further speculated that Potemkin was secretly planning to write Ms. Street's part out of the movie's final scenes.

"Categorically not," said a Potemkin spokesman. "Despite what the police are saying, we have every hope that Ally will be found alive in time to rejoin the cast before we wrap. That scene where we killed her off with a body double was just for the insurance company."

THE FINAL DAY

F our A.M. It started like any other Final Day. A rented Chrysler sat at the curb on Fairfax. Serge and Coleman sat in a curved corner booth inside the restaurant.

"Serge, I feel like crap. Why'd you get me up so early?"

"Because it's the Final Day. You have to get a jump."

Coleman unfolded a large laminated menu. "The Final Day?"

"Everything comes to a head. Loose ends tied up. Justice rendered."

"But how do you know it's the Final Day."

"You just know. Like when you're in a theater watching a movie. At a certain point you look at your watch and get a gut feeling they're about to wrap it up."

"Or when you're reading a book?" said Coleman. "And there are just a few pages left?"

"Or that."

"Serge?"

"What?"

"I don't understand this menu. It's got too many words."

"It's Canter's." Serge made a squeaking sound rubbing a finger along the dark orange vinyl. "The menu's part of the experience, like trying to crack the Dead Sea Scrolls. God, I love this place!"

"I got a hangover."

"Breakfast will cure that. It's the most important meal of the day, especially the Final Day."

A waitress as old as the restaurant came by with Serge's coffee. She opened her menu pad. Serge opened his notepad.

"Are you ready to order yet?"

"No, but I've got some questions. Which wall did Nicholas Cage shatter the ketchup bottle against?"

"I don't know. I just work here."

"He was trying to impress a date," said Serge, spooning ice from his water into the coffee. "But he got thrown out for that stunt. Good for you! *Raising Arizona* doesn't mean you can go through life slinging condiments."

"You want me to come back?"

"I think we're ready." Serge chugged his coffee and raised the plastic menu. "Coleman, you know what you want?"

"What's lox?"

"Liquid oxygen," said Serge.

"I'll come back . . ."

"No, I'll order for both of us." Serge snatched the menu from Coleman, folding it along with his own. "He'll have the corned beef, and I'll get the matzo balls with a double side of bacon." He handed the menus to the waitress. "And a refill on the coffee when you get a chance."

She left in no-nonsense shoes.

Serge leaned over his notebook and clicked a pen.

Coleman popped a beer under the table. "How does the Final Day start?"

"That's what I'm working on." Serge scribbled. "It's very intricate. Timing has to be absolutely perfect. First, we run by the police department and Vistamax, then head back to our hotel . . ."

"But, Serge, we already checked out."

"I know. We have to swing by to pick up our tail from Alabama."

"Aren't we supposed to *lose* tails?"

"Not on the Final Day," said Serge. "Otherwise they won't know how to get to the studio. They should be arriving any minute for their stakeout."

Coleman pointed across the dining room toward a thumping sound. "What's that section over there? Looks like they serve alcohol."

"The Kibitz Room. Added in 1961 with live music. Tiny dive with an old Hebrew sign, which is why it's so cool to see all these famous acts drop by for impromptu sets."

"Like who?"

"Like Slash. He used to work at a newsstand up the street."

"From Guns N' Roses?"

"Another cool thing about L.A.," said Serge. "You walk up to a newsstand: 'I'd like a *USA Today* and some gum and . . . Hey, Slash! Didn't recognize you. Welcome to the jungle. When's the new album?'"

Food came. Coffee topped off.

Serge continued writing in his notebook. ". . . And we do that, and then this happens, which leads to this—mental note to bring extra ammo there . . . and then that . . ."

"Look at the size of this sandwich." Coleman removed the cellophane toothpick. "Someone must be stoned back there."

Serge entered the brass-tacks zone, time-motion efficiency, eating with his left hand, jotting with his right, coffee gulps. Faster and faster, quickly filling several pages with small, tightly spaced print. Finally, he reached the end.

". . . And then the credits roll." Serge smiled with fulfillment and clicked his pen shut. He looked at his wristwatch. "Damn. We're behind schedule. The planes start landing any minute at LAX." He stood and threw currency on the table.

LAX

Predawn darkness at the terminal, employees with photobadges arriving, some kind of maintenance vehicle with a blinking yellow light in the fog. All the coffeepots going in the cafés. A skycap smoked on the sidewalk in front of Delta.

Flights started trickling in from the runways. An international red-eye, a private Lear.

The Lear taxied to an executive terminal. Six large men with Dixie drawls and blood allegiance to the Southeastern Football Conference sat quietly with automatic weapons in their laps. The plane taxied to a waiting limo. The men piled in.

The limo exited the tarmac behind the international airside, where six large Japanese men had just cleared Customs and marched with silent purpose for their own limo waiting outside Baggage Claim.

Ian and Mel arrived early at Vistamax.

"Did you count it?" asked Mel.

Ian set the briefcase on his desk. "Twice. It's all there."

"When do we make the handoff?"

"Said he'd call."

"Wait. What's this?" Mel noticed something in his "in" basket. An overnight article Betty had dropped off from the studio's clipping service.

"What is it?" asked Ian.

"Oh, my God! The *Tattletale*. They found out about the contract!"

"How'd it get out?"

"Who cares? We're dead!"

"You-know-who could show up at our door any minute!"

"We have to leave town!"

A knock at the door.

The brothers screamed.

Betty came in. "You all right?"

"What is it?"

"This just came for you." She handed Ian a small brown package. "The courier said you needed to open it right away. Seemed a little strange."

Ian gave her a curious look as he peeled strips of packing tape.

"There's no return address," said Mel.

Ian tore open a cardboard flap. "Audiocassette?"

A piece of paper fell out of the box and fluttered to the floor. Mel picked it up. "It's a note." He started reading out loud, then stopped. "Betty, you can go now. We're fine."

She didn't think so, but left anyway.

"What's it say?" asked Ian.

"That a duplicate of the tape is on its way right now to the police."

The brothers ran across the office to the shelves with the stereo equipment. They inserted the cassette and hit play. They listened.

"Holy shit! It's our meeting at the Polo Lounge! It's got everything!"

"That son of a bitch recorded us! The murder! The coverup!"

Mel grabbed the briefcase by the handle. "We definitely have to leave town!"

Detective Reamsnyder rushed over to his partner's desk, waving a cassette tape. "You're not going to believe this."

A vintage mustard Citroën circa *Day of the Jackal* screeched away from the Vistamax administration building and raced across the studio, toward the entrance.

A uniformed man with a clipboard came out of the guard booth. He recognized the approaching vehicle and stepped forward with a smile. He dove out of the way.

The car never slowed, smashing the orange crossing arm to splinters and scattering Ally mourners. It made a skidding right on Olive and picked up the freeway.

Ian hyperventilated and grabbed his heart. "We're dead for sure!"

"Shut up! I'm trying to think!" Mel cut the steering wheel.

They bounded down an exit ramp, scraping the guardrail, and sped south on Highland. "Anyone back there?"

Ian turned around. "So far, so good."

Mel glanced at the lane next to them. "Holy God in heaven!"

"Pull over," yelled Serge.

"Speed up!" yelled Ian.

"I'm going as fast as I can!"

"He's going to hit us!"

Serge smacked their rear fender in the traditional destabilizing maneuver. Mel spun out and violently jumped the curb at the entrance to the Hollywood Bowl.

The Sebring whipped around and parked on the far side of the stalled Citroën. Serge was out of the car in a flash. Ian went to lock his door, but Serge was quicker.

"Come with me! We don't have any time!"

The Glicks threw up their hands. "Don't kill us!"

"I'm not going to kill you." Serge pointed up the road with his gun. "They are!"

The brothers turned. Two speeding limos. The first overshot the Bowl entrance and tore up the grass, skidding to a stop. The second went even farther and had to make a fishtailing U-turn.

Serge jerked Ian from the car. "Move it!" Mel grabbed the briefcase and jumped out the driver's door. They dove in the Sebring, on the opposite side of the Citroën from the first limo. Asians in black overcoats jumped out and formed a firing-squad line. Machine guns raked the French roadster. The Sebring shot out from behind and made a squealing left back into traffic.

The Asians piled back into their limo and sideswiped the Alabama gang accelerating out of their U-turn. Both vehicles recovered and shot up an entrance ramp.

Serge glanced in the rearview at two accelerating vehicles weaving through traffic. "Good. Thought I'd lost them." He turned around and faced the Glicks. "So, how do you want this to end?"

White and woozy.

Serge turned to his side. "What about you, Coleman?"

"Hadn't given it much thought."

"We could always pick an ending from a favorite movie," said Serge. "Got one you like?"

"What about the wood chipper in *Fargo*?" said Coleman. "That was pretty funny."

Serge kept an eye on the gaining limos filling his rearview. "I was thinking *Magnolia*. Let's catch some frogs."

POLICE HEADQUARTERS

Babcock and Reamsnyder were in one of the bigger offices. Their captain had heard enough. He hit the stop button on the tape deck. "So they were in on it all along."

"Didn't plan the murder," said Reamsnyder. "But they were accessories."

"And covered it up," said Babcock.

"Approved planting that evidence in the trunk."

The captain nodded. "Bring 'em in. And get public affairs moving. This is going to be a nightmare."

The detectives stood to leave.

"Sir," said Babcock. "The kid we arrested."

"Damn." The captain closed his eyes and rubbed the bridge of his nose. He opened his eyes. "Release him. And a press conference inside the hour. The works. I want his exoneration to get no less publicity than his arrest. Do everything to restore his good name. . . . Poor kid . . ."

"You got it."

The departing detectives were almost trampled by a breathless lieutenant running in the door. "Sir, the Glick brothers! . . ."

"We know," said the captain. "We just listened to the tape."

"Tape?"

"Yeah, tape. What are *you* talking about?"

"Just got the call. Uniforms working a location at the Hollywood Bowl."

Serge smacked the steering wheel.

Coleman popped a beer. "What's the matter?"

"You see frogs all the fucking time, except when you need them. Now I don't have an ending."

"I got an ending," said Coleman.

"What is it?"

"A long time ago me and the heads went to the midnight showing of *2001: A Space Odyssey*. Ever heard of it?"

"I'm familiar."

"We were baked! At the end, this astronaut is flying through space and we're groovin' on all these psychedelic shapes zipping by, and suddenly we all go: Holy shit! The end of the universe is some old dude's room!"

"Yeah?"

"There's your ending."

"What? Some guy's room? That doesn't make any sense."

"The stoners will get it."

Serge sighed and looked up at the mirror. "Got an ending back there? You're in movies."

Quiet sobs.

"They're no help," said Serge. "I . . . wait, that's it. The ending."

He pulled into the lane for the 405 and turned south. They exited below the airport and headed for the ocean. Serge picked up Palos Verdes Boulevard and drove along the coast. Coleman looked out the window at a seaside bluff. "Where are we going?"

"It's the Big W, I tell ya!"

"The what?"

"A Mad, Mad, Mad, Mad World!"

"I loved that movie," said Coleman. "Everyone ends up at these crossed palm trees."

Serge drove another half mile. He turned left around a last bend and pointed with excitement: "It's the *Big . . . I?*"

"There's only one tree left," said Coleman. "Where'd the others go?"

Serge stopped the car and stared, slack-jawed.

Backseat screaming: "The limos are coming! The limos are coming!"

"Must have been taken out by some storms," said Coleman.

"Or a blight."

"Go! Drive!" yelled Mel. "They're almost here!"

"Now I'm depressed." Serge listlessly put the car back in gear.

"They're hanging out the windows with machine guns!"

The Chrysler slowly pulled away without urgency, bullets pinging off the trunk. The Glicks balled themselves up on the floor.

"Don't worry," said Coleman. "You'll think of another ending."

"No, I won't."

He drove aimlessly across the city, losing the will to live, not caring about the gunfire or the screaming in the back-seat. They headed inland, store signs switching from English to Asian. Heavy traffic, pedestrians, sidewalk commerce.

Coleman watched a row of seafood stands go by. "Why don't we just stop and end it here?"

"Forget it, Coleman. It's Chinatown."

Two detectives in an unmarked sedan arrived at the *Big I,* followed by five squad cars with all the lights going.

"Nobody's here," said Reamsnyder.

"Isn't this where we got the reports?"

Reamsnyder nodded. "Let me find out what's going on." The radio crackled just as he picked up the microphone. A quick exchange with the dispatcher. "Ten-four. We're rolling."

Babcock gave his partner an odd look. "Chinatown?"

"They must be heading back to the studio."

"Where are we going?" asked Coleman.

"No idea," said Serge. "I have to figure out— . . . Wait, that's it!"

"What?"

"My big ending. We're heading back to the studio."

Vigil people scattered again. Guards came out to look, then dove back in their booth as a speeding convertible with Mel and Ian in the rear seat flew through the entrance. The Chrysler bottomed out on every speed bump as it raced across the studio on narrow, one-car-wide lanes between the sets. A caveman dropped his club and pasted himself against a wall. The convertible disappeared around the corner of soundstage 27.

The guards were sticking their heads out of the booth, looking in the direction of the Chrysler, when two limos zoomed by in quick succession.

Serge zigzagged across the studio, swerving to avoid more extras diving out of the way. Revolutionary War soldiers, angels losing their halos, the abominable snowman. Passageways grew tighter and tighter until the Chrysler came to a set of steel pylons blocking the street. Serge spun toward the backseat. "What's the deal?"

"Cars can't go any farther," said Ian.

"Have to use golf carts," said Mel.

Serge jumped out of the convertible. "To the golf carts!"

They ran a hundred feet. A row of electric carts sat in numbered slots next to stage 14.

"Hey!" yelled a man with a clipboard. "You can't take that— Oh, Ian, Mel, sorry, didn't recognize . . ."

They sped off with a quiet whir.

The man with the clipboard heard a screech. A limo skidded up to the pylons. A half dozen men poured out and ran for the carts, cocking machine guns. The clipboard man backed up against a Coke machine.

"Which way did they go?"

He pointed.

The Japanese sped off.

Another screech. Another limo. Six southerners commandeered a third cart.

Serge looked back. The Japanese were gaining.

"Watch out!" yelled Coleman.

They crashed through a giant pane of trick glass two men were carrying across Broadway.

"Mel! Which way?"

"Left."

Serge took the corner on two wheels. He looked back again. "They're still there." Another cart shot out of a service alley. "Yikes!" Serge swerved to avoid the rednecks, who raced parallel down the road, aiming weapons.

"Serge . . ."

"Not now, Coleman."

"Vegetable cart!"

Crash.

Both vehicles fought to maintain traction on squished zucchini, diverting on opposite sides of a fork at the Taj Mahal.

Detective Babcock honked his horn. Reamsnyder flashed a badge out the window at the vigil people. "Move it! Now!"

The crowd parted. An unmarked sedan and five squad cars raced onto the Vistamax lot.

* * *

Serge looked back at the still-gaining Japanese. "We have to dump this thing." He steered straight for the sound-stage that formed a dead end at the end of the street. It was the largest stage on the lot, number 19, where cast members strolled in and out of the enormous, open hangar doors. They noticed Serge's cart just in time and jumped out of the way.

Inside number 19, Werner B. Potemkin sat atop a canvas director's chair, raising a megaphone.

"Annnnnnnd . . . action!"

A golf cart flew through the entrance, sailing completely over a set of metal stairs leading down to the concrete stage floor. The cart overturned and skidded on its side. Serge climbed out and pulled the others from the wreckage. "Hurry! . . ."

"Cut!" yelled Potemkin.

"I'll try," said his first assistant.

"What do you mean, 'You'll try'?"

"The scene's so complex, all kinds of valves and circuitry need to be reversed." He grabbed a walkie-talkie. "I'll call Charlie . . ."

Another cart blew through the entrance for another crash landing. A half dozen Asians crawled out with machine guns.

Serge pointed. "To the chariot." They jumped aboard and Serge cracked a whip. "He-yaw!" Horses began galloping. X-wing star fighters buzzed over their heads. Flames exploded from flash pots. "If we can just make it to those doors on the other side . . ."

The doors on the other side opened. Southerners and guns poured in.

Serge jerked back on the reins. "Whoa!" He turned the chariot around. A second chariot full of Japanese raced toward them. Serge pulled back on the reins again.

"We're trapped," said Coleman. "What'll we do?"

Serge looked around quickly. "That ladder on the side of the set!" He jumped down from the chariot and took off.

"Don't leave us!" yelled Mel.

Serge ran back to the chariot.

"Thank God!" said Ian.

Serge grinned. "Almost forgot the briefcase." He grabbed it and took off again, joining Coleman, who was already scampering up a set of vertical metal rungs to the catwalk in front of a massive control panel. The panel's technician was on a walkie-talkie with the first assistant director. He saw them coming up the ladder—especially Serge's shiny .45—and fled out the fire escape at the end of the steel walkway.

From below: "Stop or we'll shoot!"

Serge looked down: Japanese aiming guns at them.

Another direction: "Stop or *we'll* shoot!"

Serge looked the other way. Southerners.

The two groups indecisively swung guns back and forth between each other and Serge.

"Who the hell are you?" yelled one of the Japanese.

"Who the hell are *you*?" yelled a redneck.

Ian and Mel in the middle: "Help!"

"Where's our two million?" Mr. Yokamura yelled at the Glicks.

"Two million?" yelled a southerner. "That's *our* money!"

Ian pointed at the catwalk. "In the briefcase."

Asian guns swung up. "Give us the briefcase!"

A drawl: "Give *us* the briefcase!"

Mr. Yokamura flew into a rage. "What the hell's going on around here!"

Serge cupped his hands around his mouth. "The denouement!"

"You're a dead man!"

"I know you are," said Serge. "But what am I?" He walked a few steps along the catwalk and came to a bank of pressure gauges and giant red levers marked DANGER.

Nobody had ever seen Potemkin so angry, and that was saying something. He'd already smashed the director's chair and taken out a water cooler. He grabbed his megaphone, ran to the edge of the landing and pointed it up at Serge. "Who the fuck are you!"

Serge looked down and smiled. *"Mr. Mojo Risin!"*

"Who?"

". . . Gotta keep on Risin!"

"You're insane!"

"Don't you dare give them the money!" yelled Mr. Yokamura.

". . . Mr. Mo-Jo Ri-Sin! . . ." Serge began throwing red levers.

"We'll negotiate!" yelled a southerner, looking up at the catwalk. "Tell us what you want."

"I . . . just want to have some fun . . . until the sun comes up over Santa Monica Boulevard . . ."

The first assistant was screaming at Potemkin. "We have to get those people out of there!"

Potemkin was too berserk to hear. He stomped down the steps with his megaphone. "I said *cut*! Are you deaf! . . ."

"Get back up here!" yelled the assistant. "You see what he's doing on that catwalk?"

But Potemkin kept marching out into the basin. "You fuckers are ruining my movie! Who let you in here? . . ."

Cops burst through the stage entrance with guns drawn. Babcock: "There they are!"

But Serge had just thrown the last lever. Everyone froze where they stood, looking around for the source of the deep, earth-shaking rumble. Too late. They made a vain attempt to run as the concrete basin flash-flooded with three million gallons of foaming water. Broken bits of chariots bobbed as the water level continued to rise.

"*. . . Gotta keep on ri-sin'! . . .*" Serge and Coleman casually strolled through the fire escape door at the end of the catwalk and into the sunlight.

Hollywood Tattletale

Cops Release Stalker Again; 15 Die

HOLLYWOOD—In a bizarre and ironic turn of events, the director and producers of the controversial *All That Glitters* have themselves become casualties of the catastrophe-prone production.

The recovery of the bodies was delayed five hours until studio crews could drain the pirate ship basin on soundstage 19. The deceased include Werner B. Potemkin and both Glick brothers, along with a dozen actors playing the roles of redneck outlaws and Japanese mobsters during a climactic scene from *The Ten Commandments*.

The Glicks' untimely demise coincides with the shocking revelation that sealed warrants had just been issued for both brothers in connection with the kidnapping and murder of former Vistamax actress Ally Street. Police were moving in for an arrest at the time the Red Sea came back together.

Meanwhile, questions still surround sets of Polaroid photos anonymously mailed to news outlets, which depict the Glicks in a series of compromising positions. Media ethicists are divided on whether the pictures should be published. The *Hollywood Tattletale* has chosen not to print the photos, which can be viewed on our Web site.

In yet another development, police have again released The Stalker Ford Oelman (see related story, page 17). The former murder suspect was escorted from the jail shortly before noon, when police held a press conference to clear The Stalker's name.

As reported earlier, Mr. Oelman came under suspicion in the Street case because he had harassed the actress, made numerous public threats, obsessively filed court documents against the studio and had to be forcibly ejected from the property. Described as an unbalanced loner, Mr. Oelman was also found to be hiding Ms. Street's unlaundered panties in the trunk of his car.

Police said it was a mistake.

RELATED STORY, PAGE 17

Hollywood Tattletale

STALKER PAID OFF

HOLLYWOOD—The Stalker Ford Oelman has reached an undisclosed, out-of-court settlement with Vistamax Studios stemming from the actions of late producers Ian and Mel Glick, which led to his arrest for murder.

"Money can never right the injustice done to this young man, but it's a start," said Mr. Oelman's attorney, Rodney Demopolis. He refused to discuss the amount, but unnamed sources place it in the seven-figure range.

Demopolis, dressed in a sharp Armani suit and sitting in his spacious new Beverly Hills office, said he has since been flooded with clients who were previously too intimidated to come forward with complaints against several other film giants. "Apparently the old Hollywood system of exploiting the little guy is not dead." Demopolis refused to identify the studios but "you'd know the names."

Accompanying Demopolis was Vistamax Entertainment Division chief Yoshi Tagura, who read from a prepared statement: "We personally apologize to Mr. Oelman, the entire Vistamax family and loyal moviegoers everywhere who are eagerly awaiting the Christmas release of *All That Glitters.*"

The day before the civil settlement, shares of Vistamax were trading sharply downward on Wall Street, responding to reports of a massive studio shakeup, including the dismissal of two dozen top producers and executives. However, the stock quickly rebounded with confidence after Tagura named a longtime studio veteran as the new CEO.

"Vistamax is my family," said Dallas Reel, who returned from an extended leave for "professional exhaustion" to appear at the press conference and pose for a three-way handshake with Tagura and Oelman.

In addition to financial compensation, Mr. Oel-

man's settlement with the studio also involves
restoration of intellectual property rights and a
guaranteed three-film contract.

Mr. Reel announced that the first project will be
the film version of Mr. Oelman's ordeal in Tinseltown. "His story is so unbelievable and compelling
that nothing needs to be changed. We're thinking
of moving it to New York."

KISSIMMEE, FLORIDA

The Big Bamboo Lounge was hosting its first-ever cast
party.

Champagne corks popped. Music played. Laughter. The
bartender laid out toilet paper coasters.

All the players were there, the same con-artist lineup that
had pulled the oil scam in Alabama. Plus their newest addi-
tions, Serge and Coleman.

Chi-Chi and Coltrane arrived. A reunion cheer went up.

A woman named Chelsea Davidson raised her champagne glass and called the room to order for a toast. She
looked much younger—not anything like Tori Gersh without the wig, fake nose and theatrical makeup. "To Ford Oelman, without whose brilliant script we would never have
been able to pull this off."

Glasses clinked.

"Author! Author!"

Ford smiled and blushed.

"Speech!"

"Come on, Ford," said Jennifer Rosen, who played the
part of Ally Street. "This is your moment. Say something."

"Yeah, Ford," said Mark. "This was your finest script yet,
even better than the oil deal."

Ford stood up. "I just reacted. I didn't know what to do

after the Glicks screwed me and ran off my lawyer. Can't tell you how much I wanted revenge."

"It was all so perfect," said Chelsea. "The stolen cell phone, Ally's fake death, not to mention framing yourself and staging the cell phone robbery in front of your unsuspecting friends from props."

"That was key," said Ford. "The best perjury is by those who believe their own testimony."

"Remind us never to get on your bad side," said Mark.

More laughter.

"But I still don't believe it worked," said Chelsea. "It all hinged on Jennifer seducing the Glicks at the party. How'd you know they'd go for it? Without that . . ."

"It's like the snake that bites the frog and they both drown. They couldn't escape their nature." Ford smiled. "I also had a great actress."

"And I had great material," said Jennifer. Her face changed. "But I still think I should get an extra share for those two lunatics you stuck me with!"

"Lunatics!" said Serge. "What about you? Another day of that whining and there *would* have been a murder. Your bull-shit has wheels!"

"Both of you are full of crap," said Chelsea. "What about me and those crazy ransom calls. Then that shit on CNN! My head almost exploded!"

"All of you: Shut up!" yelled Chi-Chi. "This is supposed to be a happy gathering."

"He's right," said Ford, raising his glass. "I'd like to make a toast. To all my friends who came in my hour of need."

"Of course we'd come," said Jennifer. "What did you think we were going to do? We're like family."

"Speaking of which . . ." said Mark. He looked toward Serge. "How does it feel to have a half brother?"

"I nearly fainted when I read my granddad's letter," said Serge. "I couldn't get to L.A. fast enough."

"Ford couldn't believe it when I gave him the news you'd called," said Mark.

"Granddad told me all about you," said Ford. "But nobody knew where you were. Almost no chance we'd ever meet. So when Mark got the call, we thought it was some trick from the people in Alabama. They'd already started snooping, and we figured they'd gotten to Chi-Chi and the others."

A tall man with dreadlocks patted Serge on the shoulder. "Sorry about roughing you up at the Safari. No hard feelings?"

"I would have done the same," said Serge.

"But, Ford," said Chelsea, "how did you ever find your granddad? I wouldn't know where to begin looking."

"Didn't even know I was adopted until I was fifteen," said Ford. "That great family with the farm in Alabama. But you know how you just start sensing something. I mean, I'll always love them like real parents. When they thought I was old enough, they finally told me what they knew, which wasn't much . . ."

"So how did you find him?" asked Jennifer.

"That was tough. They knew my mother was from South Florida . . ." He looked at Serge. "You must have been a little kid."

"Had no idea," said Serge. "Vaguely remember her getting fat, but at that age . . . The letter Chi-Chi gave me explained the big points. A year after Dad died, she started seeing this other jai-alai player. Then he goes back to Spain before either of them knows she's pregnant. Never comes back. She was already a single mom. What was she going to do?"

"Sergio handled the arrangements," said Ford. "But after all those years, try poking around Miami with only a name. Gave up a few times. Finally Googled his name on the Internet and got a hit with a newspaper article on one of his friend's funerals."

"What a story," said Serge. He looked at the others. "So, where to now?"

"Montreal," said Chelsea. "These brokers took some friends of my parents in a stock deal."

"Acting in Canada," said Serge. "Hollywood slang for dying."

"Sure you guys won't join us?" said Chelsea. "We were quite a team."

"I'm going to stay back here in Florida for a while," said Serge. "I get jittery when I'm over the state line for too long."

"I'm hanging here, too," said Ford. "We have a lot of catching up."

"Hey!" said Serge. "You like *The Punisher*?"

"Loved it!" said Ford.

"Have I got a place to show you!"

"What are we waiting for?"

"Let's rock!"

"Slow down, you two!" said Chi-Chi. "Jesus, it's like your granddad's echo in here. Let's just relax and finish our little party."

"That reminds me," said Chelsea. "We have another toast." She raised her glass toward the framed photo on the wall over the Seven Dwarfs. "To Sergio."

"To Sergio."

TAMPA

The usually deserted downtown street in front of Union Station was jammed with humming, air-conditioned semitrailers.

The warehouse on the opposite side of the road danced with activity. A large sun umbrella shaded a director's chair with OELMAN stitched on the back. Filming had just begun on the first independent project financed by the out-of-court settlement.

Cameras from two different ground angles—and a third overhead in a cherry picker—triangulated on an abandoned brick building last seen in *The Punisher*.

A clapboard clapped.

Ford raised a megaphone. "Annnnnd . . . *action!*"

Far from camera view, across the street next to the railroad station's switching yard, sat a beat-up '71 Buick Riviera. Behind the steering wheel was Ford's screenwriting collaborator, who remained uncredited at his own request. Serge turned the page of a trade magazine.

"Hey, Coleman. Check out this article."

Hollywood Tattletale

DIRECTOR LANDS POSTHUMOUS NOMINATION

HOLLYWOOD—In a real-life success story that rivals anything ever filmed, the late Werner B. Potemkin has received an Academy Award nomination in the best director category for his swansong masterpiece, *All That Glitters*.

When first released in America, the film was viciously panned coast to coast, and had to be pulled from over one thousand screens nationwide in only the second weekend. But soon after its overseas release, the tide of reviews began to shift.

Dismissed in the States as an overindulgent, unfocused pile of steaming shit, the film had to wait upon European sensibilities to correctly interpret Potemkin's vision for a delicious self-parody of an obsessed director on the brink of madness. "I completely missed it," said Roger Ebert. "That's a testimony to his genius."

"His command of authenticity is what threw me," wrote Leonard Maltin. "The excess is so understated."

Now drawing rave comparisons to Mel Brooks's *The Producers*, the film was quickly re-released in America, shattering all box office records for a movie pulled from circulation. Monday's Oscar nomination completes the full-circle comeback for Potemkin, except for being dead.

Serge closed the tabloid and looked up at the production across the street. "The movies have returned to Tampa. All is well."

Coleman gestured with a can of Schlitz. "Is that supposed to be us?"

Across the street, two journeymen character actors ran down the front steps of the warehouse. They were the kind of actors that everyone recognizes but can't name. They didn't look anything like Serge and Coleman.

"Let's rock!"

The actors jumped in a '71 Buick Riviera with expensive restoration to make it look beat-up. The cameras followed the car as it jumped a curb and took off across the railroad tracks.

A megaphone rose.

"Annnnnd . . . *cut!*"

A NOTE ON THE TYPE

Hollywood Tattletale

STUDIO CHIEF ANNOUNCES TYPOGRAPHY BLOCKBUSTER

HOLLYWOOD—During a star-studded red-carpet gala, Vistamax CEO Dallas Reel announced plans for an ambitious, high-budget epic thriller about rival neoclassical typesetters.

The script, still in revisions, centers on the true-life eighteenth-century feud between Dutch master Baruch Leubenhoek and the Hungarian rebel Smilnik Verbleat.

Commented Reel: "It's a story that's never been told."

"And with good reason," wrote silver-screen columnist Rona Tush.

Hollywood Tattletale

SHOOTING RESUMES FOLLOWING MOVIE SET MISHAP

HOLLYWOOD—Shooting on the epic Vistamax production *A Note on the Type* resumed Monday following a four-day hiatus due to the untimely death of lead actor Keen Farris in the part of driven typographer Smilnik Verbleat.

As reported earlier, Mr. Farris was killed when a catapult malfunctioned during a scene depicting controversial allegations that a rival typemaster tried to murder the Hungarian.

Shooting was able to resume so quickly because the director had to look no further than his own set to discover a complete unknown capable of taking over the challenging role.

Ironically, the new male lead, standby carpenter Pedro Jimenez, had worked on the very catapult that malfunctioned.

"My heart goes out to the entire Farris family," said Jimenez, "but it's time to move on."

HURRICANE PUNCH
by Tim Dorsey
Available now
wherever books are sold

PROLOGUE

Editor's Note—In cooperation with local authorities, *Tampa Bay Today* is seeking the public's help in identifying a serial killer using this unprecedented hurricane season as cover for his string of grisly homicides. The following letter was just received by one of our reporters:

Dear Florida,

I am the one you seek, borne on the curling wisps of ghostly madness that crawl onshore at midnight and seep over the swamp. My glorious evil rages north from the Everglades, the living fury of the land welling up. Flushed birds fill the black sky; reeds yield as one in genuflection. I stalk across the turnpike as you sleep in your new six-bedroom abominations with screened-in pools, blissful sheep ignorant of the million alligators beyond ridiculous canals you've scarred into the sacred ground. I am the pressure drop in your soul when you finally accept, bound and gagged, that you are in The Place of No Hope, with your last breath, pitifully whimpering for the impostor that is mercy. My next sacrifice will be offered when the barometer dips below twenty-nine inches.

—The Eye of the Storm

Editor's Note—In cooperation with local authorities, *Tampa Bay Today* has decided to publish a second letter in connection with the recent rash of homicides. Based upon evidence they cannot disclose, police have confirmed that the author is responsible for at least some of the murders. However, investigators are uncertain whether this new correspondence is the work of the same person writing in a different state of mind or evidence of a second, copycat killer. A word of caution: Certain language may offend sensitive readers, but we are leaving the letter intact to increase the chance that someone might recognize the writer's syntax.

Dear Letters to the Editor,

This is the third time this month I've gotten a wet paper—what the fuck? You can fill the building with Pulitzers, but it doesn't mean dick if the guy delivering your product is on the pipe. Don't bother trying to contact me to apologize or deliver replacement papers, because I stole them off someone's lawn. All I can say, sirs, is that the residents of 3118 San Luis Obispo have every right to be prickly with your level of service.

Next: What's with giving that retardo-bot serial killer credit for every unsolved murder in this state? He doesn't possess nearly the intellect or wit to conceive the imaginative technique that police aren't divulging in the Fowler Avenue case (if, hypothetically, I knew anything about it, which I don't). But you have to admit, it was pretty funny, especially if you were there (which I wasn't). And then, what on earth were you thinking publishing his letter last week? Could you believe that trite prose? What a bunch of self-important, freshman-philosophy drivel! Sure, I went through the same idealistic phase about the encroachment of rampant development on our stressed ecosystems. And yes, people need to be killed, but not randomly. That's just wrong.

Plus: What's with letting the guy name himself? "Eye of the Storm." Give me a break! The guy's a serial killer! At the very least, his punishment should be he doesn't get to choose his own nickname. On the other hand, it's better than the dumb stuff the media always comes up with. Like a few years back when they started finding those bodies in Yosemite National Park, and you guys called him something lame like "The National Park Killer." Hey, there's no law that says you can't go back and improve a serial killer's nickname, so here's my gift to you, what he should have been dubbed in the first place: "Son of Yosemite Sam."

Finally: Why don't you run bridge anymore next to the crossword? When did that stop? Personally, I hate the game and all who play it, but seeing those little hearts and clubs in the paper each morning was a reassuring cultural anchorage. Now I constantly feel off balance, like when you take a really sound nap in the afternoon and wake up just before sunset and for a brief, terrifying moment you don't know what part of day it is: "Jumping Jesus! I've been drugged and kidnapped!" And you start checking for signs of anal violation. Know what I mean? Please run bridge.

Dissatisfied in Tampa,
Serge A. Storms

AUGUST, MIDDLE OF THE SEASON, BETWEEN HURRICANES #3 AND #4

Traffic was heavy on Tampa's main north-south artery. Several cars were flying little satin flags declaring respective allegiance to the Bucs, Lightning or Gators. A unique flag snapped in the wind from the antenna of one vehicle: a large red square with a smaller black square inside. Storm warning.

Bump. Ba-bump. Bump. Ba-bump . . .

Serge and Coleman sat through one of those ultra-long, four-way traffic lights at the corner of Dale Mabry and Kennedy. Coleman was driving so Serge could practice his new electric guitar. It was a pawnshop Stratocaster. Serge just *had* to have a Stratocaster because he was going to be "like Clapton, only better." He tuned the D string and began strumming unplugged.

Coleman held his joint below window level. "What are you playing?"

"Classic Dylan." Serge cleared his throat and inflected the distinct nasal twang. *"This is the story of the Hurricane . . ."*

Bump. Ba-bump. Bump. Ba-bump . . .

Serge stopped. The tuning was off; he twisted a knob again. "Can't tell how glad I am it's hurricane season again. I'm so pumped! I relish preparing for each new storm the way other people get ready for big football games, especially the tailgating."

Coleman took a hit from the roach secretly cupped in his hand in a way that looked even more suspicious. "Why's that?"

"Because I *love* hurricanes!" He test-strummed a cord and twisted another knob. "Everything about them. History, science, the way the community bands together in the collective memory of a common experience, which stopped when we got Internet porn. As a bonus, TV provides gavel-to-gavel coverage from those insane weather reporters on the beach. What a scream! No matter how hard you try, you can't stop watching. It's worse than crack. I just surrender and sit there for hours, like when PBS runs those Labor Day marathons on bacteria."

Coleman looked sideways at Serge.

"What?"

"Nothing." Coleman faced forward.

"No, you were going to say something."

"Don't want to judge. Just sounds like you're hoping for tragedy."

"Easy mistake to make," said Serge. "It appears ghoulish on the surface, but an obsessive interest in hurricanes actually saves lives. The more you know, the easier to react and recover."

"You're saving lives?"

"When am I not?" Serge tried another cord. "If only more people had my ungoverned curiosity. Some politicians should be going to prison for New Orleans. Remember when that FEMA wimp said he didn't know that people were stranded at the convention center until *Thursday*? Imagine being so incompetent that your performance rockets a thousand percent if someone tells you, 'Okay, stop absolutely everything else you're doing and just watch a motherfuckin' television.'"

"I want that job."

"You're overqualified."

The light turned green. They drove. Serge's hurricane flag fluttered in the breeze. "Nope, nothing would make me happier than if every storm this season obeyed my psychic commands and spun harmlessly out to sea."

Coleman stopped at another red light on the corner of Cypress. "How did you first get into hurricanes?"

"Was imprinted as a kid by Charles Chips."

"The trucks that used to deliver?"

"They'd drop off those giant, yellow-and-brown-speckled metal tabernacles of potato-chip goodness," said Serge. "Another casualty of progress."

"What's that got to do with storms?"

"Hurricane Betsy, 1965, Riviera Beach. Had a can all to myself, practically as big as me. It's how my parents bribed my hyper little butt from running around the house near the windows getting blown in." Serge tuned another string. "Ate the whole thing in the hallway while wind howled and candles burned down and a tree crashed through the garage roof. After that, hurricanes and Charles Chips went together like tonsillectomies and ice cream."

Another stoplight. Serge released the tuning knob. "There we go. . . . From the top. One and-a two and-a . . . *This is the story of the Hurricane. . . .*"

Bump. Ba-bump. Bump. Ba-bump. Bump. Ba-bump . . .

"Why'd you stop playing?" asked Coleman. "I was getting into it."

"That sound's drowning out my song. Where's it coming from?" Serge stuck his head out the window and looked up at the sky. "Are we being bombed? Is a building under demolition?"

Coleman pointed at the rearview. "I think it's that car back there."

Serge twisted around. "Where?"

"Coming up from the last light."

"Can't be." Serge rolled up his window. "That's at least a half mile. How is it possible?"

The other car grew bigger in the back window.

Bump. Ba-bump. Bump. Ba-bump . . .

Their whole vehicle shook. Metal seams hummed. Coleman tightened his grip on the vibrating steering wheel. "How far?"

"Two hundred yards and closing."

The other vehicle pulled up in the next lane and stopped at the light.

BUMP. BA-BUMP. BUMP. BA-BUMP . . .

Serge and Coleman turned to see a sunburned man with a shaved head, Fu Manchu and Mr. Clean gold earring.

"What kind of car is it?" yelled Coleman.

"Datsun," shouted Serge. "Standard package: Gothic windshield lettering, chain-link steering wheel, fog lights, chassis glow tubes, low-ride tires, thousand-watt bazooka amplifier, and those shiny, spinning hubcaps that glint in a manner saying, 'I have no investments.'"

Coleman grabbed his cheek. "I think I lost a filling."

"It's untuning my guitar." Serge's voice warbled as he gestured toward the next lane with an upturned palm. "The Death of Courtesy, Exhibit Triple-Z."

The light turned green. Squealing tires and smoke in the next lane. The Datsun raced four blocks and skidded up to another light. Serge and Coleman took their time. The music pounded louder again as they approached the intersection.

"I haven't heard this song before," said Coleman. "The only words I can make out are *fight the oppression* and *pump that pussy.*"

"He's getting on my final nerve."

"But I thought you liked rap music."

"When it's played by rappers. The gentre organically sprang forth from a culture of adversity and fortitude. I can respect that. But it also fucked up some Caucasian DNA and spawned an unintended mutant."

"Mutant?"

They eased up to the light and Serge tilted his head. "The Hip-Hop Redneck."

"Now that you mention it, I've been noticing them in disturbing numbers."

"They should work on their own sound."

"What would that be?" asked Coleman.

"More cowbell!"

"If he's going to play so loud, why does he have the windows down?"

"It's his mating call." Serge rolled down his own window and waved. "Excuse me?"

The other driver couldn't hear him.

"Excuse me!"

The driver looked around and noticed the passenger in the next car.

"Yoo-hoo!" shouted Serge. "I sure would appreciate it if you'd crank down the tunes. I believe I speak for the bulk of society. . . . No, not *up,* down. . . . Down! *Down!* . . . That's *up* again! . . ."

Serge rolled his window shut. He faced forward and counted to ten under his breath.

Coleman leaned and looked across Serge. "He's giving you the finger."

"Just ignore him. The light's green. Drive."

Coleman started to go. "But you never ignore guys like that."

"My psychiatrist says I must learn to walk away from this kind of negativity. So I focus on enjoying the future he's limited to."

Coleman glanced across Serge again. "He didn't patch out this time. He's staying right with us. . . . Now he's yelling something about your mother."

"Turn in this parking lot. Let us go our separate ways."

Coleman pulled in to Toys R Us. "He's following."

"Park here," said Serge.

The Datsun screeched up alongside. The driver jumped out and grabbed the locked door handle, banging on Serge's window. *"Open up!"*

Serge rolled his window down a crack. "You look like you could use a big hug."

"I'll fuckin' kill you!" He hopped on the balls of his feet, throwing punches in the air. *"Come out here, you wuss!"* He ripped Serge's hurricane flag off the antenna, threw it to the ground and began stomping.

"Coleman, you're a witness. Didn't I try to walk away?"

"That you did."

"Just so it's noted in the official record." Serge grabbed his door handle. "Okay, I'm coming out. . . ."

MIDNIGHT

Police cruisers and flashing lights filled the parking lot of a budget motel on Busch Boulevard. The Pink Seahorse.

Agent Mahoney was getting out of his unmarked vehicle when a newspaper reporter drove up in an oil-dripping '84 Fiero.

"Got here as fast as I could," said the journalist. "What do we have?"

"Someone's ticket got punched, and it wasn't a round-trip."

They headed for the open door of a room that was the source of all the attention.

"That motel sure is pink," said Jeff.

"It's the Pink Seahorse."

A stout police officer ran out and became ill in unpruned shrubs.

They went inside. The reporter caught a brief glimpse and jerked away. "Oh, dear God! What kind of madman . . ."

The victim was still tied to a chair in the middle of the room. Blood aggressively streaming from every natural orifice. No wounds.

Mahoney offered a hanky.

"Thanks." The reporter wiped his mouth. "What the heck happened in here?"

"Serge is what happened," said the agent. "Watch your hooves."

The reporter looked down. The entire floor was a spaghetti plate of electrical cords and cables. Miles of wire, tangled and snarled and plugging together an eclectic menu of raw electrical components and cannibalized acoustic magnets bolted to the walls.

The lead homicide detective shouted into a cell phone and slammed it shut. Mahoney approached. "What's the skinny?"

"A horror show." The detective marched toward one of his subordinates. He signed something official and handed it back. "Usually when we get a Hip-Hop Redneck in a motel room this involved, it's a meth lab. Except there are no chemicals. Just all these wires and magnets. Doesn't make any sense."

Mahoney pointed. "Why's plywood bolted over the window?"

"Haven't figured that either," said the detective. "Got our best guy on the way."

"Anyone in the other rooms hear anything?"

"*Every*one. Shook the whole motel. And the strip mall across the street. Dozens came out to rubberneck, but nobody saw anyone leave this room. That's how we know he was alone when it happened."

"Explosion?" asked Mahoney.

"Music," said the detective.

"Music?"

"Witnesses said it sounded like the Stones, but their statements differ on the album." Another aide approached with something else to sign. "The press is going to have a field day. . . ." The detective happened to notice something over Mahoney's shoulder. "You brought a reporter in here?"

"It's copasetic. He's a friendly."

"He's contaminating the crime scene."

"Jeff's hip not to paw anything."

"No, I mean he's literally contaminating it. He's throwing up."

A police officer who did not look like the others entered the motel room. He was Dipsy the Hippie Cop. Tie-dyed T-shirt, gray ponytail halfway down his back, sandals manufactured from recycled tire treads. General appearance regulations did not apply to Dipsy, because he was the department's technology wizard.

"Whoa!" said Dipsy. "Someone's been busy!"

"You know what happened?"

"Abso-fuckin'-lutely." His smile broadened as he surveyed the room. "I definitely want to rock with these cats!"